Kate Sharam

Born and brought up in Wales of English and Russian parents, Kate Sharam studied at London University before pursuing a career in advertising: she travelled all over the world while filming commercials. She now lives in Devon with her husband, two sons and three cats.

GW00542298

SCEPTRE

A Hard Place

KATE SHARAM

SCEPTRE

Copyright © 1997 Kate Sharam

First published in 1997 by Hodder and Stoughton
A division of Hodder Headline PLC
First published in paperback in 1998 by Hodder and Stoughton
A Sceptre Paperback

The right of Kate Sharam to be identified as the Author of
the Work has been asserted by her in accordance with the
Copyright, Designs and Patents Act 1988.

10 9 8 7 6 5 4 3 2 1

A CIP Catalogue record for this title
is available from the British Library

ISBN 0 340 69509 9

Typeset by Hewer Text Ltd, Edinburgh
Printed and bound in Great Britain by
Clays Ltd, St Ives PLC

Hodder and Stoughton
A division of Hodder Headline PLC
338 Euston Road
London NW1 3BH

My sons hated my writing this book for
fear they might be in it.
They are not.
All love to them both.

The boy's eyes were round and toffee brown, just like his father's. And at the moment they were wide open with the intense excitement that is the prerogative of children. Fluid, fast-stepping music billowed around the festive banquet-room and his hands pattered unrhythmically to its beat on the table in front of him. The pristine white linen was marred by the brown circle where his glass of coke had stood. It looked like a dead eye staring at him.

The boy's eyes watched the feet. The way they slid across the polished floor with the impossible ease of the water-skaters on the murky surface of the pond in his garden at home. It was as if the feet had a life of their own, a magic awareness, quite separate from the grown-up bodies that towered above them, holding so close to each other.

Step step slide, turn, step twist turn.

How did they know where to go, those feet? Was it a mysterious knowledge they were born with, or did it just come to you, like flu or body hair when you became a grown-up? How could they follow each other so exactly? Like two halves of the same sandwich. Attached by invisible jam. Why didn't they trip over each other? They were moving so fast, yet the pretty blue shoes, that felt as soft to touch as the inside of his own mouth, never missed a beat. Never stepped on the shiny black toes that had somehow turned from being the heavy, lifeless boats that dwarfed his own feet when he had shuffled round his parents' bedroom in them, into sleek flashes of bright, knowledgeable movement.

"Sam, I want some more coke."

The boy ignored his brother who was sitting at his elbow, fingers fiddling with a dead party-popper, as if to coax it back to life.

"Sa-am, Sa-aa-am. Let's get another coke."

The boy's eyes did not leave the feet. "Later, Danny, when this dance is finished."

Other feet flitted across his vision, but he held on to the blue shoes weaving their patterns among the forest of legs. Legs that were black tubes and grey tubes, with their knife-sharp creases and flat shoes, twinned with legs that were leg-shaped, flesh-shaped. Some thin as a mouse's tail, others puffed out like one of Danny's plasticine snakes. Whatever their shape, these legs ended in colourful shoes with heels and pointy toes and bows and buckles and even twinkly bits that looked like jewels.

"When will it finish?" Danny was nothing if not persistent. That's what Dad always said.

"Soon."

"I'm thirsty now."

"You'll have to wait."

"Why?"

"Just because."

"Because what?"

Sam heaved a seven-year-old's sigh of irritation, but obstinately refused to shift his gaze from the dance-floor. "Because I say so."

Having a younger brother was all very well when you wanted someone to play the earthling who must die in screeching agony when you blast him with your inter-stellar-laser-antimatter gun. But Danny couldn't always get even that right. Just recently he kept insisting that he'd had a scientist's injection to make him invincible. Invincible. That was Sam's word. Danny wasn't allowed to use it. Sam was the one who had discovered it in a comic, so it was his. Not Danny's. Sam was the invincible one.

"Aw, Sam-Sam, I want . . ."

"Don't call me Sam-Sam."

"Sam, then. Come on, Sam." The insistent voice just wouldn't give up.

It was like the time Danny had gone on and on and on at him to push him higher and higher on the swing. And then he'd fallen off. Silly dope. The thought of the gush of blood from

Danny's nose still made Sam's stomach skitter alarmingly. The mistake was that he'd given in. But not this time. He blanked the wheedling voice from his mind. The music was growing louder, quicker, the feet swirling faster as if to catch each other. Sam felt his heart do strange acrobatics inside his chest in a way that made it ache in a breathtaking jumble. His feet started to drum on the floor. The music raced, roared, seemed to leap right up to the ceiling and then came to a purring standstill.

Sam shuddered.

The feet stopped.

The blue shoes suddenly became detached from the invisible jam. They tip-tapped their way towards him across the dance-floor. His gaze travelled up from the shoes, up the flesh-legs, over the floating blue dress that gave little puffs of breath as each leg moved, and up into his mother's face. It was shining. Smiling right at him. A big, happy smile that showed her teeth. He noticed her cheeks were redder than usual, like Danny's when Sam gave him his rabbit to hold, very very carefully, in his arms. As if he had rubbed red Smarties in circles on his cheeks. His mother's eyes were blue. Not quite as blue as her shoes, but still blue. Same as Danny's. Both of them, blue eyes and blond hair.

Sam wished he had blue eyes and blond hair. He ran a hand through his neatly flattened mop of dark hair, ruffling it into its habitual unruly waves. At exactly that moment, his mother's smile turned away from him. She had glanced over her shoulder and given the smile to his father instead. His tall figure was just behind her, holding her hand, one arm still half round her waist. Sam felt himself fade into shadow and heard the one word "Mummy" called out sharply above the general murmur of voices. He looked round with a frown at Danny, before he realised the word had come from his own mouth.

"Hello, darlings, we're back again." His mother ran a hand over Sam's shoulder as she sat down next to him and gave Danny a mischievous wink. "Shall I tell you a secret?"

"Yes, yes," Danny squealed. "A secret."

She leant forward. Sam held his breath.

"Your father is the best dancer in the whole world. He makes you feel you're floating on air. Like a dream."

Sam expelled his breath with disappointment and looked up at his father, trying to imagine what it was like to be floating on air, right up near the ceiling. Like in *Mary Poppins*. His father was looking down at her, a broad smile on his face but he shifted it to include Sam. His hand came out and rumpled his son's dark hair. Sam could feel the strength in it.

"That's what wedding receptions are for. To celebrate. Drink, dance and be merry, for tomorrow . . . who knows? Certainly Susie and Giles look over the moon, as if married bliss is going to agree with them."

Sam glanced across at the woman in the Cinderella dress. She was laughing a lot, but he couldn't see why she should laugh when she had just married that man in the stiff suit and thick glasses. He couldn't dance at all. Sam had noticed his feet stumbling all over his bride's shoes, leaving dirty smears on their white material. Satin, Mummy had called it. As if you sat in them, instead of stood in them. Was there a material called stoodin, he wondered?

He looked back to his father and suddenly felt a familiar rush of pride. He didn't wear ugly glasses or look as if he'd forgotten to take the hanger out of his suit. He looked good in whatever he wore and had muscles you could see. Like an athlete. Not like his friends' dads, who were all shorter and weedier. His school mates envied him his father, and Sam liked it when he came to sports day and always won the parents' race by a mile. He liked to show him off, like Andy Fellows did with his pet lizard. Though, of course, he pretended it was nothing really and brushed off his friends' wows of admiration.

And he could dance. Like a dream, his mother said.

"You look as if you're enjoying yourself too, Sam." His father was studying his son's face closely, too closely for Sam's liking. "Why don't you go and ask Nella for a dance?"

"Yuk." Sam spat it out. "Nella is a girl."

His father laughed. "You're right. I knew there was something different about her."

"Anyway, I can't dance. I don't know how."

"Nor does she, I dare say. So you can learn on each other."

"No way, Dad."

"Go on, Sam, be an angel," his mother urged. "Go and ask Nella to dance. She'd love it."

Danny pretended to be sick over the table.

"I'd rather lie on the floor," Sam stated solemnly, "and be trampled to death by five hundred elephants."

His parents both laughed. They didn't seem to realise he meant every word.

"Well, that settles it then," his father conceded. "Nella will have to wait until her own wedding."

"No one will ever want to marry her," Sam declared. "Her teeth stick out." Fenella Torrence was in his class at school and just because their mothers were friends, she assumed they could be friends as well. He'd had to be quite rude to her in the playground to get rid of her.

"That's not kind," his mother pointed out.

"But it's true," Sam insisted.

"Teeth can be straightened."

"A brace!" Sam screwed up his face in disgust. "She'll have to wear a brace!"

"I want a coke." Danny resumed his earlier request now that he felt he had a more receptive audience. Sam was glad to be let off the hook.

His mother stood up. "All right, I'll go and get you one. One for you too, Sam?"

"Yes."

"Please," his father added.

"Yes, please," Sam echoed obediently.

His mother set off across the crowded room, weaving her way through the tables that skirted the dance-floor and headed for the bar set up near the door. Three pairs of eyes, two brown, one blue, watched her move, each swish of the blue skirt and each easy smile as she greeted other wedding guests along her path.

A long contented sigh escaped from his father and made Sam turn to study him. He was looking a bit red, the same Smartie look as his mother. From close up, Sam could see the tiny holes in the skin of his jaw where the bristles would emerge by the end of the day and the way his long brown eyelashes curved in a dense fringe. Wasted on a man, his mother always said. And sometimes she would stroke those lashes with her little finger and he would tilt his head back and seize its tip in his mouth. Grown-ups could be very silly sometimes.

As if feeling the gaze, like breath on his face, his father murmured without taking his eyes off his wife's returning figure, "You boys don't know how lucky you are. Your mother is very special."

Danny turned to look at his father with a five-year-old's scorn. "She can't play football for toffee."

Sam kicked his brother's shin under the table. But not hard enough to set him crying.

"Get off," Danny moaned and rubbed his leg.

Sam ignored him. He longed to give his father whatever it was he wanted to hear. "She's better than Nella's mum," was the best he could think of.

His father nodded agreement. "Yes, by light-years. Harriet goes round in a dream. She doesn't even know what time of day it is."

"But she wears a watch."

His father burst out laughing, a rich, rolling sound that wrapped comfortably around Sam, though he had the faint feeling he had missed something. Just then his mother arrived with the drinks, including more wine for herself and his father, but before they could raise a glass, the band started up once more.

Instantly Sam asked, "Will you dance again?"

His father hesitated. "Maybe. Not yet." He frowned, his eyebrows almost touching, the way he did when he was annoyed with himself rather than with anyone else. "To be honest, I was a bit puffed at the end of that last dance."

"Puffed?" Sam exclaimed in disbelief. "How can a dance make you puffed? You go running every day. You play rugby. You can't be puffed, Dad." He saw his mother look at his father slightly oddly and the look made Sam shut up.

"You okay, Ian?" she asked.

His father smiled reassuringly. "Of course." He picked up his glass of red wine. It swirled like blood. "Nothing a drop of this can't fix."

"So you can dance now?" Sam persisted.

His father sipped the wine.

"Don't badger your father," his mother said in that quiet voice she used when she really meant business. But what did badgers have to do with it?

"Go on, Dad." He knew he was risking her displeasure, but he wanted to see the feet perform their magic again, to watch the blue shoes and shiny black ones sweep and twirl their way round and round and round in their never-ending partnership. Jam that would last forever.

His father put down the glass. "Well . . ." He looked across at his wife.

"Go on, Dad," Sam chivvied once more. "Dance again." When his father still did not reply, Sam added, "Please." It did the trick. He had often found both of his parents caved in when he attached an earnest, quite separate "Please" on the end of a request.

"All right then. Why not?" His father stood up. "Anna, may I have the pleasure?"

He held out his hand to his wife and she rewarded him with a smile Sam would have died for. Together they seemed to float on to the dance-floor but to Sam's intense dismay, they were instantly followed by a wave of others who swept them over to the far side, where Sam could only catch a glimpse of their heads, close together, one dark, one fair. He knelt up on his chair to get a better view, but the press of bodies was too dense.

The big white wedding-dress sailed into sight and the bride looked very pleased with herself in the arms of her father. Sam watched her swish back and forth. At least her father was a better dancer than her husband. The dress reminded him of a knickerbocker-glory and he was certain that if he took a bite out of it, it would taste very sweet. Like marshmallow.

He was distracted from this inspection by a bubbling noise that seemed to growl up from the centre of the earth like molten lava. He knew what the noise meant and could not resist a glance across to watch Danny's antics. He was blowing down the straw into his drink and the bubbles were clawing their way to the top of the glass.

"They'll spill over the edge and go on the . . ." Sam stopped as, in response to a particularly hefty burst of huffing, the mass of sludge-coloured bubbles, looking exactly like giant frog-spawn, slithered down the outside of the glass, settled on the white cloth and gently expired. Danny caught Sam's eye and they both giggled. Danny blew again, energetically, but was running short of liquid, so Sam poured some of his own coke into his brother's glass. A trail of brown drips added to the interesting patterns developing on the tablecloth.

Leaving Danny to his frog-spawn, Sam returned his attention to the dance-floor. His parents had worked their way nearer to the edge where there was more room, but even from this distance Sam could see his father looked hot. Obviously it couldn't matter much, because he was smiling. Smiling down at Sam's mother and his lips were moving. If only Sam could hear what he was saying. Just then that part of the floor cleared a little more and the fast-flashing feet came into full view. Stepping, sliding, turning, mesmerising with their smooth, inch-perfect togetherness.

Sam watched and took a deep breath. He wanted to inhale the moment, tuck it safely away inside him. He squirmed forward on his seat to get closer and his own feet started to imitate the black shoes' movements, but in the privacy of under the table. He was just trying to master an intricate step-over manoeuvre when the black shoes did the unforgivable. They stumbled and landed flat on top of the pretty blue ones.

Sam was appalled.

His father could not make such a mistake. It was impossible.

Sam's eyes raced up to his face, expecting to find embarrassment and apologies there. But his father's eyes were screwed shut and his mouth was pulled tight by a clenched jaw. It took four seconds for Sam to register that it was an expression of pain. One of his father's hands was clinging to his shirt-front, the other clutched at his mother's shoulder. He must have his full weight on her because Sam saw the material round the neck of her dress tear slightly. Her arms shot out round him but the body that was his father folded over her and she could not hold him. Together they crumpled to the floor.

Sam was frozen to his chair. His feet were still twisted in mid-step, immobile and without feeling. His arms felt the same, as if they were dead. Only his heart was alive. Like a grasshopper in his chest.

The dance-floor was in confusion. People crowded round his parents, blocking them from view. The music jerked to a standstill and voices were raised. One man shouted something and another ran from the room. Sam did not realise his own mouth was hanging open until he tried to speak and found his jaw wouldn't work. A scream like an aeroplane engine tore through his ear and Danny's frantic figure hurtled past him. Others followed.

Sam was left alone among the tables. His eyes observed his brother's glass lying on its side, a stream of coke spilled diagonally across the cloth. He felt sick. Voices grew louder. "Hospital", "Ambulance", "Heart", all pierced the fireball of agony inside him.

His father was dead, he was certain. Nothing less than death could have stopped those feet. Or lowered him to floor-level. Sam recalled the look his mother had given his father when he had complained of feeling puffed. She had not wanted him to dance again. She had told Sam not to badger him. And he had ignored her. Her words powerless against his. Just to please him, his father had danced and died.

Sam knew he had killed his own father.

2

Anna Forrest was making sandwiches. She was trying to hurry but the tub of margarine was determined to make life difficult for her. The faster she worked, the sooner it would slide out of control and threaten a kamikaze leap off the kitchen counter. Out of the corner of her eye, she could see her son's hand hovering impatiently just the other side of the kitchen hatch.

Why did Sam have to do that? As if she wasn't hurrying already. And why did customers always come in together? All in a rush. If they would just space themselves out more evenly, everyone would be happier. Maybe she should put a notice on the door, no more than half a dozen customers to enter at any one time. She smiled to herself. Maybe not. It wouldn't exactly improve the flow of business into her teashop if she started rationing out the tables. Heaven knows, it had taken her long enough to get it well and truly on its feet. Anyway, she shouldn't complain about having customers. In winter she was practically dragging them in off the street.

She slapped on some cheese, a generous dollop of homemade pickle and a handful of greenery. Lettuce and cucumber on this one. Tuna, mayonnaise and spring onion on the next, prawns, watercress and tomato the next. She patted their tops, like well-behaved children, sliced them neatly along the diagonal and slid them on to plates. Then tucked a couple of tomato and carrot sections around them as garnish.

"Table eight ready," she yelled.

A face joined the hand at the hatch. The toffee-brown eyes held a mild rebuke. "No need to shout, Ma, I'm right here."

"Table eight ready," she whispered through gritted teeth.

Sam grinned. "And speed it up. The natives are getting restless." He took the plates from her, added them to the pot of tea for three he had already prepared on a tray and whisked them away.

Anna grabbed the next order-ticket with Sam's scribbles over it. "Toasted teacake and granary roll filled with banana and with . . . ?" With what? She wiggled the ticket around in the hope of a word emerging from the spider's footprints that were her son's handwriting. "With tomato?" No, that looked like a 'y' on the end. Could be a 'g' at a push. "Dressing?" What kind of dressing? She sighed in exasperation. How on earth had she managed to produce an offspring who wrote only in code?

She rumpled her short blonde hair and turned to Esther Miller who was by the stove keeping an eye on a bubbling omelette. Esther was Anna's godsend. Quite literally. One day just under six months ago, returning from an attack on the Christmas shopping list, Anna had plonked herself down in the freezing cold on a bench half-way up the High Street hill, and moaned aloud, "Please, God, please. Send me a miracle."

She had just fired her latest, totally useless assistant and was feeling as guilty as hell about it, but was desperate. Christmas shoppers needed sustenance. Her teashop right by the market square was the obvious place for weary feet to throb in peace and for time for second thoughts about whether Aunt Babs really did need another woolly bedjacket or Jason junior the latest gory game on computer. What they did not need was drinks spilled down them, sausage rolls when they ordered carrot cake or surly looks when they complained.

The girl had had to go. But Anna was then faced with the Christmas rush with only Sam on hand. He was in the sixth form now, so had Wednesday afternoons off, but the rest of the week he was only available after school and at weekends. Danny could be roped in if she bribed him enough, but only if he wasn't out training in the pool which, with the trials coming up, wasn't often. Come to think of it, desperate was an understatement.

It had been a late-night shopping evening and the High Street was ablaze with the usual fairy lights flashing their tacky Christmas message, alongside cars and shoppers jostling for space and making too much noise about it. Weighed down with carrier-bags that cut into her fingers almost as much as into her bank balance and a guilty conscience at throwing that blasted girl out into the snow in the middle of the season of goodwill, she'd had enough. She gave up and collapsed on to the bench.

Her cry for help was uttered more in a rhetorical sense than with any real expectation of divine action. She knew she would have to face trawling the Job Centre hopefuls all over again.

But Christmas was Christmas.

Beside her, a voice said, "Need a hand, love?"

Anna turned and looked at the other occupant of the bench. Beaming back at her was a smile that promised mince pies, toffee apples and how about a nice hot cup of tea to make things better? Its owner was a woman around fiftyish, hard to tell exactly, maybe older. With Father Christmas cheeks and a good helping of his curly hair. No beard though. In the icy black air, the vapour of her breath hovered around her in a smear of light like a halo. Anna had found her miracle.

Since then, Esther Miller had bustled and beamed in Anna's teashop, eyes twinkling like the Christmas elf she obviously was. She claimed to have a husband, Rudy, tucked away somewhere, but Anna was never too sure about that. Especially as Rudy was short for Rudolph, and as every kid knew, there was only one Rudolph.

"Can you make head or tail of this, Esther?" Anna waved the order-ticket under her nose.

Esther glanced at the scrawl, nodded, then returned her smile to the omelette. "With banana and with ketchup."

"Ketchup? That says ketchup?"

"That's right, love."

"In Russian or English?"

Esther chuckled and popped a stray chunk of cheese into her mouth.

"And who in their right mind wants ketchup with banana?" Anna demanded. "Must be pregnant."

"Probably just someone being awkward."

"Trying to catch Sam's attention, more like. A doe-eyed teenager with thin arms and no thighs, tossing her hair at him. And making up a weird concoction to help him remember her."

"That boy's got too much sense to fall for that."

"More to the point, he's got his A levels." Anna sliced a banana into a roll, squirted ketchup and considered adding a teaspoon of mustard. But thought better of it.

At six-thirty precisely, Anna locked the door. That gave her less than half an hour to snatch a quick shower, throw some food on the table, shoe-horn the boys out of the armchairs in front of the television and up to their desks for homework, and get herself looking half-way decent in time for Lloyd Morgan coming to pick her up at seven o'clock.

It was the same every Wednesday. Other evenings of the week the teashop remained open until seven, or even eight in the height of the summer season. But Wednesday was Chamber meeting night. She always swore she would lock up at six o'clock sharp, like it said on the door. But there was invariably some dawdler or other slurping his hot chocolate or licking the hummus off her organic oatcake. No consideration for Anna's clock-watching. Meetings of the Chamber of Trade & Commerce waited for no man. Except the chairman, of course. In the end today, she had hardened her heart against an elderly couple who had been there ages, simply ages, and bundled them on to the street still clutching the last bite of their sandwiches. Pâté and lettuce but no cucumber. It gave them wind, she had been informed in a discreet whisper.

Drawing a veil over the memory of their wide-eyed indignation, she unlocked the side-door next to the teashop and legged it up the long flight of stairs. She just about managed to pretend she hadn't noticed that the street-door was still crying out for its second coat of paint. During the Easter holidays, she had bullied and bribed her younger son into stripping the tired paint that had been battered into submission by countless toe-caps and school shoulder-bags. Danny had done a surprisingly good job on it and then sloshed on a grey undercoat in preparation for the gloss that would transform it into gleaming perfection. Unfortunately a swimming course had intervened and that was the end of that.

Was it really over two months ago?

The matt grey paint was already chipped. But Anna was getting quite successful at keeping her eyes averted. Tomorrow, she promised, I'll paint it. After I've shut up shop. It'll only take a moment. Before I bake the quiches and apple flans. Thursday night was pastry night.

"Okay, gang, come and get it."

She dumped an armful of plates on the kitchen table in the flat and heard the usual stampede. Even *Star Trek* couldn't hold them when their stomachs heard the call. Jostling and joking, the two tall teenagers burst into the kitchen, filling the room with their maleness and noise, making the hamster in its cage jump.

Danny took one look at what was on offer and moaned, "Oh no, it's Wednesday."

Anna didn't cook on a Wednesday evening. They got the scraps from the tearoom.

"You like cheese straws," she insisted.

"Yes, Ma, but not with three broken bacon-turnovers, a prawn sandwich, a clump of vol-au-vents only big enough for fairies and . . ." he prodded the contents of a plate with his finger "slices of cold pizza. It's sad."

"Don't forget the lemon meringue pie." Anna had saved it specially.

He turned reproachful blue eyes on her. "No, Ma, I wouldn't dream of forgetting that."

"Well, strain yourself and put the pizza in the microwave."

"Just great."

Danny thought nothing of a fifteen-minute run, in rain, wind or shine, to the local sports centre, followed by literally miles of slogging up and down the pool and then another race home. But the four steps to the microwave were just too much effort.

Sam grinned at her. "It's the chlorine in his brain, Ma. It makes him touchy." He pinched the prawn sandwich and wolfed it down.

"I wanted that," Danny objected.

"Hard luck, little bro. I need the fish for my intelligence quotient. Stimulates the grey matter, so they say."

"Joe says fish oil is good for the body too. I need it for my joints, he says." Joe was Danny's trainer. His every word was carved in stone.

"Too late, it's gone."

Danny continued to grumble, but as his mouth was by now full, they were spared the details.

"Here's your protein drink." She dumped a glass of his high-energy beverage in front of her son. It smelt of bananas and made her hungry. Despite his moans, Danny was half-way through a slice of pizza, still unheated.

"Thanks, Ma. You're a babe." Fed, he was in a better mood.

"There's salad and more prawns in the fridge. But I must dash now. I want a shower."

"Prawns? Mental!" Danny jumped to his feet before Sam could make a move and grabbed the bowl of shellfish that had been intended for tomorrow.

He was not as tall as his older brother but the years of swimming had broadened his back and neck, so that at fifteen he was a perfect triangle, with strong muscular legs. His blond hair was cropped short. For aerodynamic reasons, he claimed, but Anna wasn't stupid. He just liked to look laddish. Recently he had been threatening an earring, but she had won that particular battle. So far. With Danny, everything was up-front. You knew exactly where you were. His blue eyes sparkled or snapped and his full lips grinned or growled according to his latest speed times in the pool. The week his butterfly turns were giving him trouble, life in the flat was grim, but since the win at Bournemouth last weekend he had been all sweetness and light. Except where Wednesday night supper was concerned, of course.

"You go and shower," Sam urged. "We'll clear up." He scooped out a handful of prawns, tilted his head back and started dropping them from a height one at a time into his mouth. The way he used to do with Licorice Allsorts until his cheeks were bulging. "I wouldn't want you to be late for your playmates."

Danny sniggered.

Anna climbed on to her high horse. "They are not playmates. They're business colleagues."

"Whoops, my mistake." Another crustacean bomb landed bang on target.

"We discuss serious subjects."

"Oh yeah? Like where to put the hanging baskets in the town."

"And what colour the Christmas lights should be," Danny contributed helpfully.

"And whether to use stone or concrete for the new bench bases in Market Square," Sam added.

"Big deal."

"Hot stuff."

It was hopeless. She was such a sucker for their impudent grins and beautiful young faces. And they knew it. She ruffled a hand through her short hair and tried to be serious. "At least we're the ones putting the town back together. It's teenagers that destroy the litter bins, steal the signs and tear up the flower displays." Friday nights were notorious.

"Not us," Danny said quickly, conscious of the workman's yellow road-lamp wrapped in an old sweater at the bottom of his wardrobe. "I'm too busy training."

"And I'm too busy, full stop," Sam asserted. A prawn missed the black hole, bounced off a tooth and shot on to the floor. Danny grabbed it and popped it in his mouth.

Anna ignored the incident. "Okay, okay. I get the message. Both pure as the driven snow."

"Driven snow," repeated Sam, and cocked his head on the side thoughtfully. In such perfect imitation of his father that it still had the power to yank at her heart. "I wonder why they say snow is driven. It doesn't have wheels."

"Don't be silly. I'd have thought you would know better than . . ."

Their giggles stopped her and she knew she'd been had.

"Pests," she laughed, grabbed a banana from the fruit bowl and headed for the door. "I'm out of here. Don't forget to do your homework," she added. Just to remind them who was supposed to be in charge.

Her lift was five minutes late. Which was just as well, because so was she. She just had time to notice that the sun had at last deigned to appear for the first time that day and that, damn and blast, there was an incipient ladder in the ankle of her tights, before the Rover drew up at the kerb.

She climbed into its leather luxury, trying to look as bored as if she had been cooling her heels on the pavement for the last five minutes.

"Sorry I'm late," Lloyd Morgan offered by way of greeting. He was quietly Welsh, dark and muscular with Celtic blue eyes and a taste for male-voice choirs on the car stereo.

"Don't worry, we've plenty of time."

He glanced across at her with the familiar quizzical smile, but passed no comment. It was one of the few bones of contention between them. Punctuality. Her idea of being on time meant arriving five minutes either side of the deadline, whereas his meant being there at least quarter of an hour early. This divergence of ideas was inconvenient, seeing as they shared journeys to Chamber of Trade meetings every week, and had caused the occasional frisson between them. So it was a pleasant role-reversal to have him apologising for tardiness.

She returned his smile. "Problems? Making you late, I mean." She couldn't resist inserting the word 'late'.

But Lloyd didn't rise to it. "Tough day," he murmured, preoccupied, and pulled out into the spasmodic flow of traffic round the square.

Market Square was just beginning to fill up again after the lull in activity that came when shoppers and holidaymakers returned home for their evening meals. The seagulls and pigeons were still squabbling over the remains of crisp packets and sandwich crusts, but their antics were disturbed by people beginning to drift back. Long-limbed teenagers draped themselves over benches and over each other, while elderly tourists wandered out for an evening stroll in the sunshine. Eyes carefully averted from the activity on the benches.

Anna liked the square. She liked its tall Edwardian houses, the kind that sprang up all along the south coast when the advent of railways brought the smell of seaside air to the industrial towns. They sported brightly coloured paintwork and a jumble of assorted shop windows where the parlours had once been. The square itself was paved and had a soft, dusty feel to it that the central fountain and sprouting greenery did their best to dispel, but didn't quite succeed. Anna noted with pride the new hanging baskets of salmon-pink geraniums, as the car purred past.

She nodded approvingly. It was all very well for the kids to laugh, but tourists were her bread-and-butter. And theirs, for that matter. Who did they think paid for that exorbitant new pair of trainers with its air cushions, supportive heels and varying composite soles, for heaven's sake? The tooth-fairy?

A town, like a teashop, had to woo tourists, court them with smiles. Attractive bouquets of flowers were a good place to start. She'd had to fight hard for them against crabby old Lawrence Enfield. He of the dyed hair and white moustache. He had wanted the money spent on more car-parking signs. The town needed both, of course, but the purse, as always, was empty before the Chamber of Trade & Commerce had got even half-way down its list.

"Had a good day?" Lloyd Morgan asked, as he slowed down for the lights.

"Not too bad."

"Business picking up now the season is here?"

"Pretty good, yes."

"A fair number of coaches in today?"

"Of course."

"Good."

What was all this about? Anna turned to study him. No sign of anything untoward. His profile was as calm as usual; wavy dark hair smartly brushed, high forehead slightly creased by his thirty-eight years, mouth ready to smile given half a chance. Maybe just a bit tense round the edges.

"Why the inquisition?" she asked.

"Just friendly interest."

But the fleeting glance he threw her, as he slipped into gear and started the climb up the hill to the ring-road, was a mistake. After eighteen months of lift-sharing, she knew Lloyd too well. Unease was flickering in those blue eyes of his. Like Sam's when he's heard his brother is in for detention and doesn't know how to tell her.

"Out with it."

Lloyd Morgan looked across. "Out with what?"

"Whatever it is you know and I don't."

He turned back to the road and gave his attention to overtaking an elderly Volvo. More attention than it needed. "It's only a rumour I've heard. Nothing definite."

"Okay, nothing definite. So what is it?"

The glance he gave her this time, full of concern, made her heart sink. Not that bad, surely?

"It's about the coaches."

Oh no, not her coaches. Please not her coaches. The blessed, beautiful coaches that bussed in from far and wide each day, brimming with trippers looking for a quick paddle in the sea and a cheery chinwag over numerous pots of tea or beans on toast, noisy and bustling as starlings. They were her life-blood.

"Oh?"

"I heard they might be shifting their set-down and pick-up points in the town."

"What!"

"It's the Council's new idea. To reduce traffic jams."

"No!"

"I'm afraid so."

"They can't. They can't do that to me."

Lloyd smiled at her, but she couldn't see anything funny. Far from it. Without the coach trade, she would hardly have a business.

Ever since she could remember, the coaches had off-loaded in Market Square. There were three bays neatly marked out especially for them. They would then go and park for several hours down by the harbour, allowing other coaches into the square, before returning to pick up their charges at the appointed hour. A nice steady turn-round. The day-trippers tumbled off the coaches, right into the arms of Anna's Tearoom opposite, to replenish their energy levels before embarking on the town and then returning like homing pigeons for a top-up before climbing aboard once more. It was a ritual. Many of them were regulars. She had learnt their names. Knew their illnesses, for Christ's sake.

They were *her* coaches.

"It's only a rumour," Lloyd reminded her, but it wasn't very convincing. She knew it must have come from a reliable source, or he wouldn't have mentioned it to her.

"And where does this sordid little rumour say the new pick-up place will be?"

"Anna, it's not meant against you. Don't take it personally. I realise it would be a terrible blow, but . . ."

"Don't take it personally!" Anna exploded, letting her fear out in anger at him. "Of course I'll take it personally. And when my children and I are out on the streets living in cardboard boxes, I'll take that personally as well."

"Anna, you're over-dramatising. The day-trippers will still come to your place, but they'll just have to walk further, that's all. Be reasonable."

Anna didn't want to be reasonable. She wanted her coaches.

"And exactly where will they have to walk from?" she demanded.

A moment's pause, hidden in a gear change.

"From next to the leisure centre. From that car park by the beach."

"What!"

"I know it's the other end of town, but they're bound to walk up to Market Square." He took a hand off the steering wheel and patted her arm. "Even if it's just to taste those gorgeous gateaux of yours."

Anna glared at him. "Do you mean before or after they've been inside The Copper Kettle and Ye Olde blasted Cosy Teashoppe?" Her two main rivals for the town's trade lay like dainty spiders spreading their web along the route from the leisure centre at the sea-front. "I won't stand an earthly."

Lloyd concentrated on turning right across the traffic and swung into the rugby club car park. A string of under-sixteens were charging up and down the field engrossed in fitness training, as passionately as if their young lives depended on it. He pulled on the hand-brake and turned to look at her squarely.

"Anna, it's not settled yet. We still have time to fight it. I'm going to bring it up at tonight's meeting and try to swing the Chamber behind presenting objections to it. On the grounds that the beach is enough of an attraction on its own to bring the tourists in to that part of town. It's the shops in the centre that need the business. Shifting the coach drop-off spot will affect everyone. Not just you." He smiled reassuringly. "Don't go buying your cardboard boxes yet."

Anna felt silly. And selfish. Of course he was right. The other traders would be affected too. The gift shops, the card shops, the bakers, the newsagents, the pubs. All of them. They would fight it together. The Council were well known to be prats and just needed their heads screwing on straight. She had been foolish. But at least no one else had seen her little temper-tantrum. Thank goodness it was only Lloyd.

The meeting went on for ever. And ever. Upstairs in the rugby club's function room, the executive of the Chamber of Trade & Commerce, all twelve of them, sat around a large table and argued. Like a jury. Anna looked round their earnest faces and thought Henry Fonda would have been proud of them. But tonight she had no real heart for it.

"The important point is that we must be seen to speak with one voice," Lloyd reminded them all. "The Council will pay no attention to our comments if we're split down the middle."

"And just how do you intend to achieve that, Mr Chairman?" It was old Lawrence Enfield again. "The sea-front and the town centre are at each other's throats. Always have been and always will be. This coach affair is just fuel on the fire." He stroked his moustache as gently as if it were a pet cat that would purr.

"It's not a question of individual preferences," piped up Amy Court, a newcomer who had got on to the executive because she was the only one willing to take on the Chamber's precarious finances. "It's what is best for the whole town that counts."

"We *are* the town, Miss Court," the landlord from the Royal Stag pointed out with a dismissive snort. "If you've got prosperous businesses, you have a prosperous town."

"As an accountant, I am only too aware of that," Amy Court snapped.

Anna wanted to go home. She stared quite openly at her watch and decided enough was enough.

"We're going round and round in pointless circles," she said impatiently. "Let's call it a day for now." She shuffled her papers together. "But how about calling an Extraordinary General Meeting?"

"Good idea. To get the voice of the whole Chamber." Lawrence Enfield relished any opportunity to perform in front of a wider audience.

"That's certainly a possible step," Lloyd agreed.

"A waste of time," declared the man at his elbow who owned a chemist's shop in the High Street. "It would just be the same arguments all over again."

"Battle-fronts on geographical lines," Enfield chuckled.

"We can take a vote on that proposal," Lloyd said. "But before we do, I would like to make a suggestion. A compromise that we could put forward to our members."

"Mr Chairman, I really don't see that you can compromise with coaches. They're either there or they're not. Simple as that." The landlord of the Royal Stag prided himself on his blunt common sense.

Lloyd smiled patiently at him. Anna could not help admiring the way he managed to avoid looking as if he were dealing with a rather stubborn child who was refusing to drink his milk.

"Not quite that simple, John," Lloyd explained. "My suggestion is that we put forward to the Council a proposal that the coaches should continue to set down their passengers at Market Square, as they do now. But if the Council wants to avoid the traffic jams when the coaches drive to and fro through the town, then the pick-up point could be at the leisure centre car park, as proposed. That way, both parts of the town get the benefit of the visitors' custom."

Anna felt a sudden urge to crawl under the table and kiss his feet. The surge of relief in the room turned on a vociferous tap, as everyone felt the need to speak out at once.

"Brilliant idea."

"The members would back that, I'm certain."

"I don't normally believe in compromises, but . . ."

"But will the Council agree to it?"

"It would unite the town more, as well. Be darn good for us."

In the general hubbub, Lloyd caught Anna's eye and raised a questioning eyebrow. She gave him a beaming smile and a nod that rattled her brain.

"There is just one more item I would like to bring up before we take a vote on the General Meeting proposal." Lloyd summoned their attention. "It's the teenage vandalism again, I'm afraid."

A collective groan arose from the table.

3

"Feel like a drink?" Lloyd asked. He felt he deserved one.

Anna seemed tempted for all of two seconds. "No, sorry. I'd better get home and make sure those boys of mine have done their homework." She softened it with an apologetic shrug. "You know what they're like."

Lloyd did not let his disappointment show. She really was an exasperating woman. Only had room in her life for two things – her children and her business.

"Next week, maybe?" he suggested. Just casually.

"Okay."

"And don't forget to ring the *Southern Gazette* tomorrow."

Anna was in charge of publicity for the Chamber.

"No fear of that. I'll give them an earful." She had already expressed her feelings, forcefully, all the way home.

"No, Anna, it's the Chamber's considered opinion they want, as you well know. Not your personal reaction. I don't doubt for one moment that your view would make colourful copy for tomorrow's edition, but it won't necessarily help our cause."

Anna shook her head at him and said remorsefully, "Don't worry. I shall be the perfect mouthpiece. Restrained but firm."

He laughed and drew the car to a slow halt outside her teashop, giving himself time to look at her before she slipped out of his car. Her face was slender and milk-white in the darkness. He leant over, his touch light as a moth on her shoulder and brushed his lips politely on her cheek.

"Is Sam free for his driving lesson on Saturday morning?" Just words to keep her there.

"Try to stop him! Rather you than me, though."

Lloyd smiled, as if it didn't matter that her son crunched his Rover's gears into tiny pieces like mangled digestive biscuits. "I'm only too happy to teach him."

"I really am grateful. He would go ballistic if I had tried to teach him myself. Especially on my old car." Her Fiesta was feeling its age and made a show of being fragile and temperamental. It gave a vicious kick when changing from first to second gear, just to discourage learners.

"Around nine on Saturday morning? Before you open up for business."

"Better make it nearer eleven. It's Sam's turn to help me clean up the holiday flat."

"New tenants?"

"Yes. A fortnight's let. Mother and two children."

Anna rented out the top floor of her building to holidaymakers. To keep blitzing it after each letting was a chore she disliked but the flat provided a useful addition to her income.

"Thanks for the lift." She opened the door and was gone. Without a second thought.

Lloyd touched the seat where she had been sitting. He felt the warmth of her body on the leather.

The Rover's headlights followed the lane that wound down through the dark streets to the sea-front. Though only just past ten o'clock in the evening, the town had a somnolent feel, as if already tucked up in bed. The rows of neat bungalows had closed their curtains and propped empty milk bottles on the doorstep. Over their tiled roofs a blanket of low cloud was drawn comfortably, wrapping up their lives until the morning.

Only when Lloyd turned into the broad promenade that ran alongside the beach did the world change. So radically, his nerves twanged. Throngs of people and bright lights, music and traffic created the busy, dizzy atmosphere so beloved of holidaymakers. A white necklace of fairy-lights looped like luminous pearls across the night sky the length of the promenade, while the bars and cafés spilled white plastic chairs over the pavements. In the background the sea growled quietly, invisible in its blackness.

Had Anna been beside him, she would have observed it all

with approval. Business certainly looked good tonight. "Like moths to candles," he commented to himself. The fairy-lights never failed to grate on him.

Though only mid-June, the season was well under way and promising to be a good one. As long as the weather behaved itself, that is. He had a heart-felt sympathy for the residents who objected to this continental habit of night-time strolling, eating and drinking. But it gave a buzz to the place that tourists expected, now that they had seen how the other half live on the Riviera. Okay, there was the occasional lager-lout problem. He admitted that. But you had to move with the times. Business was business and the town needed every tourist it could lay its hands on. Even if it did insist on calling them all grockles.

Lloyd headed for the Weary Ploughman, an inn set way up on the cliff with a view of the coastline that made the mediocre beer worthwhile. Even in the dark, the feeling of being perched in an eyrie gave a satisfying sense of escape from the bustle below. Lloyd ordered himself a pint, traded pleasantries with the landlord and a handful of locals, then found himself a seat by the window. The bar was standard fare, with lacquered brass, lacquered oak tables and what often tasted like lacquered beer. Tonight's was no improvement.

He lit a cigarette and stared out at the dark indifferent sea below, hearing in his head the fierce surging of the waves, despite the silence of the window. Lloyd loved the sea. Loved to sail. His pride and joy was a small sailing dinghy that had won him a clutch of trophies in local races, but this season it had been tough finding the time for it. He had taken Anna's sons out in her a few times, but they had not displayed any great interest. A sad lack of taste. Cars and rollerblades were more their scene.

Which was why he had switched from sailing to driving lessons.

Lloyd watched the winking lights on a ship anchored off the coast and wondered what parts of the world she had seen. What squalls and storms she had faced, and what masters she had obeyed. As a boy, his only passion had been to join the Royal Navy, but a partly-detached retina as a result of a rugby scrum had put an end to that particular dream. So it had been engineering. Marine engineering. With sailing just for fun. Like you breathe just for fun.

He sipped his beer and wanted Anna there with him. Sometimes she came, more often she didn't. He looked at his hands, so quiet round the glass and the cigarette, and wondered how they could be so obedient. How they could bear to brush her shoulder just lightly in the car, when they were so ravenous to touch her. Such well-behaved hands.

He knew and the hands knew that they had no chance until the Chamber's dinner-dance in October. Three long months. Not that she ever danced. No, no hope of that. But the sense of occasion and the dressing-up allowed him to fuss over her, to slip an arm around her waist as they walked to the table or solicitously across her shoulder as he enquired what she would like to drink. She was always friendly, always ready with a smile for him. And he knew she needed him. Relied on him. For partnering her at functions or fiddling with that decrepit car of hers. Even for tightening tap-washers or puttying a draughty window.

But that was as far as it went. No further.

She had made that clear.

Ten years since her husband, Ian, had died, and she wasn't ready for anyone else. Christ, his divorce was only two years old and he was desperate for someone else.

No, not someone else. Not anybody else. Just Anna.

Anna with the sparky blue eyes and short blonde hair that she kept ruffling in a maddening way that made him want to straighten it for her.

Of course he'd had others. Other tries at a relationship. But time and again he found himself looking for her smile on their faces and her laugh in their mouths. So it was her sons he was wooing now. They had a direct route to her heart.

Maybe he could hitch a ride.

Sam was being irritating. He was supposed to be helping her. Three pounds fifty an hour she paid him in the teashop, but here in the flat his time was for free. For love. Good for his soul, she told him. This morning he seemed determined to torment her own instead.

"Sam, will you stop throwing that ball around and get on with the work."

He was supposed to be changing the bed-linen, but under one of the beds had found a small rubber ball left behind by the previous tenants and was now mesmerised by testing its rebound arcs off the walls.

"Sure. No problem." He bounced the ball once more, off the ceiling this time, and left a dirty smudge on it. He glanced at Anna to see if she had noticed and she pretended she hadn't. She was standing in the doorway of the bedroom, bleach in one hand, loo brush in the other.

"Please, Sam, please. Mrs Tucker is due to arrive in under an hour."

"Chill out, Ma. The flat looks great. Mrs T and *famille* will love it."

"That last couple were filthy. Grease stains and cigarette ends everywhere."

Anna hated this part of it. The cleaning up of someone else's dirt. It was bad enough coping with the sordid bear-pits that were her own sons' bedrooms; she didn't need anyone else's. But she did need their money. The holiday flat was a good earner, paid the mortgage and kept the bank manager out of her letter-box. Fair exchange, she reminded herself. And managed a smile. It spread as she looked at her son.

"No need to give me that I'm-being-very-patient-with-you grin of yours," he teased. "Look, I'm slaving away." He flapped the clean duvet cover at her.

"It's just that Esther will be needing me in the teashop, as well. I haven't got long."

"Ma, you work too hard."

She laughed. "I'll remind you of that next time you ask for that new stereo system."

"There is more to life, you know." He said it so gently, so like a caring parent to an over-diligent child. "And don't worry. Coaches aren't the be-all and end-all."

"Aren't they?"

"No."

"Thank you for that advice, oh wise one," she said solemnly. "Now will you finish doing that duvet?"

"Do you know that you're obsessive?"

"I'm afraid psychoanalysis isn't on my list for this morning. I'm too busy."

"Exactly," he grinned triumphantly at her.

She walked over to the bed and started to remove the stained duvet cover, but Sam came and took it from her hands. He towered over her. All six feet of him.

"I'll finish this one," he assured her. "But I want a shower before my driving lesson."

Anna sighed. What was it with young people and being so clean? No one talked about obsessive there. What sins were they trying to wash away? Most likely, to cleanse their pure young bodies of the sins of their parents, of their unforgivable and unforgettable mistakes. Oh no, she really was too busy for this. Mind games were reserved for later, for the long, solitary nights. This morning was for getting this blasted flat done. Sam was struggling to fit the bulk of the duvet into its new cover, but had lost one corner.

"Can't you drive dirty for once?" Anna dared suggest.

His brown eyes looked at her, appalled. "No. My hair needs washing."

That was it, of course. The hair. His glossy dark and shining glory. He wore it a bit long for Anna's liking, or his school's, for that matter. But its healthy gleam was never allowed to be tainted for more than a millisecond, so what it lacked in neatness, it made up for in bounce. Anna sometimes wondered if she was keeping Head & Shoulders in booming business all on her own.

With a final arm-wrestle, Sam tamed the duvet and raced through the rest of his jobs. Anna was cleaning the sitting-room window when he breezed in bouncing the ball, smugly announced the completion of his tasks and breezed out again. She missed him when he had gone. His company brought brightness to the dreary little flat. In the teashop, she often found herself ducking her head, while working in the kitchen, to give herself a glimpse through the hatch of his mile-long legs loping around the tables. A two-legged giraffe with a smile that melted polar ice-caps.

When he asked her customers – most of whom, predictably, were female and over fifty – if they wanted something more, their eyes misted over with secret desires that had nothing to do with food. They could not resist ordering a second slice of chocolate gateau just to have him return to their table with that smile of his. And he was only too aware which side Anna's bread was buttered, so he flirted with them shamelessly. Even the coachloads of white-haired geriatrics would primp and preen and giggle like teenagers. At times, some of the regulars could get quite raunchy with him. They would wrap an arm round his slim hips, trapping him at their table.

"Are you on the menu too?" they'd ask.

"What I wouldn't give to be fifty years younger. Then I'd show you how to really serve a lady," and they would all hoot with laughter.

Anna didn't exactly approve. But he always rebuffed their offers with such becoming blushes that they kept returning for more.

From her bird's-eye view at the second-floor window, she saw a dark blue Rover pull up outside the teashop. Lloyd, as usual, was early for Sam's driving lesson. Well, he would just have to wait for a few minutes if Sam was still in the shower. She caught a glimpse of his hand lighting a cigarette and felt the urge to warn him about passive smoking and young lungs. Just then Sam raced out of the front door, hair still wet, and folded his long legs into the car's smoky interior. Drat Lloyd and his early-bird routine.

"It's real nice, Mrs Forrest. Isn't it, Tara?" Mrs Tucker enthused to her daughter. "Real nice."

Anna was showing the family round the holiday flat. It was comfortable without being exactly homey. The sitting-room was a decent size with a view towards the sea. Not *of* the sea, she had to admit. What in estate agents' parlance would be termed 'offering sea peeps'. If you stand on the sofa and crane your neck at right angles, that is. Anna had tried to jolly things up with a smattering of lively cushions, but basically it remained stubbornly a holiday flat. 'Two double bedrooms, lounge, kitchen and bathroom with shower', as the advert went. Very succinct. She'd had to have the shower put in. Everyone expected one.

"Real nice, isn't it, Tara?" the mother repeated.

The girl hung back in the doorway of the larger room. Round-shouldered and thin, with short dark hair and a face free of make-up. She looked about fourteen and was clearly indifferent to her surroundings. Her eyes, dark and heavy-lidded, stared out the window. Only her jaw moved, chewing gum in a slow incessant motion. Her mother's enthusiasm made no impression on her, unlike her young brother who was rocketing round the rooms with frightening momentum. Like a puppy let loose in a hen-house.

"Look, Mum, look at me on my bed." The child had hurled himself on top of the clean duvet cover that Sam had struggled so hard with. Standing bolt upright in his bovver-boots, three sizes too big, he was using the mattress like a trampoline. His straight brown hair rising and falling with every bounce, like an umbrella on a showery day.

"Don't do that, Darren. You're not at home now," his mother laughed. She had a warm laugh and an easy manner that assumed instant friendship. Her small pretty features were dominated by a big bush of hair, very permed and very blonde. She didn't look more than thirty, despite her teenage daughter. "He's only eight," she offered to Anna as explanation for her son's antics.

Eight going on two and a half, Anna groaned inwardly. "Mrs Tucker, would you please remove him from . . ."

"Call me Josie."

Anna tried again. "Josie, will you please tell your son not to bounce on the beds? And especially not with his shoes on."

Little scabs of dried mud were flicking from the duvet and crumbling to a reddish powder as he landed on them. The boy was plump and round all over, round eyes, round cheeks. As if he had gobbled up all his sister's food as well as his own. His chatter ran on and on like Muzak. Maybe he's gobbled his sister's words too, Anna thought.

His mother grabbed a handful of his faded tee-shirt and yanked him to the floor. "Darren's such a live-wire," she laughed and gave him a hug. He squirmed free and started switching the bedside lamp on and off, like morse code.

Anna arranged her teeth into a smile and mentally banked the deposit money that Mrs Tucker had, reluctantly, already handed over against breakages.

"We love it," Josie Tucker enthused. "Don't we, Tara?"

The girl still did not bother to respond but continued to stare out the window. Anna thought for a foolish moment that she was interested in the view of the town, especially as it was market day, so the square was heaving with traders and stalls. Maybe something she hadn't seen before. Or perhaps it was the wisp of sea on the horizon that had enthralled her, as she came from the heartland of Sheffield. But no. The eyes were seeing none of it. The expression was blanked out into a resigned tolerance that was stretched to breaking-point. She had just turned her face in that direction to avoid contact with the other eyes in the flat, eyes that pried and probed. Anna began to get the impression that the girl was not over-keen on this whole seaside-jaunt idea.

"Enjoy your two weeks," she said nevertheless, with remorseless cheeriness. "There's lots to see round here."

"And only two weeks," Josie Tucker wailed.

Her daughter sighed. It seemed to rise right from the tractor-tyre soles of her black boots, up through her black jeans and black sweatshirt and burst out in a wave of black despair. "Two weeks," she breathed.

Anna left them to it and made her escape.

Saturday was always busy. What with it being both market day and change-over day, when sated tourists headed home with their sandy suitcases and a new batch clogged the streets, as their cars crawled round in search of their hotel or apartment. On arrival, they weren't ready for the beach yet, so they would tour the town, venting their excitement on its nooks and crannies and squealing with delight at its idiosyncrasies. Hopefully, they would do much of their squealing over a cup of tea in Anna's Tearoom.

This Saturday was no exception. The tide of eager faces had flowed in, complaining of the thin high cloud that had stolen the sun, but seemed to do very little ebbing. Anna, Sam and Esther had worked flat out all day and even Danny had been roped in for the afternoon.

"Only if you drive me over to Will's house later," he had bargained, instantly spotting that he held all the aces.

"Okay, I promise."

"And pay time and a half."

"My own son is a crook."

"And I get a piece of the Black Forest gateau."

"It's a deal." She was too busy to argue.

Will Bennett was another member of the swimming team. Together they were going to get in a session of weight training and then indulge in a night-long orgy of sci-fi by watching all three *Star Wars* films on video, one after the other. The power of the Force would be well and truly with them.

By nine o'clock that evening Anna had collapsed. Sprawled on the sofa with her feet raised up on its chintz arm to drain all the blood back into the rest of her body, her eyelids insisted on clamping shut with the force of magnets. Sam was tucked away in his room wrestling with homework. At one point she did consider getting up to make them both a cup of hot chocolate, but the idea never made it past her head. Her body had no intention of moving a muscle and remained stubbornly indifferent to any notion of thirst or motherly duty. So she gave in and skidded down the chute that opened up inside her head, into a warm nest of sleep.

She had burrowed deep into its soft layers and was in the process of dancing a fast foxtrot around the market square fountain amid a swirl of sea-mist that prevented her seeing the face of her partner, when a coach-horn blared at her. She jumped like a mongoose scenting danger and her heart hammered out an alarm that merged with the sound of the horn. It was coming closer. It blared again. And again.

Anna forced open her eyes. She was sitting bolt upright on the sofa and the telephone was clamouring at her.

"Go away," she moaned, and rummaged both hands through her hair as if to dig up some sociability from among its roots.

It continued to ring.

"Phone, Ma," Sam's voice shouted from far away.

"I hear it," she growled back and picked up the receiver. "Hello?"

It wasn't meant to be welcoming. She wanted to go back and get a look at her dancing partner's face. It had to be Ian's. Just had to be.

"Anna, oh God, I thought you were out. Anna, it's Nella here."

"What's the matter, Nella? Calm down, you sound hysterical."

Nella was Harriet Torrence's teenage daughter. Harriet had been Anna's friend ever since that day in the third form at school when three fifth-formers had cornered Anna in the lavatory and were taunting her about her mouthful of metal, enough to rebuild the Forth Bridge. Her tormentors were just about to test their theory that she would sink head-first in water by shoving her head down the loo, when the new girl, Harriet Maitland, had walked in on them. She had been tall and willowy like a frail sapling with long mud-coloured hair dragged back in a ponytail. Her face was narrow with a bony forehead, small grey eyes and a sort of disconnected jaw that made her look like a camel.

She went for them. The fifth-formers didn't stand a chance. Teeth bared, long thin arms flailing and clawing like a demented windmill, she tore them apart. They abandoned their lunchtime entertainment and scarpered as if they thought she really would eat them alive, with those camel-teeth of hers.

Anna was impressed.

The moment the tormentors were gone, Harriet resumed her mild, ruminant exterior and slightly hang-dog manner. As if apologising for living.

"Bastards," she said.

"Bastards," Anna agreed. And the friendship was made.

Over the years, Harriet had filled out a bit, coloured her hair every nuance of the rainbow, married Jonathan Torrence and endowed the world with a daughter, Fenella. Harriet and Jonathan were engaged in running a flourishing health food shop in the High Street, though Jonathan was often away giving talks all over the country, evangelising for a greener life. But Harriet Maitland still lurked inside Harriet Torrence, making her prone to sudden outbursts of emotion that swept out of control, but now too often the emotions were negative and were directed against her worst enemy, herself.

"Anna," Nella's voice was raised in panic. "She's done it again."

Oh no. Not that. Not again. Anna immediately felt guilty. She should have seen her friend's depression coming. Should have recognised the signs.

"Okay, Nella," she said, all very matter-of-fact, to calm the girl down. "I'll be right over. How bad is it? Does she need an ambulance?"

"How do I know?" The words were shaky.

But Anna could hear the anger growling through the tremors. And who could blame her? It was too much to lay on a seventeen-year-old.

"Is there much blood?"

"Not as much as last time."

"You'd better call an ambulance anyway. Just in case."

"I don't want to."

"Why on earth not?"

"Mum made me promise. That I'd never drag them into it again. Not after last time."

Oh Harriet, how could you do that to your own daughter? It wasn't fair.

"Hang on, Nella. I'll be with you in a couple of minutes."

"Hurry."

"I'm on my way."

She grabbed her car keys, yelled to Sam that she was off to the Torrences' and drove the few hundred yards up to the end of the High Street at Mach One speed. Her Fiesta groaned at the top of its voice when she pulled on the handbrake.

4 ∫

"Have a coffee." Anna placed a cup in front of Nella and an arm around her shoulders. "She'll be all right now. Just a bit sore in the morning."

"Serves her right," Nella muttered as she sipped the coffee. Its heat steamed up her glasses, so she let them slide down her nose. She had inherited her father's myopia, as well as his dark good looks. There was no trace of her mother in her, for which she declared herself, loudly and frequently, grateful.

"Don't be hard on her, Nella. When she's in depression, everything becomes unbearable."

"She's the one who becomes unbearable," Nella retorted, and burst into tears.

Anna took the coffee out of her trembling hands and placed it on a nearby table, then wrapped her arms around the sobbing child and held her close.

Harriet, as always, had been considerate about it. She had performed the ritual wrist-slashing in the bath, so there was no mess over the carpets. This time, she hadn't even bothered to fill it with water first. Maybe she was just too desperate to wait those extra minutes. But thank God, the cuts had not been deep enough. She had bled, but not profusely, so that when Nella found her, she was red but not dead. Maybe the scar tissue was toughening the skin. Maybe the knife was blunt. Or maybe her taste for death wasn't as sharp as she thought. Jonathan was away in Birmingham, so it was Anna who had bathed the wrists, sealed with surgical tape the wounds that stared up at her like hungry mouths, and wrapped them neatly in the bandages that Nella had learned to stockpile. Then Anna had gone quietly to the bathroom to be sick. Harriet lay in bed now, her long arms resting on top of the covers.

Anna wanted to be cross with her. To scold her and demand that she give thought to her responsibility to her long-suffering daughter and husband. But how could she? How could she berate her friend, when she had been so close to it herself at one time? One tiny step further and she would have been the one in the bath and Harriet would have been stuck with the job of comforting the children.

She rocked Nella in her arms and allowed herself to look at the pain that drives a person to the ultimate act of self-destruction. Not at all the pain. That would be too much even now. But a corner of it. It was a long time ago, ten years. A lifetime ago. The scab had healed at the edges but the heart of it was still too raw.

Sam rubbed his eyes. He was seeing polypeptides and microvilli everywhere he looked. The biology test was on Monday and he still had the rest of Enzymes to get through. His desk was covered with pages displaying diagrams of goblet cells, pareth cells and submucosa that made his room look like some kind of cult centre where weird rituals were performed under the spotlight of his desk-lamp. With its high-intensity bulb that his mother insisted on. To save his eyes. Never mind his eyes, what he needed right now was a high-intensity bulb inside his head.

The rest of the room was in darkness. He liked it that way. Shadowy secrets all around him. Obscured and obscuring. The hint of a life unknown, undiscovered. He put his pen down on the revision notes and let his eyes dwell on the darkness, drifting his mind along fast currents to a future that opened out into a wide, bright sea, shimmering and silver in the moonlight. He floated there in glorious freedom for all of three seconds, before dragging his mind back to his desk. He picked up the pen to emphasise the point.

Back to the amino-acids. He flicked through a thick file of what he still had to cram into his head and groaned. He was tempted to put on a CD, the latest Pearl Jam would suit his mood, but he denied himself the indulgence. He always told his mother that he functioned better with music playing in the background, but when really pushed, he knew he worked faster without it. Total focus. The denial made him feel virtuous and gave him the kick-start he needed. He chomped down on the already flattened end of his pen and gave it a good grinding with his teeth. His pre-molars to be precise.

Biology was just too full of facts. At least French and German, his other A level subjects, were less demanding. Or maybe just came more naturally to him. Oh hell, that reminded him. He hadn't done that Victor Hugo poem for French on Monday morning. The one lamenting his daughter's death. He would have to translate it tomorrow night. After his work-shift in the teashop.

His mind snatched a final glimpse of the undulating, moonlit waves and then closed down on it. Slam. That time would come. He promised himself that. This time was for the gory details of the digestive system and its crypts of *Lieberkühn*.

Anna had left Nella slumped in front of the television watching the film *Groundhog Day*. Anything to wash away some of the hurt. At least the film was a gentle tale with a positive life-message that would be good for her. No violence to add to the chaos inside her young soul.

Anna was sitting beside Harriet's bed, holding the still hand in her own. She knew Harriet was no longer asleep. Just hiding behind closed eyelids. But that was fine. Let her rest. It would take time to retrace her steps back to life. It was much harder to trudge back up the hill than down it. The slope was so slippery, with so few handholds. Anna clutched the fingers tighter and felt them give a responding flicker. One more handhold.

She wished Jonathan were here, instead of gallivanting off on some green crusade. He should be the one at his wife's bedside, comforting and cradling, providing the lifeline Harriet needed so badly. Anna knew the marriage was not always smooth, but what marriages ever were? And she had to admit it couldn't always be easy for Jonathan. But Harriet needed him. And so did his daughter.

Suddenly Harriet opened her eyes. "Anna, I'm sorry." Her voice was soft and Anna had to lean over to hear.

"You're okay now, my dear. We're all here to look after you."

Harriet's eyes gazed at her with the gentleness of a koala. "And Jonathan?"

"No, he's not back yet. But he'll be here in the morning." She squeezed her friend's hand reassuringly, as if it could make up for the lack of a husband.

Harriet gave her a very small smile. "Don't be angry with him."

"Don't be silly. I'm not angry." But Harriet had always had the uncanny knack of reading her mind. "Well, not as angry as I am with myself anyway."

"Tell Nella I'm sorry."

"You can tell her yourself. I'll call her."

"No. No, not yet. I'm not there yet." The grey eyes became uneasy. "Soon," she said and drew down her lids once more.

Anna studied the pale face on the pillow and held on firmly to the hand. It felt large and bony in her own, with long pale fingers. The whole room was pale. A reflection of Harriet. The walls, the curtains, the bedcover, all frail tints of pale, that made the room feel like the inside of an eggshell. No wonder Jonathan felt the need to inhale stronger air every now and again.

How many times had Harriet performed this ritual? Three previous attempts that Anna knew of. Maybe more that she didn't.

There was always the taboo that circled death. Or even such inefficient pleas for death. The taboo that made you unclean in society. Something dirty and shameful. People crossed the street to avoid you if death was in step behind you. Anna was only too well aware of that. When Ian had died of the heart attack, after the first generous wave of sympathy people just didn't know what to say. So they avoided you. Waited for you to get better. As if it was the plague you had, instead of a hollowed-out heart. Except for Harriet, of course. Harriet had made her talk and talk. Talk about Ian, talk about their hopes and dreams that had died on the dance-floor, talk about her fears and her loneliness. Just talk.

It had not been enough.

But the knife into the wrists had never tempted her.

No. It was to have been something fast and irreversible. Like the bath and the electric fire. No mistakes possible there and all over in seconds. She had even gone as far as filling the bath and plugging the tiny two-bar fire into the extension cable that she had run like a white trickle of death into the bathroom. The boys, so young then, were at Harriet's playing with Nella. She had told herself they would be all right, they would be happier there, content to be part of the Torrence family.

She had climbed into the bath with relief. As she stared down at Harriet's shuttered features, she remembered how the tears she had been unable to cry at the funeral had streamed down her cheeks, as if her life was already leaking out of her. The bath water was very hot but had not stopped her shivers as she sat in it. She had lifted the glowing fire, held it one inch above the water and then, after a long minute that scorched itself like acid into her brain, she placed it back on the floor.

She could not leave the children.

That was the nearest. So close, she was as good as gone. But however much she longed to follow Ian, she owed the children her life. And after that, suicide had seemed like a box of chocolates to her. A big, seductive box of Belgian chocolates that sat on her table each day and next to her pillow each night. While the boys were little, she would occasionally take the lid off and gaze with longing at the smooth, slippery surface of the chocolate. But each time the thought of the children, of their intense need for her, made her quietly replace the lid and fill her mouth with dry bread instead. Eventually, she had been able to move the tempting box to a high shelf that she only climbed up to look at very rarely, and in the end, she had shut it away in a cupboard. In the dark. Abandoned and dusty. But not forgotten. Never completely forgotten.

When Harriet felt better, they would have to talk again.

Sam had had enough. More than enough. He pushed the books away from him with a harsh gesture of rejection and a file tumbled to the floor, where it burst open. Its contents fanned like giant playing cards across the floor and Sam walked over them.

Bugger biology.

He snatched up the electric guitar from beside his bed and let rip with a burst of sound that shook the walls of the small room. It put an instant and very private smile on his face. His mouth was curved into a crescent of pure joy. He leant over, zapped up the volume of the amplifier and wrapped himself round his guitar, in the gesture of a lover. 'Black Dog' blasted into his brain and into his blood. Led Zeppelin he might never be, but in the privacy of his own room, with eyes half closed, long brown curls flicking over his face, he let his soul vibrate to the rampant rhythm. His fingers danced across the strings with a knowledge of their own and the electronic sound swept away all thought. All existence. Only music lived.

It was a nightly routine. Purging the stress of the day. Dumping all worries into the drowning pool of the music.

Only tonight it wasn't working.

He stopped abruptly and the amplifier shrieked into silence. "In your dreams," he moaned, and tossed the guitar on to his bed where it lay like a red tongue.

His back ached. The result of hours spent curled foetus-like over his desk. Vaguely, he was aware of a banging noise somewhere outside. He stretched his hands high up towards the ceiling and waggled his head around to loosen the rocks in his spine. Zilch. So he lay flat on the floor in an attempt to iron it out straight. Above him, blu-tacked to the ceiling, a huge poster of Kurt Cobain stared down at him. Now, there was a guitarist out of this world. Sam gazed up at the tortured eyes and could almost hear the riffs and chords that flowed from those late and great fingers. 'Something In The Way,' sang inside his head.

The banging continued. It was beginning to niggle.

To shut it out, he started to sing out loud and let his mind wander over the day. The driving had been ace this morning. He reckoned he was nearly ready for his test. Lloyd didn't say much but Sam was sure he was impressed by how fast he had picked it up.

"Watch out for this corner, Sam. It's extremely tight," Lloyd had warned.

"It's no hassle," Sam had assured him and cruised round it with hardly a drop in speed. Schumacher himself couldn't have done better.

Sam smiled. Driving gave control. Control and freedom. Not

long now and he'd have the car of his dreams. A Beetle. With its pear-drop body and air-cooled engine phutting behind the rear seat. Modern retro-styling eat your heart out! He had over fourteen hundred pounds saved in the Halifax. That should buy him a reasonable runner. By the end of the summer he would have earned enough to cover insurance and road tax as well. If he was lucky, there might even be enough for a quick respray. Metallic purple. Mental!

The thought sent a rush of adrenaline through his veins and he leapt up off the floor, long limbs scrambling with energy they didn't know what to do with. At the edge of his mind, he was aware that the banging had stopped. He picked up the ball that he had found in the upstairs flat that morning, gave it a series of staccato bounces off the ceiling, careful to avoid Kurt Cobain, and then seized the guitar once more and blasted out with a burst of sound.

It was ten minutes later that he finally relaxed back against the pillows and gave his fingers a rest. His ears were still rocking to the rhythm but immediately picked up a new sound. It penetrated the whole flat. The doorbell. Sam had a feeling it had been ringing for some time. He didn't want to know. But as his mother and Danny were both out, he reluctantly left his dark cave and went to the front door.

The moment he opened it, the abuse started.

"You fucking anti-social moron. You out of your drooling mind or something? Where do you think you live? In a fucking empty desert? This is a flat, for Christ's sake. What are you? Brain-dead, that's certain."

Sam stared in shock at his accuser. She was small and spiky with short black hair, about Danny's age. With very angry black eyes.

"Pardon?"

"Just shut up that noise. Or I'll come in with a sledgehammer and shut it up for you."

"Oh, I see. You mean the music."

"Yes, you prick. I mean the music."

"I'm sorry if it was too loud."

"Too loud? It was doing my head in, it was so loud. The whole place was shaking upstairs."

His mother had told him earlier that the tenant had said she was taking her kids to the cinema for the evening. Apparently she'd changed her mind. Ma would kill him if they moved out.

"I'm sorry," he offered again in the hope of calming the tempest.

"I've been banging on your ceiling for ages."

"Oh. That noise was you, was it?"

"Yes, it was me. What's the matter, are you deaf as well as stupid?"

Sam decided he'd had enough of the insults. He started to close the door. "I apologise again," he said stiffly. "I will play more quietly in future."

The door was almost shut when she stuck a foot out and pushed her face into the remaining six-inch gap.

"*You* were playing?"

"Yes."

"On the guitar?"

"Yes."

"I don't believe you." The anger had melted into surprise.

"Don't then." He wanted to slam the door but her dark little head was in the way.

"Show me," she said and pushed at the door.

Without actually resorting to a physical tussle over the door, Sam had no option but to step back and let her enter the flat. Instantly her feral eyes were everywhere.

"Nice," she commented. "So where's the guitar?"

"In my room. I'll get it."

He retreated to his room, only to find she was right behind him. She sat down on his bed as if she belonged there and looked around.

"Like Nirvana, do you?"

"Yes. Cobain was one of the all-time greats." He said it challengingly, as if he expected her to disagree.

"Was he? I only know 'Come As You Are'."

"I'll play it for you."

"No shit?"

"No shit."

Sam picked up the guitar and, feeling self-conscious in front of his new audience, played the opening bars of the song. Instantly he could see she was impressed. Confidence boosted, he blasted out the rest of the track, adding a few improvisations to cover any mistakes.

While he played, he was acutely aware that she was watching him. Not just his fingers, but all of him. That gave her an unfair advantage, as he had to concentrate on the strings. Once when he snatched a glance at her, he found her eyes travelling up his legs and he shifted his position uneasily. By the time he finished, she was sitting with her legs in a knot under her and dark eyes wide with astonishment.

"Not bad," she smiled.

"Not as good as I'd like to be."

She laughed. "You're fucking brilliant, you moron. You should go professional."

She obviously didn't know much about guitar-playing but even so, it was wild to be told he was that good.

"What's your name?" he asked awkwardly.

"Tara."

"Mine's Sam."

"Pleased to meet you, Sam," she laughed.

He knew she was laughing at him but he didn't object. He liked her laugh.

"How old are you, Tara?"

"What is this? Police enquiries?"

"No," Sam said quickly. "It's just that you act older than you look." In her black jeans and tee-shirt, she was small and slight. Her face and features were as delicate as a child's, but her eyes darted everywhere, shrewd and watchful.

She smiled at him. "I'm sixteen."

"You don't look it."

"I know. But you should see me when I'm all made-up. I can pass for eighteen then. In clubs. No hassle."

"Oh." Clubbing was a scene out of his orbit. Something suddenly occurred to him. "Were your mother and brother mad at me about the music as well?"

She smiled again and he decided he liked her mouth too. "No, they're out. They went to the cinema. Having a kebab afterwards, I expect. My brother's a fucking pig."

"You didn't want to go?"

"Out with *them*? No way. I'd rather be seen dead than in the street with that pig."

Abruptly she uncurled like a kitten and made for the door. "I'm off now."

Sam was tempted to ask her to stay longer, but the image of his mother walking in and finding Tara in his bedroom at nearly midnight was not good news.

"See you around," he said instead.

"How about tomorrow? Fancy hanging around somewhere?"

"Sure." He was trying to play it cool. "Oh no, I'm working in the teashop tomorrow. But after five o'clock I'm free. How about meeting at the beach?"

"Sounds wicked."

He had a feeling she was laughing at him again. "See you at five then." Not too eager. Chill out some.

She nodded and he watched her dark hair, spiky as a brush. With another smile, she let herself out of the flat.

5

"You're very quiet this morning," Esther Miller commented with a look of concern, during a brief lull in the kitchen.

"I had a bad night." Anna shrugged it off and concentrated on pouring two herbal teas. Her head felt as if it had a steel band around it that was tightening like a tourniquet. She had not returned home from Harriet's until four in the morning and had been too wound up to snatch more than a couple of hours' sleep.

"You should take it easy then, love. Sunday is usually fairly quiet at this hour. It won't get busy till later. Go and sit down a while. Sam and I can cope."

"I daren't stop. If I do, I'll never get going again. But thanks for the offer."

"That boy of yours is the very opposite. Bright and perky this morning. I need sunglasses just to look at him," she chuckled. "Must have had a good Saturday night."

Anna looked round in surprise and immediately regretted the sudden movement. "No, not at all. He was doing homework all evening. Some big biology test."

"Pull the other one, it's got bells on. When I was seventeen, I was out on the town on a Saturday night. I'd knock 'em dead on the dance-floor, I would, with my . . ." Her voice trailed off, appalled, as she realised what she had just said. "Oh, Anna, I'm sorry, I didn't mean . . ."

"Don't be silly. It's all right, I'm not going to collapse into tears or anything." She gave a convincing smile. "Life goes on. And so does a teashop." She pushed open the door and carried the teas out to her waiting customers.

"You bloody fool," Esther Miller scolded herself, and grated a block of cheese so fiercely that she took the skin off her knuckles.

It was an hour later, when the tearoom had filled up with tourists wanting just a light snack to last them until their half-board evening meal, that the group of teenagers cruised in. Five of them. Eyes scornful and bodies bragging their youth.

Anna was clearing a table that had just been vacated and smiled a welcome at them. They slouched over and draped themselves on the seats. Anna handed them a bunch of menus and studied them with interest. There were three boys and two girls. All around seventeen or eighteen, she would guess. The tallest boy, the one with the straggly beard, a bit older perhaps. The teashop did not attract many teenage customers, just the occasional girl out shopping with her mother and, of course, Sam's friends. Mainly boys, they would arrive en masse and huddle round a table drinking cokes until Sam had finished his shift. Getting them to talk was a bit like pulling teeth, but they always said a courteous goodbye to her with their shy smiles and deep voices. She could never resist giving them a clutch of tasty titbits to munch in the street.

But this lot was different.

A different species altogether. What were they doing here? The boys had grey complexions and greasy hair, to match their grey and greasy clothes, their eyes hard and predatory. Both girls were thin and wore a uniform of black mini-skirt and tiny sleeveless top that revealed bare concave stomachs. One girl had vague sleepy eyes and straight brown hair that hung round her shoulders, like seaweed. The other had short dark hair, slicked flat to her head. Combined with the layers of black paint round her eyes, it made her look like a seal that had decided to come ashore to mate.

"H'llo, Mrs Forrest."

The greeting had come from the seal. Anna blinked and stared at her again. It was no one she recognised.

"I'm in the flat. Above yours. Tara." The girl smiled at her with a mouth the colour of an overripe plum. Her cheeks were dusted with the same colour.

"Mrs Tucker's daughter? I'm sorry, Tara, I didn't recognise you."

Anna couldn't stop staring. Where was the fourteen-year-old? The little girl sulking in the doorway? The heavy-lidded eyes now belonged to someone else. Who was this painted stick-insect with the careless voice and bare flesh by the yard? Did her mother know? Or care?

"Are you enjoying your holiday?" Anna asked politely.

"S'all right, I s'pose," Tara shrugged.

"Would you like to order something?"

"A beer," the tallest of the youths retorted and they all laughed. As if it was a witticism.

"A spliff," another topped it and they all giggled even harder.

Anna looked at them blankly. "I'm sorry?"

"I bet you are," the long-haired girl muttered.

"Is Sam here?" Tara asked, eyes already scouting the room.

"Sam?" How did this girl know Sam?

"Sam. Your son." Tara looked at her as if she was simple-minded.

"Yes. Sam is here."

He was bringing in some boxes from the shed. Anna did not volunteer this information.

"I don't see him."

"He's busy at the moment."

The girl shrugged. "Okay. We'll wait."

"Would you like to order anything? While you wait?"

"Not really."

"I'll have a coke," the tall boy said. His cheekbones were sharp, as if there was no flesh under his skin.

"Anyone else?" Anna enquired. The smile was forgotten now.

Nobody said anything.

"Just one coke then," Anna confirmed.

"Yeah," Tara said. "And five straws. We'll each have a suck."

They all sniggered.

Anna withdrew to the kitchen.

'Like something out of Halloween," she grumbled, as she poured the drink into a glass.

"What is?" Esther asked from the sink.

"Our latest young customers. All dark and sinister and smelling of graveyards."

"Sounds weird. How's the white-haired brigade reacting to it?"

"They think they're watching the Addams Family." Anna plucked five straws from a box of them on the counter. "The girl wants to speak to Sam."

Esther was instantly curious. "Oh, yes? Who is she?"

"Tara Tucker. From upstairs."

"Tara?" It was Sam's voice from the rear door. "Is Tara here?"

Anna looked round at him, his face eager, tongue almost hanging out, and her heart plummeted.

"How do you know Tara, Sam?"

"We bumped into each other yesterday." He rinsed his hands quickly under the tap. "Is that her coke?"

"Yes."

"I'll take it."

"And five straws."

He picked them up. "Got company, has she?"

"If you count ghouls as company, yes."

Sam gave his mother a look that questioned her sanity and hurried out of the kitchen.

Anna ducked down and watched him through the hatch. Esther abandoned the washing-up and joined her in the voyeur's crouch. He went like an arrow to Tara's table. Anna saw her greet him with a smile and a touch on the hand, and the other girl look at him with interest. Like a dog would look at a bone. Sam pulled up a chair and joined them, his back firmly to the hatch, but Anna could see his determination to be one of them. As plainly as they could.

"Don't worry, love," Esther said at her elbow. "He knows what he's doing."

"Esther, he hasn't the slightest idea what he's doing. He's as green as a gooseberry and probably not much smarter when it comes to the opposite sex."

"But he's always had plenty of girls around. Like that nice Nella Torrence who worked here at Easter."

"They were girl friends, not girlfriends. Miss Tara Tucker is obviously looking for something to while away the boring seaside hours. And I have an awful feeling that my Sam is it."

Esther patted her shoulder consolingly. "It's only for a couple of weeks. Then she'll be gone. What can she do to him in that time?"

Anna was about to reply "Too much", when she saw Sam rise and return at top speed to the kitchen. Esther retreated to the sink and Anna fiddled with a pile of cups and saucers. He came in, all smiles and happy eyes.

"Ma, do you think I could finish work now? I know it's early but . . ."

"No."

The smile went out. "Aw, Ma, come on. We're not that busy and anyway, Danny is upstairs. He could fill in for me."

"No, Sam."

"Please, Ma."

"No." Anna scraped a hand through her hair. "Sunday afternoon in June is always busy and Danny is doing his homework. I don't want to disturb him. It's hard enough getting him down to it in the first place. So, sorry, but the answer is no. You did agree to work today."

"But . . ."

"No, Sam. I need you here."

The happiness had gone. He stood and stared at her for a minute, his jaw mulish, then turned and left the kitchen without a word. The set of his shoulders declared his hurt. A moment later, the five teenagers stood up and made for the door. Through the hatch Anna watched Tara lay a farewell hand on Sam's arm, dark purple nails sinking into his flesh like claws. She whispered something to him and he nodded, smiling. No shortage of smiles for her. Then she was gone. Sam stood and watched her walk past the window with her companions. As soon as she was out of sight, the mulish set of his jaw returned.

Just at that moment Danny galloped into the tearoom kitchen. "Anything to eat? Can I have some of that strawberry thing?" He pointed at a creamy strawberry shortcake.

"No," Anna snapped.

Danny stared at her, his blue eyes startled, and made a speedy exit.

The telephone rang. Anna leapt from her chair and picked it up. It might be Sam.

"Hello, Anna."

It was only Lloyd.

"I hope I'm not disturbing you."

"No, not at all."

She had been sitting in front of the television. The screen was flickering with figures in some comedy that Danny was watching, but she had been paying little attention. There seemed to be a lot of shouting and false laughter, but what it was about she had no idea. Danny had finished his homework and done several hours in the pool, so he was flaked out on the sofa enjoying the antics on screen with the pleasure of the self-righteous.

Anna had been watching the clock.

Sam was not back yet.

It was only ten o'clock, so she couldn't complain that it was exactly late. But it was Sunday. School tomorrow. He usually stayed in on a Sunday night. After completing his afternoon shift in virtual silence, pointedly avoiding all eye-contact with her, at five o'clock on the dot he had taken his jacket and gone.

So no, Lloyd was not disturbing her. She was already disturbed enough.

"I've arranged a meeting. About the coaches."

Right at this moment, her worries about the coaches seemed light-years away.

"Good." It was all she could think of.

"The borough planning officer, George Paige, has agreed to come on Wednesday evening to discuss the matter with the Chamber's executive."

"Good."

"I bumped into him when I was taking my boat out today. He's got a motor launch in the marina."

"Oh."

"Says he's willing to talk to the full executive, but I thought it would be a good idea if we have a chat with him beforehand. So I've invited him over for a drink tomorrow night.''

"Good."

There was a pause.

"Are you okay, Anna?"

"Yes. Fine."

"Good," Lloyd commented, and she could hear the irony in it. "So I'll see you around eight o'clock."

"What?"

"Eight o'clock. At my place."

"What?"

"Haven't you been listening?"

"Yes."

"We're seeing George for a drink to discuss the coaches. At my house. Eight o'clock tomorrow." He said it all very slowly and clearly.

"Right."

" 'We' means you and I."

"Me? Why me?"

She felt his sigh whisper down the line. "Because I thought you wanted to be involved. I can ask someone else if you don't want to . . ." He let it hang.

"No." Damn it all, what was the matter with her? She needed those coaches. "No, Lloyd. Of course I'll come."

"Good."

"I'll be there at eight."

"Just before would be better. So we can discuss our approach before he arrives."

"Right."

There was another pause and Anna wondered if she could hang up. Sam might be trying to ring.

"You okay, Anna?"

"Yes. Fine. 'Bye." She hung up.

As she stood there, wondering how she could have been so obtuse with Lloyd, she heard a key in the lock and Sam breezed in. Head high, shoulders broad and a confident strut in his step. All puffed up and his face full of colour like a courting mandrill. With a brief but friendly "Hi, Ma," he headed for his room and shut the door.

Anna went back to the sitting-room, lifted Danny's hulking feet off one end of the sofa, sat down in their place and rested them gently back on her lap. Danny did not even notice.

"Ow, it's freezing," Tara squealed, and scuttled back on to the sand.

"Wimp," Sam laughed at her and kicked a spray of sea foam in her wake. It arced towards her like a glistening rainbow in the sun and she squealed some more.

Sam was standing knee-deep in the waves, tempting Tara to pluck up courage and take the plunge, but she was proving extremely reluctant.

"It's only cold for a couple of minutes, until you get used to it," he assured her, and patted his hands over the surface of the water as if to demonstrate its compatibility.

A dog hurtled past her, a black-and-white spaniel, and threw itself into the sea with ecstatic glee.

"See," Sam cajoled, "it's great."

"It's all right for him, he's got a fur coat," Tara laughed and hopped back a couple of feet to avoid the ripples of surf.

He still liked her laugh.

She was wearing a bikini, black and skimpy, emphasising the milky whiteness of her body. She looked even smaller in the great outdoors and her thin limbs very vulnerable. Like spindly twigs that would snap if he pressed them between finger and thumb. He wondered if her skin had ever seen the sun before, it was so pale. Almost translucent. Like tissue paper. Her breasts and bottom were small, firm curves that he felt the need to touch, and he thrust his hands into the cold water again to control their over-heated fingertips.

He dragged his eyes away from her, in the hope of dragging his mind away from her curves, but when he glanced up at the sky, his eyeballs were instantly hammered into jelly by the glare of the sun. The day was hot and had lured holidaymakers to the beach in droves. They milled around the ice-cream huts, sweltered behind windbreaks with their paperbacks growing increasingly greasy, dug sand out of their hair and blithely let the children risk life and limb on the sea in their inflatable dinghies. Bodies littered the sand like sweet-papers, all stretched out on towels and rapidly basting to a tortured shade of strawberry.

Sam was used to it. His crowd of friends often hung out at the beach at the weekends and he thought nothing of a half-mile swim in the sea. The salt water made it easy. Though recently he'd had less opportunity, as he was putting in more hours at the teashop. That Beetle would soon be his. But already his back was tinged to a golden biscuit colour and his chest-muscles looked fit and well developed. Not quite up to Danny's standard, but quite passable. He had noticed Tara eyeing them with interest.

"Come on, a bit of water won't hurt you," he called out to her.

"No, no, it's cold-cold-cold."

Sam wondered why girls had to squeal and hop around so much. But already he recognised that it was generic to the species. Like the way they run from the knees down and flap their hands at the same time. The only way he was going to get her in the water was by brute force. Abruptly, he charged out of the waves, setting her squealing again, grabbed her round the waist and dragged her back into the sea with him, ignoring her high-pitched protests until they were standing waist-deep in it. Only then did he release his hold on her.

"You pig," she yelled at him and scooped handfuls of water into his face, making his eyes sting. "You stinking pig," but she was starting to laugh.

"Come on, you're wet now. Let's swim."

He flipped on to his back and performed a sharp back-crawl for a few metres. But she did not follow. Just stood there looking forlorn. He kicked himself back to her side.

"What's the matter?" He could see her nipples clearly under the black bikini now that she was cold.

"I can't swim."

"What?"

"I can't."

"I thought everybody could swim."

"Well that's where you're wrong."

"It's easy in the sea. The salt does all the work."

"In your face, fish-head."

"I'll help you."

"How?"

"I'll hold you up."

Her heavy lids flickered and her tongue ran over her lips, tasting the salt. "Okay."

Before Sam was aware how it happened, he had an arm around her and was holding her flat on the surface of the water. Her waist was tiny between his hands. And very soft. Her feet and arms flailed about, making a lot of noise and splash, but no real progress. He talked to her quietly, calming her jerky actions, smoothing them into the semblance of a stroke. No panic, no rush. Just slow, sensual movements. Her body rested light as a dragonfly on his hands. She was kicking freely and laughing a lot, spitting out water in disgust. He walked her slowly through the water, letting it bear more and more of her weight without her realising. From where he stood just behind her shoulders, his eyes wallowed in the pleasure of gazing at the wet skull-cap of her hair on her small delicate head, at the curve of her spine between her shoulder-blades and at its rise into the black strip of her bikini-bottom. The sun on the water gilded her form into an exotic shimmering fish.

A child suddenly streaked across their path, pounding out a fast front-crawl and breaking the spell. Tara panicked. Lost it completely. She shrieked, struggled and went under.

Sam seized hold of her arm. He pulled her up, spluttering and coughing. She clung to him, arms wrapped round his shoulders, and he realised he had walked her almost out of her depth. He held her close, closer than necessary, and took his time returning to the shallows. Her cheek was cold against his shoulder, her teeth chattering. He liked her need of his warmth. Of him.

On the beach, he hunted for the spot where they had left their clothes. His were school shirt and trousers because it was Monday and he was supposed to be in a French lesson. It gave him a kick to know he was missing it; skiving off was not something he had so far been prone to. But he had been easily persuaded to meet Tara on the beach today. Especially after yesterday evening. It had been really brilliant, even with those friends of hers in tow. She had met them in some pub in the town and seemed to like to hang around with them. Sam wasn't so keen, but it didn't stop him having a great time yesterday, walking into bars with his arm round Tara, laughing with her, smoking with her. Kissing her. She had wanted him to go on to a club with them, but he had said no and gone home.

It had felt childish. And Tara had teased him. But he knew his mother would be in a real state if he hadn't. For that matter, she'd be in a real state if she knew about today.

Sam ran across the beach, holding Tara's hand, weaving their way through the array of bodies until they found their clothes.

"We didn't bring a towel," Sam pointed out and shook his hair like a dog.

"That's no problem," Tara laughed, and skipped off among the windbreaks. A few moments later she was back. In one hand was a towel. In the other a camera.

"Here you are."

She tossed the towel to Sam, but he would not touch it and it floated down on to the sand. She held the camera up to her eye and took a picture of him staring at her, open-mouthed.

"Hurry up, get dressed," she said, and wriggled into her shorts. They were denim and very short.

"Tara, where did you get that camera? And towel?"

She grinned up at him. "Where do you think?"

"You stole them."

"Of course. It's easy."

"Tara, no. It's not right. That's someone's holiday camera."

"Don't be such a wanker. Get a move on." She stood on tiptoe and kissed him full on the mouth. "This camera will buy us lunch."

It bought them more than lunch. It bought her an amber necklace and him a CD. The camera had been an expensive Pentax and a back-street shop that dealt in second-hand goods had given her seventy-five pounds for it. Sam had waited outside, uneasily skulking in a doorway while she did her bargaining inside, careful to keep out of sight in case the trader recognised him. He felt acutely jumpy about the whole scene, but could not deny the buzz of excitement it gave. It was like Tara herself. Dangerous. On the edge.

Afterwards, his stomach was too uptight to touch the pizza she ordered. They were sitting at one of the outdoor tables watching the tourists drift along the promenade. An abundance of sea, sun and sand seemed to have spread smiles on the stream of faces until, right opposite them, a little child threw a tantrum and chucked his plastic bucket on to the road where it was promptly squashed to a green pancake by a passing car. The child screamed in protest and received a heartfelt smack from his mother.

"That's the trouble with families," Tara commented. "When you're young, you can't get away from them."

Sam sipped his coke in silence.

"I'd give anything to get away from my pig of a brother." She blew a cloud of smoke at him. "What about yours?"

"He's all right, I suppose."

"What's up with you? Still sulking about nicking that camera?"

"You shouldn't have stolen it."

She closed her heavy eyelids and murmured, "Give me a break."

"It belonged to someone else, Tara. Not you."

She laughed, but Sam shut his ears to it.

"Sam, you are a prick. A snobby pompous prick. Life is about taking what you want. Nobody is going to give you anything in this world. Don't you know that yet?" She leant forward and ran a finger over his lips. It tasted of salt.

He jerked away and frowned at her taunting eyes. She was so sure and so knowing. What had those eyes seen that he hadn't? Her world was so different from his. He stood up, pushing his chair over. It rolled towards the road.

"I'm leaving," he announced.

She looked up at him and gave a small smile. For a moment he wondered what was going on inside that dark little head, but then she laughed. And this time he didn't like it.

"Running home to Mummy again, are you?"

He picked up the CD from the table, and threw it at her lap. It bounced off and he heard its plastic box crack on the pavement.

"You can keep your spoils," he shouted, and stormed off up the promenade. Behind him he heard her voice, light and laughing.

"Give Mummy a big kiss from me."

He hated her. But he hated himself more.

6

Even with the sunroof open and the windows fully down, it was hot in the Rover. The leather was scorching to the touch but Lloyd had no wish to miss out on that rich, animal smell that only leather could greet you with each time you opened the door. Pure caveman gratification.

He had just finished a hectic morning and had emerged for a pint and a breath of sea air. Some decent ozone to replace all that nicotine in his lungs. He had spent the first part of the morning working on the prototype of his next design and the second part fending off eager customers desperate to update their boats. Not that he should complain. Business was booming. But he was an engineer at heart, not a salesman. He had set up his company twelve years ago to design and build speedboats and each year it had continued to expand, ignoring the rigours of recession and exchange rates. Much of his business was now for export, especially to Italy where speed was in their blood.

He wished a drop of that speed could be transfused into the car in front of him. A smart BMW 525 with an elderly man almost asleep at the wheel. He was crawling along the promenade at ten miles an hour, while his wife admired the view of the stretch of sea on her left, infested with sails and seagulls, and on her right the palm trees and watering-holes. She did not think to look behind her. The sun was directly overhead and Lloyd could feel its rays frying his brain. He prayed for a parking space to open up and swallow the old man. That, or a convenient whale.

Instead, a mild commotion on the pavement just near the BMW distracted the aged couple's attention and slowed the car down to the speed of a disabled snail. Lloyd had his hand over the horn to hoot his impatience, when he suddenly realised that one of the ubiquitous white plastic chairs, the kind no self-respecting pavement café could bear to be without, had tumbled into the road. He braked to a standstill and waited for his brain to self-combust in the heat.

A tall teenager was striding away from a table where a scrawny young girl was laughing. Laughing and shouting something after him. Something not very pleasant, judging by his stiff and resentful back. A passer-by obligingly snatched up the offending chair, so that the BMW and its elderly occupants could resume their crawl along the promenade, and as Lloyd's car crept up behind the teenager, there was something familiar about those lanky giraffe legs. The mop of brown hair confirmed it. He wound down the window.

"Like a lift, Sam?"

Furious eyes turned on him, their anger still raw. But it was quickly held in check when they recognised the speaker.

"Cheers."

Lloyd had learned to take that as code for yes and pulled to a stop. "Hop in."

Sam did not so much hop as lope in, and soon had his legs folded into the confined space. He said nothing, but turned his face away and glared out of the side window. It was fully open and the faint breeze ruffled his curls. There were bright spots of scarlet on each cheek and Lloyd was not sure whether it was the sun or the anger at work. He was wearing what were obviously school trousers and a white shirt, open at the neck and with sleeves rolled up. Lloyd assumed the school tie was bunched in his pocket.

"No classes today?"

The toffee-brown eyes flicked across, as if to check on Lloyd's level of concern, and returned to the side window. "My French teacher is ill."

Lloyd let it pass.

"Are you heading home?"

A very definite shake of the head. "No."

Another small silence seemed to blow in on the breeze that was eddying round the inside of the car now that its speed was picking up. The old man and his BMW had finally pulled over on a yellow line.

"Fancy a drink then? I was just off for a pint and a sandwich at the Weary Ploughman. Care to join me?"

Sam looked round, surprised. He nodded. "Thanks."

Not exactly garrulous, Lloyd thought, but it was a start.

Neither of them mentioned that he was under-age.

The bar was full, so Lloyd led Sam out on to the terrace. It was more private there. Perched on the cliff-top, it benefited from a gentle breeze that rippled up from below, bringing with it the refreshing tang of the sea. Lloyd placed the two beers on one of the available tables and sat down to enjoy the view. A sweeping panorama of the coast, with the sea sighing its siren call, extended as far as the eye could see. Stretching out his legs, he gave a deep sigh of contentment. Not a bad version of it, anyway. He watched the boy out of the corner of his eye to see if he was taken in.

Sam dumped the plate of sandwiches he was carrying on to the table with the drinks, and followed suit with the chair and the legs. The red smudges on his cheeks had sobered to a dusky pink. He sipped his beer and stared at the view, but Lloyd had a feeling his eyes were seeing only what was inside his own head.

He let him wind down for several minutes, then commented, "It's tough living in a woman's world."

At least it caught the boy's attention. He even smiled. And nodded his agreement.

"Can't live with them. But can't live without them," Lloyd said, and was pleased to see the boy laugh. He obviously hadn't heard that old chestnut before.

"It's true," Sam responded with feeling. "It's impossible to get it right with them. They mix up the rules."

"The secret is to let them think you're playing by theirs. But in reality, never give up on your own."

"That's what Ma is always banging on about. Being straight with yourself."

"She's right."

Sam gave him a dirty look and started in on the sandwiches. Lloyd wondered what Anna had done to be in her son's bad books. Or vice versa. He'd bet his beer that the scrawny kid at the café table had something to do with it. He knew Anna was often quite strict with the boys, but at other times was, he felt, too indulgent with them. She saw their point of view too often. Even if it meant overriding her own convenience. He smiled to himself and took a sandwich before they all disappeared. That's Anna for you. Boys first, teashop second and everybody else, including himself, a very poor third. How was he to stand a chance? Maybe if he developed acne and a higher voice and started attending school again, she would sit up and take notice of him. Blast the woman.

The boy kicked at a snail that had been foolhardy enough to venture out of the shrubbery. "I'm thinking of getting a job somewhere else this summer. Instead of the teashop."

"Yes." Lloyd nodded in what he hoped was a sage manner. "In some ways that might be a good idea. Give you an insight into a different business."

"No white-haired old biddies."

"That's a point."

"With younger people."

"I can see the appeal."

"And no Ma." Sam's foot jerked out and sent the snail sailing back into a bush, as if to emphasise the point.

Oh Anna. My poor Anna.

It must have been hard for her after her husband died. On her own with young kids. She had worked her guts out, he knew. First taking in summer lodgers to keep a roof over the family's head and then selling her home to buy a teashop and the flats. No one could deny she had built it up into a good solid business. And done a really fine job on the boys at the same time. The only trouble was, Lloyd could see she was frightened to let go. Still tended to tie them too tightly to her apron-strings. He wondered if the scrawny girl had nipped up with a sharp pair of scissors.

He lit himself a cigarette and blew smoke at the sea.

"May I have one?"

He glanced across and saw Sam looking at him. Oh hell. How could he reject such a request for male bonding? It was better than tree-hugging, for heaven's sake.

"A cigarette?"

"Yes."

Sam looked as if he expected censure. Or even a lecture. Maybe that was what he wanted. To shock.

"Certainly." Lloyd pushed the packet and lighter across the table. "Help yourself."

Sam did so and the way he held the cigarette between wooden fingers told Lloyd he was still new to the game. He recalled that the girl in the café had been smoking.

"Finding a holiday job somewhere else is probably a good idea, Sam. But you will have to give your mother plenty of warning. So she can find someone else to replace you."

Their eyes met and the words that were left unsaid passed between them.

Sam sighed, "I'll break it to her gently."

"It's only fair."

"I guess so." He sipped his beer. "It's just that I feel I'm choking sometimes."

"I know. It's normal. I did at your age."

Sam's eyes relinquished their focus on his inner turmoil. "Really? So what did you do about it?"

Lloyd relaxed back in his chair and knew a soppy smile had crept on to his face. "I bought my first boat."

"I should have guessed. It figures."

Lloyd warmed to the memory. "I worked all hours. Delivering milk and papers in the morning and groceries after school. God, it was bloody cold in winter, I can tell you. But there wasn't much else for a fifteen-year-old in those days. I only earned a pittance though. You lads today don't know you're born. Three pounds an hour and you complain it's slave labour!"

Sam laughed. It pleased Lloyd to hear it.

"So how did you afford the boat?"

"I shouldn't tell you really. Your mother would complain I was setting a bad example."

That made Sam lean forward with interest. "What did you do?"

"I went up into the attic, where my mother had all her treasured possessions stored – she was paranoid about burglars – her best china, silver knick-knacks she had inherited, even a set of golf clubs. One by one, I sold them all."

"No shit!"

"That's exactly what I ended up in. The shit. I had one glorious month on that boat on the estuary at Penarth before I was found out."

"What happened?"

"My father skinned me alive and I was grounded for a month. Allowed out to go to school, but nothing else."

'And the boat?''

"She was sold. They got some of the silver back, but that was all."

"That's what I call street cred."

"That's what I call stupid. I didn't have a hope of getting away with it," but he joined in Sam's laughter. "Anyway, it was immoral," he added quickly. "They weren't mine to sell."

Sam abruptly turned away and frowned down at his foot. The offending shoe looked innocent enough to Lloyd, but boys' minds, as he well remembered, were a maze of unpredictable swings and roundabouts. All those hormones chasing each other.

"The point is, Sam, you have to decide what you want for yourself and go for it. Not for what anyone else wants for you. Only you can make those decisions. My father wanted me to join him in his glove-manufacturing business but I knew that was not for me. It had to be boats." He downed the last of his pint and glanced at his watch. "Maybe if you do decide to take a break from the teashop in the holidays, I might be able to fix you up with a job in my boatyard."

Sam looked up, brown eyes eager as a puppy's. "That would be brilliant."

"It would just be grubbing around with the boats. Nothing glamorous."

"Fantastic."

"Good." Lloyd was always on the look-out for converts. "I'll speak to your mother."

Sam laughed. "Rather you than me." He reached out to take the last sandwich, but remembered his manners. "Do you want the sandwich?" he offered.

Lloyd decided to take it. That was the least the boy owed him.

*　　*　　*

Anna was asleep in Lloyd's car.

The informal drink with George Paige, the borough planning officer, had gone well. Lloyd was satisfied he had got his message across loud and clear, that a compromise over the coaches would be in everyone's interests. Including the town council's. Unless they wanted insurrection and dead bodies in the street, that is.

No, he couldn't complain about George. It was Anna who was the problem. George had been early and she had been late, so it had got off on the wrong foot from the start. Not that she had been anything but charming. A bit too charming to George, he felt, but he wasn't going to nit-pick. George had lapped it up and agreed with each word she said, refilling her glass with Lloyd's wine at every opportunity.

It was the wine that did it. The moment the door finally closed behind George, with his assurances of agreement still ringing in their ears, she had curled up in Lloyd's armchair and gone to sleep. No chance of discussing Sam then, that was obvious. He had never known her drink before. Not more than a sociable glass or two anyway. He wasn't sure how much she'd had this evening, but it was certainly a darn sight more than that. He wondered if the cause was Sam. Or the uncertainty over the coaches. Or just plain old loneliness. So he had draped a rug over her and let her sleep.

At first he had sat quite close and watched her. He watched the way her eyelashes rested on her cheeks, the way her fair hair fell in wisps over her forehead, where the creases of recent days had relaxed into silky smoothness. When he looked closely, he could see the very fine down on her cheek and a tiny scar he had not noticed before just in front of her ear. But it was her mouth he watched most. Soft, moist and uttering little wuffling noises that made him want to kiss it.

It was when she started moaning faintly in her sleep that he decided he was intruding too blatantly on her vulnerability. It was altogether too intimate. He was stealing her privacy, uninvited and unwanted. He withdrew to the kitchen and made himself a coffee, before sitting down and finishing off some paperwork. It was over an hour later that she woke.

"Lloyd, I'm so sorry."

Her voice was thick with sleep, or maybe drink, and her eyes blinked blearily as she ran a hand through her hair. She reminded him of a tousled rabbit caught in his headlights.

"That's okay," he smiled. "Feel free."

"What time is it?"

"Almost midnight."

"Oh hell, I'm sorry. How unforgivable."

"Not at all. Don't worry. You were tired."

"Tired as a newt, you mean," she said and laughed, a good-natured easy laugh that was infectious. The sleep had helped. "And no, no coffee. Thanks all the same. I must get home."

So he had driven her home. She had wanted to drive her own car but he had pointed out, very delicately, that she was over the limit. The Rover was now sitting outside the teashop and she was fast asleep again, her head wedged against the window for support. For a moment he listened to her breathing. Soft and regular. Too sweet to last.

"We're here," he said gently.

She woke with a start and jerked upright. "Oh Lloyd, I'm sorry. My Sleeping Beauty routine again."

"You said it," he agreed.

She smiled sleepily. "Thank you," she said, and opened the door.

Lloyd thought it safer to see her up all those stairs to the flat over the teashop, so locked the Rover and accompanied her. He even risked a steadying hand round her waist, which she did not object to. Whether that was because she was unaware of it or just grateful for its support, he preferred not to ponder as he climbed the stairs. She was wearing a light summer frock in some silky material that felt good under his hand and that stopped short just above her knees, giving him a good view of her legs as she went up the stairs ahead of him. Nice legs.

"Thanks, Lloyd," she said again as she unlocked the door, but as she still had a tendency to sway in the wind, he reunited his arm with her waist and steered her through to the kitchen. She seemed to be slowly falling asleep once more on his arm as she walked, but the sight of a large page of paper propped up on the table prodded her awake. There was a message scrawled on it.

Even before she snatched it up, Lloyd had read it.

"Gone out. Won't be back tonight." Signed 'Sam'. No love. No explanation.

Anna sank down on a chair, put her head in her hands and started to cry.

"Anna, he's a young man. Grown-up now. He just wants to spread his wings."

"I know that." She had finished crying and was prowling round the table. "It would be all right if it was one of the girls from school. One of his own kind. But not this girl. Not this Tara. She'll poison him."

"No. Give Sam more credit than that. He's too bright to let that happen."

"You haven't seen her, Lloyd. There's something rotten about her." She flipped her hair off her forehead as if to flip the girl off her son. "Like part of her is dead inside. Dead and decaying."

"I still say no. Don't forget, he's his mother's son."

Anna halted her stride and smiled gratefully at him. "Thanks."

"So stop fretting. He'll come back in the morning, very sheepish I dare say, and you can tear a strip off him if you must. But don't be too hard on him. He's not a child any more."

Anna looked at him and he saw her eyes slowly fill with tears. "He is, Lloyd. He is. He's my child."

He took a step towards her but she shook away the tears and replaced them with anger. "And what about school tomorrow? And homework? What does he think he's playing at?"

Lloyd quite suddenly found himself annoyed with Anna. The boy wanted to be a man and she was still tying ribbons in his hair. Couldn't she see he needed to break free? Free from playing the Boy Wonder. Free from her. The poor kid had conformed too much already to her expectations.

"He's just sowing a few wild oats, Anna, that's all. Surely he has the right to do that."

Anna slumped down in a chair and shook her head at him. "Not when he has A levels next year."

"For heaven's sake, see things straight. That is twelve months away. This girl is here for just two weeks. Can't you at least give him that?"

Anna stared at him and he saw her blue eyes change, as she retreated from him.

"You don't own him, Anna."

"I am aware of that."

"He's far too well brought up to do anything really stupid. Just let him have his fling and when this kid has gone back home, he'll be his old self again. A bit older and wiser maybe. But still the Sam you love. And hardly the worse for wear. You'll wonder what all the fuss was about. It's just normal teenage stuff."

She listened to him politely.

"We'll see," she said, then stood up. "Thank you for bringing me home." A courteous dismissal.

Lloyd picked up his car keys and left.

Anna kept her finger on the doorbell. She could hear it ringing relentlessly. At first there was no other sound, but eventually it provoked a shout of "I'm coming, for Christ's sake."

The door opened a crack.

"Mrs Tucker, I apologise for disturbing you, but I'm looking for my son, Sam. Is he here? With Tara?"

"No, he's not," Josie Tucker groaned and started to shut the door.

Anna put her weight against it. "May I come in and talk to you a moment?"

"Do you know what bloody time it is?"

"Yes. I realise it's early but I need to speak to you."

"It's six o'clock in the morning, for Christ's sake. That's the middle of the night in my book." But she gave Anna a patient nod. "Look, come back later, will you, and we'll talk then. Okay?" Again she tried to close the door.

"No, it's not okay, Mrs Tucker. I need to speak to you now."

There was a pause during which Anna could see Josie Tucker working out whether she could get away with slamming the door in her landlady's face and deciding the odds weren't in her favour.

"Oh, all right. If you're that desperate. But not for long, mind." She stood back and allowed Anna to enter the flat.

Given a wider view, Anna could not help noticing that her tenant's hair was even bushier than usual, sending branches out in all directions, and a faint whiff of stale perfume tracked her every move. She was wearing a skimpy short nightdress in black satin which revealed heavy breasts and equally heavy thighs. With no make-up and her face still full of sleep, she looked older. Old enough to have a teenage daughter. Her smile was as amiable as ever.

"Thank you, Mrs Tucker."

"Josie, please."

"You say Sam is not here?"

"That's your son, right?"

"Yes."

"No, no Sams anywhere in sight." She smiled expectantly, obviously hoping that was the end of it.

"Are you sure?"

"Of course I'm sure."

"Do you mind if I look?"

Josie Tucker's amiability lapsed. "Of course I bloody mind. Are you calling me a liar?"

"No, not at all. I just wonder if he came in without your knowledge."

Josie relaxed. "Oh, I see." She chuckled. "Sneaked in for a night of passion, you mean."

Anna gritted her teeth. "Something like that, yes."

"No, no point. Tara's not here either. See for yourself if you like."

She led Anna to the bedroom containing the two singles. One was occupied by the bed-bouncing son, splayed on his back with arms and legs spread wide in abandon and rumbling snores issuing from his open mouth. The other bed was empty. Unmade and unoccupied.

"See? No Tara. No Sam," Josie Tucker whispered, so as not to wake her son from his dreams. She chuckled again. "Can't really blame her. Who'd want to sleep with that?"

They returned to the front door. The woman was really being extremely helpful, considering it was such an unreasonable hour. Yet Anna disliked her.

"Do you know where they are, Mrs Tucker?"

"Probably went to some nightclub and then dossed down in a friend's flat somewhere. Tara did mention she'd met some kids with a place near the harbour. That'll be where they are, you can bet your bottom dollar on it."

"Do you have any idea where near the harbour?"

"Not the faintest." She peered at Anna more closely. "In a tizz about it, are you, love? Don't you fret. Your Sam will come home when he's good and ready."

"Mrs Tucker, don't you worry about Tara? A sixteen- or even seventeen-year-old is still young. We should know where they are."

The woman laughed, "Good Lord, love, I gave up expecting to be told where Tara was going years ago. Little minx she is." She leaned forward and whispered confidentially, "Suspended from school she is at the moment."

Anna felt cold inside. "What for? What did she do?"

"The usual."

"What's that?"

"The same as most of them get caught for. Drugs." After one look at Anna, she added quickly, "Don't look so green round the gills. It was nothing heavy. So don't you worry. I've brought her down here to get her away from the bad crowd she was running with back home. Real dead-beats they were. And I can see your boy is a good clean lad. I was really pleased when he popped up here to see her yesterday evening. I said to her . . ."

"He came up here?"

"Yes." She smiled indulgently. "Apparently they'd had some kind of a tiff earlier. But they're as thick as thieves again now, the pair of them."

Anna winced. If only she had stayed at home last night. Not gone to Lloyd's.

"Sam is not allowed to spend the night out unless I know where he is," she said stiffly. "He has always let me know which friend he is staying with before."

"That's a bit tight, isn't it?" Josie Tucker reached out and patted her visitor's arm. "No need to worry your head about what they get up to. I always make sure Tara is well stocked up with rubbers." She threw back her head, bouncing her bush of hair, and laughed boisterously. "I remember all too well what young love is like."

A deep male voice issued from the second bedroom. "Josie, for Christ's sake, cut that cackle, will you? I'm trying to get some sleep."

"Sorry, love," Josie called back, and smiled with no hint of embarrassment at Anna. "A friend of mine," she explained. Then added brightly, "A very new friend."

Anna backed out of the door. "If Sam turns up here, will you send him down to me? Please."

"'Course, love."

Anna thanked her and made her way back downstairs, leaving her tenant to her very new friend.

7

Anna was not looking where she was going. Her eyes were on the shivering leaves of the tall poplar trees. They stood in a regimental row alongside the river at the back of the supermarket car park and reminded her of France. France was big on poplars and she had been intensely happy there. When Sam was small, and she and Ian had tried to make a go of the self-sufficiency scheme. They had bought a tiny battered old farm in the Dordogne and filled it with goats, ducks and hens, as well as dear Belle, an anaemic-looking cow. Anna smiled at the trees and remembered the old Charolais with a tug of affection, her hide sweet and musty, as Anna's cheek rested on her warm flank, while fingers coaxed out the milk.

It had been too good to last. Harvests failed and eggs did not pay for electricity. The money-men had moved in and the family had returned to England. Ian had gone into tennis coaching and sports goods, while Anna had produced Danny.

"Watch out, will you? Bloody women drivers."

Her supermarket trolley had drifted into the path of a man reversing a Peugeot estate from its slot in the ranks of cars, and now threatened its paintwork. Anna had no inclination to dredge up an apology but put her laden trolley into reverse.

The wind shimmered across the poplar leaves like sunlight on water and Anna stood watching. It was easier than watching the wind in her own life. A week ago when she had stood there with an identical trolley, watching the trees with identical eyes, the world had looked a sunny place to be. She had been humming as she unpacked the trolley into the Fiesta boot and toying with the idea of one day taking a cruise down the River Nile. When she could afford it. One day when her coach came in. That had made her laugh and she had dropped a pack of six eggs on the tarmac. A dog on its way to the riverbank had lapped them up and wagged his tail like a propeller.

Today Anna found she did not want to move. She was standing, hand on the trolley, just staring at the trees. Her car was a few yards away, but she had no desire to reach it. It was as if her life was becoming unravelled, and while she remained still the unravelling had stopped. The moment she moved she knew it would start up again. She had waited for Sam to come home all night and all morning, but there had been no sign of him. No key in the lock, no ring of the telephone. Nothing. Normally she went to the supermarket early on a Tuesday morning, but she had delayed it and delayed it, in the hope of seeing him arrive back at the flat. In the end, during the lull in the teashop after lunch, she had driven over and made a quick dash round the aisles. Now all she had to do was drive home again. So why couldn't she make it to the car?

"Hello, Anna. You're not usually here at this hour."

It was Harriet Torrence. Behind her crawled Nella, pushing a trolley as if it were a ball and chain.

"No, I'm later than usual. I was busy this morning."

Harriet took it to mean the teashop was busy, so smiled encouragingly. "I'm glad business is brisk. Any news on the coaches?"

"No, not yet. There's an executive meeting of the Chamber about it on Wednesday."

"I rely on you and Lloyd to make them see sense. We can't afford to lose those tourists up our end of the town." She laughed, showing her camel teeth.

Anna was pleased to see her friend so full of good cheer, but she wondered what had triggered the swing of mood. How could someone attempt suicide one day and be so full of laughter less than two days later? As if letting out the blood had let out the demons. She noticed Harriet was wearing a long-sleeved blouse to cover the bandages on her wrists.

Anna suddenly realised Harriet was still talking.

". . . and so I'm taking advantage of Nella to do the donkey work for me."

Anna recognised the narrowed eyes and clenched jaw of incipient rebellion in a teenager. She smiled at her. "Hello, Nella."

"Hi."

"No school?"

Nella drew in a long, patient breath. "Mum has just been telling you. I had a dentist appointment."

"Nothing gruesome, I hope."

"No, just a check-up." She was staring at the contents of the trolley as she spoke, as if tins of catfood made a more conducive companion. Less hassle, fewer questions. "Mum says the trolley hurts her wrists."

Harriet beamed at her. "Isn't she wonderful? Aren't I lucky?"

"Yes," Anna said, keeping it minimalist.

Nella threw a quick scowl at her mother from under her dark eyebrows and flicked her hand through her thick mane in the gesture beloved of all long-haired teenagers. "Shall I unload now?" She held out her hand for the car keys.

"Thanks." Harriet passed them over and watched her daughter slouch over to where the 2CV was parked, trailing the trolley. "She's still annoyed with me," she said in a lowered voice to Anna.

"So I see."

"I'm just sitting it out and feeding her ice-cream. That usually does the trick."

"Harriet, she's seventeen, not seven."

Harriet smiled slowly and shook her head. "Is there much difference?"

"Yes," Anna said with feeling. "You don't have to tiptoe round them on eggshells when they're little."

Harriet's dove-grey eyes studied her with concern. "Oh yes? So which of the boys is cutting up rough?"

"It's Sam."

"Good heavens, that's unlike him, the blue-eyed boy. What's he been up to?"

"Oh, just being a pain."

"Adolescents are experts at that."

"Come on, Mum." Nella's voice carried from twenty metres away.

"Give me a call," Harriet urged, and just for a moment her bony fingers rested on Anna's shoulder. "We can have a moan together."

Anna nodded. "I will." She looked across the busy car park, and the sight of Nella leaning against the car, twirling the keys in an impatient circle, prompted her to add, "Maybe you could ask Nella to have a chat with Sam at school. They're good friends. To find out what's going on inside his head."

"I can try. I'll ask her, but Lord knows whether she'll oblige. Though she should, because she owes you one." Harriet smiled gently. "We all owe you one."

Then she turned and trotted off towards the twirling keys.

He was back. The moment Anna entered the flat she knew he was there. His jacket hung in the hallway.

"Sam?" she called.

There was no answer.

Keeping one eye on the door to the sitting-room, she dumped her shopping on the floor and quickly ran her fingers through the jacket pockets.

Nothing.

Unless you count a few sweet papers and a comb. Feeling like a criminal, she picked up her bags and carried them through to the kitchen.

"Sam?" she called again.

"I'm here." His voice came from his bedroom.

Petrified of finding Tara there as well, she pushed open his door. But no, he was alone. Sprawled out on his bed in shorts and tee-shirt, playing on his brother's Game Gear. His brown eyes smiled up at her and suddenly she found she could breathe more easily. It was as if her lungs had been struggling through treacle and had abruptly broken free. She wanted to hug him. Instead she leant against the door-frame. No invasion of his space.

"I was worried, Sam."

He looked up again from the electronic mayhem in his hands. "Worried? Why? I left a note telling you I wouldn't be back." All wide-eyed innocence.

"You know I like to be told where you'll be. It's only fair, Sam.

I didn't even know you were going out at all. Until I arrived home and found the note."

He returned to the game. "I didn't know myself until after you had left."

"Who were you with?"

"Oh, various people. No one you know."

"Tara Tucker?"

He kept his attention firmly on the miniature screen. "Yes, she was one of them." Elaborately casual.

"And where did you stay?"

"At a friend's flat."

"Where?"

"Oh, come on, Ma. That's enough of a grilling. It was just a night out, that's all. No big deal." He looked tired. Grey shadows made his cheeks seem old. He rubbed the down on his chin as if it were stubble.

"You're supposed to be at school today."

"I know. But I'm honestly too knackered." He turned to her and gave a mischievous grin that knocked the last of her anger on the head. She was so pleased that he was home. "Don't dob on me to Mr Berry, will you?" Mr Berry was the head of the sixth form. "I'll have a bath and then get some sleep, so I'll be okay for school in the morning. You can write a note saying I had a sore throat or something."

Anna stood up straight. "I certainly will not."

"Aw, go on." He dumped the Game Gear and swung his lanky frame off the bed. He stood in front of her, rested both hands heavily on her shoulders and looked down into her eyes. All very serious. "Ma, I know what I'm doing. So don't get on my case. Just leave me in peace. I haven't forgotten all the lectures on the evils of drink, drugs and sex. So there's no need to worry over me. Save that for your coaches. Trust me. Okay?"

Her eyes were on a level with his throat and she could see the blue edge of a lovebite not quite hidden by the tee-shirt. That plum-coloured mouth of hers had been eating his skin. She looked away, up into his father's eyes.

"Okay, Sam. On condition you miss no more school, get your homework done and keep within house rules. That means no nights away, except at weekends. Even then I must know where you'll be. Your other activities are your own business.''

''Thanks,'' he said.

She wanted to put her arms around his adolescent body and hold him tight. But he stepped out of reach and whistled his way to the bathroom.

It didn't take her long. As soon as she heard the splashing noises that announced Sam was in the bath, she started her search. His room was the usual mess with yesterday's clothes littering the floor. She hunted through his trouser pockets, his bedside cupboard, the shoulder-bag dumped by his pillow, and had a quick flick through his clothes in the chest-of-drawers. Even the underwear. But other than an old Valentine card from a girl in his class at school, she came up with nothing.

She didn't know exactly what she was looking for. Feared to admit it even to herself. But as she rummaged through his personal possessions, she just hoped for something, anything, to give her some clues as to what he had been doing. When she had searched his jacket in the hall, she had felt guilty. But not now. This time the guilt had gone. The question of whether she should or shouldn't be doing this, no longer arose. He was her child and she was protecting him. From himself, if need be.

In his desk drawer she found his wallet. There was something intensely intimate about a wallet. Such personal territory. But Anna did not hesitate. Children were not allowed privacy. Privacy was something you earned as a grown-up, she told herself. And whatever Lloyd might say, to a mother a child is a child. They get bigger and older. But grown-up? No. So she opened it.

Inside were only a few coins. Where was all his money? But in the back she came across some night-club flyers and an identification card. It bore a photograph of Sam, putting on his serious face in the hope of looking older, and stated that he was a member of Exeter University students union. The date of birth made him eighteen. She wondered how much he'd had to pay for it and what sleaze-bag had supplied it.

In a separate compartment she found a pack of condoms. Two were missing. She read the description on the pack: the sheath with knobs on for extra stimulation every inch of the way! What had happened to plain old feather-light? And where had he got hold of these? Maybe they were the ones Josie Tucker supplied for her daughter, acquired over a boisterous giggle in some Sheffield sex-shop. To titillate her very new friends, no doubt.

Anna didn't know whether to be grateful or more miserable. At least, she tried to reassure herself, he had that much sense. God only knew what the girl might be infected with. She returned everything to its correct compartment and was careful to replace the wallet exactly where she had found it in the drawer. She tried the other side of the desk, a small door to a section that she knew had always contained his music tapes and CDs.

It was locked.

She tugged at the door but it would not budge. She shook it harder and the whole desk responded by leaping wildly, so that Sam's pens dived on to the floor like well-trained soldiers. She picked them up, gave the desk one last resentful thump and left the room. As she walked past the bathroom, she could hear Sam whistling, as merry as mistletoe.

The traffic was heavy in the centre of town and Lloyd was going to be late. It annoyed him intensely. He had arranged to meet the borough planning officer at the leisure centre to inspect the bays that would be allocated to the coaches in the car park. The meeting was for four-thirty, but despite leaving his office in good time, he had been telephoned on the mobile by his secretary and asked to call in at the printers in the High Street. The latest sales brochures for their recent speedboat design were ready to be collected.

So now his time had ticked away and with it his patience. Tourists were clogging the streets. A cool breeze was producing the kind of weather that was ideal for the town. Dry and bright enough to tempt holidaymakers out of their hotels, but windy enough to drive them into the shops and cafés. It wasn't that Lloyd objected to their rosy faces packing the pavements. It was just their cars that got up his nose.

He had missed lunch altogether. A hiccup in the workshop had kept him up to his elbows in engine oil for several hours and his stomach was now growling like one of his speedboats at full throttle. He had filled up on cigarettes instead and his throat felt fit for sandcastles, rather than sandwiches. After a quick detour down a rat-run that was frequented by locals but kept a masonic secret from grockles, Lloyd pulled into the leisure centre car park. Four-thirty-four the fascia clock announced. Damn its liquid crystal.

Lawrence Enfield from the Chamber executive was standing by the entrance door, very dapper in sports jacket, cravat and cavalry twill. His moustache looked well stroked. Lloyd wondered how long he had been waiting there.

"Hello, Lawrence. I got caught up in traffic. No sign of George yet?"

"He has just pulled in over there."

Enfield nodded in the direction of the bottle-bank in one corner, where the borough officer was unloading a carton of glass containers. Mainly wine empties with the odd gin bottle thrown in. They could hear the nerve-grating crashes as he dutifully sorted them by colour before hurrying over to them and apologising for the delay. George Paige had ginger hair and a ginger face that at the moment was wearing a look of disappointment.

"No Anna Forrest?" he enquired. "She said at the meeting on Wednesday that she wanted to inspect the site allocated to the coaches here today. I told her it would be this Friday."

"She sends her apologies," Lloyd informed him, "but she has been detained by business."

So hard luck, George, and tuck your tongue back in.

In fact her actual message had not been quite so calm and businesslike. She had rung him in a panic that morning to say she would be stuck in the teashop all day. Sam had announced over breakfast that he would not be doing his usual Friday afternoon stint between four and six o'clock. No explanation. Just that he would be out. Apparently she had reasoned with him but got nowhere. On the phone, her voice had sounded halfway between murderous and suicidal, and he could picture that blonde hair of hers rumpled to death by frustration.

"Well, that's a shame," George Paige muttered, as he led them off to the far end of the car park.

Lloyd listened to the list of facts and figures that George reeled off, numbers of coaches and times of turn-around. The meeting was more a gesture of co-operation than anything else, but Lloyd asked a few relevant questions, just to show willing. He left the long-winded speeches to Lawrence Enfield. When they finally ran out of steam, Lloyd thanked George for his time and information, put in a request for full consultation with traders before any final decision was taken, and set off towards his Rover before Enfield could think up any new issues to take them round the track once more.

A shiny face, with extremely short blond hair and a pair of wide shoulders that looked as if they were stuffed with coconuts, greeted him with an amiable, "Cheers, Lloyd."

It was Danny Forrest, just emerging from the leisure centre, towel under one arm and smile over his face. The training must have gone well. "Hello, Danny. Can't you at least have the decency to look worn out after all that swimming?" Lloyd teased. "Even a little tired would help."

Danny grinned, his eyes bloodshot from immersion in chlorine and bearing panda imprints around them where the goggles had been. "I'm exhausted," he declared, looking the picture of energy.

It reminded Lloyd of his far-off rugby days in Wales, when a hard match left him battered and bruised and on a high that even the space-shuttle couldn't reach. Adrenaline rushes were few and far between these days. Too few and too far between. A fierce wind in his sail on a rough sea could still get his blood charging like a prop-forward, or even a blast across the waves in his latest racing boat, throttle wide and salt spray rearing all around him. That certainly got the juices flowing. Especially if he had been shackled to his office all day. He cast a covetous glance in the direction of the marina and decided the wretched piles of paperwork crawling all over his desk would have to wait. The weekend could start an hour or two early.

"You're certainly looking fit, Danny. Any competitions coming up?"

"You bet. A really heavy one in Wales. It's going to be tight."

"In Cardiff?"

"Yes."

"I used to swim in that pool as a teenager. That was before the nicotine demon got me. But you'd better watch out, they produce some great sportsmen."

Danny looked at him as if he were from Mars, then broadened his shoulders and jeered, "They haven't a hope. We'll flatten them. Out of sight."

"No chance." Lloyd let his Welsh accent thicken. "If it's Welsh muscle you're up against, you don't stand a chance in hell, boyo."

"In your dreams," Danny countered, and they both laughed to bridge the nationalistic gulf.

They had reached the Rover and Danny gave the front tyre a hopeful kick. "Going past Market Square, are you?"

"No, I'm not. But okay, hop in."

Danny was in the passenger seat before Lloyd could change his mind.

It was while they were stuck at a traffic light which had fallen asleep on red that Lloyd asked casually, "How are things at home?"

Danny was fiddling with the electric windows, sliding them up and down like guillotines. "Okay."

"And Sam?"

"Oh, that. He's hardly ever at home."

"So I gather."

"Ma's really uptight." A fly gave its wings a breather by landing on the edge of the rising pane of glass and was promptly squashed as it slotted into the metal frame. Danny slid the window down again and flicked off the remains. It left a yellow smear. "She's just waiting for Tara to leave."

"That's not for another week though, is it?" The lights at last obliged and trickled on to green.

"I know," Danny chuckled and opened the glove-locker, clicked it shut, then opened it again. "Sam is having a mental time, but he says Ma is doing his head in." A few more clicks, then he started on the electric side-mirror.

"What's Tara like?"

"No idea really. Seems all right. I've only spoken to her twice. Once on the stairs and once on the beach." He glanced quickly at Lloyd and rattled on at speed, as if to cover a mistake. "She's not exactly a babe, but she's nice enough, I suppose. She's nothing like girls at school. They're all giggly and speak properly. She doesn't half swear a lot." The last was said with open admiration.

"Have you tried speaking to Sam yourself? Talking the situation through with him?"

"No."

"It might help."

Danny shrugged and the mirror gave Lloyd a close-up view of the side panel of his car. "I could give it a go, I s'pose. But he's not around much."

"He might even appreciate it, you never know."

"Or I might get my face thumped."

"Try it."

"Okay. If you think it will help." Danny abandoned the switch and looked round at Lloyd. For that one moment he let slip the brightness from his forget-me-not eyes. "I don't like Ma and Sam to be at each other. Not like this. I wish Tara was gone."

"Then let's do something about it. You speak to your brother and I'll have a word with your mother."

"It's a deal." The brightness bounced back and his fingers took up where they had left off.

Lloyd put his foot down in the hope of getting his car to Market Square while it was still in one piece.

The telephone jangled and Anna's body jerked like a calf on the wrong end of a cattle prod. An electric shock that jumbled the mind and scrambled the senses.

God, my nerves are shot.

She picked up the receiver with no wish to speak to anyone.

"Hello, Anna, it's me."

"Harriet." Anna had been meaning to call her. "How are you feeling?"

"No need to fret, my friend. All is sweetness and light. Even Nella is beginning to talk to me again."

"Good for her."

"And Jonathan is full of plans for preventive measures. He thinks my problem is that I am out of touch with the earth. That's why I lose myself in too many air currents, too many whirlwinds of emotion."

"Is that what *you* think?"

Harriet laughed, somewhat self-consciously. "Who knows? Anyway, would you believe we're buying a field over in Wadham? Good soil and not too damp, the way it is nearer the river. We're going to cultivate it. Digging and planting, hoeing and harvesting. But we haven't quite decided what to grow yet. Jonathan says it will put me in touch with the earth-bound currents. Make me more stable."

"Sounds to me like he is the one who needs stabilising."

Harriet chuckled. "No, Anna, he's being great. Very concerned and wanting to help. And you never know, it might work. I've got to try."

Digging together, growing seed together, watching and worrying, and then reaping the benefit together. Like having children. Yes, it would work. It was the togetherness that could make it work.

"Sounds fun anyway, Harriet. I wish you both luck, I really do."

"Thanks."

Anna suddenly felt very lonely. So isolated, she might as well be at the north pole. Her skin felt cold and she shivered.

"What I was actually ringing about was Sam. How are things going?"

Anna couldn't even begin to talk about it. Not even to Harriet.

"Bearable."

"I asked Nella to speak to him and she says it's nothing. Just a casual thing. A holiday romance. Nothing for you to worry about."

Anna clutched at the straw. "Is that what Sam said?"

"Seems so, yes."

"That girl is not important to him?"

"No. So you've nothing to worry about."

Anna could almost feel the waves of comfort, the desire to

help, flowing down the line from Harriet. "Thank you, Harriet. And thank Nella from me."

"I will. So cheer up. It seems Sam's got it all under control after all."

"I hope so. Sorry, but I must go now. Something is over-cooking in the oven. Thanks again. Take care." She hung up. Her arms wrapped around her own body and rocked it gently.

It was worse. Worse than her fears. And God knows, they were bad enough already. Either Sam was lying or Nella was lying. Why? What were they hiding? She could feel the hairs tingling on the back of her neck and for the first time in many years was suddenly consumed by the belief that the burden of bringing up children was too great for one person. A beloved burden it may be, but on your own, there was no one to catch it when you dropped it.

8

The room was dark because the light-bulb that hung nakedly from the ceiling had expired with a sharp pop. Nobody had replaced it. Sam moved his head, very carefully in case it became disconnected from his body, and looked round the gloom. Dim shapes of people he supposed he must know moved in front of his eyes and he wondered if they were aware that they all had haloes. Glittering spiky haloes that reminded him of sparklers on bonfire night.

He felt great. Really great. Much calmer now. He tucked an arm tighter round Tara who was asleep, curled up beside him on the floor. She is a petal, he thought, pale and fragile and infinitely touchable. He bent his head to sniff the bare skin of her shoulder. It smelt of strawberries in the sun and he gently licked a small spot, expecting it to taste sweet and sticky. The tang of dirt and dust was a disappointment to his tongue and he wiped it on his arm in disgust. It was because they were lying stretched out on the carpet. Zack's carpet. It was grey and threadbare and harboured unknown stains and odours that only a few days ago would have worried him. Now he knew better. Infinitely better.

Zack and Sparky were somewhere around but they weren't bothering him. Not yet anyway. And he could hear Tammy's high voice whining about something. Probably after more of his pills. He had a feeling a voice he didn't recognise was calling him, but he shut his eyes and blocked it out. He didn't want it to be his mother's. Not after that last row.

Calmer now. And peaceful. His heart wasn't hammering to get out of his chest any more. He ran the fingertips of one hand down each of Tara's ribs and imagined he was playing the piano. Chopin's Minute Waltz, just like his piano teacher had instructed, with a light, flowing touch. The fingers rebelled and set off to slide up over the arc of her hip and down the smooth steep curve of her bottom. Soft as a bird's wing.

Tara was the only occupant of his head. He knew that was the way it was, and though he had struggled against it at first, he now accepted it as inevitable. She swirled round in his brain, dizzying him with her movement. At times he saw her like a cuckoo in there, growing bigger and stronger each time she managed to push out another egg to smash it to pieces on the ground beneath. He smiled, lying there in the dark room, because he knew he didn't want any other eggs. Not any more.

Tara was like no one he had ever known. Free and flying unfettered across the sky, looking down on the insects crawling below. Sam didn't want to be an insect.

"It's for you," Esther Miller said and handed over the telephone receiver. It was on a small desk at the back of the teashop. "Sam's school."

She took the tray of dirty dishes from Anna's hands and disappeared into the kitchen. Eavesdropping was not one of her failings. If Anna wanted her to know, she would tell her. A couple of coaches from Reading had just off-loaded in the square and their occupants were already homing in on the scones and pots of tea. The apricot flans were also going down a treat and Esther was glad she had come in early this morning to help out with baking them. Especially as Anna was looking so tired. Unlike that merry old bird in the corner. The one with the Carmen Miranda hat and the equally fruity mouth. Sounds as if she's been topping up with something stronger than tea, Esther chuckled, then she set about the hot chocolate, hoping Anna would get her skates on.

A call from the school was a rare occurrence and Anna was uncertain as to what to expect. "Hello?" she said cautiously.

"Hello, Mrs Forrest. This is the school secretary. I have been asked by Mr Berry to ring you. He just wants to query a note he received."

"A note?"

"Yes, a sick note."

Anna held her breath.

"It said Sam has flu and that is why he is not at school." She paused, but receiving no response continued, "Mr Berry was not happy about the signature." She coughed slightly awkwardly. "He suspected it might not be yours."

"How long has Sam been away from school?" Anna asked.

"Ten days. Since Monday of last week."

Ten days. He had not been to school for ten days. Ever since he first met that girl. That Tucker girl. He had been lying to her all this time. Going off in the mornings with his lunch money, coming home around four as if completing a school day, spending an hour or so in the teashop and then going out in the evening. She had chivvied him gently at first, but when it had no effect she had positively insisted that he stay in to complete homework, and that when he did go out in the evening, he should come home earlier. Midnight was too late with school next morning. When he disobeyed her and returned at all hours, she had remonstrated loudly but clung for comfort to the fact that he was still attending school each day. But it had been a sham. All a sham.

"Mrs Forrest?"

"I'm sorry."

"Can you therefore confirm it? Did you send in the note to say Sam is at home with flu?"

"No. No, I did not." Sam would hate her.

"So the note is a forgery?"

Anna could hear the woman's ill-concealed amusement.

"It is not funny," she shouted down the line. "My son is in trouble and it's not funny." She slammed down the receiver and the whole telephone skidded off the desk and on to the floor with a plastic crash. It lay on its side, whirring complainingly. She left it there.

She flew up the stairs two at a time. Right up to the top floor. Her fist banged on the door, too angry to find the bell.

"Mrs Tucker," she called loudly. "Mrs Tucker, I need to speak to you." Bang, bang. "Open the door." Bang.

If the woman was out, she would wait on this spot until she came home again. Wait and bang, wait and bang. Wishing it was Tara Tucker's face she was banging.

Abruptly the door opened. "What's all the fuss about, for heaven's sake?" It was Josie Tucker, neat and tidy in a linen suit with short skirt. "Mrs Forrest, it's you. What's up? Is there a fire or something?"

"Mrs Tucker, I want to talk to you," Anna said firmly and walked into the flat.

The week was not going well for Lloyd. To begin with, some idiot crunched the front wing of his Rover and turned out to have neither insurance nor MOT. Sod's law. His assistant then compounded matters by breaking his leg in a rock-climbing accident and taking to his bed. What the hell was the silly fool doing dangling from a rope down a cliff-face in the first place? Then an urgent delivery of manifolds went missing and threw the workshop into panic, so that he had to waste half a day on one end of a telephone tracking it down.

The boatyard was in the throes of the usual summer rush and he had spent the last two days working on noise reduction for a cabin cruiser, instead of out testing the sweet new hull of his beloved speedboat. An altogether different kind of challenge and one that he relished. Cabin cruisers were by nature living-quarters as well as water-transport and there was a constant plea for greater sound-dampening. He was only too aware that any effort spent in reducing noise in a boat was worthwhile. Noise induces fatigue, which in turn reduces human efficiency.

His foreman in the yard, Dave Taylor, objected to anything that deflected him from work on the sleek sailing-boats that he loved to build and was at present sulking under beetle-black brows and the battered peak of his trawlerman's cap. Admittedly, the smaller boats did present more of a problem when it came to noise because there was less space to install proper insulation panelling. But for Lloyd a boat was a boat, and he loved them all.

The paperwork was altogether a different matter. Right at this moment his accountant was sitting like a spider in Lloyd's office, waiting to trail his spindly limbs all over the boatyard books. It was the part of the business that Lloyd loathed. Figures and files and forms, fit only for stuffing down the taxman's throat. A wasted morning, as far as he was concerned. With regret he swept his hand along the cruiser's hull and patted her flanks as if taking leave of a favourite racehorse, grabbed a deep lungful of sea air and blue sky, then headed indoors.

His office was not up to much. A desk, two chairs, metal shelving stacked high with marine books and in the corner a drawing-board. That was about it. No frills. A place he avoided if he could. Most of his design work was done at home with a brandy in one hand, a cigarette in the other and a vision in his head. His secretary kept trying to pin up glamorous posters of powerboats and sailing yachts in surging seas. "To remind visitors what we're about," she pointed out. But he had no time for them. If he wanted to see a boat, he looked out the window.

The chair opposite his desk was occupied by a small, slight man with thinning hair that he tried to counterbalance with a bushy moustache.

"A lovely morning, Lloyd." The accountant greeted him with a contented smile and outstretched hand.

"It was. Until you turned up," Lloyd said, and his companion laughed, under the misapprehension that his client was joking.

Lloyd's secretary scampered in with biscuits and coffee and a large clean ashtray. The accountant eyed it with dismay, so she opened the window wide and instantly the sound of machine tools from the workshop drifted in on the scent of a sea breeze.

"Thanks, June," Lloyd said, more comfortable now that his boatyard had taken a step in through the window.

"Give a shout when the ashtray's full." She treated him to a snide grin and hopped out pretty smartly when he threatened to throw the offending article at her.

June Fairley had worked for Lloyd for four years, ever since leaving school at sixteen. Though she liked to pretend she was a fluffy blonde with a giggle that belonged to a five-year-old, her mind was as sharp and efficient as one of Lloyd's electric saws.

She dealt with everything that Lloyd did not wish to be bothered by, all the business incidentals that had nothing to do with boats. Her own passion for speed had been hijacked by motorbikes and nothing Lloyd could say or do would tempt her out in one of his boats. "Too risky," she would declare, before leaping astride her Kawasaki.

Lloyd lit a cigarette, sat himself on the window-ledge where he could watch the boats on the slipway, and remembered to nod whenever the accountant seemed to require an affirmative.

It was only later in the day when June reminded him it was Wednesday, that he remembered the Chamber of Trade & Commerce meeting. Those damn coaches. He would have to draft an official statement for the executive to approve, so that the Council could now make its final decision. There had been considerable representation from the beach and harbour areas, the Council had informed Lloyd, for a return to the original intention of shifting the coaches over to the leisure centre car park, lock, stock and barrel.

Lloyd groaned to himself. That meant more trips around the coast in cruisers and seductive speedboats to sway the vacillating councillors. No bribery, of course. They would jib at that. Just gentle persuasion. A few perks and warm brandies all round. It had worked before, it would work again. On the whole they meant well, but some were unquestionably in it for the glory. Damn those pompous pricks. And damn their undying devotion to the sound of their own voices. Though he had to admit, even the Chamber had its fair share of those. He constantly assured himself he had not become one of their number, and if ever he caught himself talking of being 'pro-active' or searching for a 'window of opportunity', he gave his ankle a wicked kick under the table and shut his mouth. It was amazing what a long table and a gavel in the hand could do to the brain.

The thought of the meeting tonight reminded him of Anna and he felt the familiar kick of desire for her. He had rung her several times at the weekend in the hope of a word about that six-foot son of hers, but each time he had only got Danny. Lloyd had a feeling she was skulking out of reach of anyone except

Sam and he felt a twinge of concern for Danny. The Chamber pow-wow would be a good opportunity to corner her. But when he rang her at the teashop to suggest a drink after the meeting, he met with a stone wall. How about before the meeting, then? Apologies, but no. She would not be able to attend at all this evening. Sorry. No excuses. Just sorry.

Lloyd hung up. Anna never missed meetings. What the hell was she up to?

It was late when Lloyd set off for home. Nearly eleven and he was dog-tired. For the millionth time he decided that people were their own worst enemies.

The Chamber executive had been in full flight tonight, as if the divisions over the coaches had opened up old wounds and old enmities. It had started with an innocent enough remark from Amy Court about wanting street entertainers to add to the fun of the Summer Festival that they were arranging for August. That had led to a comment on the poor organisation of last year's Carnival and then all hell had let loose. A firework display Guy Fawkes would have been proud of. Lloyd had eventually grabbed them all by the scruff of the neck, given them a darn good shake and imposed an enforced truce.

But as he drove home, acutely aware of the empty seat beside him, he wondered whether it was worth the effort. The Chamber did a great deal for the town, as well as representing its collective business-voice, so it was in all their interests to pull together. But would they ever learn? After a night like tonight, he felt they could all jump off the end of the pier and he wouldn't care a jot.

On a sudden whim, he pointed the Rover down towards the harbour. There was a full moon that vied for brightness with his headlights and created unaccustomed shadows that loomed out of the darkness. As he pulled into the horseshoe curve of the harbour, the ancient sea-walls reared up like guardians of the marine cradle. The tide was high and the waves gently rocked the moored boats with a lullaby of sighs and rattling masts. He rolled down the window and just the smell of the salt air soothed the tight coil of his nerves. He could feel it slowly unwinding, slurring the tension inside him like an old-fashioned gramophone running down. He parked the car by the harbour wall and looked out over the harsh lights of the town for only a moment. His eyes swung away hungrily to the silvery sheen of the sea where the water swayed under its shawl of moonlight.

To hell with the town. And even more, to hell with women. A boat you could rely on.

Ten minutes later his racing dinghy was on the water, sail unfurled, and the night wind was lifting the sleek bow through the waves.

His sleep was as rough as the seas in his dreams. Endlessly he tossed and turned in his bed, twisting the sheet into tight knots as he fought the storms, until finally, with sails reefed and tiller lashed to one side, he let the winds take control. Then a lull of sorts descended and his rest achieved a precarious peace.

By five o'clock he was awake again. His eyes felt gritty with salt and he took a long, scalding shower. Only then did he feel up to giving the day the once-over. Outside the window, the early-morning sky was streaked with feathered fingers of blood-red where the dawn had left its imprint on the clouds. The cool breeze of the night before had picked up to a steady westerly wind that swayed the yukka palms in his garden and rattled the crowding wisteria against the windows of the house. After his third cup of black coffee, Lloyd was just starting to feel almost human, when the doorbell screeched at him. He looked at his watch. Not yet six o'clock. What early bird was looking for worms, he wondered?

He opened the door and in front of him stood the last person he expected to see.

"Sam." Lloyd stared hard to make sure he wasn't still seeing phantoms from the night before. "Sam, what the hell do you want at this hour?"

"Can I have a talk with you, please?" The words were mumbled awkwardly, but his eyes were focused on Lloyd's with pin-point intensity and there was no way Lloyd could turn them down.

"You'd better come on in, then." He stepped aside to let the boy into the hall but Sam hung back.

Lloyd waited for enlightenment.

Sam's eyes had found Lloyd's shoes and were now addressing them. "I've got someone with me."

"Anna?" It came out before Lloyd could stop it. Bloody stupid, of course it wouldn't be Anna.

"No." Sam's feet shuffled, as if contemplating flight. "It's Tara."

Oh hell. Anna was going to love him for this.

"You had better bring her in as well."

Instantly a small dark head popped into sight behind Sam's shoulder and her slight figure leant against his, as if frightened to allow daylight between them. Lloyd nodded a greeting to her, then turned and walked into the kitchen where the coffee pot offered sustenance. He had a feeling he was going to need it.

"Coffee?" he asked them when they were both standing uncomfortably in the middle of the room.

They nodded in unison.

"Sit down."

They did as they were told.

On closer view, Lloyd was forced to sympathise with Anna. The girl did not look good news. He had been inclined until then to believe that Anna was making a fuss about nothing, but now that the girl was sitting in front of him, he could understand why a mother would be getting uneasy. There was a sly, deceitful look about her face and her dark eyes were jumpy as hell. But her body had a softness and a fragility that gave it a vulnerable appeal and made him understand why Sam sat so close to her, as if protecting her.

"Well, what can I do for you at this ungodly hour?"

He placed the coffees on the table in front of the two teenagers but neither touched them. The girl's right hand sneaked out across her body and entwined itself tightly in Sam's right hand, while her other hand was tucked into the back of his jeans. It created a tight, possessive circle around him. Lloyd wondered if she chanted spells as an encore.

"It's about the job. The job in your boatyard. That's why we've come," Sam said, his voice tense and nervous.

"You have materialised on my doorstep at six o'clock in the

morning just to ask for a job in the summer holidays?" Lloyd asked incredulously.

"Not quite."

"Not quite what?"

"It's not quite for a summer job."

Lloyd could see it coming. That girl had warped the boy's mind.

"I need a job right away. A permanent job."

"And what about school?"

Sam straightened his back and lifted his chin in a gesture that was so reminiscent of his mother that it almost made Lloyd smile. "I've left school."

"Why on earth would you do a damn fool thing like that?"

It came out in a rush. "Because I've decided against university. If I had a job in your boatyard, I could learn engineering in a really practical way. Not all theory, like school is. I would be in a job and earning money."

"You've got it all worked out."

"Yes, I have. I've thought about it." He stopped and his brown eyes pleaded with Lloyd. "I would work very hard, I promise. You wouldn't be disappointed."

"I'm sure I wouldn't, Sam."

"Does that mean it's yes?"

"Hey, slow down. Let's have a good look at this." Lloyd had remained standing, leaning against the dresser, and now studied his early birds carefully. They both looked tired and somehow disorientated, as if they had lost touch with the world outside themselves. Their clothes were the usual blend of black and grey, giving their skins the ashen pallor that Lloyd knew the youth of today seemed to admire as much as his own generation had admired mahogany suntans. He lit a cigarette to lubricate the sluggish brain-cogs, but did not offer one to the teenagers.

"And what does your mother have to say about this, Sam?"

"She doesn't know."

Lloyd had suspected that was the case. That after a bust-up with Anna, they were trying to get to him before she did. "Don't you think you should discuss it with her first?"

Sam's jaw hardened and his fingers fiddled with the silver rings on Tara's hand. "No, I don't. It's none of her business now. I've left home."

Lloyd took a long pull on his cigarette and said quietly, "That's not a sensible move."

Sam's eyes retreated to Tara's fingers and he fiddled harder. The silence stretched out uncomfortably and was only broken by the girl. She spoke for the first time.

"It's his mother's own fault. She asked for it, didn't she, Sam?"

Lloyd had to admit she had an enticing voice, all silky and low, as soft as cat's fur. But if she uttered one more word against Anna, she would end up in the harbour.

He made a point of addressing just Sam. "What happened?"

The response caught him by surprise.

One moment the boy was sitting at the table quietly twiddling the girl's rings, trying to handle the situation in a way he believed was adult and mature. But the next, he exploded. Like a fizzy can when it's shaken. Burst into an outpouring of emotion straight out of a two-year-old's temper tantrum rule-book.

"She had no right, none at all. Behind my back she did it. Without even talking to me. Just because I'd missed a bit of school. Who does she think she is? Some kind of god or something who decides what should and shouldn't happen to people? It was wrong, fucking wrong, and so yes, she did ask for it. I don't want to live under that roof any more. Never again. Never. She had no right to interfere in my life." The words ran out and he drew breath. "No right at all."

Lloyd let the dust settle, then asked calmly, "What did she do?"

Sam stared angrily at the girl but said nothing. As if the words were too awful to be spoken. It was Tara who supplied the answer.

"She tried to bribe my mum to take me home right away. Not wait till the end of the holiday. She even offered to pay for a fortnight in Spain instead."

Oh God, Anna. You've really lost it this time.

"Can you believe the fucking nerve?" the girl continued, rolling her dark eyes upward in exaggerated horror.

Lloyd was just about to bring up the fucking nerve of

stick-insects who snaffle sons from under their mother's nose and tempt them out of school, when Sam burst out with, "That's why I need the job. To get a flat for us. Tara is staying here. With me. Not returning to Sheffield. We want somewhere together."

"Half the places won't take anyone on DSS," Tara added.

"And where are you staying at the moment?"

"At a friend's flat," Sam volunteered. "But he didn't come home last night, so we couldn't get in."

"So you've been out on the streets all night?"

Sam nodded sheepishly. "Yeah."

Lloyd shuddered inwardly. "It's tough, Sam, when you decide to take care of yourself. But there's no need to start on the treadmill so young. You could finish school first."

The boy shook his head adamantly. "No way. I want out."

"I can see that."

"So is it yes?" the girl asked with a plaintive smile for Lloyd and a rub of her shoulder against Sam.

"Is it what you really want, Sam?"

The girl and the boy stared at each other and she touched his mouth with a finger, caressing his lower lip with an intimacy that was too raw. Lloyd felt like a peeping Tom.

"Yes," Sam said. "It's what I really want."

Lloyd took his time, smoked his cigarette and looked at the expectant young faces.

"All right, Sam. If it's what you want, a job in the boatyard is yours."

The massive smile on the boy's face suddenly made him look no more than fifteen. A schoolboy still. "That's brilliant. Really ace. Thanks a ton." He hugged the girl to him and she planted her dark lips on his, like a champion's trophy.

"But don't think this is a cushy number, Sam. I'll expect damned hard work out of you, and to start with your salary won't be up to much."

"That's okay," Tara answered for Sam. "We won't need much." She turned to the boy. "Will we?"

"No," he said, and their eyes smiled at each other.

Oh God, what the hell did that mean? Love may satisfy them but it wouldn't pay the rent.

Abruptly Sam became more serious and asked Lloyd with sudden suspicion, "What if Ma objects? Will you chicken out?"

Lloyd did not care for the chicken implication.

"No, Sam. If I say you've got the job, you've got it. I'll expect you to start on Monday. Eight-thirty at the boatyard. Leave me to deal with your mother."

Sam had the grace to look shamefaced. "Sorry, I didn't mean to . . ."

"Let it go. But you had better learn now, Sam, that if I say something, I mean it."

"Right. I get the message."

"Good." Lloyd stubbed out the cigarette. "Now, do either of you two want some breakfast?"

The girl shook her head and sipped her coffee, but the boy smiled a hopeful yes. Half an hour later, after two bowls of Weetabix, an orange juice and four slices of toast, he declared himself 'full as a beer barrel' and rolled himself out the front door. The girl still had a hand tucked into the back of his jeans, like an umbilical cord.

"Does your mother know your present address?" Lloyd asked as they were leaving.

"No," Sam said fiercely.

"I see. Well, I'll expect you on Monday morning. Eight-thirty sharp."

"Cheers. I'll be there."

Like Siamese twins, attached by flesh and bone, the pair drifted away.

Lloyd closed the door and went back to the kitchen to light himself another cigarette. The image of Anna trying to bribe the girl's mother kept slipping into his head. It made him smile. The more he thought about it, the more he liked it.

9

"How could you?" Anna demanded. "How could you encourage him like that?" But it was almost a whisper.

It made Lloyd sick in his stomach to see she was too distressed even to shout at him. He sat down on the sofa beside her and tucked his hands under his legs to keep them off her. She was wearing a very old, frumpy dressing-gown and he thought she looked adorable in it. He had driven over to her flat right away despite the early hour and she had opened the door immediately, as if she had been pacing the floor the other side of it. Willing Sam to return.

"Anna, I didn't do it to encourage him. I offered the job to keep contact with him."

"Without the job, he might have stayed."

"No, Sam has obviously set his heart on going. This way will mean we can keep in touch. As long as he is in my boatyard you can be certain he is earning sufficient money, so is not destitute in some gutter. And as his employer, I will automatically have his address."

Anna nodded. "I suppose you're right."

She was sitting very still beside him, very stiff and upright, as if holding herself together by a fraying thread. Her gaze was fixed on her bare toes and it seemed confused, as if they were strangers she did not recognise that had come uninvited into her home.

Lloyd allowed one hand out to pat her knee, but only very gently. "I'll work his butt so hard he won't have the energy for any antics with Miss Tucker the rest of the time."

It earned a smile, small, but a smile. She turned to him and her blue eyes looked utterly exhausted. As if she had not slept for a week. She rested both her hands lightly on his arm and left them there. Lloyd kept perfectly still in case any movement frightened them away.

"I am grateful to you, Lloyd. More grateful than I can say." Her fingers gave his arm a tiny squeeze. "It's an enormous relief to know you will be keeping an eye on him." She attempted another smile but it did not quite work. Instead her eyes filled with tears and quickly she looked down at her hand to conceal them from him.

It irritated him, unreasonably, that she was staring at her wedding ring.

"I thought I had lost him," she murmured.

"No hope of that, I'm afraid," Lloyd said, assuming she was referring to her son and not to the ring. "You can't get rid of kids that easily."

She glanced up in surprise, but instantly saw the concern behind his teasing expression.

"Do you really think he'll ever come home again, Lloyd?"

"Not yet maybe. But eventually, yes, when he's got this girl out of his system."

"Or when he can't stand dirty socks any longer."

He smiled. That was better. "My money is on the socks."

She ruffled a hand through her unkempt hair, leaving his arm feeling bereft. "When you've invested half your life in someone, it's sheer hell to watch them chuck it all away."

"Think positive. He's a bright kid. He's seventeen and big and ugly enough to stand on his own two feet. He'll be okay." He made it sound convincing.

Anna lifted her head and a sharp hiss of anger escaped. "God only knows what drugs and diseases she'll get him into. Why does he want her so much? What's the attraction of someone like that? She's just a scrawny drop-out, for Christ's sake."

"Maybe that's the attraction. She's different. He's breaking out of the middle-class strait-jacket, rejecting its solid hard-working morality."

Anna objected to that and jumped to her feet. "Are you saying that I . . ."

"No, no, Anna. Don't get touchy. I'm not saying anything. Just searching for reasons. The same as you."

She prowled round the room a couple of times, then resumed her seat beside him. "I'm sorry, Lloyd. I don't mean to yell at you."

"Feel free. Pretend I'm Tara Tucker and get it out of your system. But I'll hide the kitchen-knives first."

She managed a laugh. "It's ironic, isn't it? It's the mothers who neglect their children who get all the flak. But what about the mothers who over-indulge them? So often it's easier to say yes. To avert the risk of conflict. We all know kids benefit from firm treatment, but I assure you they don't thank you for it."

"No parents like to be hated, Anna."

She shook her head and put a hand over her eyes. "I got it all wrong, Lloyd. I thought we were okay, but underneath it couldn't have been, could it? Or he wouldn't have gone off on his own like this. I made a mess of it and it will remain with him for the rest of his life."

"Rubbish." Lloyd gently took her hand away and pulled her towards him. "No, Anna, you didn't do it wrong. Quite the opposite. Sam's a fine boy. He's just a bit screwed up at the moment."

She leant against him and burrowed her face into his shoulder as if she could find atonement somewhere in there, and he wrapped his arms around her. Her body felt small and shivery, but so desirable his arms thought it was Christmas.

"It's a case of teenage hormones meet sex and independence. He'll outlive it, Anna, I assure you."

She moaned faintly against him and he stroked her hair. It felt soft and feathery, the way he'd always known it would. He smoothed it, ruffled it, then smoothed it again. Teenagers had not yet cornered the market on sex and hormones.

Danny kept wandering from the television to the fridge and back again. It was driving Anna up the wall but she didn't say anything. She even sat with him through *Top Of The Pops*, the ultimate in self-sacrifice. As she watched the gyrating bodies on the screen, she could not help wondering how much their raucous lifestyles were responsible for. If modern youth insisted on making heroes of such people, so many of whom seemed to believe indulging every debauched whim was a sign of greatness, then what possible hope was there?

She looked across at her younger son with his perfect skin and clear eyes and reminded herself that these strange teenage animals, half child, half man, only existed for a few short years. Lloyd was absolutely right, it was a phase. But a phase that could undermine the rest of their lives.

Danny usually went out with a group of his friends on Friday night after his training was finished, but tonight he had mumbled something about not feeling like getting up to speed. Instead he had roamed around the flat with the pointless energy of a hamster in its wheel, until Anna was so angry at Sam that, had he walked in at that moment, she would have thrown him out.

Eventually she heard Danny meander into his brother's room and strum a few inexpert chords on the electric guitar. At least that was one glimmer of hope. The fact that Sam had left the guitar behind. He had actually taken very little with him, just a few clothes, his CD player, a handful of beloved CDs and the old acoustic guitar that he rarely bothered with now. It could of course mean that he was waiting until he had a place of his own before moving out all his belongings, but she hung on like grim death to the idea that it meant he did not intend to be gone for long. She didn't care if she was kidding herself. It helped.

"Anything to watch on TV tonight?" Danny had arrived back in the room and the first thing she noticed was that he had changed his tee-shirt. He was wearing one of Sam's. The black Pearl Jam one he had bought at the concert at Wembley. She remembered how Sam had come home wearing it last summer, proud and excited after his very first pop concert.

"Nothing worth watching." She flipped him the television paper.

He caught it, skimmed through what was on offer and dropped it on to a chair dismissively. "Just crap."

"Danny," Anna objected, but only half-heartedly.

She knew he was hurting. It was obvious. First his father, now his brother. Both had deserted him. So what was he supposed to feel? Guilt? Anger? Confusion? Oh Danny, join the club. I'm so very sorry, my sweet amphibious child. I have really messed it up for you as well, haven't I? She had tried to discuss Sam's behaviour with him but he had clammed up, unwilling to talk about it.

She stood up and roamed the room, fidgeting with ornaments, realigning pictures, wiping a speck of dust off the most recent swimming trophy. Danny's silver cups, all sixteen of them, sat in shining splendour on a cabinet in the corner and she promised herself yet again that she would one day buy a glass case for them all. She had never been a great one with the Silvo. She threw a glance at Danny out of the corner of her eye and saw that he hadn't moved. He was just staring at the empty television screen and kicking with the tip of his shoe at the carpet in a desultory manner.

"We're a pair of miseries, aren't we?" she commented with a smile.

One dimple reappeared. "Speak for yourself. I'm fine."

"Well, speaking for myself, I'm feeling very restless and need some physical activity to burn it off. What about a walk down to the beach?"

"Nah, I'm knackered after training."

"Okay, something less strenuous. I know, get out the juggling balls."

For a moment she thought he was going to say no. But he stopped kicking, flexed his arm muscles and disappeared. A few seconds later he was back with the brightly coloured balls. The boys had each been given a set of juggling balls last Christmas, and both she and they had spent hours and hours over Boxing Day and the New Year acquiring and perfecting the skill of juggling three balls, and eventually even four. They had become quite competitive with each other, timing to see who could keep it going the longest. There was nothing Danny liked better than competition.

"You're on," he said and tossed her one tube.

She lifted out the bean-filled leather balls and after a couple of false starts, got them going. There was something very soothing about the bizarre activity. Partly the rhythm, partly the intense concentration that blocked out all else. Danny had a grin on his face and was keeping pace with her. She just hoped she could give him a decent run for his money before her elbows started to ache.

Anna stripped the bed with an animosity that the bed did not deserve. She intended to burn the sheet. Cut it up into tiny, pointless strips and set fire to them. Flames would destroy all trace, all trace of their last occupant, curling the girl's imprint into black fingers of spite. And when there was nothing but ashes remaining, Anna would flush them down the loo. Back into the sewers.

She attacked the flat with an energy that meant she could get out of it quickly. It was Saturday morning and the Tucker mother and son had, thank God, finally gone. The new tenant was due in after lunch, a Mr N. Steed, who had booked in for a month. Most summer bookings were for no more than a week or two at a time, but Mr Steed was more than welcome to a month. It meant less paperwork and less cleaning. The Tuckers had left early in the morning to catch the first train, and Anna had got the impression that Josie Tucker was as eager to go as Anna was to see her gone. But for different reasons. Earlier in the week Josie had clearly been tempted to accept the offer of the foreign holiday that Anna could ill afford, but had explained, regretfully, that she couldn't speak for her daughter. Now that Tara had, as she put it, 'shacked up' with Sam, she was eager to be off. Anna could almost see her heels shaking off the dust of her wilful daughter and her maternal conscience beaming smugly in the knowledge that Tara was Sam's problem now.

"We'll keep in touch," Josie Tucker had said, smiling her amiable smile. "I've got your telephone number."

"And I have yours," Anna replied pointedly, but what good it would do her she couldn't imagine. The woman clearly had no intention of picking up the phone.

As she pushed the wheezing Electrolux round the carpet, adjusting to the minor explosions as hairgrips, cherry stones and peanuts struggled against the suction, she steered her head clear of teenagers and thought about Lloyd instead. She was enormously grateful to him. But he must think she and her family were totally round the bend. Certainly not his concern.

Yet he had been so thoughtful, so ready to help Sam. In fact, now she thought about it, he had been very much on Sam's side. All that stuff about giving the boy control of his own life, letting him spread his wings and learn by his mistakes. At one point he had actually come out and said she was too protective, too clinging.

That had stung.

She didn't care that he might be right, it had still stung.

It was all very well for Lloyd, he'd never had children. How could he even begin to understand the bond?

Easy to say let go when you had nothing to hold on to. Like this weekend. Lloyd had taken off abruptly on his own, as if the world was suddenly too much to bear. She knew he would be, as usual, heading for Wales, to a remote river in the back of beyond somewhere where the fish were biting. He would camp in the battered old tent he'd apparently had since his student days, and block out the world. Not so easy for some of us. Anna could picture him up to his thighs in his kinky rubber gear standing like a heron in the freezing cold of the fast-flowing waters, watched only by a couple of black-faced sheep who could think of nothing better to do. If he was lucky an irritated kingfisher might flash its gaudy wings at him.

Anna felt a tug of envy.

He had actually invited her to join him on one of these jaunts last spring, but he had said it with a laugh. As if knowing that she wouldn't had made it safe to ask. Anyway, there was no way she could have left the boys and the teashop. Even if she'd wanted to.

The vacuum-cleaner nozzle chased a ball of fluff down the back of a sofa cushion and came up with a pair of lacy black panties. Anna slung them into the bin-bag.

Maybe that was it. Maybe Sam was a surrogate son for him. That would explain why he was so concerned. So keen to offer the job and keep in touch with him. The thought made her want to cry again, so she abandoned the vacuum and started on rearranging the furniture back to its original positions, which at least did demand a modicum of concentration and might put a stop to the thoughts. But when everything was finished and she had jumbled the cleaning equipment back into her bucket and the laundry under her arm, she found her mind wandering back to Lloyd. Anything to avoid Sam.

Lloyd had never talked much about his life before she met him. A bit about Wales but he never mentioned his marriage. Nor his divorce. But she had heard gossip. Malicious most of it. About his wife. Her affair with a divorced doctor had been the talk of the Chamber and when she had finally shipped off to Ireland with him, the Chamber had been incensed. The good burghers of the town might frequently be ready to slit each other's throats, but they were surprisingly protective of their own. Anna had never met his wife but she did sometimes wonder about her. There was no trace of her in his house, which over the past couple of years he had systematically redecorated, room by room, colour over colour. As if painting her out of his life. And rumours reached Anna every now and again that he was dating someone new.

Yet it was clear to her that he was not looking for a permanent relationship. Why else would he spend so much time on herself and on the Chamber? Sometimes she even thought he was using her as a convenience. Not that he was ever obvious about it. Quite the reverse in fact. He had been wonderful to Sam. And always good company and a good friend to her. But she had a sneaking feeling that it suited him to be with someone who made no demands on him, someone he could fuss over and then walk away from with no strings. Maybe his wife had tied him up in too many knots.

But then, maybe it suited Anna too.

Except when the blasted man decided to stick his nose in too far and told her how to bring up her own kids. Possessive, he had said. Clinging. What the hell did he know?

She let herself into her flat, intending to snatch a wash and brush-up and a change of clothes in time to join Esther in the teashop for the mid-morning hordes. But the moment she set foot in the hall, a shroud of misery settled on her, so heavy that she wanted to curl up on the floor and expire.

There wasn't time for that.

She hurried towards her bedroom, bustling her body into action against its will.

And suddenly he was there. Sam. Standing in the doorway to his room. Tall and straight and unbearably beautiful to her eyes. The last words they had spoken to each other before he stormed out three days ago had been harsh and strident, words that tore at each other and drew blood. She would have taken them back a thousand times if she could.

"Hello, Sam," she said gently.

"Hi, Ma." A tentative smile, as if testing the waters. "All okay? Been doing upstairs?"

"Yes."

"A new tenant?"

"Yes. He arrives after lunch."

Why on earth were they talking about the flat?

"Danny not in?"

"No."

"Training at the pool?"

"Yes." She wanted to hug him, but his eyes said no. She kept a safe distance.

"I just came by to pick up a few things."

It was then she noticed the electric guitar in his hand. The sight of it about to walk out of her house wrenched something loose inside her. She stepped nearer him, near enough to touch.

"Have you found a flat yet?"

He shook his head and she noticed his hair was lank and greasy, its curls subdued to a matted nest.

"Sam, you could come home."

He smiled patiently but his eyes drew up defences. "No. No, I couldn't. Can't you understand?"

He was asking the impossible. But she let no hint of it show. She took a tiny step back from him, just to show willing and said easily, "Of course I do, darling. Spreading your wings, making your own mistakes. Controlling your life. All that and lots more."

"Exactly." He looked relieved.

Damn Lloyd and his words.

"It's wonderful about the job in the boatyard, isn't it?" she said with a show of enthusiasm.

"Brilliant."

"Good luck with it next week."

"Cheers." He started to move back into his room. Away from her.

"Sam."

"Yes?"

"Sam, do you need anything? Money? Food?"

A roof over your head?

"No," he said, and there was a curt edge to the word. "Nothing."

Nothing from me.

"All well then? Everything under control?"

"Just great."

"I'm glad for you, Sam."

His toffee-brown eyes looked at her and for a moment said the thank you his tongue could not.

"Hello, Mrs Forrest."

It was the girl. The appalling Tucker girl. Here in her house. Here in Sam's bedroom. Suddenly entwined round his arm and smiling a secret, intimate smile up into his face. Instantly Sam had eyes for nothing and no one else. It turned Anna's stomach to see him so in thrall to this creature. She felt like an intruder in her own home. How long had they been there?

"We're just off." Sam turned and picked up a bulging backpack off the bed, while the girl carried a holdall. Her dark-painted gaze watched Anna with an expression of such taunting amusement that Anna wanted to scratch her eyes out.

"Won't you stay for a meal, Sam? There's pasta in the fridge. Or a drink of something?"

"No, Ma, nothing." They moved hurriedly to the hall, eager to be gone.

"Sam." Anna touched his shoulder lightly, she could not help herself. "Please keep in touch. Let me know where you'll be living. And if you need anything, I'm here."

He grunted something that might have been a yes or even a thank you, though she doubted it, and left. The girl did not bother to mutter a goodbye but her spare hand was tucked into the back of Sam's jeans as if it belonged there.

Anna shut the door quietly and in the kitchen uttered a shriek of relief. It woke the hamster who came out of his nest to stare at her with sleepy eyes.

Sam was all right.

Sam had come home and spoken to her.

They were friends again. But as she started to replay every

frame of their conversation in her head, she could not help wondering whether he would have just taken his belongings and left without seeing her, if she had been only ten minutes longer upstairs.

In the boatyard, Dave was introducing his new assistant to the mysteries of gudgeon pins and connecting rods.

"Are you paying attention, lad?"

"'Course I am."

"Don't look like it."

"Well I am."

"Seem half asleep to me," Dave mumbled, and took up where he'd left off in his explanation of the component parts of an engine.

But he kept a wary eye out. The boy looked dead-beat on his feet. The first few days he had turned up on the dot all eager to learn, well-trimmed and halyards tight, but now look at him. Fit to keel over. What's the matter, didn't the kid sleep nights? And he didn't look none too clean no more. As if he hadn't washed properly since he'd started. All that oil and grease needed a bloody good scrub with detergent each night, not just a lick and a promise. A real nice lad he was though, and not stupid neither. But he'd better sort himself out pretty smartish or he'd end up inside the machinery instead of leaning over it.

At the other end of the busy boatyard near the slipway, Lloyd was working on a ketch that had collided with an inexperienced motorboat but he was keeping an unobtrusive watch over the kid. Very low key because the last thing he had time for was playing mother-hen.

But he was uneasy.

Sam seemed to be sliding further and further out of reach. The yard was working flat out this month and could not afford to carry any passengers. Not even Sam. Lloyd prayed Dave was getting through to the boy and then returned to his business. There were a dozen or more boats laid up on hard-standing, in for immediate repairs and alterations. One neat little yawl had lost the top of its mainmast in a recent stiff westerly and the jumper-stay had taken the mizzenmast with it. Must have given them a nasty fright. But what do you expect if you insist on carrying your intermediates too tight? Incompetent handling gives the sea the chance it's looking for and then you're done for. Briefly it occurred to Lloyd that this was equally true of relationships. But at least boats didn't walk out on you after you'd treated them well.

10

The summer suddenly seemed to settle into its stride, and several days of unbroken sunshine brought a steady march of holidaymakers beating a path to the south coast's door. Or doors, in the case of the town shops that benefited from the invasion. Market Square heaved under the combined assault of sandalled feet, and Anna's Teashop offered a tempting refuge from the heat that shimmered off the walls and pavements.

The tearoom was in the shape of a dog-leg with a wide bay window in the front and a small terrace sprouting wrought-iron tables, bay trees and pampas palms at the back. Anna had never been a gardener. A mellow expanse of York stone with no more than a hint of greenery thrown in was much more her scene. A few window-boxes of black-eyed pansies, the odd geranium pot and a couple of ready-planted tubs was her absolute limit. Even then she usually managed to water them to a slow and soggy death. As a child she had been recruited by her father into a mowing and hedge-clipping regime that had scarred Sunday mornings, and put her off for life any patch of lawn larger than a postage stamp.

The inside of the tearoom remained pleasantly cool during the heat of the day, armoured against its onslaught by metre-thick walls and the protective oak beams. They soothed scorched eyeballs without darkening the mood. An assortment of blue-and-white china on display round the room, from willow-pattern tureens to chubby Victorian teapots and vast antique platters, gave the teashop an air of delicacy that was echoed in the folds of the curtains and the white embroidered table-cloths. People came there for Earl Grey in china cups and gateaux with cake-forks instead of milk-shakes in plastic beakers with fries on the side and a straw that tasted like a silicon worm in your mouth.

It was Saturday morning, and the early-rising sun was doing its utmost to lift Anna's depression but failing miserably. She had even set herself to polishing all the brass in the teashop as occupational therapy, but the only result was black fingers and an admiring comment from Esther Miller when she arrived.

"You must have got out of bed on the right side this morning. Busy as a bee you've been and it's not even nine o'clock. Those brass shire-horses look a picture, don't they?" Esther beamed.

"I'm just going to run up to Harriet Torrence's shop. I want a few things there. Won't be long."

"Take your time, love. I can cope here."

As Anna hurried up the hill, it seemed to her that Esther was always telling her these days to take her time. Did that mean she was constantly in a rush? Dashing from one job to the next so that no gaps could open up between them? Anna made herself slow her pace. It was the gaps that frightened her. She might fall into one and never climb out.

The Torrences' place was not busy yet. It was called Nature's Basket, which always made Anna think it was suited to basket-cases, but she kept that thought to herself. It was a long narrow shop with shelves densely packed with sugarless and gluten-free products and with names like tahini and tabouli, while near the door mouth-watering aromas of freshly baked breads and cakes wafted to tempt you in. Anna always made a point of buying her honey and jams there, and could never resist the avocado hummus which she had a tendency to eat by the spoonful like ice-cream.

"Hello," Harriet greeted her. "How are you?" The quick ripple of concern in Harriet's eyes told Anna she was not looking her best.

"Surviving," she replied, with a smile that indicated that was as far as she wanted to go.

Harriet nodded, and slowly moved her jaw back and forth in the way she did when she was thinking hard. "Nella says she saw Sam last night."

"Where? Where did she see him?"

"At some nightclub in town. I couldn't get much out of her except that he was okay. You would think they were guarding MI5's most sensitive files the way these kids keep their secrets."

Anna picked up a wire basket. "Who was he with?"

"That thin girl."

"Tara Tucker?"

"That's her name. Yes, with her."

"Anyone else?"

"Oh Anna, I'm not sure. Nella was so cagey. It sounded as if there were a few others with them, but whether they had just bumped into them on the dance-floor, I honestly don't know. I have to put my hand down my daughter's throat sometimes to get any words out of her."

"Thanks anyway." Anna gave a small shrug. "It all helps."

A customer came up to the till with a handful of packets, so Anna left Harriet to it and walked over to the honey shelf. Danny was a great honey-eater. He dolloped it on his cereal, on his toast and even into his special protein drinks. At least it was better than the chocolate bars which his friends seemed to consume at a teeth-rotting rate. She dumped two jars into her basket and moved further along the shelves, hardly registering what her eyes were browsing over.

It was the telephone call last night that had gummed up her mind. She had rung Lloyd to ask how Sam was getting on in the boatyard and what his new address was. Lloyd had been evasive on both. What was going on? She hated being kept in the dark. When she had pushed him, Lloyd had eventually admitted that Sam had not turned up for work that day. And no, he still did not have an address for him. Sam had given them her own address above the teashop, as he claimed he did not know exactly where he would be staying each night until he found a place of his own.

The thought of her son drifting round with his backpack and guitar and dossing down on any old filthy floor made her want to cry. Or throw something.

"Hello, Mrs Forrest."

She turned and it took her a moment to recognise the owner of the voice.

"Oh, hello, Mr Steed." It was her new tenant from upstairs, a fair-haired man in his mid-thirties. She noticed he had a packet of rice cakes tucked under one arm. How anyone could eat what looked and tasted like polystyrene doorsteps, she did not know. He was looking at her slightly oddly and she suddenly realised she was holding a jar of babyfood in her hand. She would have laughed if there had been any laughter inside her. Instead she replaced it amongst its siblings and gave him a polite smile. "Are you enjoying your holiday?"

"Yes, very much. The light is wonderful here."

She remembered that he had told her he was an artist, so she presumed he meant for painting.

"Good. Have you been going out and about to sketch?"

He told her of the places he had found with the kind of settings he wanted, like the shingle coves the other side of the headland, the woods that tumbled down to the sea at Holme Point and the crumbling ruins of the fort at Watcombe. His enthusiasm for his subject was endearing, but after she had suggested that he also try the waterfall up at Maypool, she excused herself, picked up a packet of spinach pasta-shells and headed for the till. Harriet beamed at her, teeth like well-scrubbed tombstones.

"And *who* is that?" she asked in a whisper.

"My new tenant."

"Lucky you."

Anna stopped putting her shopping on the counter, one hand still clutching the pasta, and stared at Harriet in surprise. "What do you mean by that?"

Harriet gave her a look usually reserved for the simple-minded. "Are you blind or something?"

Anna turned to where Nick Steed was cruising the chilled cabinets. She took a good look at him. He was tall, angular and very blond in a Scandinavian sort of way. Long nose and pale blue eyes. A little close together but very intense. As though searching for answers in everything. His mouth was wide and very defined, and Anna was sure the teeth under it would be perfect. Floppy fair hair gave him the air of someone younger than his age.

Anna turned back to Harriet. "Okay, so he's attractive."

"Attractive and available?"

"How on earth would I know?"

"Let's put it this way. Has he got a Swedish dolly in tow, all Timotei hair and legs up to her nose?"

Anna laughed despite herself. "No, he hasn't." She kept her voice low. "He's down here on his own. To paint."

Harriet raised one eyebrow. "And you say he's sleeping above you?"

"In the *flat* above me, Harriet. Don't get your hopes up. I'm not in the mood for men, gorgeous or otherwise."

Harriet stopped teasing. "So I see."

"Don't sound so mournful."

"You're the one who's mournful, Anna. You've grown too thin and you've got shadows under your eyes that my cat Sooty could hide in."

"Thanks a lot. That makes me feel a whole heap better."

Harriet smiled sympathetically, gave Anna her change, placed the purchases in a bag and added a jumbo slice of carrot cake from the window. "Here, spoil yourself a bit. You certainly look as if you need it."

"Thank you, Harriet. You are kind. Rude, but kind."

She left the shop and headed back down the High Street. Danny would enjoy the cake.

Later that evening Anna decided to torment herself.

Danny was well entrenched in his pit with three friends, music blaring in perpetual cacophony and electronic games-machines draining her electricity at a rate of knots. She did not expect to see any trace of them again until morning. She went to her bedroom, to the bottom of the wardrobe, and dug out the photograph albums. She sat on the floor and started flicking through the pages. Her eyes pored hungrily over the sight of Sam grinning at her from behind a snowman, Sam winning the high-jump, Sam displaying his arm in plaster after he fell out of a tree, and Sam pink and gap-toothed in the bath with Danny when he was six. If she couldn't see him in the flesh, she would make do with shiny paper versions of him.

After an hour she rose and poured herself a good slug of gin with only a trickle of tonic and ice. Equipped with the drink as anaesthetic, she returned to the floor in front of her wardrobe and went in for more torture. From the very bottom of the pile she pulled out two thick albums. The first one fell open at a spread of camping photographs. In the middle of the page was a close-up of her husband. Of Ian. So young and handsome and oh God, how she'd adored him! With a massive sunflower in his mouth and that infectious laugh in his eyes that even now made her grin back at him. They had been only seventeen and already engaged. Just after her eighteenth birthday they were married and by nineteen she'd had Sam. There had never been anyone else for her. Only Ian. Ian Forrest, rugby captain at school and the idol of half the sixth-form girls.

They had been inseparable. Every weekend throughout the winters she had shouted herself hoarse on the touchline for him, completely unaware of the blocks of ice that housed her feet. In summer she had spent whole weeks in the cricket pavilion or the practice nets, while in turn he had yelled his encouragement at her on the tennis courts with a passion that even then had made her blush.

The last photograph in the album jogged a memory that she'd thought was long since buried, one of Ian water-skiing and giving a bravado performance with matching wave to the camera. They had been camping in the New Forest and Ian was showing off his newly acquired aquatic skill. A split-second after the photograph was taken, a motorboat in learner hands had smashed into him and he had spent six weeks in hospital. An Egyptian mummy, she had called him when he was swathed in bandages and he had laughed, clutching his broken ribs. Abruptly, layer upon layer of images that she thought forgotten started to unreel in her head. It was like a box of tissues. When she pulled at one memory, it brought another one with it.

After another hour and another drink, the ring of the doorbell buzzed across her thoughts. It took a few moments for the unwelcome sound to penetrate through the curtain of memories. She stood up out of the circle of albums and suddenly realised her cheeks were wet with tears and she was surrounded by crumpled tissues. How long had that been going on?

She scrubbed her face dry on her sleeve as she hurried through the flat. It might be Sam. No, of course not, Sam had a key. Keys can be lost. But it was without any real surprise that she saw no sign of her son when she opened the door. It was Nick Steed, her tenant from upstairs.

"I'm sorry to disturb you, Mrs Forrest, but I've had a slight accident."

Anna's gaze travelled down from the penetrating blue of his eyes to his hands. One was cradling the other. The left one was swathed in one of the peach hand-towels she had bought from M & S only a month ago. Small circles of blood were seeping through it.

"Oh my goodness, what have you done?"

"Slit it with a knife, I'm afraid."

She stepped back quickly. "Come on in."

He walked into the flat. "I've come away with no first-aid kit, of course. Not even a pack of plasters."

"Looks as if you might need more than just a plaster on that."

He followed her through to the kitchen and meekly submitted to her ministrations, but she had a feeling he was amused by her gritting of teeth and little rumblings of dismay. She had never been good with blood. He had been slicing bread. Using the surface of his hand as a plate, he had attempted to cut a slice of bread in half with the serrated bread-knife. How could a grown man be so stupid? The metal teeth had zipped through the bread and carved a deep trench diagonally right through the flesh of his palm. It made her toes tingle just to think about it. But she did a reasonable job on it. Maybe it was the two gins she'd had earlier that helped.

She bathed it, TCP-ed it and when he refused to go to the hospital for stitches, stuck sticky strips across it to close the wound. It was while she was binding it up with inexpert twists of the bandage that Nick Steed's probing gaze started to unsettle her. It asked too many questions. She silenced it with one of her own.

"Feeling better, Mr Steed?"

"Please call me Nick."

She nodded and snipped at the bandage to tie a knot. "I'm Anna."

"Well, Anna, I am feeling very much better. All thanks to you. It took me by surprise, all that blood. Like strawberry jam gushing on to my bread. I've always had a liking for jam.'' He laughed and put a finger on the knot for her to tie again.

"That's a bit macabre, isn't it?''

"Not at all. I love vivid colour, and blood is particularly vibrant – especially when it's your own.''

They were sitting at the kitchen table, a battered old pine rectangle that had seen better days, but as every scratch and dent told a tale about the boys' activities at each stage of their childhood, Anna could not bear to part with it. She packed the first-aid equipment back into its box.

"Are your paintings very vivid?''

"Some of them, yes. Mainly the portraits. Less so when I paint scenery. I like to absorb the mood of the place and use that to dictate the colours.''

She nodded, but wondered how he differentiated between the mood of the place and his own mood.

"Are you any good?'' she asked. When you'd staunched a man's life-blood, you had a right to ask such a question.

But he did not seem to mind. "Yes,'' he said without any hint of boasting, as if she had asked him if he could swim. "I am very good.'' Aware that she might be sceptical, he added, "You can come up and see some of my work, if you want.''

Suddenly, she was frightened.

She had just been making conversation, doing her Good Samaritan act. That was all.

She back-pedalled fast.

"I don't doubt your word,'' she said and stood up, as if announcing the end of the discussion.

But he did not take the hint. He sat and smiled at her with those eyes of his that seemed to see inside her head. "Any chance of a coffee?'' He waved his bandaged left hand at her like a white lollipop. "It won't stop me painting but might make coffee-making a bit of a chore.''

How could she refuse?

"Of course. Or would you prefer something stronger?''

"For the shock?'' He smiled gently. "I think you're the one in shock.''

Damn the man.

"No, not at all, I'm fine, just not used to so much blood, that's all. A pin-prick and I'm usually flat on the floor. When the boys were young and used to come home with gory holes all over the place, knees drooling blood, I'd get Harriet to . . ." She shut up. She was talking drivel. Just building a wall of words.

"Then I thank you again for being my Florence Nightingale."

She nodded acknowledgement and turned away. "Coffee it is."

She cursed herself for behaving stupidly. What on earth was the matter with her? Over the years she had become adept at brushing off any man who had shown any interest. Why was this one getting under her skin? She remembered the photograph albums lying open on her bedroom floor and wondered if they had performed some cathartic rite over her that had prised apart a chink in her armour. Perhaps she was the one who needed the bandages.

While she busied herself with the cups and grinder, Nick chatted to her. Like you chat to a nervous animal, with a soothing, settling flow of sound to reassure and calm it. About what he had seen of the town, about its abundance of ancient trees that she had not even realised were old, and about the dog that ran off with one of his sable brushes at Holme Point. That had made her laugh. She knew he intended it to and for that she was grateful. Laughter had been a rare commodity in her life just recently.

She set the coffee on the table and sat down opposite him, where she could look at him. He must be around her own age, but to her he seemed younger. Maybe it was the boyish good looks that belied the lines that were beginning to indent his smooth skin, or maybe it was the air of passionate interest in everything that he wore like a cloak. His curiosity had not been blunted by the brick wall of adulthood. She could almost feel his curiosity about herself, but she side-stepped any questions, however well mannered they might be, and instead asked openly about his own life. It came out in little chunks. Early childhood with his grandmother in Denmark. Art school in Kent. An exhibition last year in London. A period in advertising which he hated. Sales to a New York gallery. And sandwiched in between, a mention of a wife and later of a divorce.

In exchange, she amused him with tales of the Chamber of

Trade & Commerce. Stories about its eccentricities, its factions and frictions and its dedicated fight for the welfare of the town, like a parent defending its wayward child. She told him of the new plan they were putting forward for the redevelopment of a patch of wasteland by the harbour into a safe park for children to play, and of the battle to persuade the Council to refurbish the ailing multi-storey car park.

"Lloyd Morgan, the chairman of our executive, is like the tide," she laughed, "slowly wearing away the planning officer's resistance." She didn't mention the coaches. It was a bit too close to home.

Before she realised, it was almost midnight and they were staring at an empty bottle of wine. The mood was broken by Danny popping his head round the door, staring goggle-eyed at his mother's late-night visitor and disappearing again with an embarrassed mutter about needing more rations before morning.

Nick Steed rose to his feet. "I've kept you up late. Thank you for the nursing and thank you for the talking." He smiled at her, while his eyes studied her face. "I enjoyed them both."

"You're welcome," she said and, as she shut the door behind him, she murmured again to herself, "You're very welcome."

Headlights zigzagged through the darkness.

"You're crazy," Tara squealed with delight, her voice high on the chemical cocktail that streamed through her blood. She had wrapped an arm around Sam's neck and was kissing and nibbling at his ear, unable to keep her hands off him. He felt her saliva on his cheek like tears.

"Leave off him, girl, or you'll have us in a ditch," Zack yelled from the back seat, but it only made them all laugh and shout further encouragement both to Sam and to Tara.

Sam was driving the car.

It was a black Golf GTi that had just enough space for all five of them. Sparky was the one who knew how to twock a car, who could get it going. He was good with cars. Cars and locks. Neat, capable hands that spoke their language. He was small and freckled with bushy hair and bright, nervous eyes that reminded Sam of a squirrel.

Sam swung the wheel just in time to miss a telegraph pole and the girl in the back shrieked with ecstatic terror. The radio was blaring out night-time heavy metal and everyone was shouting. Noise was filling up his head. He could feel the level rising inside his brain and he began to worry that he might drown in it. A bend loomed ahead out of the darkness and he hit the horn. It made every one of his passengers jump out of their skins and he laughed. He liked being the one in control.

The road was a country lane, hedges and ditches each side and scarcely enough for two cars abreast. But the GTi was piss-easy to drive. He held it in third and gunned the motor until it leapt under him. Admittedly, he had never driven at night before and the engine was racier than he was used to in Lloyd's Rover, so that he had already lost it once and swiped off a wing-mirror. But who needed mirrors in the dark? He touched the brakes to scramble round a corner and swung the car back into the middle of the road.

He was out to play chicken.

That was the whole idea. Zack, the tall one in the back with Sparky, had dared him. Zack was an ugly bastard with pale eyes that slimed your soul but he was being useful to Sam. Showing him the ropes. And now Sam would show him something. A long straight section of road opened up and a pair of headlights blinked at them.

Behind him, Zack let loose his hyena laugh and yelled, "Go get him, Sam."

They had found their chicken.

Sam crushed his foot down on the pedal and the car leapt forward eagerly, rushing to meet its playmate. Rain had started spitting on the windscreen and the approaching car began to dissolve into a watery blur. Its horn was sounding angrily out of the darkness, warning the Golf to move over.

Sam struggled to find the wipers and dislodge Tara from his arm. His heart was battering at his chest-wall but his head was cool, eyes steady and when at last the wipers swept his vision clear, he was ready for the test of nerve. He gripped the wheel firmly. King of the road, centre square for him. No way was he backing off. The oncoming headlights flashed wildly at him and above the screaming of his companions, Sam could hear the screeching of brakes. He hung on. Hung on to the middle of the road. Black hedges rushed past on either side and then the headlights filled his vision.

It was here. This was his moment.

At the last second he shut his eyes and waited for the impact. It came with a hideous screeching of metal. But not head-on. At the very instant when the cars should have torn into each other like snarling wild-cats, the chicken found a field gateway and scurried into the small gap. The GTi gouged its doors down the side of the other car, tearing off mirrors, paintwork and metal trim, but then he was past. The road was his. Unstoppable. Sam had broken the chicken's nerve.

"Way to go, man!" shrieked a voice from the back seat. "Wild!"

"Fucking mental!"

"Piss on that chicken. He's dogmeat."

"I was shitting myself," screamed the girl, "you bloody maniac."

And Tara was all over him.

He pushed her off and fought to control his hands. They were shaking. So badly he could hardly hold the wheel. He eased down on the speed a touch, not so much that the others would notice but enough to give him time. Time to get back in control. His tongue was as dry as ash in his mouth and he could feel his body covered in sweat. It was slithering down his spine.

A hand came over from the back seat and thumped his head. "You are one hell of a driver, Sam."

It was Zack.

And he was right. Sam knew he had proved it. He started to laugh, louder and louder, and they all joined in until they were shrieking and rolling on the seats. Sam was the one calling the shots. Whisking the car round curves and streaking like lightning along the straights, until he swung up on the dual-carriageway that would carry them back to town. The rain was beating harder now, splintering in the glare of headlights that sliced yellow tunnels through the darkness. It was nearly one o'clock in the morning and the traffic was sparse, so Sam pushed up the speed.

The GTi gave more so effortlessly that Sam floored the pedal and the special alloys sent up a curtain of spray behind them. He let it cruise, fast and furious, leaving the few other cars standing.

It was Tara that did it.

She suddenly scrabbled in his pocket, the one where she knew he kept the pills. It took him by surprise and he looked round at her. The moment his eyes were off the road, his foot was automatically on the brake. The car went straight into a skid.

He had no idea what to do.

Suddenly the dream was a nightmare. The rear of the car swung round and they were travelling at a terrifying speed facing the wrong way. Beside him Tara's scream was tearing his eardrum. He jabbed at the brakes. On off, on off. There was the squeal of rubber as the tyres fought to grip on the wet road. He swung the steering-wheel in the opposite direction but it only made the skid worse. Everything was out of control.

The rear of the car slammed into the central barrier with a force that tore off great chunks of metal and shattered the windows. For a split-second it raced along the barrier with an ear-splitting scream of metal, dragging off both bodywork and speed. Then it let go, catapulted across the two empty lanes and nose-dived down the embankment.

11

There was rain on his forehead. Sam could feel it streaming down into his eyes and across his cheek. There seemed to be a big black hole where his brain should be that was pulsing and drawing him into it. He felt a leg being sucked in first, then the other and slowly his body. He knew he was going to suffocate if it reached his chest. Frantically he tried to flail his arms, to grab hold of something to halt the slide but they would not move, just lay there waiting to be swallowed up. When the black hole reached his neck, he started to cry.

"Bugger off," he shouted out at it.

The black hole took no notice. It closed over his mouth, his nose and finally over the top of his head.

"Bloody joy-riders. Why is it they never quite manage to kill themselves? Just make a bloody great mess of everything for others to clear up."

The words trickled into Sam's ear, along with the rain, as he lay on the ground. His head hurt. So badly he wanted to shout out but he had just enough awareness to clamp his lips tight together.

"At least no one else was hurt this time. No poor innocent bastard mown down while out for a walk, like last weekend over at Highfield."

The voices continued, but moved further away and Sam concentrated on getting his brain working. He felt sick, great heaving waves of nausea that were rising up from his stomach. He opened his eyes a crack and instantly felt slightly better. The swirling in his head came to a standstill and memory began to seep back.

The car. He remembered the car. And Tara. Where was Tara?

He was lying on his back on grass and the sky was black above him, a heaving dirty black that was spitting rain down on him. He flexed each foot and hand carefully and though it sent spikes of pain shooting into his spine, he knew they were all okay. It was his chest that hurt. His chest and his head.

He moved his head a fraction to one side, ignoring its objections, to bring the voices into his field of vision, and instantly his heart went berserk behind his sore ribs. Two policemen stood nearby. Their big feet were at his face-level, while their fluorescent jackets made his eyes ache. He shut them for a second, tried to settle his heart-beat and then opened them again. The feet were still there. Not far behind them, the Golf lay on its side, its body-lines distorted into grotesque shapes. Sam felt sorry for it.

"Where's that bloody ambulance? It should be here by now." The policeman was getting wet and did not like it.

"Don't fuss. I know there's a smear of blood on the other seats, but whoever it was must have scarpered. This kid is knocked out cold, but he's still breathing all right. A bit cut about, but doesn't look too bad to me."

"Since when have you been a doctor?"

Sam heard the first policeman laugh. "God, you're a pain tonight. The trouble with you is you need to get laid. It's making you a right arsehole to work with."

"You're dead right. But I haven't a hope. At eight months pregnant, my wife won't let me lay a finger on her." He stamped his feet against the cold and the frustration. "I'm calling in about that bloody ambulance again."

Both pairs of feet moved out of Sam's sight and soon he heard the crackle of a two-way radio. Very gingerly, he twisted his head further round until he found the two policemen again. The big burly one was sitting in their white patrol car on the top of the embankment talking on the radio, while his partner leant in the door, listening.

Sam seized the moment.

He rolled over on his side and pushed himself up to his knees.

Instantly his head exploded and his stomach shot into his mouth. He vomited on to the grass, terrified the policemen would hear, then staggered to his feet. Another wave of nausea hit him and he felt himself sway as his vision blacked out, but he fought his way through it. He tried to take a deep breath, but his ribs objected, so making do with shallow gasps he stumbled off into the darkness. He kept close to the undergrowth that ran in a tangled ribbon along the base of the embankment, because though it made his path hard going, it gave him plenty of cover.

After a few minutes he heard the voices. Raised in alarm. The policemen were searching for him. Not far behind, he could see their torches raking the bushes. He hurtled on as fast as his shaking legs would carry him, scratched by brambles and torn by branches, but soon realised the torches were gaining on him. He allowed himself a moment's break to be sick once more, then choosing a particularly dark spot, hauled himself painfully up the embankment. The road was almost empty, both carriageways, except for the police-car parked a few hundred metres further down. In the distance he could see the ambulance approaching.

Rising panic robbed him of breath but he forced his legs into wobbly motion once more and made a dash for it across the road. He scrambled over the central barrier, but caught his toe in its top ridge and went flying flat on his face into the fast lane. Headlights raced down on him, a horn and brakes screeched and the dark shape of a car swerved round his prone figure into the slow lane. He saw its brake-lights pull to a stop.

Sam dragged himself to his feet, focused his mind on nothing but escape and made for the grass bank opposite. He crawled over it, through a narrow screen of trees and found himself behind a row of back gardens. He had just enough sense to peer over them through the blackness and rain, searching for one with a toolshed, and after three attempts managed to climb over the wall. The shed was not locked, just bolted, but his fingers were trembling so violently it took him several minutes to get it undone. Eventually, drenched and exhausted, he collapsed inside, curled up on the floor and fell straight down into the black hole inside his head.

*   *   *

The night gave no respite. The wind snatched at the trees and threatened to tear off any roof-tiles unwary enough to leave a gap for it to find. Anna lay in bed in the dark listening to the rain rattling against the window. She couldn't sleep, however hard she tossed and turned, her mind charging round in tight circles that whirled through her head like elusive frisbies.

Oh Ian, why did you go?

It wasn't right. It wasn't right to leave me behind to cope with all the mess.

She turned on her side, thumped the pillow into submission again and tried to blank out the thoughts. But it was no good. They lurked in every corner, leaving no place to hide. At the beginning of the summer she had been so full of high hopes, had thought everything was going so smoothly, yet within a few short weeks her whole life had been tumbled upside-down.

Her business was under threat.

And Sam had gone.

Just like Ian, without a word of warning. Every child had to leave the nest eventually, she knew that. But not this way. Not abandoning all the plans and expectations they had built together. Not hurling himself in with a low-life that would rot all decency out of him. Rot his mind with their poisonous drugs and his future with their hopelessness. What chance did his beleaguered sense of morals stand against them?

Sam, my precious Sam, how could you make such a choice? What about all the years that went before? Were they worth nothing? A wasted effort?

Anna threw off the bedcover and padded to the bathroom to brush her teeth again. It felt as if they were covered in a slimy film of decay that she just could not manage to shift.

Damn that girl.

Damn Tara Tucker.

But as she ran the water and cooled her wrists under it, she could not help wondering whether there was something in Sam that would have made him seek out that path anyway. With or without Tara. Something that made him desperate to get away from herself, as far away as possible.

So what the hell had she done to him?

She scrubbed her teeth until her gums hurt, then flung herself back into bed and dragged the duvet in a tight ball around her. Whichever way she stared at it, the future looked broken into shattered fragments that she could not piece together. She used to be good at jigsaws as a child. But not this one. This one was cutting her fingers to ribbons.

Sam had dropped out.

She opened her eyes and glared at the dark shadows, willing herself to open her stubborn mind to that knowledge. He had chosen to leave her and in the process had made it abundantly clear he did not want her in his life. She had given some excuse to his school, implying that he would soon return, but she knew she had to face up to the fact that it was a lie. That all dreams of education had been shredded.

Of course she still had Danny. Her adorable aquatic son. But Danny had always been more independent, a typical second child. More self-reliant and less in need of her mothering. She recalled the first day she took him at the age of four to swimming lessons in the local pool and it was as if he had found his natural element. He slid into the water as though he had been waiting for that moment all his short life. In the very first lesson, he had dragged off the hated orange armbands, ducked under the water and wriggled like a squat torpedo towards the opposite wall. His miniature lungs had burst before he reached it and forced him to bob up to the surface, but totally undaunted he had thrashed out in an efficient doggy-paddle. His teacher had scolded him and thrust the orange tourniquets back on his rebellious limbs. But he quickly learnt to yank out the stoppers with his teeth and by the end of the second lesson had discarded them completely. Once free and unfettered, he instantly acquired a rare grace in the water. It was the power of his swimming that Danny was proud of, but for Anna it was the sheer elegance of his stroke that she had always admired.

So where did that leave her now?

Alone.

For the first time with no one under her feet. No children to put first, to chivvy and fuss over, to feed and to worry about. No one.

Except herself.

Was that part of the trouble between her and Sam? That she envied him? He was probably even at that moment curled up in his Tara's arms, encircled by her warmth.

Ian, where are you when I need you?

But instead of the laughing brown eyes that had stared at her earlier from the album, her mind conjured up a pair of vivid blue eyes, eyes which were just a little too close together and which seemed determined to probe right inside her head.

The cobwebs were like net curtains draped across the window. So when Sam forced open his eyes, the glare of the sun was diffused to a soft sheen that painted the shed with an amber glow it did not deserve. It was packed with a variety of muddy garden tools, a wheelbarrow crippled by a flat tyre, rusty paint-pots, several cartons overflowing with assorted debris and in the corner, observing him with bright interest, a large rat.

Sam made a startled movement that sent the animal scurrying out through a jagged hole in the floorboards and a bolt of pain tearing through his head.

Everything hurt.

His whole body felt stiff and sore, as well as cold, despite the early morning sun. Very carefully, he eased himself into a sitting position and examined the damage. He was battered all over and his knee had been skinned in the fall on the roadway, but it was when he lifted his tee-shirt to inspect his chest that he found out why his ribs felt like they had been kicked by a horse. The impact with the steering-wheel had left its mark. A violently purple and black bruise was spread like a dinner plate with legs over his chest. He winced when he touched it with his fingertips. He made an effort to keep his breathing shallow. Just don't let any ribs be broken, please.

For a fleeting millisecond, he felt the urge to crawl into his clean and comfortable bed at home and be nursed back to health by the same hands that had got him through chicken-pox and mumps, and that god-awful Asian flu last winter. But it was for no more than a second. With an effort that momentarily cost him his sight he yanked himself up on to his feet, swayed dangerously, but refused to go down again. He had to get out of here fast.

It was then he noticed the blood. A frightening amount of it. Half-dried and staining the floorboards a dark maroon. Maybe it was that smell that had attracted the rat, the smell of a wounded animal. For the first time he studied his clothes properly and found blood-streaks all over them. Reluctant to touch his head in case it set the pain screeching to a higher decibel level, he ran his fingers with extreme caution over his face. It was caked with dried blood that came off in flakes under his nails and that seemed to have come from somewhere up in his hairline.

Sam could feel his hair thick with matted clots that had dried into stiff spikes. Thank God his hair was brown, so the blood would hardly show. But what to do about his face and clothes? There was no chance of walking through the town looking like the survivor of a chain-saw massacre without getting picked up, early morning or not. He stared miserably out of the grimy window and wondered what the hell to do. Maybe he could stay here until night and slink back to the harbourside flat in the dark. But what if the sun tempted the shed-owner into a bout of gardening? The police would be round before Sam had even made it over the wall.

The police.

Something suddenly occurred to him.

Frantically he hunted through his jacket pockets. The pills were gone. His wallet was gone. And all his ID with it, including his Halifax and fake student-union cards. He leant his head against the cool of the window, careless of the cobwebs, and knew he was done for. The police as good as had him already. They had taken his wallet and probably were at this very moment banging on his mother's door.

He felt furious with himself. So what now?

His only hope was to get away. To leave town and make a run for it.

But Tara. Where was Tara?

She couldn't have been badly hurt in the crash or she would not have been able to get out of there before the police arrived. Zack and Sparky as well. Dimly, he recalled the policeman mentioning blood on the seats. But not much. So they had baled out and headed for home. They would be at the flat now, he was sure. And were they laughing at him? Laughing at him getting caught by the fuzz first time out.

The hell with them, he wasn't caught yet.

The anger kicked his bruised mind into gear and he realised he was actually staring out at a garden that had a washing-line. On the line hung a row of disembodied white shirts and against the greenhouse stood a watering-can that must be half full of water from the previous night's rain. Sam did not know what time it was because his watch had gone – why on earth had the police taken that? – but judging from the sun's angle, it was still really early. With luck, the occupants of the house would be asleep.

Two minutes later, he was washing the blood off his face and hands when a dog started barking inside the house. Sam took no chances. He grabbed two shirts off the line, one to dry himself, the other to wear, and threw himself over the back wall. His ribs screamed blue murder but he ignored their protest and made a run for it, heading downhill in the general direction of the sea.

To keep his mind off the thudding pain in his head every time his foot hit the pavement, he thought of Tara. She had abandoned him. Left him for the police to find. As if he was nothing to her. His feet thumped down harder on the pavement to drive out one pain with another.

"Sam, my Sam, I knew you'd come."

Tara threw her arms around his neck and squeezed him to her until he almost blacked out. She helped him into the flat, her tiny frame struggling to support his weight, until he collapsed on to the grimy sofa.

"You look as if you've been run over by a train," Zack commented without concern. He was stretched out in a chair with a bandaged arm resting on his lap. "Tara is getting good at playing nursemaid."

"Is it bad? Are you hurting?" Tara's dark eyes looked glazed and Sam wondered whether it was shock or if she was on acid. But her anxiety soothed the edges off his despair.

"I just need somewhere to hide. The police will be after me. They took my wallet."

Tara fluttered beside him and gave a childish giggle. "Don't be silly, Sam. Look," she reached into her jeans pocket, "I've got it. And your watch." She snuggled her head against his shoulder and ran a hand over his lips and down his throat. He noticed then that her arm and one cheek were covered in tiny scabs, nicks from the flying glass.

"You took my wallet?"

"Yeah. I wasn't going to let those filthy pigs find out who you were."

"And the pills?"

Her smile widened and she patted her pocket. "Safe with me. I've got more sense than to let no pig get his snout into them." She laughed, high-pitched as a bat's squeak, and then asked, "So how did you get away from the fuzz?"

Sam's head was beginning to swim and her face on his shoulder seemed to be sliding away down a tunnel.

"I just ran," he mumbled.

"You're okay though, aren't you, Sam?"

"Fine," he muttered, just before he was sick over her feet.

12

The sun had drawn the grockles out in force. The beaches were sprouting multi-layered sandcastles and sandwiches, but the shopkeepers in town were not wildly pleased to see such blue skies, as it meant their potential customers were all dipping their fingers into the sea instead of into their purses. But with luck, a cool breeze might spring up later in the day to drive them inland.

As Lloyd drove round Market Square, he saw a sunburned group of tourists disappear inside Anna's Teashop and he was tempted to park and follow suit. He was going to have to talk with her about Sam. The boy had not turned up at the boatyard for days and the job could not be held open indefinitely.

But now was not the right time. Now he was on his way to Bristol. A competitive company had contacted him about a possible merger. It was a small business but with a good reputation. It also built racing-boats but had run into financial trouble after the death of the designer who had set up the company. Killed in an accident in one of his own speedboats. His son was trying to make a go of it but, without the vision and experience of his father, was struggling.

The idea had possibilities.

This first meeting was a tentative sounding-out of their situation and expectations. A look at their books and production methods would come next.

The Rover narrowly avoided a pedestrian in the High Street who seemed determined to make this holiday his last. After a warning blast of the horn that made the surrounding pedestrians jump, Lloyd headed out of town and sped north towards Bristol.

The roads were crowded with the summer flood of traffic, but most of it was travelling in the opposite direction, aiming for the south coast. It was a long day, but the meeting went well and Lloyd was impressed by the company's set-up. The next step was to get the accountants involved. Lloyd's gut reaction had been a positive one, but he kept his farewell noncommittal, already manoeuvring to hold the price down.

As he drove home, joining the crawl southward this time, his head was full of plans and share-offers. The son would have to go, but the production manager seemed very sound. Efficient and capable, as well as a fifteen-year history with the company. Lloyd was certain he would be an invaluable manager of the new business. There were economies to be made in the sales force, of course, doubling up with his own highly motivated team, and they needed a lesson in marketing; but Lloyd was sure, if the figures proved attractive, he could make a success of it.

He wound his window further down, letting warm air swirl sluggishly through the car as it hovered in the wake of an HGV that was struggling to make the hill. The merger would mean more demands on his time, more travelling like this between the two companies, keeping tabs on them both. Did he want that?

Of course he did. He was ready for a new challenge. It would mean some changes, new staff. That consideration brought his thoughts full circle to Sam Forrest.

What the hell had got into that boy?

Lloyd felt a twist of concern in his stomach, and it caught him by surprise. The boy was Anna's child, not his. What he did with his life was up to him. Everyone made mistakes, and Sam would work his way through this one and out the other side. Eventually.

Lloyd stabbed at the accelerator and swept past a surprised Volvo with more gusto than was strictly necessary. He eased himself back to a sensible speed. The trouble was that he was uncomfortable when it came to children. They had a mind of their own and no amount of reasonable advice would prevail once they had set their stubborn hearts on a hell-bent dash in the opposite direction.

Like Sam. Silly, senseless Sam.

The kid had everything going for him, yet was determined to

mess it up by running with the kind of low-life that were born losers. It was such a waste. A totally pointless waste.

The Rover reached a stretch of dual-carriageway and pulled at the leash, so Lloyd gave it its head. The early-evening sun was glaring in through the open window but the speed of the car provided a cool, buffeting breeze that reminded Lloyd of the joys of sailing. For the millionth time he wondered how anyone could bear to live away from the sea. They must be out of their land-locked minds. The image of taut sheets running before a stiff wind of six or seven knots suddenly swooped into his head, filling him with the sense of elation that the sea never failed to bestow. Escape from all worldly woes.

He lit a cigarette and filled his lungs with smoke as readily as if it had been the salt wind. For Anna there was no escape. No amount of sailing could bring release. Not when you had children.

It was something Lloyd was not used to and he regarded it with a certain unease. Awe even. That lifelong commitment. His own wife had not wanted children. She had been so involved in her career as a biochemist that there had been no room for the distraction of bawling babies. That discovery had come as a shock. At first he had tried to persuade her otherwise, but when she proved adamant, he had taught himself to get used to the idea and for a while had actually enjoyed the illusion of freedom it gave. She'd had her cats to cuddle, all five of them, and he had his boats. And the fishing for when he got really uptight.

But the crack had widened to a gap, and the gap to a gulf, and then the marriage was living on borrowed air. It had only been a matter of time. A question of when, not if. He pictured her now ensconced in Killarney with her doctor and her research, and he wished her well. No hard feelings. Not any more. He let his mind wander back to Anna, as he pulled his foot off the accelerator at the sight of a police car ahead and allowed the speed to rub off without use of telltale brake-lights.

Anna would never put chemistry before children.

Would she put *anything* before her children?

So was he beating his head against a brick wall? And if she did ever drop her guard, would he want to take on her children?

Sam and Danny. They may be nice kids, but living with them was something else.

Whoa. Hold your horses.

His foot jabbed on the brake, as though to slow down his thoughts.

One step at a time.

Just like the new company he'd been looking at in Bristol, a merger sounded like a great idea, but you had to take each stage carefully and keep your eyes wide open. No problems there. When he was around Anna, there was nothing he liked better than keeping his eyes open. To watch the way she moved, so alertly and with an eagerness to handle life. The way she gave you that smile of hers, as if including you in her private world. And the laugh that tickled your innards and made the moment roll over inside you.

As he passed a sign that told him he was only fifty miles from her, Lloyd smiled. In his head, she smiled back at him.

By the time he arrived at the boatyard, everyone had gone home. His desk had disappeared under an avalanche of circulars and letters during his brief absence, but his secretary, ever aware of his aversion to paperwork, had arranged it in piles of descending urgency. A pad of telephone messages sat in pride of place. Bearing in mind the lateness of the hour and the growling of his stomach, Lloyd decided to tackle just the phone messages.

An hour later, they all had dutiful black lines through them and he'd had enough for one day. His mind was slowly settling into concrete. He poured himself a quick scotch to dilute the mix, and before he was tempted to start sifting through the paperwork, he had his racing dinghy in the water and was gone.

The breeze was light and it took him a while to coax her into action, tacking frequently to catch each breath for maximum headway, but once free of the protecting arm of the coast, the wind stiffened to a decent south-westerly and he could put her through her paces. The movement of the boat under Lloyd massaged the kinks out of his spine and the wind carried away the concrete blocks from inside his head, leaving it feeling light and fresh, despite the late hour.

It took no time at all to sweep round the headland into the next cove, the neat bow hissing through the water at speed. High pressure had swept the sky clear of clouds and the sun was slipping down over the horizon, leaving in its wake a dazzling trail of golden footprints across the sea. From there he had a good view of the Weary Ploughman. It was perched up in its eyrie on the cliff-top and the sight of it reminded his stomach that he had not eaten since snatching a sandwich for lunch. He swung the helm to come about and set off back towards the headland, but as he glanced astern he noticed two figures sitting on the rocks at the water's edge.

One was Anna.

He would know her at twice the distance.

The other figure was that of a man. Close beside her. For a moment Lloyd clung to the assumption that it might be Sam or even Danny, but this man was fair where Sam was dark and had hair too long for Danny's. A large book or something similar was in the man's hands and they were studying it. For a split second Lloyd was tempted to sail closer, to hail them from the boat and drive a wedge of words between their two bodies. But even as he watched, Anna put her arms up round the man's neck and kissed him on the mouth.

Lloyd tore his eyes away, pulled hard on the tiller and ran before the wind.

Lloyd was on his third scotch before he started to slow down. And on his fourth before he noticed it was completely dark and he was the only one left on the terrace of the Weary Ploughman. The damp air had driven all others into the bar but the candle on each outside table continued to glow and flutter inside its glass tube with the same erratic syncopation as the pulse in Lloyd's head.

Anna and Sam Forrest, they made a right pair. Mother and son. Neither knew what they bloody wanted. Both say one thing and do another. And he had been stupid enough to get hooked by both of them. Well, not any more. Painful or not, he was yanking the barb out of his mouth and swimming free. The drinks kept coming.

"Hello, Lloyd, what are you doing out here in the dark all alone?"

Lloyd made an effort to focus his gaze, and after wandering off in the wrong direction at first, it finally found the face that went with the voice. It was Anna's face. Looking flushed and happy.

"Hello, Anna."

She was wearing navy jeans and a navy shirt with a white scarf at her throat, and he felt an overwhelming urge to shanghai her on to his boat and sail off into the sunset. Beside her stood a man with blond hair and arty good looks that Lloyd took an instant dislike to. His hair was too floppy, he was too tall and his eyes were too close together. Sure sign of a criminal, Lloyd's mother had always told him. A wise woman she was, who had sadly not taken her own advice about avoiding strangers and had run off to America with one as soon as all the children had left home. His father still attended chapel each Sunday and the pub each night, as if he'd never noticed she had gone.

"This is my new tenant, Nick Steed. He's an artist." Anna turned to smile at him. "Lloyd is chairman of our Chamber of Commerce."

Her words slid like slivers of glass into his brain. Is that all he was to her, for Christ's sake? A chairman? What happened to 'a good friend who is helping me save my son'? Or even 'the man who gives me lifts and takes me out for a drink when I'm feeling down in the dumps'? Just the chairman of the Chamber. Cool and distant and strictly professional.

To hell with them both. He drained his latest glass.

"Nick and I have been up at Schooner Cove," she continued. "He's been painting it."

"And what colour have you been painting it, Nick? Bright red perhaps? Scarlet shingle with purple rocks would be interesting."

Nick smiled politely. "Anna means I have been painting a picture of it."

"I know precisely what Anna means."

"It's damp out here. Shall we go back inside, Anna?"

"Get me another large scotch, will you, Nick?" Lloyd asked too loudly and tossed a ten-pound note on the table. "And a gin for Anna. That's her usual tipple." He didn't offer Nick Steed a drink.

Anna shook her head and frowned slightly. "Not for me, thanks. Nick has bought me wine already." She was holding a stemmed glass in her hand.

"As you wish. Just one for me then, Nick, old pal." He saw Anna and Nick Steed exchange a glance and it goaded him further. "Don't look so concerned, Nick. The lady is quite safe out here in the dark with me. I won't jump on her bones, if that's what you're worried about." He grinned at the discomfort his words put on the face of the other man. "I expect you're aiming to do that yourself."

"Lloyd!" Anna exclaimed.

"Run along, Nicky, and fetch me my drink. I'm celebrating a merger of minds. Boating minds." He laughed loosely. "Or is it gloating minds?"

"Lloyd, you're drunk," Anna said stiffly.

Lloyd smiled and his cheeks felt like rubber. "Bull's eye."

"You certainly don't need another drink. You've had enough."

"I am not one of your sons. I'll do as I please."

He saw her wince.

Why had she come here with her Mr Steed? It was Lloyd's pub, she knew that. God knows, he had brought her here enough times, bought her drinks and shared her woes. So what was the point of bringing her tenant here, except to flaunt in front of himself? Look, Mr Chairman, look what I've hooked myself, a blue-eyed fish whose bedroom is only inches away from my own.

"The drink, Mr Steed. Please."

Nick Steed hesitated.

Anna sat down at the table and asked with concern, "Would you like me to order you a taxi home?"

"All I want to order is that drink."

Anna shook her head at her tenant and stared for a long moment at Lloyd. In the shadows she looked to him like the chiselled angel he would wish to have carved on his tomb, her short blonde hair like a wind-blown halo round her head.

"Have you had a bad day, Lloyd?"

"No, not yet. But it's getting worse by the minute."

She frowned again, lines creasing the forehead that had so recently lain asleep on his sofa. He could have kissed it then. He wanted to kiss it now. But someone else's lips had beaten him to it.

"Is something the matter, Lloyd?"

"Yes."

"What is it?"

The candle flickered in the cool breeze and for a moment Lloyd watched as her eyes seemed to grow huge in her face. Now he thought about it, her eyes did seem larger these days, her cheeks thinner. It was not hard to guess the cause of that. New love had taken away her appetite, made her hungry for flesh still on the bone, instead of on the plate.

Lloyd yanked a cigarette from the packet on the table and lit it after several attempts. "The only thing the matter with me is that I need that drink."

The tenant intervened. "You sound like you've had quite a few already. Enough is as good as a feast, Mr Morgan, so we'll put you in a taxi." He let his hand rest lightly on Anna's shoulder at the mention of 'we'.

It was the hand that did it. So possessive, so familiar.

Lloyd sat forward. "The one thing I do not need is your clichés, Mr Steed. Or your interference. So why don't you take them both elsewhere?"

Anna turned her face up to her companion with an apologetic grimace. "Nick, I'm sorry."

He returned the smile with so much understanding, it made Lloyd want to chew him up and spit him out.

"It's okay, Anna, it's the drink talking," Nick Steed said.

Lloyd stood up, but found it wise to hold on to the table. "Like hell it's the drink. I can see exactly what you are, drunk or sober. You're down here on holiday and looking for someone to warm your bed."

"Lloyd, stop it." Anna was sounding angry.

But his tongue did not know how to stop. "You and your son are both the same, Anna." He dropped into his chair once again and tilted his head back until the stars whirled violently above him. He drew on his cigarette and tried to make them stand still. Anna was on her feet, glaring down at him and in the darkness her eyes looked almost black.

"And what precisely do you mean by that remark, Lloyd? In what way are Sam and I the same?"

He did try to make his tongue shut up, but it took not a blind bit of notice.

"You're both in too much of a rush."

"Too much of a rush for what?" she asked icily.

"To jump into bed with the first person who gets under your guard. Poor judges of character."

"And I suppose you're the one who knows what is best for us?"

Lloyd nodded, setting the stars swirling again. "Yes."

She leant forward, her face only inches away and he could see the hurt in her eyes. His fingers wanted to stroke her hair.

"What do you know about relationships, Lloyd Morgan? Just keep your nose out of my life. And out of Sam's too. Your track record is not exactly a shining example for him to follow, is it? Maybe it's you who are the poor judge of character. Especially of your own."

"Where's that drink I ordered?"

"Go and hide in your boats and your fishing, then you don't have to get involved. That's what you want, isn't it?"

"Anna, he's drunk." Nick Steed put a soothing hand on her arm. "There's no point saying all this. Leave him alone."

At that moment a waiter came out to clear the tables and Lloyd waved the money at him. "Bring me a large scotch, please."

Anna stood very rigid, staring at Lloyd and breathing heavily. Abruptly she turned and stalked off.

Nick Steed commented quietly, "I don't know what that was all about, but was it really necessary to be so rude to her?"

"Piss off."

Lloyd watched the tall streak disappear into the bar, then leant forward and blew out the candle.

13

It was the next evening that Danny decided to go for a run. He had tried pumping the weights in his bedroom but still felt restless and unable to settle. The long summer holidays had only just started and already he was bored. He had mooched around the flat for another half hour or so, getting under his mother's feet in the kitchen, but in the end had opted for the run.

The moment he stepped outside the door, he felt better. He also noticed for the first time that the door had acquired a coat of glossy navy blue and wondered when his mother had done that. At least it meant she wouldn't nag him about it any more. His legs set off in an easy lope carrying him down towards the sea, and the wind in his face whipped away the tensions that were cobwebbing his mind.

It was Ma who was doing it. Messing up his head. She was making such a hassle of this Sam thing. It wasn't that she was going on about it or anything, but he could see it all smouldering underneath. Like she was bubbling lava inside. He got hot just being around her. She'd been a bit better since the tenant from upstairs had been hanging about, but this morning she had dropped a glass and started to cry. Oh shit, that really screwed him up, to see her cry. He hadn't known what to do. He'd put an arm around her and she felt really small. Like she was shrinking in the tears. It had only been a minute or so, and then she'd stopped and tried to laugh about it. But it hadn't worked.

He kicked out his legs to stretch further, run harder, racing away from the memory. He pounded over the pavements relentlessly. The sun was falling lower on the horizon and when finally he settled down to a steadier pace along the promenade, he saw

his elongated shadow on the ground ahead of him like a lazy
Gulliver. The sea air smelt good, and the flat run round the
curve of the harbour and on to the marina emptied his head of
all thoughts. Nothing but the rhythm of his legs and the breath
in his lungs.

It was the sight of the breakwater that broke that rhythm. He
felt his muscles tighten. Sam was sitting on the stone parapet,
his back towards him. The shape beside him was a girl and her
hair was short and dark. He slowed his pace to an uneasy trot.
To give himself time to think. Should he go up to them? Go and
say 'Cheers, bro. Hi, Tara. Stop screwing up my life, will you?'
Or should he turn now before they looked round and saw him?
He felt sweat break out on his chest and wished he was in the
swimming-pool where you could just put your head down and
block out the world. The whole world. Just you and the water
and the clock. The only way to go.

At that moment, the girl turned. She instantly saw him and
waved. It wasn't Tara. She was wearing glasses. It was Nella
Torrence. With her dark hair pinned on top of her head. She
gave him a big smile and he grinned back. Relieved.

"Hi, Danny," she called out.

Sam was looking now. Suddenly he leapt to his feet, trotted
over and fell into step beside Danny. Danny noticed a long dark
scab high on his brother's forehead and was about to ask if he
had been knocking some sense into himself, when Sam upped
the pace.

"Call that running, bro? Slow-worms crawl faster," Sam
laughed and took off, loping ahead.

Danny lengthened his stride, fresh adrenaline swamping tired
muscles and he caught up with his brother. For a hundred
metres they went at it full pelt, scattering pedestrians and
seagulls indiscriminately in their path. Step for step, shoulder
to shoulder, they held each other. Then Sam peeled off, clutching
his ribs and laughing. He headed back to Nella.

"Not bad for a slow-worm," he called after Danny.

Danny kept up the speed until he was out of sight, then struck
out to the left to cut back across town. He let his muscles take it
easier while he pumped oxygen into the aching body machine
and let his mind wrap itself round what had just happened. He

was glad to have seen Sam, glad Sam had chosen to race with him, but as he recalled the lanky figure of his brother, it seemed to him it was scrawnier. Greyer, somehow. Not surprising really, without Ma's baking. Danny started up the hill at a faster pace and began to wish he had stopped and spoken with him, but Sam had shown no inclination to talk.

Maybe Danny was too much a part of what he had left behind. Next time, he promised himself, next time whether Sam wanted it or not, Danny would make him talk. He did not want to lose his brother.

Anna was alone in the kitchen. Danny was still out on his run. She had tried to busy herself but was sick of baking.

Sick of everything.

Sam, oh Sam, where are you now? What are you doing with that black-haired creature from the sewers? Is she putting her dirty little paw-prints all over the whiteness of your soul? Paw-prints that will never wash off. No matter how hard you scrub.

Anna still had not got over last night. Sharp little darts of misery kept sticking in her skin whenever she thought of Lloyd. Did he really have such a low opinion of her? Voiced in front of Nick Steed, as well. She had been so embarrassed and so furious. Lloyd had been lucky not to get her wine over his head. Not that he'd have noticed, he was so drunk.

Damn the man.

He had no right. No right at all to talk to her like that. Nick was the only bright spark in her life right now. The couple of hours with him out at Schooner Cove yesterday, watching while he painted, had been a welcome oasis of calm. They had not talked much, just occasional exchanges that kept contact but did not disturb. There had been no need for more. She had sat on the rocks and thrown stones to the waves and thought about nothing. A tiny pool of peace in which she had floated with relief.

Until she bumped into Lloyd Morgan, that is.

It had been the most natural thing in the world to end the pleasant evening with a drink at the Weary Ploughman. It had a glorious view out over the sea that she knew Nick would appreciate, but unfortunately it was rather too dark by the time they arrived there, so he did not get to see much of it. But he did get to meet Lloyd Morgan.

What on earth had got into Lloyd?

She was grateful to Nick for being so understanding. He had brushed it aside and when she had finally calmed down, he had opened a bottle of wine in his flat and she had sat and listened to him. He had regaled her with stories of a three-month tour of Canada the previous year, of encounters with caribou in the uplands of the George River and an irate racoon in his backyard that made her laugh.

Nick was good for her.

And she liked the feel of him. Of his touch on her hand, of his arm round her waist. Of his lips on hers. The first time he kissed her, it had taken her by surprise and she had drawn back, but he had held on to her and gradually, brick by brick, her defences had crumbled. It was ten years since she had been kissed like that. Until that moment, she had not realised how much she had blanked out during those lonely years, how much she had denied herself. How sheer bloody wonderful it was to be in the arms of a lover. Not that he was her lover in the strict sense of the word. Whatever blasted Lloyd might think.

No, it had not gone that far. Not yet.

Against her will, her cheeks blushed at the memory of the caresses. She was a grown woman, for heaven's sake. No need to blush at the fact that her body had responded to the touch of his fingers like a dog to the hand that pets it. Her skin had been starved of such affection for a whole decade and had reacted with electric quivers and shivers, while deep inside a vibrant ecstatic pulse had taken over. And Nick had been patient, not rushing her.

The telephone interrupted her thoughts.

"Hello, it's me."

"Harriet, I'm glad you've called."

"Why's that?"

"I'm feeling grouchy."

"What's happened now? News of Sam?"

"No, none at all. Except what you pass on from Nella, which are slim pickings."

"What then? Not the coaches?"

"No, our apathetic council always drag their feet when it comes to decisions. Don't worry about that. They'll come up with something any day now. And we have to look on the bright side. It means the coaches continue to use the square for the time being."

"So what's the grouchiness about?"

"It's just that I had a row with Lloyd last night."

"That's not like our chairman. What happened?"

"He was drunk and became bloody offensive."

"Good Lord, I wish I'd been there. It would have been fun to see those smooth-talking gloves of his coming off."

"Not for me, I assure you. Let's drop the subject. Tell me instead what you rang me about."

"I'm being nosy."

"That's nothing new."

"I saw you down at the flower-market this morning."

Anna knew what was coming but played innocent. "Yes, I go there regularly for posies for the teashop tables. You know I do."

"Ah yes, but you were not alone."

"True. There were lots of people there."

"Anna! Don't be difficult. You know exactly what I mean."

Anna laughed. "You *are* being nosy."

"Come on, come clean. It was that blond hunk from upstairs, wasn't it? The one you were talking to in my shop. I don't believe his arm around your waist is normally stipulated in the tenancy agreement though."

"We're just friends, Harriet." Anna started to blush again and was glad Harriet could not see her.

"But *good* friends, by the look of it. I presume he's not with you right now or you wouldn't be feeling grouchy."

"No, he's not. He had to nip back up to London. Just for the day. To make arrangements with a gallery up there."

"Of course, I remember now. A Michelangelo type. You've got great taste."

"Don't be such a snob."

"I tell you what, pop up here now and I'll pour you a glass of something to cheer you up, while you tell me all about your protégé. Jonathan is up to his eyes in stocktaking, so he won't disturb us."

Anna hesitated, but found herself shrugging agreement. "Okay. Just to shut you up. Danny is out training at the moment but he's got his key with him, so I'll just leave a note. I'll be with you in a couple of minutes."

"Good, I'll get the corkscrew ready."

"Thumbscrew is more like it," Anna laughed and hung up.

Anna closed the door behind her and stepped out on to the pavement. The sun had slipped down out of sight behind the somnolent sandstone of the Methodist church, while a cool breeze rustled up the street and headed into Market Square to chase its tail round the benches. She glanced at her watch. Almost nine-thirty. She tried to take a deep breath but without much success. It felt as if an elephant had taken up permanent residence on top of her chest. That was the tension. She had grown so used to the pounding in her head that she hardly even noticed it any more. A chat with Harriet would do her good, release some of the demons.

The cat from across the road spotted her, a regular source of titbits, and made a beeline for her legs. He was a sturdy ginger tom with ears like lacework and he promptly proceeded to weave between her ankles with plaintive mews. Anna crouched down to tickle the speckled throat and immediately a dark shadow spread like black oil over herself and the cat. She looked up to see a tall figure blotting out the light. For a gut-wrenching second she thought it was Sam.

She rose to her feet and stared into pale eyes that seemed drained of all vitality. It was his scraggly beard she recognised. This was the greasy companion who had come with Tara Tucker into the teashop that Sunday when they had started to suck her Sam down into their sordid world. She hated him even before he spoke.

"You're Sam's mother, aren't you?"

She was surprised to hear that his voice had a thick Devon accent. She had not noticed it in the teashop, but then her attention had been focused on the girl. It just went to prove that the big cities did not have a monopoly on candidates for the underclass.

"Yes, I am."

"Thought so."

She wanted to bombard him with questions, to learn if Sam was all right, eating properly, sleeping properly, working, enjoying himself. Everything. But the words jammed in her throat.

"Don't suppose you hear much from him," he commented.

She shook her head, waiting for more.

"Want to?"

"Of course. How is he?"

He smiled and she felt disgusted. It was a smile full of malice and greed. There were yellow stains on his teeth and his cheekbones threatened to cut through the skin, so paper-thin did it seem. His hair hung in lank threads to his shoulders, and the black sweatshirt and jeans could not hide the fact that his body was made up of bones and very little else. He edged closer to her and she could smell him. A rank acid smell that caught at her nostrils and made her want to step back. But she held her ground.

"So we can help each other out," he said through the smile.

"Just how do you envisage that?"

"Simple. I'll bring you news of Sam. You pay me. I'm Zack. And if you want me to protect him, you pay me more."

Oh God, Sam, is this your friend? Or your enemy? And protect you from what? From gangs, maybe. From violence. From whores carrying Aids and from drugs carrying death.

"How do I know you're even in contact with my son?"

The smile dropped. "Trust me."

"Why should I do that?"

"Because he's living in my flat."

"With Tara?"

"That's information." He held out his hand. Black lines were traced like cobwebs along the creases of his palm.

Anna rummaged in her bag, pulled out her purse and handed over a ten-pound note. Danny's lunch-money for the week. Zack crumpled it up and shoved it into his pocket. A minuscule spark of life crept into his eyes.

"Yes. With Tara. We share the flat with a few others." He brought back the smile. "All friends together."

"Is Sam all right? Tell me, how is he?"

"He's riding the clouds, lady."

Oh God, why couldn't he talk English?

"What's he doing for money? Is he working?"

The laugh, when it came, was reeking with scorn. "No, your little boy is like the rest of us. On DSS."

"Please tell me the address of the flat. I would like to speak to him."

"That's not for sale." He tapped the side of his nose in a confidential gesture. "Got to keep my golden egg safe in its nest."

"Will you give Sam a message from me then? Tell him that I . . ."

"No, can't do that neither. Or he'll know I've been yakking with his tasty little Ma." His eyes slid down from her face and came to rest on her breasts. "Very tasty indeed."

She felt dirty, as if the filth in his mind had brushed against her. "You are revolting."

He laughed, genuinely amused, and gave her another dose of the yellow teeth. "That's not the point, is it?"

"No," she said briskly, "it's not. So what are you offering me in exchange for my money? I am worried about Sam."

"Like I said, lady, I can protect him. Show him the ropes. Keep him out of trouble."

Oh, please God, keep him out of trouble.

"Very well. But I'll only pay if I believe you are telling me the truth."

"The truth? What is truth?"

"Something you may be unfamiliar with. But I do want to hear about Sam, to keep in contact with him. So tell me what he has been doing."

"Nothing much."

"That's not worth ten pounds of my money."

Zack's eyes followed the cat as it strolled back across the road. He seemed to be losing interest in her, as if the money had been his sole aim and now that he had it in his pocket, his focus was already on which drugs he would use to wipe his mind tonight. Next time she would demand an exchange of information before handing over the cash. She prodded his foot with her own to regain his attention. Her hand could not bear to touch him.

"I want to know what he has been doing. My money buys me that much."

He turned to face her once more and said nastily, "Your money has bought you just this – Sam's okay and dossing in my flat with his girl Tara. That's it. If you want me to keep an eye on him, you cough up more."

Anna hated this. This black wraith of a man with his poisoned mind and leeching words. She loathed his power over her. And even worse, oh God even worse, his influence over her son. Without a word, from her purse she pulled a five-pound note and held it out.

He laughed, high-pitched and derisive. "That sucks, Ma. You'll have to do better than that."

She added a second five pounds to it. "That's all I have with me."

He took it. "Next time, come prepared."

"So when will I see you again?"

"Sometime."

"Come soon."

"Maybe."

"Tomorrow? Monday?"

"When I'm ready, lady."

"If we have a deal, I will expect you here on Monday. Otherwise the deal is off."

"Don't give me no hassle, lady." His pale eyes screwed up into slits of hostility. "Or you'll regret it."

An explosion went off inside Anna's head. Completely unexpected and totally deafening. For a split second she glanced around, thinking the noise was in the street, before she recognised that it was the roaring of rage in her ears.

She snatched the two notes from his hand. "Go to hell," she hurled at him. People on the pavement turned to look. "Go back to the sewer where you belong. I don't need you. And neither does my Sam."

She stormed away from him and his rank smell, and headed straight towards her car.

14

She knew she was asking for trouble. It was dark and the area around the harbour was not well-lit. Anna had already lost her bearings twice in the tangle of back streets and alleyways that wound away from the waterfront, and she was now in danger of again missing the road she was searching for.

Albert Street. That was what the boy on the harbour wall had told her. He was the twenty-fourth teenager she had shown Sam's photograph to, the one she always carried in her purse that showed Sam and Danny laughing together, with Sam's arm round his brother's neck, throttling him. It had been taken on Danny's birthday. Only last April, but now those days seemed light-years away. The boy had said he recognised the face, didn't know the name, but thought he lived somewhere in Albert Street.

She had asked directions in a pub that was all smoke and stained ceilings and, if she had followed them correctly, it should now be somewhere close by. The streets were narrow and the houses leaned in on her in rickety terraces with front doors that opened straight on to the pavement. Even in the dark, Anna could see that most of them were run-down, but every now and again a sill would boast a window-box that had about as much chance as Custer's last stand. Occasionally, as Anna walked briskly past a lighted window, she could hear raised voices and once, the sound of a child crying. It tugged at her own fears and she had to quicken her pace.

Dark shapes seemed to loom in every doorway until she forced herself to stare directly at them and found they were no more than shadows. Her heart rattled against her ribs when suddenly a door slammed and hurrying footsteps burst out behind her, but the man only gave her a curious glance and then was past her and round the corner. It was almost eleven o'clock at night and no woman in her right mind would parade these streets alone. With relief, Anna found a chipped sign that announced Albert Street was the dog-leg road that ran off to the right. She turned into it and then faced the problem that she had been postponing until this moment. How was she to find which house the flat was in?

She could knock on every door.

A risky option. Especially at this hour of night.

So what was the alternative? To stand in a doorway and wait until Sam or Tara emerged from one of the houses? They were probably already curled up asleep, dreaming their dreams and – what was it that creature had called it? – riding the clouds. Anna pictured them in each other's arms, the girl's naked skin against her son's lean young body, and the image was enough to make her stride up to the first door. She banged the knocker, hard.

By the eleventh house she had grown used to the comments and the suspicious stares.

"Your fancy-boy, is he, love?" one woman had asked with a smile, while another just slammed the door in her face. A swarthy man wearing only boxer shorts and chest hair invited her in for a drink, but several others tried to be helpful and studied the photograph carefully. But each time it was the same: no, sorry, never laid eyes on him. It was the twelfth door that was opened by a pretty young girl with long straight hair who smiled as soon as she was shown the photograph.

"Yes, I know Sam. He's living four doors along at Ben Carter's house." She pulled a face. "With those weirdos. That girl of his never lets him out of her sight. Worse luck!"

Anna thanked her profusely and headed for the door that was indicated. It was no different from any of the others, its flaking paint emphasised by the shadows thrown by the nearby streetlamp. There were two doorbells. Neither had a name beside it. She stepped back and looked up at the windows for a light, but all were totally black, as black as the sticky ball of tar that felt as though it was suffocating the back of her throat. Despite the warmth of the evening, she found herself shivering. She stamped her feet twice, then stabbed a finger at the lower bell.

Inside the house she heard it ring, but no one seemed to react. There was no other sound. Anna pressed it again, waited and pressed it again. Maybe everyone was out. Or more likely, asleep. A car raced down the road behind her, twanging her taut nerves. She was just about to start on the higher bell when, without warning, the door opened abruptly and the narrow hallway was filled by a burly man in his mid-forties. His hair was cut to an even centimetre all over, as dense as a mole's fur. Ben Carter, she presumed.

"What d'you want?"

Anna went through her routine. "I am looking for my son, Sam Forrest. I believe he lives here." She held out the photograph.

The man hardly glanced at it. "It's bloody late for calling."

"I'm sorry to disturb you at this hour, but it is urgent. Is Sam here?"

"I've got to be up by five in the morning. I don't need you or your son waking me up when I'm trying to sleep."

"So he does live here? Sam Forrest?"

"Did."

"Did? You mean he's gone?"

"Chucked the lot out, I did. A couple of days back."

"Do you know where they went?"

He looked at her more closely and narrowed his eyes. "Owed me money, they did. Haven't paid no rent for weeks."

Anna understood the hint and pulled out her purse. She kept it shut in her hands and asked again, "Do you have any idea where they went?"

"I might have." He stared at the purse.

Anna opened it and took out the two five-pound notes she had reclaimed earlier from the greasy teenager. She held them out to him. "It's all I have with me."

He reached out, yanked the purse from her grasp and looked inside. With a disgusted grunt he removed the few pound-coins in it, took the notes from her hand and returned the purse. "Not enough but better than a spoke up the jacksie." He shrugged and pocketed the money.

Anna contained her annoyance with difficulty and asked for the third time, "Do you know where they went?"

Noisily the man scratched the stubble on his chin while he thought about it. "Bloody layabouts, the lot of them. All bone-idle parasites. Left the place like a pigsty." He flexed his shoulders, as if wanting to let loose on someone. "I was glad to see the back of them."

"Did they say where they were going?"

"When I threw them and their trash into the street, they muttered something about intending to crash out at a friend's place. Somewhere near the police station. They thought it a real laugh to be on the law's doorstep."

"Is that all you can tell me? Somewhere near the police station."

"That's it."

"But that could be anywhere round there. Don't you know the road?"

"No. We were not exactly on friendly terms."

"You know nothing more? That's it?"

He nodded his bullet head. "That's it. Except to say your son is a bloody disgrace and you should be ashamed of yourself as a mother."

He shut the door in her face.

It took Anna some time to find the way back to her car. She ended up walking two sides of a triangle, indifferent to the shadows she had feared earlier. It was the shadows in her head that frightened her now. Which was why she did not notice the two figures sitting inside her car until she opened its door. Instantly they slid out the other side, her radio-cassette under one arm, wires dangling. They faced her, unruffled, from the far side of the Fiesta, two young boys, no more than sixteen years old.

"Give that back immediately," Anna ordered them as if it were Danny and his friend pinching a strawberry tart.

The one holding the radio waved it at her and taunted her with a laugh that made her want to slap him. "Come and take it from me if you want." He held it out to her.

Tonight of all nights, Anna did not need a couple of car-thieves in her life. It didn't help that she knew Sam could be doing exactly the same thing with his new-found friends, somewhere in the town. She stormed round the bonnet of the car and caught the wrist of the teenager, but before she could seize the radio from him, his partner gripped both her arms from behind, fixing her as helplessly as a butterfly on a pin. She started to cry out but before any sound had escaped, the one with the radio had his mouth clamped on to hers, his tongue thrusting against her lips and his free hand exploring her breast.

Without hesitation, she bit him.

Her teeth came together hard and she tasted blood.

The teenager screamed. A high terrified shriek of pain. He leapt back, clutching his mouth, and blood gushed between his fingers. It looked like black treacle in the darkness. Then he came at her. She struggled to free herself, but the boy behind held her rigidly and she stood no chance. The fist thudded towards her face and she took the impact on her cheekbone. She felt a tooth snap and the pain rocketed up into her head, but before she had time to shout for help, the fist rammed twice into her stomach. She lost her breath and her supper at the same time. The hands that gripped her arms pushed her roughly to the pavement and left her there.

Swirls of nausea swept through her body and into her brain, misting it with fear, but she had the sense to keep still, crouched on the ground. She did not want him to strike her again. It had shocked her so much she couldn't even cry. But it was the humiliation that was worse than the pain. A torrent of curses and abuse hailed down on her.

"You fucking bitch, I'll kick your teeth in for you."

Who was this person who could inflict such fear in her? Some snotty-nosed kid no older than Danny. Yet here she was cowering in front of him. With a sudden surge of anger, she jerked herself to her feet and faced her attacker in the dark street.

"Don't you dare touch me again," she said, and for a moment it stopped him in his tracks. "Get away from me or . . ."

The boy with the bleeding lips let loose a punch that caught her in the throat and sent her sprawling back on the pavement, gasping for breath. He brought his face down close to hers and hissed, "The trouble with you, lady, is you can't see when you're finished."

It was then Anna realised he was holding a knife in his hand. He pricked the point of it against the soft skin just below her right eye.

"Maybe," he said, giving her a smile that turned her stomach, "it would be better if you didn't see at all."

The other boy was giggling behind him.

Without taking her eyes from the one with the knife, Anna slowly sat up. She felt the blade nick her skin, but only the surface.

"Not even you," she said in a firm voice, "would want to do anything so appalling."

For a hideous second, she thought he was going to prove her wrong, but then he jumped away from her and set about attacking the car instead. He danced round it, stabbing the knife repeatedly into each of the tyres and dragging its blade along the coachwork with shrieks of satisfaction. When another car's headlights swung into the road, both boys froze, then skittered away into the darkness. Anna could hear the sound of their running feet fading out of her life. The car swept past, unaware of her hunched figure among the shadows on the pavement.

Wretchedly she crawled the couple of yards to her car, hauled herself up on her feet, opened the door and collapsed on to the seat. She closed and locked the door behind her, then leaned over and slammed shut the passenger door that the thieves had left open. When she had locked that one as well, she began to feel safer. It was only then that she put her arms and her head down on the steering wheel and wept.

The telephone was ringing. Lloyd had only just got to sleep and it took an effort of will to reverse the slide into peaceful slumber.

"Hello?" The word was riddled with annoyance.

"Lloyd, it's me, Anna."

"Anna." It came as a shock. He had been dreaming about her. Instantly he was concerned. "Anna, what's the matter?" She never telephoned him at this hour. He peered at his bedside table where the clock was flashing eleven forty-five at him.

"I'm sorry to disturb you, Lloyd." She said it very formally, as if from a long distance. The row they'd had at the Weary Ploughman came crashing back into his head. They had not spoken since. "But I do need your help."

Lloyd wondered what the effort of asking for assistance from him was costing her.

"What can I do for you?"

"I need a lift."

"A lift?" She had woken him up at nearly midnight just to ask for a ride. "What's wrong with your own car?"

There was a short silence and suddenly Lloyd knew this wasn't about cars. "Are you all right, Anna?"

"Yes, I'm fine." No warmer than before. "But my car has had its tyres slashed. I've tried to ring for a taxi but I can't get hold of one."

Lloyd was out of bed in one swift movement. "Where are you?"

"In a phone-box in Seaway Road. Near the harbour."

"I'll be there in five minutes. Don't move."

"Thank you." She hung up.

Oh God, she sounded as if she was talking to her bank manager. What the hell was she doing in that area at this time of night anyway? As he tugged a sweater over his head, he recalled that Sam was living somewhere round there. What on earth was she up to now? Surely she hadn't gone down there on her own at night. The woman was just stupid enough to risk her neck like that. As he grabbed his car keys, there was one consolation that allowed him a brief smile – if she was telephoning him for help, it meant that the artist fellow wasn't with her.

Anna waited in her Fiesta in the dark. An occasional car swept past, its headlights picking out a cat on the garden wall opposite, indifferent and immobile. Each time she thought the driver would be Lloyd. When the Rover did arrive, she watched it pull up outside the telephone kiosk a hundred metres down the road. Relief made her hands shake.

She climbed out of her seat, appeasing the aches and pains by moving carefully, waved an arm and called out, "I'm over here."

For a moment she thought he hadn't heard, but when the headlights started to roll towards her, she locked her car and waited in the road for him. Despite her determination to remain calm, she felt the tears gathering and could think of nowhere she would prefer to cry than on Lloyd's broad shoulder.

The Rover pulled up and Lloyd jumped out. He looked annoyed. "What on earth are you doing out alone on these streets at this hour?"

He was standing close to her and even in the muted light of the streetlamp she could see the rigid tension in his face, as if he was struggling for self-control. It confused her. Belatedly, she recalled that they had not been speaking to each other recently. She had turned automatically to him for help but it was obvious that he was still angry about the other night. Oh hell, she shouldn't have rung him.

"I am not a child to be told where I can and cannot go, Lloyd," she snapped, disappointment making the words sharper than she intended.

They succeeded in driving him a step back from her. "Are you all right, Anna? Not hurt?"

She opened her mouth to tell him what had happened, to shout abuse at her attackers and to moan that her face and stomach hurt like hell, but all that came out was, "I've got toothache."

For a fleeting second she thought he was going to laugh, but instead the muscles of his face relaxed and he commented, "I'm glad that's all."

His eyes scoured her face and she turned the throbbing cheek away from him. "Look what the bastards have done to my car. I know it wasn't up to much, but they've ruined it."

The Fiesta did look forlorn, small and squat on its deflated tyres, its paintwork raked by deep scratches, as if it had gone a few rounds with a particularly large tom-cat.

"I had better drive you to the police station first. You'll have to report it."

"Won't tomorrow do? I don't feel like going through all that now."

He was giving her that look again, those Welsh eyes of his intent on her. As if her pain would show in a telltale lump. She bent to study the damage to the car more closely.

"Anna, are you sure you're okay? Tell me what happened."

The unexpected gentleness in his voice caught at the frail threads of her self-control and set her on the verge of tears again. But if he was so grumpy when all she had asked for was a lift home, then blast the man. He could keep his belated sympathy.

"I came looking for Sam, but he was out. He's staying with a person called Zack. When I got back to my car, I found it like this."

"Did you see anyone?"

"A couple of teenage boys were running off with its radio."

He studied her face, nodded but said nothing.

She hoped her cheek was not giving too much away. "Okay, the police station it is," she shrugged and headed for the Rover.

Anything to get this horror story over with quickly. Deprived of a shoulder to cry on, she just yearned to curl up in bed with a handful of paracetamol and a pillow for comfort. She'd had years of practice at it.

Why on earth hadn't she told them?

As Anna put her key in the street-door and waved a curt farewell to the Rover, she wondered what was the matter with her. Why had she been so reluctant to admit to the attack on herself by that vicious kid? The police had questioned her about the marks on her face, but when she opened her stupid mouth it told them that she had tripped and fallen over on the road while chasing the thieves. What had possessed her to tell such a lie?

She shut the door behind her and leaned against it. It felt warm and supportive against her back. Oh Lord, was she really reduced to seeking comfort from doors? The thought was embarrassing but did not manage to shift her away from its glossy paintwork. At first she had told herself she did not want to admit to anyone that she had behaved so foolishly. She had asked for trouble and found it by the boot-load. That wasn't something she felt she wanted to confess. Especially not to Lloyd. Not the way he was tonight, acting as if he had the right to order her around.

But that was not the only reason. No, not the real cause of her stupid lie. She could feel the sharp pricks of the truth like a coil of barbed-wire inside her. She leant her head back against the door and shut her eyes, but before she could shuffle her thoughts into some kind of acceptable order, the image of the blank space in the centre of her mantelpiece in the dining-room jumped out at her. As if it had been lying in wait.

Sam was the real reason.

Sam was the name on each spike of the tangle of wire in her guts. The police had told her that over sixty per cent of burglaries were drugs-related. What if he was stealing, like those teenagers tonight? Taking radios and wallets, maybe even cars, to feed himself and his girl, to feed a habit and a warped sense of fun. Somehow, she was certain in her own head that by lessening the guilt of the boys who had attacked her, she was at the same time reducing Sam's guilt. Saving him from himself.

That was rubbish and she knew it.

She opened her eyes, pushed herself off the door and started up the stairs. If Sam was stealing, he deserved to be punished. And she was sure he *was* stealing. Two days ago the small clock had disappeared from her mantelpiece, the black marble one that had been a wedding gift from Ian's parents. And before that, the silver frame from the hallway and the mother-of-pearl bowl from the window-sill.

Sam still had a key.

Of course, she could change the lock, but she didn't want to. It would be like shutting him out of her life. But what if the girl had taken the key from him? Or that thin slimeball who had tried to extort money from her? What if they were coming into her home without Sam's knowledge?

Oh God, she couldn't keep going round in circles like this. She had to speak to Sam. Absolutely had to. But how? Look at the disaster she had made of tonight.

Just as her footsteps reached the door to her flat, she heard the fragile clink of glass on the stairs above. She turned quickly and peered up into the shadows. Nick Steed was sitting on a step half-way up the flight of stairs that led to the holiday flat above, a welcoming smile on his face and a glass of red wine in his hand. On the step below stood another glass and a half-empty bottle of wine.

"Hello, Anna, I've been waiting for you."

Lloyd was concerned about Anna. She had asked for his help and then refused to accept it. He had, of course, driven her to the police station and then home, but that was as far as it went. She had kept him at arm's length, cool and polite as a stranger. Yet he could see how she was churned up inside. She should have had more sense than to go knocking around those harbour streets in the dark. They were bad enough in the daytime, for heaven's sake. How would Danny and Sam feel if anything happened to her?

For that matter, how would he feel?

As he accelerated away from the teashop, he pushed the Rover into third gear with a sharp jerk. Bloody awful. That's how he'd feel. But he knew how stubborn she was. If she had set her mind to finding that son of hers, nothing was going to deter her.

It was gone midnight and the streets were dark and empty. At the crossroads a solitary Micra skidded to a halt alongside him and then shot off from the lights before they had even changed to amber. Lloyd made a sudden decision. Instead of turning right to take the road that led to the warmth of his bed, he pointed the Rover's chrome grille down towards the promenade and the town's night-life.

Music was playing softly in the background while Nick Steed told Anna about the exhibition he was putting together in London. When she arrived home, he had taken one look at her, led her gently upstairs to his flat and placed a glass of wine in her hand. His enthusiasm for his subject was infectious. The exhibition was in a recently opened gallery in Chelsea and the organisers were new on the scene, which meant a constant stream of loose ends and panicky phone-calls. Half a dozen of his paintings from the summer's marine exhibition in Plymouth were supposed to have arrived by rail, but had gone astray somewhere en route, so that Nick had spent much of the day tracking them down.

"Thank God for the miracle of the telephone," he laughed as he poured Anna another glass of wine and described how he had eventually traced his errant paintings to Edinburgh. "Taking the Highland tour, it seems."

"What were they doing in Edinburgh?"

"They were sent by mistake with a consignment of artwork to Scotland, but should right now be making the return journey to the centre of London." He held up two crossed fingers. "I'm relying on the gallery owner to get his act together and add them to the display without further mishap."

"You're taking it all very calmly, Nick. Don't you get uptight at the loss of something precious to you?"

He raised his glass to her and smiled, the blue eyes fixed on hers. "Yes, I do. That's why I couldn't bring myself to stay away from here any longer."

His meaning was unmistakable.

Shivers skipped down Anna's spine, making her forget her toothache. She sipped her wine to moisten her dry mouth and said lightly to fill the silence, "I know just what you mean. I can't bear to be away from the sea for long either. It's as if it becomes a part of you and without it your lungs won't breathe properly."

The blue eyes stared at her quietly.

"You've captured something of that magnetic quality in your painting of Schooner Cove."

Still he said nothing.

"It's that feeling of the sea being the cradle of life, a source of peace and yet in perpetual motion. And then there's the danger that lurks just beneath the surface, as if . . ."

Nick was waiting for her to stop.

She shut up.

He smiled at her. "You talk too much."

"Only when I'm nervous."

He sat down on the sofa beside her and for a fleeting second Anna wondered if Sam had sat here with Tara. His hand picked up hers, his lips brushed her fingers and then kissed her mouth, long and slow and unbearably delicious.

"There's no reason to be nervous."

No reason. No reason at all. Except for the fact that she was terrified. Terrified of the changes that had torn her cosy life to shreds. Terrified that she'd make a fool of herself, terrified that this desirable man would be disappointed in her after ten barren years; and more than anything else, terrified by how much her body wanted him.

"I'm not nervous," she lied against his lips, and slid her hands under his shirt. His body felt so male and so extraordinarily touchable that her hands would not stop caressing.

"Open your eyes, Anna."

She had not realised they were shut.

She opened them and found his eyes so close to hers that it made her heart jump. Did she want anyone that close?

"That's better," he murmured as he kissed her nose, her bruised cheek and then her mouth. "Now you can see what you're doing."

His arms were around her, his body hard against hers. There was no doubt in her mind that he wanted her, cared enough to race back from London for her. No one else cared. Not Sam. And certainly not Lloyd. And Danny thought of nothing but swimming.

So why not?

Why bloody not?

The noise was not what Lloyd needed. It pounded off the walls and bounced off the ceiling until the whole nightclub was reverberating with sound. It made it almost impossible to hear anybody talk. Nevertheless, he slogged his way round the room, buttonholing anorexic young men and stick-like girls and shouting his questions at them. Most had already had far too much to drink to have all their faculties functioning, but were generally as helpful as coherence would allow.

"Sam Forres'? Naah, never 'eard of 'im," one shaggy-haired

boy responded to Lloyd's repeated question, but his girlfriend volunteered, "Don't we know a Forrest? Somebody Forrest. Or was it Forrest Somebody? Yeah, that's right. Forrest Gump." She looked proud of her effort.

The other teenagers in their group fell into their beers laughing and a blonde girl with acne explained blearily, "He's in a film, you moron."

"Oh," the girlfriend smiled sweetly at Lloyd. "Sorry."

He continued his trawl of the tables. This was the third nightclub he had been in and was larger and louder than the others. The Purple Parrot it was called and with good reason. Everything was painted a vibrant purple, with multi-colour parrots perched in plastic splendour on every possible surface. The club consisted of a huge high-ceilinged room seething with bodies, a music pulse that vibrated up through the feet and flashing lights that scorched the eyeballs. At one end, a neon disco-consul blasted out the choice of band under a weird purple halo. A closer version to Dante's Inferno, Lloyd could not imagine. But the kids were loving it. And loving each other. Judging by the way they were draped over one another's flesh on the dance-floor. The place was a heaving mass of overheated bodies with only one thing on their minds.

Lloyd had no qualms about disturbing them. He would yank them out of each other's arms, remove lips from ears and replace them with his own.

"Sam Forrest?" he would yell only a millimetre from his victim. "Do you know him?"

A vague shake of the head was the usual response before the limbs clamped together again. After shouting Sam's name against the tide of noise until he was hoarse, Lloyd fought his way over to the bar and rewarded his throat with a cold beer. It was the first sane thing he'd done all night. Despite the efforts of the air-conditioning, the air in the club was as hot and humid as a night in the tropics and he could feel the sweat running down inside his shirt. He had no intention of taking much more of this. There had to be easier ways of finding the boy, but right now he couldn't think of any. Admittedly, right now he couldn't think, full stop. The inside of his head was blasted to a pulp and any sanity had trickled out his ears. So when yet another rowdy group of adolescent males took up the space next to him in the hope of catching the barman's eye, instead of doing the sensible thing of downing his beer and making for the purple exit, he turned to them and started in on the Sam-routine again.

"Do any of you know Sam Forrest?"

The teenager nearest him blinked like an awakened dormouse and shrugged to indicate he had not heard.

Lloyd tried again at full volume. "I'm looking for Sam Forrest."

The boy nodded, but that was all.

Lloyd leant closer. "Do you know him?"

The boy nodded again.

Lloyd did not get his hopes up. The boy looked as if he had reached the stage where he thought he knew everything.

Lloyd repeated, "You know him?"

The boy stared at the beer in front of his questioner and licked his lips. Lloyd pushed it along the bar, but kept a hand on the glass.

The boy blinked again and got the point.

"Yeah, I know Sam. Sells nice cakes in his shop. He was in my class at school, but . . ." The rest was lost in a mumble that did not penetrate the sound barrier.

"Have you seen him tonight?"

"Yeah." The boy's hand reached out and joined Lloyd's on the glass.

"Where?"

"At Veronica's."

Veronica's was another club. Down by the harbour, it was not as sprauncy as this purple monstrosity and catered for a slightly older clientele. Lloyd had started his search there but speedily moved on.

"How long ago?" Daft question. The boy was probably not fit to know five minutes from five hours. But his informant blinked at his watch, did some kind of slow-motion calculation in his head and eventually came out with, "Forty minutes ago."

Lloyd was impressed. He released the beer.

"You saw him there just forty minutes ago?"

The boy took two gulps of the beer and smiled blissfully.

"Yeah, with a girl. Tiny she was but real watchable the way she danced."

Lloyd yelled a thank you and went in search of non-purple air.

Anna was in his bed. She had postponed the moment of disrobing until Nick disappeared into the bathroom, then she slipped hurriedly out of her clothes and scooted under the duvet. By the time he returned, she was discreetly covered, sipping a glass of wine and trying to look nonchalant. He seemed momentarily surprised at the speed of her transference into bed but let it pass without comment. Instead he stared at her with open desire and started to unbutton his shirt.

"You look adorable," he smiled at her. "More tempting than any apple."

Anna could not stop her tongue drying out or her heart racing. She watched his long, naked back curve over as he bent to flick off his shoes and when he removed his socks, his jeans and finally the sunshine-yellow underpants, she could not take her eyes off him, off his long rangy limbs and his narrow hips. And, drawing her gaze like a magnet, off his visible erection, that outrageous quirk of biology that proclaimed exactly how he was feeling about her.

Something started to ache deep inside her.

She wanted him more in that moment than she ever remembered wanting anybody in her life. Even Ian, all those years ago. So was this love? Is this how it had felt?

She couldn't remember.

"If you keep staring like that, you'll make me blush," Nick smiled, with no hint of self-consciousness.

"Blush all over?"

"No, only my cheeks. All of them."

They both laughed, easing the tension a few notches. Anna placed her wine glass safely on the bedside-table, threw back the duvet and slid down on to the pillow. "It's your turn to stare now," she said, praying she wouldn't be the one to start blushing.

She stretched out her hand to him and he joined her on the

bed. As his lips and his body began to caress her own, she felt herself relax. Like riding a bicycle, it all came back to her.

Lloyd stood at the bar, glass in his hand. A different bar, a different glass, but otherwise the place was much the same. Too much noise and too many people, all gyrating and distorting in the frenetic spasms of blue light that beamed down on them like messages from outer space.

Veronica's nightclub was not quite as flamboyant as the Purple Parrot, but made up for it by pounding out the music a few decibels nearer the glass-shattering point. The predominance of blue lights gave the dance-floor a strange underwater feel that was emphasised by the spray of foam bubbles that descended from above like surf every six and a half minutes. Lloyd knew it was exactly six and a half minutes because he'd timed it. Leaning up against the bar, there was nothing better to do. The average age of the dancers made him feel fractionally less like Methuselah than he had in the Purple Parrot but nevertheless aware of a vast gulf that he had no desire to bridge. So far, he had not managed to find Sam. He had gone through his table-trawling repertoire once more with no result and had retreated to the bar to study the dance-floor from behind a cooling pint.

"Lloyd Morgan, what are you doing here? I didn't think this was your kind of scene."

The words were shouted into his ear and he turned to find their owner. Gleaming like headlights back at him was a pair of enormous eyes, avocado green with golden twists of light in them.

"Deborah, what a pleasant surprise. It's good to know there is at least one other sane human being in this place."

Deborah Milton laughed and shook her long mane of red hair at him. "I'll take that as a compliment. You never were one for clubs, were you?"

"No, I prefer to keep my eardrums intact."

"You're probably right. I've taken to coming here most weekends and it always takes me a couple of days to stop shouting at everyone." She laughed again and slipped an arm through his. "But it can be fun, you must admit."

Lloyd suddenly remembered why he had split with the delicious Deborah Milton more than a year ago. She couldn't keep her hands off any succulent man that wasn't hers. At this moment she probably had some poor sucker in tow who had been dumped like a parcel in a corner, to be collected later. The music switched to a slow smooch and the dense pack on the dance-floor shuffled closer. Lloyd downed the last of his beer and smiled invitingly at the green eyes.

"Shall we fight for a square inch to stamp our feet on?"

"I'd love to." Anticipation added to the flush on her cheeks.

Lloyd led her on to the floor, trying not to look too much like a devious rat. Anna, you had better be appreciating this self-sacrifice. He smiled to himself as he felt Deborah melt against him, as silky as a kitten and twice as playful. Some sacrifices really took it out of you.

"What are you grinning at, Lloyd?" She pulled his head down so that her lips could brush his ear.

"At you, my gilded lily."

"You do talk rot sometimes," she breathed, and rolled her hips against his. He let his hand slide further down the curve of her back. "Like old times, isn't it, Lloyd?"

"Except we used to manage to avoid places like this."

She gave him full-beam with the eyes. "So what are you doing here now?"

"Looking for someone."

"Someone special?"

"Of course."

"Me?"

"Who else?"

She laughed and snuggled close again. "I always did love it when you lied to me." Her arms lay like gentle boa-constrictors round his neck. "Don't stop now."

"No risk of that." Lloyd rested his cheek on the soft curls of her hair that gleamed purple in the blue light, and for a second let himself dream that it was a short bouncy crop of blonde silk against his skin. But the perfume was too heavy-handed and the nails too sharp on his neck. Anyway, Anna would have been yakking on about the blasted coaches while she danced. It always amazed him the way she could at the same time combine practical and sexy in one package, totally unaware of its effect. She had no idea that trotting round the teashop with her little pinny and notepad, she looked good enough to eat.

"You could at least do it discreetly."

Lloyd dragged his gaze away from the other dancers. "Sorry?"

"The searching for someone else."

"Don't get me wrong, Deborah. I'm only looking for a young teenager."

"Cradle-snatching is your scene now, is it?"

"A young male teenager."

"Oh, I see, a real change of scene."

He laughed and, using his back as a battering ram, inched deeper into the hard core of the dance-floor. A short couple edged out of his path, leaving a brief gap behind them that Lloyd steered into and used as a base for a fresh reconnaissance. Immediately his eye was caught by a tall figure with dark curls, but it had the wrong face. The crush of bodies had reached the stage where Lloyd felt he knew several of them intimately, including the men, when a cheek turned and he suddenly caught sight of the girl.

The small dark head and nervous black eyes were unmistakable. For a micro-second, she stared back at him and then ducked behind a passing shoulder. Lloyd did not stand on ceremony. He broke loose from Deborah's entangling embrace, abandoning her with as much reluctance as a sinking ship, and forced a solitary route through the dancers. Several sharp elbows and explicit adjectives accompanied his progress, but he took no notice. He did not intend to lose the girl. That meant he had to reach her before she escaped from the dance-floor.

He was under no illusion about her intentions. The dark eyes had contained recognition, but also dislike. No way was she going to hang around waiting for him to pin her down but was already on the move. Lloyd knew all he had to do was get his hands on the girl and Sam would eventually materialise nearby. Hey presto, mission accomplished. He was closing in on the girl. Her small frame did not possess the strength required for effective path-scything and as she squeezed round the final couple that swayed between her and freedom, she made the mistake of trailing one hand behind her.

Lloyd lunged forward and seized it, stopping her in her tracks. But she was no slouch when it came to self-defence and instantly turned, hissing at him and sinking her teeth into his wrist.

"If you don't stop that, I'll yank those fangs of yours right out of your head." Lloyd growled at her, but she took no notice, concentrating only on biting deeper into the offending flesh.

With his free hand, he grabbed a handful of her hair and was threatening to pull it out by its spiky roots when, above the music, he heard a threatening voice.

"Leave her, Lloyd."

Sam Forrest was standing just beyond the edge of the dance-floor, muscles bunched, ready to lash out.

Both of them knew the youth did not stand a chance, but the girl had served her purpose, so Lloyd released his grip on her hair and on her hand. She rewarded him with a last malicious nip on the wristbone and darted behind the six-foot frame of her protector. Lloyd felt an urge to reach round him and shake an apology out of those sharp little teeth, but decided it might not exactly improve his rapport with her boyfriend. Sam was already glaring like a moody water-buffalo that had had its mud-hole disturbed.

"What do you want?"

"Hello, Sam."

"Why are you here?"

"I want to talk to you."

Even Sam realised it was impossible to carry on any kind of conversation that did not involve straining vocal chords in that welter of sound, so backed off and allowed Lloyd to choose a route through the tables to the door. The girl was in tow, one hand tucked into Sam's back pocket. In the foyer the air tasted like spring water and Lloyd felt his eardrums bound back into shape.

"So?" Sam demanded, but his belligerence was now only skin-deep. In the brighter light, Lloyd thought he looked tired.

"I want you to come with me to see your mother."

"At this time of night?" Abruptly, alarm had made him

look younger. "What's the matter? Is something wrong? Is she hurt?"

"No, Sam, but she could have been. She went looking for you this evening round the harbour and had her car vandalised. It could easily have been herself that was attacked."

Relief made the boy sulk. His jaw jutted stubbornly in mirror-image of his mother. "It would have been her own fault. She should leave me alone."

"That's not the point, is it? She wants to talk to you. Just talk, that's all, and she won't give up until she finds you. You know what she's like."

"Tell me about it," Sam moaned, and both pairs of male eyes met in understanding. For a second, Lloyd thought the young face was going to break into a smile but it put the brakes on just in time. Nevertheless, the atmosphere had changed.

"Only a talk, Sam. No more."

The boy's shoulders gave the answer before his tongue. They shrugged as if it didn't matter to him one way or the other.

"So you'll come with me now?"

"I s'pose so."

Lloyd marched him out of the club, with the girl still attached, before she could change his mind.

The drive was conducted in silence. The streets were almost empty and the traffic-lights were in an obliging frame of mind, so it did not take more than a few minutes. Lloyd made no attempt at small-talk once he had the pair captured in the back of the car. That's what it felt like. As if he had netted and caged a wild species that bore no relation to human beings as he understood them. In his rear-view mirror he could see the girl's thin arms entwined round Sam's like ivy and he could hear the rustle of their low, spasmodic whispers. Once outside the teashop, he parked the car and Sam produced a key for the side-door. Lloyd was interested to note that the boy still carried it around with him.

"It's two o'clock in the morning," Sam said in a whisper, and opened the door quietly, as if he had been out too late.

"She won't care, Sam," Lloyd pointed out and led the way up the stairs. Tara trailed behind uneasily.

At the door to the flat, Lloyd decided to ring the bell rather than use the key, to give Anna time to rouse herself fully before facing Sam. But after two long bursts on it, there was still no sign of movement. Danny would of course be sunk in the torpor of the well-fed and well-exercised, but he expected Anna to react more alertly. Especially after her experiences of this evening which he was sure had shaken her badly. After one more ring, he resorted to knocking on the door and called loudly, "Anna, wake up, I've got Sam with me."

At first there was no response and Lloyd wondered whether to let Sam use his key after all. Perhaps Anna had found trouble getting to sleep and had resorted to a knock-out tablet. He wouldn't be able to hang on to the kid indefinitely, as the girl was already making impatient noises as if preparing for flight, but he had no intention of letting them trickle through his fingers now he'd got them this far. Just when he needed Anna to complete the picture, she was playing hard to get. Christ, that was all he needed.

He rapped harder with every intention of waking the dead and shouted once more, "Anna, Sam's here."

Almost instantly there was the sound of a door opening and the light on the stairs above them flicked on. Footsteps in a hurry fluttered down towards them.

"Sam."

It was Anna.

Lloyd had turned and was staring up at her. Her feet were bare and so were her shoulders. Around her body was wrapped a long green bath-towel, so that she looked for all the world like a slender chrysalis that had sprouted a tousled blonde crest. Had Lloyd been a buzzard, he would have gobbled her up.

But behind her on the stairs stood the tenant. In nothing more than a maroon dressing-gown. Shock rippled through the hallway.

"Sam, I'm so glad you've come," Anna said softly, but when she turned to thank Lloyd, he was already taking the downward stairs two at a time.

"Lloyd," she called after him, but he was gone.

Outside in the dark of the deserted street, he gunned the Rover's engine and was just about to drive away when Sam seized hold of the door-handle. The boy held on and ducked his head to peer in through the side glass. Lloyd slid down the window.

"Lloyd," the toffee-brown eyes looked at him pleadingly, "don't be hard on her."

Lloyd stared back at him, wishing the young face was a fair-haired one with close-together eyes that it would give him the greatest of pleasure to rearrange. "Why not?" he demanded curtly. "You are."

The window drew shut between them and the Rover pulled away from the teashop into the night.

16

The next two weeks were busy for Lloyd. He spent them commuting between his own business and the one in Bristol, setting the merger in motion and keeping a sharp eye on every turn of the wheels. His accountant nit-picked his way through the company's books and pronounced them salvable, while Lloyd brought the two yard-managers together to start on ways of amortising costs. He kept himself in motion. If he didn't stay in any one place for long, nothing could catch up with him and that way, he reckoned he could keep one step ahead of the game.

Except, of course, it wasn't a game.

He was at his desk and had just finished arranging a meeting with the bank for the following week when his secretary reminded him, "Don't forget lunch with the Priestleys."

June Fairley was used to jogging his memory. She had plonked herself on the corner of his desk and was flicking through the pages of her notepad, checking off his commitments for the week. She was wearing a short skirt that emphasised her good legs, but Lloyd wasn't in the mood for women, with or without legs.

"I hadn't forgotten," he grumbled.

Jack Priestley and his wife, Emma, were clients. Extremely wealthy ones at that. They changed their boats like other people change shoes. At present Emma was on the look-out for something as tight and trim as her new face-lift, so Lloyd had invited them to lunch at the Park Hotel to tempt out their cheque-book over a glass of Moët. A mug of instant in his office was not quite their scene.

He looked up from the pile of paperwork that seemed to

pursue him wherever he went. "I hope you haven't forgotten that you're coming as well."

"As if! It's not every day I get invited to pig out in a place like that."

"It's not just for the meal that you're invited, you glutton. You're supposed to be gleaning sales techniques and developing client relationships, all part of the new expansion programme. We need every client we can get, so be on your best behaviour."

She laughed. "Aren't I always?"

Lloyd was spared comment by the ring of the telephone which removed June from his desk. He spent the next hour wrestling with documents, so that it was with a sense of relief and a clear conscience that at twelve-thirty he was walking down the High Street with his secretary, making for the Park Hotel. The pavements were a jostling crush of tourists that boded well for the town's traders and the sight of them reminded Lloyd that tonight was the gathering of the Chamber of Trade & Commerce. He had made a point of being in Bristol for the last one, leaving his deputy to run the show, but when he checked over the minutes of the meeting, he had seen that Anna had not turned up either. No doubt she would give tonight a miss as well.

The pavement widened to accommodate a dusty looking palm tree and a bench around which the crowd slowed and thickened, and June had just started on her hobby-horse of what about the rights of residents in this blasted town when she suddenly found herself several paces ahead of her boss. He was standing as still as if he had shot roots down into the pavement, staring at a couple of vagrants busking by the palm tree. She could see nothing about them that was worth his attention. They were just a scruffy boy and girl wearing the usual grimy black and with eyes that avoided contact with the rest of the world.

The boy was tall with a mass of curly hair and there was something vaguely familiar about him but June couldn't place it. He was playing a guitar, better than most of the drop-outs who litter the streets, but just the sight of him set June's hackles rising. You could hardly walk through any town these days without being accosted by one of the idle bums. And the girl was no better, with spiky black hair and a silver ring through her nose, as if waiting to be tethered. She was singing to the music but her voice was too light to attract attention. Leeches on society, the pair of them.

Lloyd had stopped staring and was walking briskly past her, so that she had to hurry to catch up with him. She was thankful to see he'd had more sense than to give the beggars any money, but they did seem to have stolen his tongue. He was silent during the rest of the walk to the hotel, and throughout the meal it was obvious that his conversation with his clients was an effort. Damn the blasted teenagers, they spoiled everything.

Sam watched Lloyd Morgan walk away. His guts were screwed tight with humiliation. To vent his feelings, he struck a few strident chords and earned a kick from Tara. She hated the singing bit and always threw a moody when he made her take part, but it didn't half increase their haul.

Thank Christ, Lloyd hadn't given anything. That would have been the end. It was bad enough as it was, on the street. Sam had pretended he didn't notice him and concentrated on some fancy fingerwork on the strings to attract a family of passing holidaymakers. Anything to block Lloyd from view. A child placed a twenty-pence piece on the square of frayed cloth. It was part of an old blouse of Tara's, maroon velour, and lay on the pavement in front of them with its smattering of coins.

"Thanks," Sam smiled at the kid who beamed and scuttled back to his father. "You mean old skinflint," he added to the man when he was out of earshot. "My guitar-playing is worth a hell of a lot more than a stinking twenty pence."

But they added up, all these coins. Nearly nine pounds they'd made yesterday and last Saturday they'd reached the dizzy heights of seventeen pounds sixty-two pence. That was the only reason he kept putting Tara and himself through this humiliation.

"Some people are so mean, it really sucks," Tara said sulkily and leaned against Sam's shoulder. It hampered his playing but he didn't much care.

"I'm hot and hungry," he declared, while his fingers took up with 'Stairway to Heaven'. "And I need a smoke."

"Let's pack it in for today then." Tara rubbed her cheek against his shoulder. "I've had enough."

Sam was tempted but knew it would be a mistake. Tara was always trying to duck out of the busking but it was the nearest he could get her to any work and it kept her off the pills for a few hours. A stack of joints didn't do anyone any harm but he'd had a couple of nasty trips while popping pills and was steering well clear of them, though he knew Tara was overdoing them and it scared him.

"No, not yet, Tara. The middle of the day is our best time. Give it another hour. I know it sucks, but we need the dosh."

"Screw the dosh, Sam. I can get more than we make at this in a week, if you'd just let me do the shops again."

Sam stopped playing. "Don't be dumb, Tara. They've got cameras everywhere now. You'd get caught again."

"Aw, Sam, come on. I'd be careful. I'm too quick for those fat-arsed tortoises. In and out. They'd never catch me." From her jeans pocket she pulled a tin containing some Rizlas, a tobacco pouch and a small packet of weed wrapped in clingfilm. She started skinning up behind the protection of his shoulder. "This street-work is the pits."

"So is starving."

She rolled two thin reefers, more expertly than Sam could have done, stuck a roach in each and handed him one. They gave up on the music and sank down to the pavement, their backs resting against the palm tree, warm and prickly in the sun. As they smoked, they stared at the legs marching past, a forest of moving limbs, and for some reason they suddenly triggered in Sam the memory of the swirling legs on the dance-floor at the wedding all those years ago. A pulse of pain, as palpable as a sharp stab in the heart, shuddered through him and he tugged hard at his newly bleached hair to distract his thoughts.

"Just now, wasn't that guy going past the one who's friendly with your mum?" Tara asked.

Sam thought she hadn't seen him. "Who do you mean?"

"The one who was dumb enough to give you a job at the boatyard. The big dark guy that nearly broke my wrist in the club."

"Lloyd Morgan."

"Yeah, that's the one. He went past, didn't he?"

"I didn't notice."

"Like hell."

"Okay, so he went past. So what?"

"So nothing."

"I don't need him. Or his money."

"He had a woman with him."

Sam could feel the smoke in his lungs smoothing the jagged edges of his irritation. This Northern Lights mix that Zack had got hold of was something else. He stroked the back of Tara's neck. "That's nothing. She works in his office."

"Yeah, it's always the same. Boss takes secretary out for quick shag, then objects when she wants a raise." She laughed childishly behind her hand, at the unintended double meaning.

"You've got shagging on the brain. Lloyd's too busy for that."

"Don't talk rot. She was all dressed up and they were off somewhere to get it together, I bet you."

For some reason, that idea annoyed Sam. He stood up. "Bugger this, I'm packing it in."

Tara brightened instantly. "Great. Suits me." She scooped up the cloth and the coins. "Come on, let's go back to the flat." She entwined an arm through Sam's. "I know Zack wants to talk to you about something."

Sam slung his guitar over his shoulder, grabbed a kiss from Tara to quieten his conscience and dropped the dregs of his joint into the gutter.

"Oh yes? What does he want?"

"A spot of help, I think."

"More like help out of a spot," Sam said and they both giggled.

"Open it."

"I can't."

"I said open it, you bastard," Zack snarled. The point of the blade jumped an inch nearer the man's throat. "Don't jerk me around or you'll be eating this steel. Open it. Right now."

The man was shaking. Sam thought he looked as if he was going to faint. Or have a heart-attack.

"I haven't got the k-k-keys to the safe," the man whimpered, fear breaking his words. His glasses lay crushed on the floor and sweat was trickling from his bald forehead.

"So where are they?" Zack demanded. His pale eyes left no doubt about the pleasure he took in his work.

"In the back room."

"Where?"

"In the boss's desk."

"Then get them." The knife indicated the door at the back of the shop.

"The desk is kept locked. Mr Porter has the k-key."

Mr Porter was the owner of the off-licence and earlier Sam had watched from across the road as he left to share his lunchtime sandwich with the pretty manager of the shop next door. They had chosen this place because there were no cameras.

Zack grabbed a bottle off the nearest shelf, smashed it against the wall sending an explosion of glass and red wine over himself and his victim, then thrust the business end of the jagged bottle to within a millimetre of the man's face.

"You get that desk open in two minutes or even your mother won't recognise you when I've finished with you."

At the door, Sam was scared. It wasn't meant to be like this. Just straight in, empty the till and straight out again. That's what Zack had said. No trouble of any sort. The knives were just to frighten them, that's all. But now it was all going wrong. The till had been almost empty because Mr Porter had transferred the money to the safe, just before he left the shop.

Sam looked at the knife in his own hand. It was only a short stubby fruit-knife, but its blade looked as if it meant business. He wanted to drop it and run.

Oh shit, what had he got himself into?

His job was just to guard the door. But he should have stuck to saying no. Definitely no. But Zack had made it sound so simple and Tara had been so excited by it, she couldn't get enough of him. He knew it was a bad idea right from the start. He could feel his palms clammy and his mouth like sandpaper. He wiped a hand on his jeans and prayed that nobody else would come into the shop. Zack had taken the assistant into the back room now and was trying to open the desk that contained the key to the safe.

Sam watched the passers-by outside on the pavement and willed them to stay out there. He must be out of his mind. Completely insane to get involved in this. But he knew he could not walk out now, not without Zack. More noises and voices came from the back room.

"Come on, Zack, hurry up," Sam called out and was appalled to hear that his own voice sounded as jittery as the man's. "Let's get out of here."

Zack's head snapped round the door.

"For fuck's sake, kid, why don't you go ahead and announce my name to the whole world?"

"Hell, I'm sorry, I didn't mean to."

"Use your frigging brains, kid." He disappeared again.

Sam hated him. He hated Zack's guts. This was a nightmare. One he didn't know how to wake up from.

He should just walk out.

No way. Don't even think of it. You're Zack's partner.

Like he was Tara's. He used to keep watch for her and block the security cameras' view while she pocketed stuff. Easy stuff. Gifts, handbags, clothes, all things they could sell on quickly. He never liked it. But he couldn't stop her, so he'd had to protect her. But she still got caught. In the supermarket, for fuck's sake, just taking out a bottle of Malibu in her shoulderbag. Too careless. The police were called and it got real scary, but in the end they just gave her a caution. Since then he had been adamant. No more shops.

Until this.

Come on, Zack, come on. We've got to clear out of here.

He glanced again at the street-door and his heart stuttered to a standstill when he saw a middle-aged couple standing outside, hand against the glass, ready to give it a push.

No, no, don't come in.

They took no notice. The door swung open and they walked right past him with the polite smile of strangers who want to keep it that way. The man was the one who saw the knife. The woman, in her broad-beamed suit and shopping shoes, was too intent on heading for the shelf of French Burgundy. The man's eyes shot wide open and his mouth uttered a faint mew, that made his wife turn.

"What's up with you, Philip?" She held up a green bottle for his inspection. "How about this one?"

Then she saw her husband's face. Her gaze followed his and ended on the knife. Immediately her eyes were on Sam's, reminding him of his form-tutor at school when she was assessing what level of resistance she was likely to meet from a rowdy pupil.

"Philip, I don't know what this young man is up to, but I suggest we leave." She took her husband's arm and started to steer him towards the door. The bottle was still in her hand.

"No." Sam raised the knife and pointed it directly at them. He had been told to prevent any customers from leaving the shop. "Stay where you are." Fear made his voice more aggressive than he felt.

The woman looked at him steadily. She must have been about fifty, grey hair neatly permed and a mouth that was accustomed to control. "Young man, I have no wish to be involved in whatever crime you are committing in this shop."

"You are already involved."

"My husband and I are going to walk out of here. Don't try to stop us or you will be in even greater trouble than you are already."

"I warn you," Sam said, "stay where you are and you won't get hurt." It sounded convincing enough to his own ears.

Just then the sound of Zack's voice raised in anger came from the back room, followed by a thump and a cry of pain. The woman's eyes remained fixed on Sam.

"Maybe your friend has other ideas."

Sam lifted his voice in subdued panic. "Come on, for Christ's sake, let's go." This time he remembered not to use Zack's name.

The woman would not give up. "We are leaving now." Again she moved towards the door, dragging her husband with her.

"Don't," Sam shouted. "I'm warning you."

"What will you do, young man? Stick that knife in us?" She smiled at him calmly. "I think not."

At that moment Zack hurtled out of the back room, stuffing banknotes into a canvas bag, the flick-knife still in his hand.

"We're out of here," he yelled, but stopped long enough to seize a couple of bottles of vodka off a shelf and thrust them with the money into Sam's arms. "Who the hell are these?"

"Customers. They just came in. I was keeping them here, like you told me."

"Good kid."

The middle-aged couple were standing quietly, having decided to wait for the thieves to leave first.

"Don't you fancy playing hero and having a go at us?" Zack taunted the man, waving the knife at him. "Come on, let's see what you're made of."

Sam shoved the money and vodka into a carrier-bag from the counter and brushed past Zack. "I'm off."

But Zack was enjoying himself. He lifted a handful of the man's shirt-front and slit it open with the knife. The man stood very still.

"I bet you've always fancied a pierced nipple, haven't you?" The blade nicked a drop of blood from the tip of the man's nipple.

The wife reacted instantly. "You scum, get your filthy hands off him." She launched herself at Zack, seizing his arm and swung the bottle at him.

Sam did not see precisely what happened next. There was a struggle and the woman sank down with a soft cough. Blood was pumping out on to the floor. He stared at the crimson knife in Zack's hand.

They both ran.

17

"Hey, bro, what are you doing here?"

Danny had just arrived home from the gym after an afternoon of weight training and the first thing he saw when he walked into the flat was his brother. Sam was huddled in front of the television screen where two cooks were expounding on the secrets of the perfect soufflé. No way could he really be getting his mind round that rubbish.

Danny dropped his kitbag on to the floor and gave it a goal kick that sent it skidding between the legs of the coffee-table.

"Eat your heart out, Shearer," he crowed. "Ma is busy downstairs in the teashop," he added, in case his brother was waiting for her.

Sam looked round, as if startled by the voice, and the expression on his face shocked Danny. It was so full of jitters.

"What's up, Sam?" Danny sat down in the armchair opposite him and tried to keep the concern out of his voice. But the unease was too infectious and he could feel it already spawning in his own guts. "What's the matter?"

"Nothing. I just felt like coming home."

"Missing me too much, were you?" Danny tried the usual banter.

"Get a life."

"So why are you back here?"

Sam hesitated. "For fresh clothes."

"Too pongy even for you, are they?" Danny was relieved to see his brother respond with a small smile. Maybe things weren't so bad, after all.

Sam's eyes retreated back to the television to watch one of the cooks whipping egg-whites into Ski Sunday peaks.

"You've dyed your hair," Danny commented, stating the obvious. His brother's long shaggy curls had been transformed from their natural dark brown to graded streaks of blond that had the effect of making him look oddly vulnerable. Danny had always known his older brother to be the solid one, the dependable one, the one who had his head together, screwed on real tight. But somehow the breakdown of the dense mop of hair into separate ripples of colour seemed to shred that solidity into wisps of straw. Danny gnawed at his thumb-nail. "When did you get that done?"

"Yesterday."

"Did you dye it yourself?"

"Tara did it."

"Takes some getting used to."

Sam just shrugged. Hair was obviously not something that interested him at the moment. Danny wondered where Tara was, but didn't want to ask outright.

"I've been up at the gym."

Sam looked at him blankly and his eyes blinked twice as if making an effort to take in the mundane details. "Did it go okay?"

"Yeah, great. I was working on my pecs today. It's triceps tomorrow. They've got a new machine in the gym that's really wicked."

He was simply making conversation, any conversation, just noise to divert his thoughts from the fear that he'd seen crouched in his brother's eyes.

"No pain, no gain," Sam said automatically and stood up, as if to leave the room.

Danny didn't want him to go. He had missed his brother. Sam looked so thin that he seemed inches taller. It would really do Ma's head in when she saw him, especially with the blond hair and all.

"Do you want me to tell Ma you're here?" Danny asked, to delay his departure.

"No. Not if she's busy. I'll just hang about till she comes up."

"No rush then?"

"No."

"How about a film?"

"What?"

"On video. Let's watch a film. As you're not in a rush. Like we used to."

For the first time Danny saw Sam's eyes shift away from whatever was going on inside his head and focus properly on himself. The jitters retreated a few steps.

"Sure. Why not? Like old times."

"Which film?" Danny asked.

They both smiled.

"The usual?" Danny grinned.

Sam nodded and picked up the remote-control gadget that was lying on top of the television. "Go find it, little bro."

Danny descended on the cabinet where the video films were stored, tumbled them all out on to the floor and selected the one with the most dog-eared box. On its cover was written in Sam's hand the single word *Predator*.

"I haven't seen Nick around so much lately," Esther Miller commented. She had just baked a jacket potato in the microwave and was spreading it with prawns and coleslaw. She didn't approve of the microwave but had been talked into making use of it by Anna. "Has he gone back up to London again?"

"Just for a couple of days, to fix the final details at the gallery." Anna pushed two plates of scones with clotted cream towards the hatch.

On the tearoom side, a pair of female hands with painted nails appeared briefly, placed the plates on a tray, thrust another order-slip through to the kitchen and disappeared. No cheery smile, nor cheeky quip. Just a girl doing a job she didn't much care for.

"Oh yes, of course," Esther noted. "The exhibition."

"All art and fart."

"Anna!"

"Well, critics are so full of hot air, aren't they," she chuckled. "They just love the sight of their words in print. They're bound to give Nick a hard time."

"Let's hope not. How is he finding life in the hotel?".

"A bit isolated."

Nick Steed had been ousted from Anna's holiday flat last week by the arrival of the new tenants with their inflatable crocodile and sunbleached windbreak. The month had passed too fast and he wasn't ready to leave yet. Anna had managed to find him a cancellation room in a colleague's small hotel, but she missed him in the flat above. Missed him popping his head round for a chat or inviting her up for a glass of wine in the evening. She missed the attention. But if she was honest, really honest with herself, she was relieved that he was more remote now. Ever since that one night when she had climbed into his bed and been dragged out of it by Lloyd and Sam turning up on her doorstep, the relationship had not been the same.

Her head was a tangle inside and she ran a hand through her hair, as if to pull out the thorns. She saw her companion watching her.

"Don't look at me like that, Esther."

"Like what?" the older woman asked innocently.

"As if you know what's in my head better than I do."

Esther laughed, making her broad bosom sway. "So when is the exhibition due to start?"

"The grand opening is on Monday."

"Are you going up to London for it with him?"

"He has invited me."

"That's not what I asked."

Anna slid a slice of cheesecake on to a plate. "Of course I want to see the exhibition. His paintings are wonderful, they deserve a good show."

"So are you going?"

Anna turned her back towards Esther and busied herself at the sink. "It depends on whether I can get someone to stand in for me here."

Esther's grey eyes rested for a long moment on her employer, but she said nothing. Instead she set to work on the next order.

Anna was aware of the silence. To fill it she said, "Don't worry. I won't leave you in the lurch. I'll ask Nella. She might be able to help out with a few extra hours."

Nella Torrence had been working at the teashop since the

beginning of the school summer holidays and was due in any moment for the start of her shift. Harriet had offered her daughter a job in the health-food shop but had been turned down flat. Once out of sight of her mother, Nella dropped the surly looks and displayed a diffident manner and shy smile that was infinitely more attractive to customers than the bored eyes of the girl taking their orders out there at the moment.

"Teenagers," Anna sighed, "make an early grave look more inviting than any lottery jackpot."

Esther gave a nod of sympathy. "No word from Sam?"

Anna shook her head and concentrated on buttering a teacake. She had got Esther off the sticky subject of Nick Steed only to land on a stickier one.

"No."

"Give him time, love. And don't fret so much. Sam is a decent boy and he'll sort himself out in the end. Anyway, it can't get any worse."

"Is that a promise?"

At that moment Nella Torrence walked into the kitchen to start her shift, her long hair neatly held back by a black ribbon and her face slightly flushed from hurrying. "Hi, sorry I'm late." She pushed her spectacles up her nose and tied a little white apron round her waist. "It's great to see Sam is here. When did he get back?"

Anna stared at the girl, annoyed that everyone seemed determined to bring up the subject of Sam.

"What?"

"Sam. Upstairs."

"Nella, what are you talking about?"

"I just saw him. He walked past the upstairs window as I crossed the road. I waved but he didn't see me and I thought . . ."

Anna did not let her finish. She thrust the butter-knife and teacake into the girl's hands, shot out of the kitchen and took the stairs two at a time.

Oh God, he's wearing an earring. Just one, in his left ear. Like a tag, a label, declaring his allegiance to mass stupidity. Anna wanted to tear it out.

"Hello, Sam." She kept it so casual, she wondered if she was overdoing it. "It's good to see you."

She had made a point of walking into the kitchen first as if she had returned to the flat to collect something she had forgotten earlier, and only then did she allow herself to look in on the sitting-room. Both boys were watching that dreadful film they were so keen on and Sam was clutching a glass of something clear that looked suspiciously as if it might have come out of a gin or vodka bottle.

Worse, much worse, his hair was blond. Badly streaked into albino rat-tails. All his childhood he had bewailed the fact that he wasn't fair-haired like herself and Danny. So now he had gone and granted his wish, wiped out his father's genes.

Sam looked round at her, and instantly neither the hair nor the earring mattered one jot. Her heart ground to a halt. He looked stunned. Eyes tormented into total shell-shock.

Oh Sam, what have you done to yourself?

"Hello, Ma."

That was it. Nothing more. He returned his eyes to the screen.

She was willing to wait. When he was ready, he would talk. Please God, let him talk to her. She retreated to the kitchen, made them all a mug of hot chocolate, then placed herself quietly in a chair to sit out the film.

At one point, Danny commented, "I thought you didn't like *Predator*."

"I don't."

He frowned slightly as if trying to make sense of that, but not for long. A transparent alien was oozing luminous blood in the jungle and demanded his attention.

Sam kept his face turned rigidly away from her.

He did not eat much that evening, only picked at a few scraps of chicken and pushed most of it away. He looked painfully thin, even his fingers were like sticks, and Anna had to suppress the urge to shovel food at him. When he announced that he would be spending the night at home with them, Anna felt a surge of relief that was immediately swamped by a sense of disaster.

"Sam, has something happened? Please tell me if you're in any kind of trouble. Maybe I could help."

They were standing in the kitchen together and Sam scowled at the cup of coffee in his hand instead of looking at her. "Why do you immediately have to assume there's trouble?"

"Because you seem upset," Anna said gently.

"I'm not upset."

"Good, I'm glad. So does that mean there isn't any?"

"Any what?"

"Trouble."

He shrugged and dumped the cup in the sink. "Nothing much."

How much was nothing much?

"And Tara? Is she okay?"

"Yes."

Anna waited to see if more followed but nothing did, so instead she told him about Harriet Torrence's plans to cultivate organic vegetables in her therapy field, and started to clean out the hamster's cage. Sam cradled the fragile ball of fur in his hands while she scraped out Hammy's musty bedding and a slight smile appeared as he stroked its twitching petal-pink nose. Anna felt like wringing its smelly little neck. How come Sam had a smile for his bloody hamster but not for his mother? But by the time the cage was all ready for its occupant once more, she had talked some sense into herself and gave the hamster a particularly big peanut to make up for her stab of jealousy.

After that, Sam drifted away to his room, shut the door and that was the last she saw of him for the evening. He did not seem to have brought anything home with him. There were no dirty clothes lying around, no toothbrush or comb or CDs, no possessions of any sort. As if he had decided to come on impulse. While she played cards with Danny who was eager to improve his poker skills, she kept wondering what had prompted that impulse.

She didn't sleep. In bed she tossed and turned, eventually got up and made herself a hot drink that she did not want, reeled off her list of jobs for the next day and even tried counting the number of customers she had served that morning. Nothing helped. Sleep refused to come. She lay in the dark thinking of Sam and was grateful that he was, however briefly, safe under her roof.

It was nearly three-thirty in the morning when she heard his bedroom door open and footsteps whisper along the corridor. A visit to the bathroom she presumed, but when they did not stop but kept right on going, she suddenly panicked. Sam, don't you dare creep off in the middle of the night without even saying goodbye. She sat up, paralysed midway between intending to leap out of bed and yet not wanting to frighten him off, when a light tap pecked at her door.

She slid back down under the duvet.

"Ma, are you awake?" Very soft and barely audible above her heartbeat.

"Yes, come in." She strove to keep it sounding sleepy and relaxed.

The door opened and a rectangle of light from the corridor slipped into the room. The tall silhouette of her son followed it and headed for the end of her bed, where he perched with his knees tucked under his chin. It was a double bed, so he could choose his own space without running the risk of invading hers, unless he wanted to.

"Hello, Sam."

"Feel like talking?"

"It beats counting sheep."

In the dark the expression on his face was hidden from her, but a smear of light from the corridor brushed across one cheek and highlighted the hated earring.

"Sam, I know we've had our differences this summer, but it's nice to be friends again." She almost added 'like old times', but decided it might make him cringe. Anyway, it wasn't a bit like old times.

"Yes."

"Is there something particular that you want to talk about?"

"Yes."

She waited.

Nothing came. There was just the soft scrape of his light

stubble as he rubbed his chin back and forth across his knees.

After a few minutes, Anna said softly, "Sam, just start at the beginning and tell me what has happened."

She heard his breathing quicken its pace and knew that whatever it was, it was at last coming to the surface.

"Ma, I'm in trouble."

"Tell me about it."

"You'll think I've let you down."

"No, Sam, never that. And maybe it's not quite as bad as you think."

"Ma, I'm in trouble. I mean real trouble."

Anna let that sink in and tucked her hands under the duvet to hide their trembling. "In what way are you in real trouble?"

"I'll go to prison."

"No, Sam, no. What on earth have you done?"

"They'll put me in prison."

"You're not eighteen yet, too young for prison."

"You don't understand." His voice was shaking. "They chuck you in a young offenders' place first. And then prison. In a cage no bigger than Hammy's."

"Oh Sam. Please just tell me what happened."

He rolled on to his side on the bed in a tight, prickly ball at her feet and the words that came out of his mouth were incredulous, as if he could not believe them himself.

"I did a robbery with Zack. It was an off-licence. A woman got stabbed."

Oh no. No, no, no. Not murder.

"Did you stab her? Or did Zack?"

It had to be Zack. Please, make it Zack.

"Zack."

Anna breathed again, a short ragged breath. "Then it need not be so bad for you."

"It happened so quickly. She struggled for his knife and suddenly there was blood everywhere. It was hideous. I keep seeing it every time I shut my eyes." His voice choked and then whispered, "Ma, I'm scared."

She reached out to him. She stroked his head, as if he were still a child afraid of the dark. The feel of his hair was foreign to her, greasy and lank under her hand, and she was glad its bleached streaks were hidden by the shadows. When her fingers touched his cheek, the bones felt naked and unprotected, and she murmured, "I'm here," as if that could stave off the demons.

Sam moaned and put his hand over hers, clasping it firmly against his cheek as he lay curled on her duvet. "I need help."

"I'll help you, Sam. In every way I can."

"Promise me, Ma, promise."

"I promise. We'll sort this out together." Years of training had made her an expert at picking up the pieces.

She felt his grasp on her hand tighten and knew he'd had about as much as he could take for tonight. He had forced the words out of his throat and the pain of it had scraped him raw. Anna could not help thinking about the pain of the woman who had been stabbed, wondering how her family were feeling tonight.

Gradually Sam's breathing lost its shallow uneasy rhythm and acquired the regular whisperings of exhausted sleep. It was disturbed every now and again by a prolonged groan that startled her each time and indicated that the nightmare had pursued him into his dreams. She lay quietly, her hand still enclosed by his, and made no sound when, an hour later, Sam shuddered back to consciousness and slipped silently off the bed. He padded back along the corridor to his own room and shut the door.

There was no Sam at breakfast. Danny shovelled down the usual mountain range of scrambled eggs and toast, but looked at his mother oddly, which made Anna think she must look as rough as she felt.

"You okay, Ma?" he asked when he surfaced for air.

"Yes, I'm fine."

"You look kind of funny."

"Rubbish, of course I'm okay. What about you? Are you pleased to have Sam home?"

"You bet. Is he staying?"

"I don't know. I don't think he has decided yet what his plans are."

Danny poured himself a third glass of orange juice. "What about Tara?"

"I don't know that either. Did he mention anything to you about her? Whether they have split up, maybe?"

"Naah, don't get your hopes up. Nothing like that. He just said she'd dropped out of sight for a while. And before you ask, I don't know why and I don't know where." He replaced the juice carton in the fridge and helped himself to some hunks off the roast chicken that was sitting invitingly on a shelf. "Sounds like she's dumped him, if you ask me."

"Now you're the one getting my hopes up. But I expect he'll tell us if and when he's ready."

"S'pose so," her younger son muttered doubtfully, and wandered into the sitting-room from where Anna soon heard the squawk of television cartoons emerging. Wasn't he too old for that rubbish yet?

She dumped the dishes in the sink and, with a hopeful "Get the washing up done, will you, Danny?", grabbed her purse and was out of the flat. The newsagent was only a few doors up the road, so within minutes she was standing in the street clutching the local morning newspaper in her hand and fighting hard to breathe right as she flicked through its pages.

Nothing.

No mention of a robbery. Nor of a murder.

Maybe it wasn't as bad as Sam thought. Could it be that he was mistaken about what had happened? Oh yes, and maybe hamsters might fly. She scrunched up the paper and threw it into the nearest bin. The obvious answer was that the news had not reached the printing presses in time but no doubt the afternoon edition was already clearing a centre-spread for it. Violence always made good copy.

Anna headed back home. There was a business to run. And Sam had to be talked to.

She spent a couple of hours in the teashop with Nella and Esther both chivvying her for details that she could not give.

"Has he finished with Tara?" Nella wanted to know.

"He hasn't mentioned her to me yet, so I honestly don't know." Seeing the young girl's mouth droop with disappointment, she added, "But I'm hoping that he might have come to see sense at last."

Nella pushed up her glasses and frowned as if she suspected Anna was keeping something from her. "Can I take my coffee-break now and go upstairs to see him?"

"No, not yet, Nella," Anna said quickly. "He's asleep."

"Oh, later then," Nella said and mooched away with her order-pad, every twitch of her body declaring her dissatisfaction with yet more arbitrary adult rules.

Anna gave Sam another half-hour and at eleven-thirty she went up to the flat to wake him. But she need not have bothered. He was already in the kitchen eating a bowl of cereal at the table. Despite the sleep, in daylight he looked just as bad as last night, and the shadows under his eyes seemed even worse. She noticed he was not wearing the earring.

He looked up and managed the hint of a smile when she walked in. "Hi, how's business downstairs?"

"Busy."

"Good."

That was the extent of his gesture towards a conversation. He attacked the Bran Flakes with a grim determination that indicated duty rather than inclination.

"Would you like some eggs?" Anna enquired, and was surprised to receive a nod and a grunt that sounded as if it might be a please.

She cooked him eggs, bacon and toast, and then made coffee for them both. When she put the plate in front of him, he scowled as if he could hardly stomach to look at it, but ate it without murmur. Anna sat down opposite him with her coffee and tried not to stare at the bleached hair.

"It's good to see you eating well," she commented.

He glanced up briefly from a forkful of bacon. "I'm fattening myself up on purpose. Like a turkey for Christmas."

"Sam!"

He looked at her and his brown eyes were deadly serious. "Okay, not for Christmas. But for an identity parade."

She stared at him, appalled.

He shrugged and returned to his bacon.

After a long silence that wrapped round the table like a

shroud, Anna said, "Sam, I need to know the truth about what happened."

He nodded and finished his toast, and for one insane moment she thought he was going to tell her it was all a joke that he had concocted with Tara. But one look at his face brought her back to reality. His gaze was fixed on his coffee as if seeing the robbery again enacted in its dark swirls, and when he spoke, his voice was unsteady.

"It was Zack's idea. And I went along with it. I knew it wasn't right but I let him persuade me. Dumb idiot! I must have been out of my mind." He thumped the table with the flat of his hand and his coffee jumped threateningly in response. He picked it up and drank a mouthful, then proceeded to tell his mother the details of what had happened in the off-licence.

Anna listened in silence.

She kept thinking that if only she had managed to talk to him that night Lloyd had brought him to the flat, then perhaps none of this would have happened. But she had been out living her own life, upstairs in Nick Steed's bed, so Sam had turned and walked away from her. Straight into Tara's embrace and Zack's criminal clutches. At the end of his account, he hung his head and fiddled with a strand of the hideous locks.

"Sam, what you did was terribly wrong."

"I know, Ma. The whole thing was insane. I feel gutted about that woman." He looked up suddenly. "But it wasn't me who stabbed her. Honestly. It was Zack."

"I believe you, Sam."

"I'm sorry, really sorry. I wish I could undo it."

"So do I." She reached out a hand to rest on the table between them, holding out a lifeline.

For the first time, she saw tears gather in his eyes and he blinked them back fiercely. He put out a hand and held on to hers with a firm squeeze. "Thanks, Ma. Thanks for helping me."

"We haven't started yet. It's time we got down to business. Where do we go from here? A solicitor, I think."

"No." Sam snatched his hand away and jumped to his feet. "No solicitors."

"Don't be foolish, Sam. We have to try to salvage what we can out of a situation that is already bad. Don't make it worse."

"I say no solicitors. Solicitors mean police."

"Sam, haven't you done enough that's immoral? Stop right this second. Of course we have to go to the police."

"No. No police. You promised you'd help me. That means no police and no solicitors."

The realisation of what he intended hit Anna like an express train. "Sam, you would be making things worse for yourself."

"No police."

"You are already in real trouble. The only possible course of action now is to go to the police. Tell them everything that happened. If Zack was the one who used the knife, then he is the one who will be punished for it. Not you."

"Ma, what planet are you on? I took part in a robbery with violence. No way am I going to march up to the police and hold out my wrists for the handcuffs."

Anna wanted to shake some sense into him.

She stood up. "Of course you must. Go to the police and tell them what happened and how little you were involved. The man in the shop will surely back you up with his version of events. But Sam, you must go to them."

He just stared at her with a tilt of the head that said it all.

Anna went over it all again. In detail she explained the reasons, argued how he must accept the consequences of his actions and even underlined how black it would look when the police eventually came knocking on his door. Sam listened in silence until she had finished.

"No police."

It was then that she exploded.

"Sam, you and I are going round to the police station right this minute and you can continue the argument with them!"

"Calm down." He spoke quietly and slowly as if to a wayward child. "I am ready to admit to you that what I did was wrong. And I'm really sorry for it. But I am *not* going to make things worse by confessing to the police. That's final. But I've worked out exactly what I *am* going to do. I'm going to keep my head down. Here. In this flat. I need your help. I need shelter. You've got to hide me." His jaw softened in a smile that threatened to melt her soul. "Please, Ma. Please."

Anna hardened her heart.

"No."

"Think about it. I'll go and see if the lunch-time newspaper is in the shop yet, and while I'm gone, just think about what it would be like to live in prison." He disappeared in a flurry of limbs.

Anna sat down and thought about it.

Sam took longer than she expected. When finally he did return, he looked positively buoyant.

"Ma, she's not dead," he announced the moment he stepped through the door. "The woman is in intensive-care but her condition is stable. Her name is Mrs Rachel Anstey. She's a magistrate, for Christ's sake."

Anna rested her head on her hands to still its dizzy pirouettes.

Sam spread the paper flat on the table for her to read. "Look."

It was plastered right across the front page. Violent attack by two teenagers. The black headline somehow made it all unbelievable again, as if she were hearing about someone else. Some other mother's son. But Sam was reading aloud the details.

" 'Two youths, believed to be aged between 17 and 20, entered an off-licence in Bruton Street at 12.15 p.m. yesterday, both carrying knives. They forced . . .' "

"Both?"

Sam glanced up from the paper and blushed fiercely. "Yes, I was carrying one too."

"Oh Sam!"

"I didn't intend to use it, honestly. It was just for show."

"But it makes it so much worse for you. It looks like premeditated violence."

Sam ducked his head back to the paper. "I know," he muttered, and continued reading out loud, faster now. " 'They forced the assistant, Mr John Hale, to open the safe from which they stole £900. During their escape, a customer, Mrs Rachel Anstey, a local magistrate, was stabbed in the stomach and her husband, Mr Philip Anstey, was slightly wounded.' " Sam looked up again. "Slightly wounded! Who's he kidding? He received a tiny pinprick, that's all."

"Even a pinprick is too much."

"Oh yes, of course it is, I know that, Ma," Sam backtracked fast. "It's just that he's blowing it up into something much bigger."

He continued to read, " 'Mrs Anstey was taken to Warborough Hospital where she underwent an emergency operation. She is now in intensive-care but her condition is said to be stable. The police are looking for two youths. One is described as tall and thin with long dark hair, a slight beard and unusual pale eyes. He was wearing black jeans and a black tee-shirt. The other is also tall and thin with blond curly hair worn quite long and was wearing blue denim jeans and a black tee-shirt with a Pearl Jam motif.' Oh shit, I've got to get rid of that shirt!" He pulled a chemist's package from his pocket. "And I'll get this done."

"What is it?"

He opened the bag to reveal its contents. A packet of hair-dye. That's why he had taken so long on his trip to buy the paper.

"I'm going to go brown again." He walked over to the kitchen drawer and lifted out a pair of scissors which he held out towards his mother. "Will you cut it first?" When he saw her hesitate, he added, "Please, Ma. I need it real short."

So Anna cut it. She knew she shouldn't, but she did. She worked in silence in front of a mirror, snipping shorter and shorter at his urging. By the end of twenty minutes, the blond curls lay like dead wings on the floor and his head was covered by a dense velvet that didn't even have a wave to its credit.

"Thanks, that's perfect." He rubbed a hand over his blond crop and nodded solemnly. "I'll dye it now."

"Sam, this isn't right."

Suddenly, taking Anna totally by surprise, the veneer cracked and her son started shaking. "What is it you want, Ma? To send me to prison? To shut me behind bars with a slop-pail and drug dealers for companions. With weirdos who screw young boys in the showers for fun. Is that what you want for me? Because that's exactly what I'll get if you go to the police."

Anna said softly, "You should have thought of that before you committed the robbery."

"But I didn't. I know I should have, but I didn't. I just did not think of the consequences. But all I did was just stand there by the door. That's all. Does that mean you want to send me to some stinking prison?''

''No,'' Anna said vehemently. ''No, Sam, of course I don't. I couldn't bear you to go to prison. You know I couldn't. But it's where you deserve to be, you stupid, stupid fool.''

And she started to cry.

Sam came close to her and awkwardly wrapped his arms around her shuddering shoulders. ''Then help me, Ma. Help me.''

18

Once Anna had made the decision, she set about changing Sam's appearance. First she dyed his hair and when it was transformed into a glossy brown moleskin, she began on his face. Using tweezers and ignoring his grunts of protest, she plucked his heavy eyebrows to a lighter, younger look, then made him shave off his stubble, pull back his shoulders and dress more smartly. The whole time, she kept feeding him. Cheeses and chops, jacket potatoes and apple crumble, chocolate and milkshakes. Anything that would fatten him up at top speed. And it worked. Within only a few hours his face seemed to be losing that distinctive boniness that was the stamp of street-life, and softer curves padded out the telltale angles.

When Danny bounced in at five o'clock after swimming the day away on a training course in Weymouth, he blinked with surprise.

"Hey, bro, cool haircut."

Sam shrugged. "I got sick of the surfer look."

"What does Tara think?"

"She hasn't seen it."

"Oh yeah? Out of the scene completely, is she?"

Sam turned away and rummaged in the fridge for a yogurt, so Danny did not press the point and went off to take a shower. Anna had listened to the exchange, appalled at her own short-sightedness. She had been totally absorbed all day in Sam. What about Tara?

"Sam, where is Tara?"

"I don't know." He tried to shrug it off again, but a mother was not as easily discouraged as a younger brother.

"Tell me what went on. After the robbery. You ran, but then what?"

Sam turned to face her but kept his eyes on the spoon that was stirring the yogurt in his hand. "It doesn't really matter, does it?"

"Yes, it does. I have to know the rest."

Sam popped a purple cherry from the pot into his mouth. "Nothing much happened. We met up with Tara at the church. Like we'd arranged. It was too dangerous to go back to the flat, so we agreed to split up for a few weeks." His breathing was coming fast, as if the memory was too tightly laced with fear. "Until everything is quiet again."

Anna stood very still by the window. "Are you telling me that you intend to gang up again with them if you get away with this?"

Sam's eyes lifted to hers for the first time. "No, I'll never run with Zack again. I promise you that."

"And Tara?"

He shook his head and his gaze dropped back to the yogurt. "I'll see."

Anna prayed that he would indeed see and left it at that.

It was seven-thirty in the evening when Nick Steed rang the bell and announced, "I'm back."

It should have been a relief to see him, a breath of normality sweeping aside the feeling of conspiracy that hung like a sour odour in the flat. But instead, it just cranked up the tension. Anna had said nothing to Danny about the cause of Sam's return, but he wasn't stupid. He must have known something wasn't right. She invited Nick in and received the usual martyred look from her sons as they switched off the television. They remained the obligatory three polite minutes in the room, then made themselves scarce.

"Sam is looking better," Nick commented when the door had banged shut behind them. "Given up on life on the streets, has he?"

Anna nodded. She did not want to talk about Sam.

Nick chuckled. "Kids are soft these days. A bit of hard living won't have done him any harm. Toughen him up."

"I don't want him toughened up."

He looked at her, surprised at the abruptness of her tone, and headed on to safer territory. "Has trade been good in the teashop? Did you have a busy day?"

Yes, oh hell, yes, she'd had a busy day. But not in the teashop.

"Yes, thanks. This sunny weather attracts tourists to the seaside like flies."

"Did anything interesting go on while I was away?"

"What do you mean?" she asked, instantly suspicious.

"I didn't mean anything in particular, Anna. Why so prickly tonight?"

She rubbed a hand over her eyes. "I'm sorry, Nick, I'm just tired, that's all. I didn't sleep well last night. Tell me about the exhibition instead."

That did the trick. Immediately Anna's sons and teashop dwindled into also-rans and he launched into a prolonged description of the final preparations of the exhibition. She was treated to a blow-by-blow account of his disagreement with the gallery owner over lighting arrangements and the details of every painting's precise juxtaposition on the walls. At the end of an hour, she was still struggling to keep her mind away from visions of knives and prison cells, but tried to concentrate on what Nick was saying. He was in the middle of telling her about which art critics had been invited to attend the opening on Monday, when a police siren wailed its way into the High Street. Anna's heart thumped to a standstill. She held her breath and waited for it to stop outside her door.

It drove on past.

Her heart picked itself up again and raced away as if in pursuit. She simply could not force herself to sit still one more second. She stumbled to her feet and asked Nick if he would like a coffee.

"Good idea, my throat's getting dry."

Anna said nothing but walked into the kitchen. He followed her and continued the steady flow of his side of the conversation while she made the coffee and poured it into mugs. When she handed one to him, he commented, "You're quiet tonight."

"I'm just a bit tired. You know how a day on my feet drains all activity from my brain." She dredged up a convincing smile and was pleased when he laughed. Already she was on guard every second, ready to insist that nothing had changed during the last two days.

Except that her son had returned home.

Nick put an arm round her waist and kissed her blonde head. "What you need is a break. The trip up to London for my exhibition will do you good. You'll enjoy it. By the way, I thought that instead of going up by train, we might as well use your car instead. It will save money on fares."

Money.

The word suddenly shouted in Anna's brain.

Money.

Where was the money?

She put down her coffee and hurried to the door.

"Anna!"

She stopped in her tracks. "Sorry, Nick. I've just remembered something. I really must have a quick word with Sam. I won't be long."

"Can't it wait?"

"No, sorry. Not this. Drink your coffee." She disappeared before he could ask more questions.

Sam was lying on his bed, flat on his back with one arm draped across his eyes. He might have been asleep, but Anna doubted it. She shut the door behind her.

"Sam."

Reluctantly, he removed the arm and rolled his head to one side to look at her. "Has Nick gone?"

"No, not yet."

"Oh. Danny told me that Nick has a painting exhibition opening in London on Monday."

"Yes, that's right, but I want to talk to you about . . ."

"Because I was thinking. If you want to go to it, I could fill in at the teashop for you while you're in London." He made the offer shyly.

It took Anna by surprise.

"Thank you, Sam. That's kind. I haven't decided yet. I'm not sure if it's a good idea for me to go. Especially now."

"It's up to you. But don't miss it because of me." He draped his arm back across his eyes.

"That's not what I came to talk to you about."

"Oh, Ma, please don't start on again about going to the police. And I won't shop Zack to them either, so don't ask me. There were no cameras, so . . ."

"Sam, where's the money?"

"What?" He removed the arm again.

"The money. The nine hundred pounds that you stole. What happened to it?"

He whipped over on to his stomach and buried his head under the pillow. "It's gone." The words emerged indistinctly through the feathers.

"Gone where?"

"Away."

"Sam, don't hide." Anna sat down on the bed and pulled the pillow off his head. "What do you mean, 'away'?"

He rolled over to face her. "We dumped it. When we met up by the church, we agreed it was too dangerous to hang on to it. We thought the woman was dead. The police would be too tight on our tails. So we chucked it in a dustbin."

"A dustbin in the street?"

"Yes. Outside someone's gate. The money was in a plastic bag, so nobody would find it."

She stared at him. "Sam, that's very hard to believe."

His toffee eyes widened with hurt. "It's the truth."

"But Zack and Tara knew they would need the money while in hiding. They wouldn't have thrown it away."

"We were scared, Ma. We thought Zack had murdered that woman. All we wanted to do was get rid of anything that connected us to it."

She wanted to believe him.

"Sam, are you lying to me?"

"No, honestly I'm not." He sat up, placed one hand on

each of her shoulders and brought his face close to hers, as if to impress the truth into her mind by physical force. "I'm telling you exactly what happened. We hid the money in a bin and ran. Come on, Ma, get real. Why should I lie to you now?"

She let herself believe him. "Okay, Sam, okay, I'm convinced. But it was a stupid thing to do."

He patted her back reassuringly. "It's all right, don't worry about it. The money has gone and even if it is ever found, it can't be traced to me."

"Oh Sam, this is too hideous to be true."

"Don't, Ma."

"You should have had the sense to give the money back to the people you took it from."

He pulled a face and tried to smile. "Oh yes, that would have been great. Walk into the shop and say 'Here's your money back, sir. It was all a mistake.' They would have us in handcuffs before we'd got to the door."

"There are other ways of doing it."

He fiddled with the gold chain round her neck, winding it round his thumb. "It's too late now. It's gone." He looked earnestly into her eyes. "I am sorry."

Anna took a deep breath and let it out slowly, as if it might wash away some of the nightmare. "I know," she said. "So am I."

When she returned to the kitchen, Nick Steed had gone.

Lloyd Morgan was at a tourism forum. It had started at nine-thirty in the morning and at midday was still in full flow. Seated round a long rectangular table, it was one of those meetings where everyone had a lot to say but not an awful lot of listening was going on. The problem was, as always, persuading local businesses to put their hands in their pocket to finance new schemes. The group of ten men and two women were made up mainly of representatives from the town's hoteliers and traders, and was chaired by the head of the tourist board, Tim Brearey. The subject under discussion was security.

"Closed-circuit television is the only answer to those teen-agers," Lloyd pointed out to those dragging their feet. "We'd be mad not to get it installed."

Lloyd was attending the meeting to put forward the Chamber of Trade & Commerce's point of view and was well aware that it was in the business community's interest to tighten up on the security systems. That meant investment.

"It's the cost," Tim Brearey said for the third time. "Of course we all know that cameras will deter the kind of drunken vandalism that is such a menace to our town, especially at weekends. But the question is, is it feasible?"

"Exactly. Is it feasible?" a hotelier echoed. "Can we afford it?"

Lloyd was tired of these short-sighted objections. "It's a matter of having to. And it's not as if we have to cover the whole cost ourselves," he reminded them. "We've got the guarantee of a chunk of government and council funding, so let's get on with it while the offer is on the table."

"I'm totally behind you, Mr Morgan," the older of the two women said enthusiastically. "It's common sense that we need to make that kind of necessary investment, if we are to protect our town. My shop has been broken into three times already this summer and every time the culprits got away scot-free."

"The vandals were at it again last night. There was another shop window smashed on the sea-front," a deep voice informed them.

It belonged to Inspector Matlock. As guest speaker to the forum, he sat at the head of the table, faintly intimidating in his dark police uniform. His sandy hair and freckled skin did nothing to soften the impression of the critical eyes and the straight, unbending mouth. At forty-two, he had seen too much that was unspeakable, and the alert intelligence had hardened into a pessimism that was set in concrete.

"The banning of alcohol in the streets this summer has made quite a difference to the vandalism levels," the inspector continued. "But when the nightclubs empty out in the early hours, all hell is let loose. Nevertheless, the main problem is still drugs."

"Behind my break-ins, you mean?"

"Yes. This is where the CCTV will prove a major deterrent. It won't get rid of the criminals, but it will drive them elsewhere, out of our town."

"Wasn't that robbery in the off-licence the other day the result of drugs?" one of the hoteliers asked with interest. "John Hale, the assistant there, told me the dark-haired boy seemed as high as a kite."

"And Mr Hale is an expert on such matters, is he?" Inspector Matlock asked coolly.

"No," Lloyd intervened, "of course not. But he has eyes in his head and can recognise erratic behaviour when he sees it. I hear that the woman who was stabbed has identified a mug-shot of her attacker. Is that so?"

The inspector debated with himself whether to release such information. In the cause of good relations within the community, he eventually nodded. "Yes, that is true. Both Mrs Anstey and her husband have picked out his photograph."

"Any chance of catching him soon?" the music-shop woman asked.

"We are doing all in our power to trace him. He is a known drug-addict who requires a high cash-income to pay for his habit. Naturally, he has gone into hiding now but I have no doubt that we will winkle him out soon."

"What about the other boy?" Lloyd asked. "Is he on your books too?"

The inspector frowned and tapped a dissatisfied finger on the table. "No, no joy there. But we are following up on leads, dredging through the usual cess-pools. We'll come up with his name any day now, I promise you."

The group of faces round the table all smiled encouragement.

Lloyd was climbing into his Rover in the car park when the inspector strode over and offered a parting comment. "Went well, I thought."

"Yes, it did. I like your idea of introducing radio links into the shops to report cases of truancy from school. It will be useful when the new term starts next month. I'm sure I can sell that idea to the Chamber of Commerce members."

"Good. That's what we need. The more co-operation we receive, the better."

"Of course, we have to work together on this. Today I think

we convinced the waverers that CCTV is worth the investment if it helps make our streets safer.''

Inspector Matlock nodded agreement. ''I'm relying on you, Lloyd, to bring the rest of the town's traders and businessmen round to seeing sense. I know they listen to you. God only knows why.'' His ramrod mouth took on a slight curve which Lloyd knew from experience was intended as a smile.

''Maybe they like the way I bang their heads together,'' Lloyd laughed. ''Don't worry, Anthony, I'll bring them into line. We cannot afford to tolerate this level of crime. The town may look like a millpond to tourists, but underneath . . .'' He let the words hang.

''Damn drug-pushers,'' the inspector snorted.

''But step by step, we're getting there. Kicking and screaming it may be, but I swear I'll drag this town out of its apathy. By the scruff of its neck, if need be.''

Another snort from the policeman was meant as approval. ''A few more cases of violent robbery might buck up their ideas. But it's a heavy price to pay. And in the meantime, low-life filth like Zack McCauley can go around stabbing women in off-licences because there isn't enough surveillance from security cameras to scare them off.''

''With a bit more arm-twisting, we'll soon put an end to that,'' Lloyd assured him. ''Leave it with me and I'll deal with it.''

''Thank you, Lloyd.'' The inspector gave a final handshake, straightened the peak of his cap and strode back to the perfectly good Scorpio that it grieved Lloyd to see ruined by the red stripe running along it like luminous jam.

It was only as Lloyd was driving through the car-park gates that it occurred to him where he had recently heard the name Zack.

Lloyd sat at his desk smoking a cigarette and thought about it. In the newspaper the description of the second youth involved in the off-licence robbery had stated that he was blond. Tall, thin and blond. The last time Lloyd had seen Sam, he had been busking on the pavement with the girl. Without question, he was tall and certainly thin, but more to the point, he had been blond. His hair

was bleached into horrible matt streaks that changed what was
a goodlooking boy into a straw scarecrow. And he was running
round with a kid called Zack.

Poor Anna. She had no idea what her son was mixed up in.

Lloyd blew a skein of smoke at the ceiling. He had not seen
Anna recently. But he had bumped into Harriet Torrence at the
bank and she had told him that Anna was still seeing the tenant
but that he had moved out to a room elsewhere in the town. Her
grey eyes had been squeezed into bright nuggets of concern and
her long face drooped even further as she confided that Anna
was going through 'a rough patch'.

As if he didn't know.

But jumping into bed with Nick Steed did not solve anything.
It still stunned him. He kept telling himself it was a good sign
because it meant she had finally crawled out from under the shell
of the past. The trouble was that his heart was too damn stubborn
to see it that way. Instead it kept reminding him of that last time
he had laid eyes on her. The night of the nightclub disaster, when
he had disturbed her antics with that tenant of hers and she had
descended the stairs towards him. Gift-wrapped in a towel.

Lloyd shook his head to shatter the image and, making an effort
to ignore the splinters embedded in his brain, concentrated on
the matter in hand. Sam. Sam and Zack McCauley.

What the hell was he to do about them?

19

"He's acting real weird," Nella Torrence remarked to Danny. "He's gone all neat and tidy, and polite as hell in the teashop."

"I know, don't tell me about it. It gives me the creeps."

Danny started to reel in his line. He was fishing off the long arm of the breakwater but wasn't having much luck, so he had welcomed the distraction when he saw Nella cycling along the promenade walkway. He had waved his one and only fish at her and in response the bicycle had wobbled its way along the crest of the breakwater towards him. Now she was leaning on her saddle, peering down with distaste at Danny's pot of maggots, seething and bubbling like white lava.

"God, that's revolting." She grimaced as Danny speared three of the fat, undulating bodies on to his hook.

"Don't be such a girl," he mocked, and cast his line out over the choppy water. There was a sharp breeze churning the sea into short hard waves and chasing evening strollers into pubs and cafés. "Anyway, Sam doesn't want to talk about what he's been doing all summer. So I don't ask. If he's decided to come home and go all smart and geeky, that's his business."

"He's not geeky. Just extremely polite. I bet your mother loves it."

Danny slid his rod on to its stand and thought about that. "You'd think so, wouldn't you? But she doesn't seem to. She's even more uptight than when he was away. She watches him all the time. As if she expects him to sprout green tentacles or something at any moment. All very weird."

"Well, I'm glad he's come back."

Danny picked up a maggot and threw it at her, provoking a

shrill shriek of panic. "You're bound to be glad, aren't you? We all know you fancy Sam."

"Danny Forrest, shut your lying mouth."

But Nella blushed so furiously that she bent over pretending to examine the silver-green scales of the solitary mullet, swinging her long hair into a dense curtain that hid her cheeks.

Danny did not even notice. He was still pondering the situation between his mother and brother. Something was wrong. And judging by their jumpiness, whatever it was, it was bad. But they had shut him out. Both of them. It really annoyed him the way they were keeping it all to themselves, as if he wasn't part of the same family. That really sucked, that did.

"Sam was working in the teashop today and the old biddies just loved him," Nella commented. "I asked him if he was going to be working there permanently, but he said he didn't know. I got the impression he wasn't that keen. What do you think?"

Danny gave his reel a few sharp twists and watched the line jump. "I have no idea. You'll have to ask him."

"Mmm," Nella murmured thoughtfully. She dumped her bicycle on the ground and perched herself on the edge of the concrete breakwater with her legs dangling over the grey sea six feet below. "My mother says that your mother is expecting him to go back to school next term. Is that a fact?"

"Dunno. Probably."

Nella flicked back her hair to look over her shoulder at him, dark eyes curious behind the spectacles. "What's up with you?"

"Nothing."

"Like hell. He's only been home a few days and he's already got up your nose."

"He hasn't."

"Yes, he has. I can tell."

"No, he hasn't," Danny insisted, and yanked the fishing-rod off its stand.

"Has."

"Hasn't."

Nella picked up a stone, hurled it out over the sea and waited for it to hit the water and drown. "The trouble with you Forrests is that you're all so pig-headed. Stubborn as mules, you are."

"At least I don't have ears like one, like someone I could mention," Danny retorted, and started to reel in the line.

"You bastard," Nella laughed good-naturedly, but because she was sensitive about the length of her ears, she picked up the pot of maggots and emptied it into his fishing-box.

"Yuk," she exclaimed, fascinated by the writhing mass that coiled itself round the hooks, floats and other oddments in the box.

"Girls!" Danny moaned with exaggerated irritation. "They do a guy's head in."

He finished reeling in his line and plonked himself down on the ground beside his box where he started picking out the maggots one by one.

As he did so, Nella asked very casually, "Danny, have you heard what's happened to that girl Sam was hanging around with?"

"He told me she's not on the scene at the moment."

"So they've split?"

"It looks like it."

"Or has she just cleared off home for a while? She's from up north, isn't she?"

"Yes. Sheffield or Scunthorpe or somewhere like that."

"So what do you think? Are they planning to get back together again?"

Danny had no idea, but because he didn't want to hurt Nella, he shook his head. "I doubt it. I mean, just look at him. All smart and tidy. Not exactly the image that matches Tara any more, is it?"

Nella smiled and steeled herself to pick up one of the maggots. "That's true. If he carries on working in the teashop and goes back to school, it'll be just like before, won't it? Before he got caught up with that crack-head." She tossed a wriggling maggot into the sea.

"How do you know she's into crack?"

"Dope, crack, smack, whatever, she's into them, I tell you. You didn't see her in the nightclub. She was flying high, Danny, sky-high."

Danny did not want to ask but made himself. "And Sam?"

Nella flicked her curtain into place and muttered, "I couldn't tell."

Danny had had enough of this conversation. "Fancy a swim?" He knew she would say no.

"No."

"I'm going for one." He abandoned the maggots, stood up, stripped down to his boxer shorts and poised to dive off the breakwater into the sea.

Nella emptied the fishing-box upside-down on the ground, then started picking the angling equipment out of the mobile mass of larvae and replacing it in the box. The expression on her face looked as if she were sucking a lemon. "I think he's changed inside. Really changed. So even if he is trying to go back to the way things were before, it won't work. Will it?"

Danny pretended he hadn't heard and launched himself out into thin air. His dive was clean and graceful, and almost silent as his taut body sliced into the sea. The water was dark and murky and, as he kicked to swim deeper, he could see nothing clearly in any direction.

Lloyd felt a draught of cold air as he opened the door of his office. Everyone had finished for the day and the boatyard was slumbering peacefully after the frantic activity of working hours. He treated himself to a gentle stroll round the sleeping hulls, stranded out of their natural element like beached dolphins. The touch of their sleek functional lines gave him a frisson of pleasure and for a moment he was tempted to slide one down the slipway, but resisted the urge. He stood at the water's edge and studied the waves under the pearly sky, watched them form and break and frisk away as if inviting him to play.

"Not tonight, Josephine," he murmured affectionately and turned his back on them.

The drive to Anna's teashop did not take long, as the evening traffic was light. A blustery sea-breeze had driven the tourists off the promenade, to gather like magpies in the shops still touting for business in the High Street despite the lateness of the hour. It was on his fifth circuit of Market Square that he succeeded in finding a parking place and as he walked the short distance to the flat, he didn't hurry. He was aware that his reception might not be the warmest. Earlier in the afternoon he had telephoned and left a message with Danny that he would call round to see Anna this evening, but was prepared to find she might not be there. She had been avoiding him recently and he did not trust her not to do so again.

Danny opened the door. "Hi, Lloyd, come on up." His hair was wet as if from a shower or a swim.

Lloyd followed him up the steep flight of stairs to the flat, envying the mountain-goat legs ahead of him that leapt up two at a time.

"Ma," Danny called out, "it's Lloyd."

Lloyd was left alone for a moment in the sitting-room and its appearance as always made him smile. It was so like Anna. Honey-coloured and soft with chintz and silks, but its prettiness was saved by the strong lines of the furniture and the solidity of its dark woods. And even by that hideous collection of china cats that she loved so much. Danny's swimming-togs lay by the door where he had dumped them and a pair of trainers had been abandoned on the sofa. Lloyd was inspecting a framed photograph of the boys, taken about five years ago by the look of their cheeky grins, when Anna walked into the room.

His heart plummeted at the sight of her. She was painfully thin and her eyes were flat and expressionless. They gave him a plastic smile.

"Hello, Lloyd. How nice to see you."

"Anna, how are you?" He took her offered hand and it felt as hollow as a bird's wing in his own. He held on to it.

"I'm fine. What about you? How's business?"

"Frantic, thank goodness."

"Good, I'm glad," she said, retrieving her hand.

They sat down and he was aware that she kept the coffee-table squarely between them. Maybe she was remembering their recent differences. Yet he had the feeling she was genuinely pleased to see him, an impression gained from her mouth which remained soft and mobile, escaping from the tyranny of the Barbie eyes.

"How is the teashop doing this month?" August was the high point in any tourist season. "Packed with thirsty grockles, I hope."

She nodded but he didn't think she was really listening. Behind the eyes, her mind was off elsewhere. Lloyd took his time, letting her settle whatever dust-storms were clouding her thoughts. He chatted about the Chamber meetings she had missed and the discussions over refurbishing the old car park, talked about the recent carnival and told her of Lawrence Enfield's argument with the town planner over the Council's delay in announcing the decision about the coaches' pick-up and set-down stations.

"You know how pompous he can be when he tries," Lloyd said, filling up the time. She was less nervous now, her limbs losing that stiffness that made him think of a high-wire act. The tension rigid in every muscle. He wondered if she was aware how obvious it was. "I can't seem to get it into Lawrence's thick skull," Lloyd continued, "that putting the planner's back up is not the most successful way of achieving what you want. Or more to the point, what the Chamber has put forward as a sane compromise."

She smiled and this time some of the plastic had peeled away. "That's Lawrence for you."

"All mouth and no mind."

She laughed, but it didn't reach the eyes. "I hear on the grapevine that you're buying a company in Bristol."

"That's true. I'm expanding my business and at the same time eliminating a competitor."

There was a tight little pause before she asked, "Not thinking of deserting us, are you?"

"No."

"I'm glad."

"How did you get to hear about it?"

"Esther Miller told me. She got it from her husband who apparently plays darts with the brother of one of your mechanics."

"It's always the same. You can't even pick your nose in this town without everybody learning about it."

She shuddered. As if he had just drilled into a nerve. Maybe she realised she would be the last person to hear what her son was up to. Mothers and wives were always the last to know.

Lloyd took a deep breath and plunged in the deep end. "Have you seen anything of Sam recently?"

To his surprise, instead of becoming more agitated, she grew very still and gave him a calm smile that made his innards lurch. It was too practised to be true.

"Yes, I have."

"Really? That's great. How is he?"

"Back to normal now, thank heavens."

"Normal? What do you mean?"

"As normal as any teenager is capable of being, anyway," she said with a light laugh.

"Do you mean he has dropped out of the drop-out scene?"

"Oh yes. Completely."

"Since when?"

"Since last week."

"And Tara Tucker?"

"That's all over. It was just a passing phase. You know what teenagers are like. I shouldn't have got into such a tizz about it. You were right when you said it was just his way of finding greater independence, breaking free from the apron-strings and all that." She smiled at him with such a good imitation of gratitude that Lloyd almost fell for it. "I should have listened to you."

"So where is he now?"

"He's here. Don't look so surprised. After all, this is still his home. I'll call him in and you'll see what I mean." She stood up and from the door called, "Sam, would you come in here for a moment, please?"

A minute later, Sam walked into the room.

Lloyd absorbed the shock. Then he rose to shake hands with the demure young man before him.

"Hello, Sam. Nice to see you again. You're looking well."

"Hi, Lloyd. Thanks, I'm fine."

And fine he certainly seemed. There was no resemblance to the scruffy urchin who had been busking in the street for the odd coin and looking as if he would entwine his fingers as skilfully round your wallet as around his guitar. This upright young citizen looked as if the only time he'd get his hands on your money would be in a bank. Working as a cashier.

Anna was smiling at Lloyd, eyes and all this time. "You look surprised."

"I am."

"Doesn't he look respectable?"

"He certainly does."

Sam shuffled uncomfortably but maintained a polite expression and steady eye-contact. No furtive secrecy here. And suddenly it dawned on Lloyd.

Anna knew.

There was no need for him to tell her because she already knew. He should have known better than to underestimate her. He sat down heavily and nodded thankfully when she suggested a drink. Hell, he needed a cigarette but it was against house rules. Sam took a seat opposite him and stretched out as if relaxed, but his eyes were alert.

It explained everything.

Explained the impregnable force-field Anna had built around herself, explained her son's transformation from sleaze to sleek in five easy lessons. The street-wise partner in an armed robbery had disappeared off the face of the earth, and in his place Anna had created this respectable youth with his neat haircut and neat manners, well-filled cheeks and ready smile, who didn't look as if he had ever in his life even seen the inside of an off-licence, let alone robbed one.

Lloyd knew she wouldn't get away with it. Not once Zack McCauley was caught and started singing for his supper. But Christ, you had to admire the woman's guts. The fact that she was aiding and abetting a criminal, breaking the law and risking the consequences, had not deterred her one jot.

Oh, Anna, this is crazy. There will be two of you in court, not just one.

He abruptly realised Sam was talking to him and had asked a question.

"I'm sorry, Sam, what did you say?"

"I asked how the new boat was going. I expect you're really busy at the yard."

Though Lloyd's brain was struggling to slot the cogs back into working order, he was still capable of role-playing quite as well as any seventeen-year-old.

"Yes, I've had a glut of orders for the new racing-boat, so everyone at the yard is chasing round like dogs with two tails."

"Dave likes the sailing-boats best, he told me when I was working with him."

"Dave's an old stick-in-the-mud. Anyway, now that I'm taking over the company in Bristol, we'll concentrate most of the racing-boats up there and deal with the sail-boats and running repairs down here. It makes more sense." His enthusiasm leaked out irresistibly. "We're all very keen."

"It sounds exciting."

"It is." Taking advantage of Anna's absence with the drinks, Lloyd leaned back in his chair, offering no threat, and commented, "Talking of sense, I'm glad you've seen it at last. It's been an eventful summer for you."

The boy had the grace to blush. Not quite street-hardened yet. "Yes, it was."

"And what triggered the change of heart?"

The hesitation was covered by a soft sigh, that Lloyd had to give the boy credit for. It was very effective. How much of it was Anna's coaching, he could only guess.

"It was when the guy I was sharing a flat with wanted me to take part in a robbery he was planning. It suddenly hit me like a ton of bricks what a prick I was being. Out of my mind to be caught up with someone that dumb. So I just left."

"As simple as that?"

The boy gave him a look of wide-eyed innocence. "As simple as that."

It was good. Very good. A story that covered the fact that people knew he was an associate of Zack's, but explained why he had upped and left to return home so suddenly. And if Zack named him as an accomplice in the off-licence crime, Sam could deny it and put it down to malice because he had refused to help in the robbery. Not the total denial that a panicked seventeen-year-old might have gone for, but a clever partial truth. It had Anna's fingerprints all over it.

Just at that moment she walked in with a scotch and soda for Lloyd and herself. And a glass of milk for Sam. The sickly treacle was starting to feel like something oozing out of a Disney fantasy.

"You can overdo it, you know," Lloyd said.

They both stared at him, alarmed.

"What?" Anna asked. "Overdo what?"

"The soda."

He saw them both relax.

"Sorry, Lloyd, did I spoil it for you?"

"It's just that I like it straight, Anna. Not drowned in rubbish to disguise it." He looked at her and waited for a reaction.

"I know," she said. "I know you do."

The doorbell rang.

Everything was left unsaid.

Anna rose and left the room. Sam and Lloyd stared at each other but no word was spoken. A moment later Anna returned. Nick Steed was with her.

"Surely the boys are old enough to look after themselves for a couple of days. They don't need you here to hold their hands."

"I know, Nick, but the teashop does. We're rushed off our feet right now. I'm sorry but I just can't leave it in the lurch tomorrow."

Nick Steed put an arm round her shoulder, but she stiffened. "No, Nick, the answer is no. My mind is made up. You'll have to go without me."

Nick sat back on his half of the sofa and picked up his coffee. His blue eyes were drawn even closer together in a frown as he sipped the Colombian brew and Anna expected another argument, but all he did was give a slight shake of his head, as if dislodging a fly.

Lloyd had left almost immediately after Nick's arrival. He had downed his scotch, said a curt farewell and gone. A confusing cocktail of disappointment and relief had gone straight to Anna's head and left her bad-tempered. She'd had no trouble voicing the decision she had been postponing all week, that she had no intention of going to Nick's exhibition in London. Nick had reacted predictably. Hurt and surprised. And then annoyed. But she did not have the energy or the inclination for a session of ego-massage, not today. Nor any other day, for that matter.

"Your exhibition will be a great success with or without me, but my business won't. Not when there are a dozen coaches booked into the town that day."

"It's your sons really, isn't it?"

"No, it's not because of them. I've told you, it's the teashop."

That was when he had pointed out that the boys could survive perfectly well without her and that the business would certainly not collapse if she deserted it just for two days.

That was, of course, absolutely true. Undeniably so. But it wasn't going to change her mind. She couldn't leave Sam. Not now. Not even for one day. What if the police came calling and he said all the wrong things to them? Of course they had rehearsed and rehearsed till Sam was climbing the walls, but he might panic and get it all wrong. She knew the police were not allowed to question a minor without an adult present, but they wouldn't wait for her to come back from London. They'd just stick a social-worker in the room and get on with it.

No, London was out of the question.

Anyway, it wouldn't be fair to Nick. She enjoyed his company and lapped up the unaccustomed attention like a cat does sunshine, but if she went away with him to London, he would expect her to adorn his bed again and she did not want that. Once was enough. More than enough. It might have been lust that drove her to leap between his sheets or maybe just plain old-fashioned loneliness, but sure as hell it wasn't love. She had become depressingly aware of that reality the moment she came down the stairs that night and saw Sam and Lloyd waiting for her. Yet she was fond of Nick Steed. More than fond. And it wasn't as if she didn't want to see his paintings. She did. But what she did not want was to give him the wrong signals. It wasn't fair. But neither was it fair to blame him for being the one who had tempted her away that night, when she should have been there for Sam.

To hell with fair!

"Shall I open a bottle of wine?" Anna offered by way of amends.

He accepted it for what it was and smiled. "That would be nice."

She stood up. "Don't worry, the exhibition will be a great success, I'm sure. You don't need me."

"Maybe not. But I do want you."

She bent down and kissed him softly on the mouth. "We

can't always have what we want, Nick. But a glass of wine, I can do."

He held on to her hand, preventing her leaving. "And what is it you want, Anna? Have you worked that one out?"

She responded with what she hoped was a light-hearted laugh. "I'm still working on it."

She extricated her hand and escaped to the kitchen. There was only one thing she wanted right now and that was to see Sam safe, safe and sound, and back at school studying for his A levels. Unhampered by the fear of a knock on the door or the slam of a prison gate. That was what she wanted and that was what she was going to have. If it took every lying breath in her body.

As soon as Nick had left, Anna checked that Sam and Danny were preoccupied in their bedrooms, received a tetchy "Stop fussing," and made for the telephone in the hall. She had picked it up and was half-way through dialling the number, when a thought struck her. Her hand froze over the button, then tugged indecisively at her hair. She replaced the receiver.

"Boys, I'm just popping out for a while. I won't be long," she called, and received faint grunts of acknowledgement.

Market Square was quiet and dark, except for the picturesque Victorian streetlamps that created pools of soft light. Anna set her sights on the far side of the square and hurried past the central fountain where illuminated Niagaras cascaded down on to a pontoon of beer-cans. The civic corner of Anna's mind, which refused to keep its mouth shut even though she was otherwise occupied, made her hope that the cleaner would have them out of there first thing in the morning.

When she reached the telephone kiosk, it was unoccupied. She slotted in a few coins and dialled the number that was scribbled on a scrap of paper in her pocket. It rang, and with each repeated buzz her heartbeat picked up its pace.

"Good evening. Warborough Hospital here. How may I help you?"

"Hello, I'm calling to ask about Mrs Rachel Anstey."

"Do you know what ward she is on?"

"She's in intensive care."

"One moment, please."

A whirr and a click and then another cool voice. "Hello, Sister Hyde speaking."

"Hello, I want to enquire about Mrs Rachel Anstey. To find out how her condition is."

"Are you a member of the family?"

"Yes. I'm Mr Anstey's sister-in-law. I'm up in Oxford and only heard about the attack this evening. How is she?"

The voice became more user-friendly. "We've had such a lot of enquiries from the press and the general public. Well-meaning most of them are, but they do take up our time, so I have to check on callers."

"Of course. I quite understand. But how is Rachel?"

"Making good progress. She's still in intensive and her condition is being carefully monitored, but she is quite cheerful and doing well."

Anna breathed a silent sigh of relief. "Thank goodness. I was worried about her."

"Shall I tell her you called?"

"No, don't disturb her now. I'll write to her tonight. Thank you for your time."

"You're welcome."

Anna hung up.

'Good progress' and 'quite cheerful'. Thank God for small mercies.

20

It was at four o'clock the next morning that Anna decided to ring a solicitor. She lay watching the billowing shadows of the curtains at the open window and kicked the suffocating duvet off her feet. The night had turned hot and clammy, as if stoking a furnace somewhere in the distance, and Anna had lost interest in sleep. She was thinking about Lloyd.

He had asked a lot of questions. Too many questions. She ran over them in her head and tried to fit them into a pattern of casual interest, but they wouldn't oblige. Instead they stuck out dangerously like alarm signals. And then there was the final "You can overdo it, you know."

What did he mean by that? Obviously not simply a reference to the soda in his drink.

Oh shit, had he guessed?

But how could he? She had given him no clues. And he wasn't a mind-reader, for Christ's sake.

Yet, when she came to consider it, he had always been uncannily good at knowing what she was thinking. And feeling. Maybe that was it, he had picked up on her fears. But even so, it wasn't possible to jump to a connection between Sam and the robbery.

How could he?

After the traumas of the last few days, the sight of Lloyd Morgan standing like the Rock of Gibraltar in her sitting-room had been so reassuring. She had felt the urge to borrow those solid shoulders of his, to lean heavily and selfishly on them. She had done so in the past. And if they were broad enough to carry the burden of sluggish starter-motors and exploding microwaves, why not armed robbery?

Because he was childless.

He would not understand that she had no choice. That she was caught between Scylla and Charybdis, jammed between a rock and a hard place with nowhere to go. It was impossible to ignore the fact that he was a pillar of the community and pillars, by definition, don't bend. Sam would be up before the judge and never mind his howls of remorse. Rub the puppy's nose in it and the blighter won't offend again, no sir!

Lloyd Morgan, how could you be so heartless?

She was being unfair and she knew it. In recent Chamber of Commerce meetings hers had been one of the most vociferous voices against the soft treatment of young offenders. Yet look at her now.

She rolled over, wrestled her pillow into a more amenable lump and made the decision to ring a solicitor first thing in the morning.

At nine-thirty she was back in the telephone kiosk. It was Monday, so the refuse-collection lorry was trawling the street and stinking out the air-intake of any car foolish enough to get stuck behind it. Otherwise the square was quiet, with no one around to cast curious glances at her use of the kiosk when she had a perfectly good telephone in the teashop.

The solicitor was in Stratford-upon-Avon. His name was Gerald Courtney and she had come into contact with him when he had set up a trust fund for her after her mother's death. That was nearly eleven years ago, exactly six months before Ian died. Her father had married again, sold the house to move in with his new, much younger bride and placed Anna's share of the inheritance into a trust fund. Over the last ten years she could have done with that capital more times than she cared to remember, but her father had been adamant.

"You'll only blow it all on some hare-brained scheme like that farm in France which you and Ian tried to make a go of. A steady income is what you need, just to make sure you and the kids don't starve."

The income from the fund was too small to make much difference to her life one way or the other, but she had to admit it had bought the boys an occasional holiday that she could not otherwise have afforded and certainly they had not starved. She did not have much contact with her father now beyond irregular phone-calls and an annual weekend trip with the boys to visit him, as well as the Stratford Theatre and Anne Hathaway's cottage. A crash course in culture. The stepmother kept a polite distance.

Anna dialled the number of Courtney, Watts & Caine's office and informed the young woman who answered that she wished to speak to Mr Courtney.

"What is it in connection with?"

"I wish to discuss a criminal case with him."

"Who shall I say is calling?"

"Mrs Nicholson."

After a brief wait, she was put through.

"Mrs Nicholson, how may I help you?" The voice was cheery and up-beat, a deliberate attempt to dispel the stuffy haze that hung round solicitors like body odour.

"I have an academic query, Mr Courtney, that I hope you will help me with. Let me explain. My son is in the sixth form at a local school and is studying philosophy. They spend a lot of time debating moral issues. At present he is preparing a project on a theoretical criminal case. I wonder if you would be kind enough to tell me what the legal outcome of the robbery in his project would be. He would appreciate it very much."

Mr Courtney smiled. She could hear it in his voice. She remembered him as tall and slim with intelligent grey eyes and mousy hair combed flat against his narrow head, and she knew he would enjoy playing the well-informed professional expanding the horizons of the little woman.

"Of course, Mrs Nicholson. Always happy to be of assistance to the younger generation. What are the circumstances of this theoretical robbery?"

"Two boys, one is seventeen, the other twenty. They go into a shop to steal money. The seventeen-year-old stands inside the door, guarding it while the other boy takes the money from the till. About a thousand pounds in all. A customer comes in and during a struggle with the twenty-year-old, the customer is stabbed. What my son needs to know is what would the sentence be for the seventeen-year-old."

"Well now, let me think for a moment."

Anna let him think. She had in the past so often rung vicars, fire-stations, librarians and even the police station to find information to feed both Sam's and Danny's homework projects that she did not doubt that he would believe her story.

"Has the boy had any previous convictions?"

"No, none at all," she said, maybe a touch too quickly.

"No trouble with the police of any kind?"

"No."

"That would certainly count in his favour."

She waited for more.

"The customer was stabbed, you say."

"Yes, that's correct."

"How seriously?"

"A stomach wound that needed intensive-care treatment, but not fatal."

"Mmm, that's not good. Did the younger boy know that his companion was carrying a knife?"

"Yes, he did."

"Then that's more serious. Armed robbery is regarded as a very serious crime indeed. The sentence would be quite heavy despite the boy's age and history."

"What if the boy gave himself up to the police and supplied them with information about the one who did the stabbing? Would that help his case?" Anna had to make a real effort to keep her voice neutral.

"Yes, it would help a little. But the fact that he knew the other boy was carrying a knife is quite damning, I'm afraid. He would receive a sentence of between two and four years' detention, possibly even more, depending on the exact circumstances of the offence."

"But he's under-age." Anna quickly corrected her tone to one of only mild interest. "It seems rather harsh to me. I thought children under eighteen were put on probation and given community work or something, rather than detention."

Gerald Courtney gave a superior little laugh. "No, don't underestimate the severity of the offence, Mrs Nicholson. He would be sentenced to one year in a young offenders' institution until he was eighteen and then be expected to serve the rest of it in prison.''

''I see.''

''Those are the realities of a criminal life, I'm afraid. It would have been even worse if the lad had been carrying a knife himself, so this theoretical boy is lucky he wasn't stupid enough to go that far.''

Anna had difficulty swallowing.

''Thank you for your help, Mr Courtney.''

''My pleasure. I would be interested in seeing the project when it is completed, if that's possible, to see what your son makes of it.''

''Certainly. No trouble. I'll send you a copy,'' she said, and hung up.

Well, now she knew.

The rest of the morning she spent in the teashop. Nella Torrence and Sam were on duty and Anna found every opportunity to bite their heads off. When Sam was slow to clean up a table after one group of customers had left, she snapped at him and was almost disappointed when he declined to snap back. She felt like having a bloody good row with him.

''What on earth has got into you?'' Esther Miller asked when they were alone in the kitchen. Her gentle eyes were reproachful. ''The kid can't do a thing right today.''

''Today or any other day, the way I feel just now.''

''Poor Sam.''

''More like stupid Sam, selfish Sam and even string-him-up-by-the-thumbs Sam. But not poor Sam.''

Esther put down the plate she was holding and came to stand in front of her boss. ''What's the matter, Anna? He's safely home now, and is working here where you can keep an eye on him. That's what you wanted, isn't it?''

''Yes.''

''So what has he got up to now?''

It almost came out. The words were on the brink of spilling

out of her mouth, so desperate was she to share them with someone. But she plugged the dam just in time.

"Oh, nothing much," she said, and forced a remorseful smile. "I'm still cross about him going off with Tara Tucker for the summer, I suppose."

It must have sounded convincing because Esther looked relieved. "Well, don't be too hard on the lad or you'll drive him off again." She patted Anna's arm reassuringly. "Sam won't go far wrong. He's a good boy and a real credit to you, so stop fretting."

Anna smiled brightly. "You're right of course. But you know what mothers are like. By the way, can you hold the fort here for a moment? I just want to go upstairs for something."

"Okay, go ahead. But don't be long because it's packed out front there."

"I won't."

She rinsed her hands and hurried up to her flat where Danny was still snoring under his duvet. She headed straight for her own bedroom, threw herself face-down on the bed and clamped the pillow tight round her head to stifle any sound. After five minutes of that, she got up, washed her face and flicked a comb through her hair, then remembered to telephone the art gallery.

"Hello, Anna," Nick Steed exclaimed, his voice on a high. "It's going great guns. Everyone is here."

Everyone except herself. As she listened to his excited report on numbers of art critics and sales, she could not help wishing she had gone with him. To be anywhere but here. But she shook that thought out of her head, congratulated him on his success and rang off. She must get back to the teashop. But before doing so, she decided to fetch the car keys from her desk because she would have to drive over to the supermarket later. The desk was in the hall and was as usual swamped with paperwork that needed attention. She quickly opened the right-hand drawer and scooped out the Fiesta keys. She was just shutting it again when something caught her attention. A thick red rubber-band that should not be there.

*   *   *

Sam was rushed off his feet but did not let it show. He had learned that if you move smoothly, people do not notice that you are moving fast. And he never hurried the customers as they dithered over their orders.

"So what's it to be, girls? The Black Forest gateau is particularly good today." He added a smile of encouragement.

"You could tempt me to eat anything," grinned one of the six customers at the table and they all laughed raucously.

The girls were in fact women of at least fifty and probably nearer sixty who came in regularly off one of the coaches. It always amazed Sam that whereas society frowned on elderly men who were lewd or suggestive, dirty old women could get away with murder. And they loved to be called girls.

"Sam."

Sam turned to find Nella at his shoulder. She was carrying a laden tray and the steam from the hot-water jug was misting her glasses.

"Your mother wants you upstairs. Right now."

"What for?"

"I don't know. She just telephoned down to the kitchen and asked Esther to pass on the message."

"I can't go now. I'm too busy."

He glanced back at his table of girls and saw that they were all following the conversation with interest.

"Go on, Sam," urged a white-haired woman with a large liver-spot on her forehead. "You do what your mother says, like a good boy. Mothers are always right, aren't they, Alice?"

Alice, next to her, giggled her agreement.

Sam did not appreciate being made a mummy's boy but smiled with apparent amusement. "Shall I take your orders first, ladies?" He withheld 'girls' this time.

"No, you can go now, Sam. We haven't quite decided what to have yet. Your pretty girlfriend there can come and take our order when we're ready."

"I'm not his girlfriend." Nella blushed and took her tray elsewhere.

Alice giggled again. "Silly boy, you should get your arms round that one before she slips away."

Sam said with a teasing smile, "I'd rather get my arms around you before you slip away." It set them all off into boisterous merriment once more. He left them to it.

To be summoned away from the customers by his mother was unheard-of. It scared him rigid. This jumpiness was really getting to him. Every time the doorbell went or the telephone rang, his heart hammered as loud as a war-drum inside his chest. Each time he expected the police.

He wondered if it was the same for his mother.

The door of the flat was ajar and in the hall his mother was standing stiffly next to the desk, a drawer lying open and an elastic-band in her hand. Her face was very still but he knew instantly that there was big trouble. She only clenched her jaws together like that when she was really furious. He kept a safe distance from her.

"What is it, Ma? What's happened?"

"My money. Where is my money?" she asked in a low, angry voice.

"What?"

"The money that was in this drawer. It's gone."

It was like a kick in the stomach. "Ma, I don't know anything about any money. I haven't touched it."

"There were three hundred pounds in this rubber-band inside this drawer. I put it there two days ago and now it's missing."

"You think I took it?"

"Did you?"

He stared at her incredulously. How could she ask such a question?

"No, I didn't." He did his best to keep it polite but even to his own ears it sounded sullen.

A long silence stretched between them, but Sam refused to be the one to break it. She should believe her own son.

"Sam," she said eventually, "how can I know whether to believe you?"

"Because it's true."

"But can I trust you?"

It was said so sadly and with such a depth of disappointment that he felt his guts grind sickeningly. That hurt like hell.

"I promise you I never have and never would steal from you, Ma. Never. I know you think I lived on thieving while I was away, but I swear to you I didn't. Honestly. I made Tara stop pinching stuff as well."

His mother's eyes searched his, as if trying to peel back the skins of self-protection. She always thought she knew him so well. But this time she was way off the mark. He wanted to storm out in a blaze of self-righteous anger, but he knew he had forfeited that right. He stood and suffered her gaze.

"So what did you live on? What paid for your food and your drugs?"

He let the reference to drugs pass. Safer not to get into that. He was going to have to tell her now what they'd used for dough. He didn't want to but had always known it would have to come out sooner or later. He held her gaze.

"My Halifax savings."

Her eyes widened. "But that money was for your car. A Beetle."

"I know."

"How much is left?"

"Nothing. It's all gone."

"All the fourteen hundred pounds?"

"Yes."

There was an awful pause and for a second he thought she was going to shout at him, but instead she gave a long sigh that seemed to carry all the anger out of her.

"Oh, Sam, what a waste. After all your hard work to save that much, and now it's all gone. All your dreams."

For the first time Sam dropped his eyes and stared at the carpet. "I sold my electric guitar as well." He said it quickly, because the words hurt.

His mother said nothing for a while, but he continued to study the carpet. Even a blank carpet was better than looking at her face.

"And the rest of your things? What happened to them?"

"I left everything behind. I didn't want to risk going back to the flat. Anyway, someone will have flogged them all by now."

Suddenly he heard the drawer shut with a sharp click and he looked up. She had turned away from him and was fiddling aimlessly with some papers on the desk when she asked, "Sam, have you gained something from all this mess? I would like to think that you've enough sense to have learnt by these mistakes. Then all this pain won't have been pointless."

Oh shit, she was going to give him a lecture on morals. Right now, he didn't need that one.

He stepped closer to her and touched her arm to make her look at him. "Yes, Ma, I've learnt. The hard way. But it was my own fault, my own doing. I know that and I don't blame anybody but myself. So don't dump it all on Tara or Zack. Every decision, right or wrong, was my own."

"But why, Sam? Why did you do it?"

"I'm still asking myself that."

"And what answers do you come up with?"

Sam was not ready to talk. Not yet. So he opted for the easy one. "Because I fell for Tara in a big way. Nothing else mattered."

"And now? Do you miss her?"

Sam shrugged it off. "But you needn't worry that I'll ever get caught up in something like that off-licence business again. I won't. And I did not take your money from that drawer." He leant forward and kissed her cheek. "I've hurt you enough already."

She held on to him for a split second, then let go of him. He was grateful for that.

"Okay," she said abruptly. "So who did take it?"

"I don't know." But fears hovered in the back of his mind.

"It has got to be one of them, hasn't it? Tara or Zack. One of them must have a key. It's possible, isn't it?"

"Yes, it's possible."

His mother nodded and picked up the telephone directory. "What we need is a locksmith. Today."

Sam watched her flick through the pages and guilt prickled his scalp. "Ma, I'm sorry."

This time she shrugged and turned to smile at him. "It's only money. I'll take it out of your wages."

Danny had been woken by the raised voices as he lay in his bed. He didn't hear what they were saying but their tone was obvious even to a dimwit. When they finally stopped, he went and ran himself a shower. He was due down at the pool in an hour and had to get his warm-up exercises done before then or Joe would start yelling at him. Joe Todd was a trainer who believed in total commitment.

As he turned off the stinging spray, he wished he could turn off the stinging inside himself as easily. He hated the way Ma and Sam were behaving, treading round each other with the politeness of strangers. That's why the row was really weird, but maybe it meant that they would get back to normal now. Sam still wasn't talking, just going round being so fucking polite, it stank. Whatever it was he had done, he must be feeling hellish guilty about it, and Nella was right when she said he'd changed. He had. And Danny didn't like the change. Sam was different. Less his brother. Harder somehow. As if something inside him had been toughened and sharpened.

Danny pulled on his tracksuit, raced through the exercises and breakfast, said a speedy "I'm off now" to his mother in the teashop, then set off for the leisure centre. As he ran, he shed the unease that dogged him at home and focused his mind on the swimming to come. He should have eaten his breakfast earlier, of course, but he wouldn't let on to Joe about that. Two or three hours in the pool and he would have clipped those butterfly times down to match Will Bennett's, on that he was determined. Will had grown over an inch this summer and it had set him flying.

Danny jogged across the car park of the leisure centre and noticed that the sun was glinting off the rows of windscreens that crouched sleepily in neat rows. It bleached out his vision uncomfortably, so he hopped over a railing that edged the kerb and was walking in the shade of the building when three figures suddenly peeled themselves off the wall in front of him.

Danny stopped. These guys were not here to ask the time. The one in front looked mean. He was thin and scrawny, but his pale eyes were looking for trouble. In his hand was a bottle.

21

Anna was expecting Danny back from his training session, but he was late. It was already five o'clock. Probably he had gone off to Will Bennett's house and would give her a ring later, asking to be allowed to spend the night there. As there were only a few days before the start of the new school term, she wouldn't begrudge him a final fling. Especially as the mood at home was not exactly the merriest. She had tried to pretend that everything was normal, but not for a minute did she think she was fooling her younger son.

"All finished, Mrs Forrest." It was the locksmith. "You take good care of the keys this time."

"I will, don't you worry, Mr Bates. I appreciate your coming out so promptly. I wouldn't have slept comfortably tonight knowing that someone might have found my keys."

"Can't be too careful these days," he said in an accent thick with cider and skittles. "Gone is the time when people would hand in lost sets of keys at the police station. Nowadays they go around trying them in locks in the hope of striking lucky."

They were standing at the street-door. Across the road a police car pulled up and reversed expertly into a small parking space. Anna's heartbeat went into instant overdrive but she reminded herself that the police did actually have other duties to perform and that she couldn't spend the rest of her life having palpitations every time she saw a blue uniform.

"They won't strike lucky here. Not tonight," Anna said, dragging her gaze away.

"It's a real disgrace the way all these young people on DSS from all over the country are being dumped in the hotels in seaside towns. It may keep the hotels in business, but it's ruining everyone else's. Not right, it isn't."

"They certainly don't do much for mine. Tea and cakes are not quite their . . ." She hesitated. The policeman was walking off up the High Street, looking very young and keen. ". . . scene."

"Scones and clotted cream are the wife's favourite. Every Sunday afternoon she bakes a batch of fruit scones and we have them with –"

"Excuse me, Mrs Forrest?"

A man was standing at her elbow. He was tall with crinkly fair hair and reminded Anna of a young Michael Caine without the glasses. Cheerful face and observant grey eyes.

"Yes?"

The man flashed a badge discreetly. "May I have a few words with you?"

The locksmith decided to make himself scarce. "Bye now, Mrs Forrest. Take care of those keys."

"I will. Thank you."

The man waited until he had gone and then said very politely, "I am Detective Sergeant Crawford. Could we talk somewhere in private, please?"

No mention of Sam. So maybe it was just that her road tax was out of date or she had run through a red light. And maybe she believed in the tooth-fairy. She found herself resenting the policeman, the way he had crept up on her in plain clothes as if to catch her out.

"Certainly, Sergeant. But I am rather busy now. I have to get back to my customers."

"It won't take long."

Couldn't possibly be serious then, could it?

With a heartbeat that had dropped to merely manic, she started to lead him upstairs. "What's it about? Not going to haul me off in chains?" she laughed.

The response was a tolerant smile. Perhaps he'd heard that one once too often.

"I would just like to ask a few questions. We're making enquiries and . . ."

"Enquiries about what?"

They had reached the flat.

"I need to talk to your son, Sam Forrest."

A sharp pain ricocheted inside her chest.

Sam wondered how his mother did it. So affable and smiling, acting as if nothing pleased her more than to sit and chat with a goodlooking young detective at the end of a busy afternoon.

"Would you like a cup of tea, Sergeant? Or a cold drink, if you prefer?"

"No, thank you, Mrs Forrest. What I'd like to do is ask your son some questions. About Zack McCauley." He turned to Sam and added, "He is a friend of yours, I believe."

Sam's mouth was bone-dry. "Yes." He licked the inside of his lips to stop them sticking to his teeth. "He was."

The detective's grey eyes watched him so closely, Sam felt like he was on the wrong end of a microscope.

"Was?"

"Yes. But not any more."

"And what caused the break-up of the friendship?"

Sam's mind went blank. Oh shit, everything they had rehearsed was gone. He tried to swallow but nothing happened. His eyes dropped to the policeman's gleaming black shoes and stuck there.

"Sergeant Crawford," his mother's voice rescued him, "why all these questions about Zack McCauley? What's it all about?"

The sergeant's gaze unpinned from Sam and rested with professional courtesy on his mother. "McCauley has been identified as a suspect in a robbery and we are trying to discover his present whereabouts. Your son's name was given to us as someone who shared a flat with him this summer." He turned like a homing missile back to Sam. "Is that true?"

Sam nodded to the shoes.

"But my son is finished with all that now. It was just a summer fling. He is living at home again and preparing to return to school. You haven't seen Zack since the row, have you, Sam?"

Sam seized the cue and his brain kicked into gear. With the return of the practised script came the return of speech.

"No, I haven't. And I don't want to either."

"You had a row with him?" asked the detective sergeant. "When was that?"

"Last week."

"Which day last week?"

Sam paused, as if needing to think. "Thursday."

"And you parted company?"

"Yes. I left his place and came home. I've been working in my mother's teashop since." He remembered to give his mother a smile.

"So Thursday was the last time you saw McCauley?"

"Yes."

"Morning or afternoon?"

"It was in the morning. I walked out because I . . ." He swallowed with difficulty and hoped like hell the detective would think it was because of recalling the row. He made himself look into those sceptical grey eyes and burst out angrily with, "Because I didn't want to hang around with a shit like him any more."

There was a tense silence while Sergeant Crawford jotted down a few notes and then asked, "What was the row about, Sam? We are trying to trace his movements on that Thursday and it would help us to know what was going on in his head."

Sam was careful not to look at his mother. "He owed me some money."

"Is that all?"

He shrugged and stared again at the black shoes, but did not answer.

"Sam, was there something else you quarrelled about? I advise you to tell the whole truth. You seem to have been this boy's friend and we are looking carefully at all his friends and associates."

His mother sat bolt upright, as if offended. "Detective Sergeant Crawford, I hope you are not implying that my son is a part of whatever this McCauley is caught up in."

"That's what I'm here to find out, Mrs Forrest."

"Well, I can tell you that Sam came home around eleven-thirty that morning. He was still upset about the row. The boy owed him money and refused to pay up, but I think it was just the last straw in a relationship that was already doomed."

"Is that so, Sam? Was that all the disagreement was about?"

It wasn't hard to let himself appear nervous, but he took the two quick breaths like they had rehearsed, as if reluctant to let the words out. "No, that wasn't all."

"What else did you fall out over?"

Sam let it come fast now. "He wanted me to do a job with him. He kept on and on about it, that I owed it to him for using the flat. But that was lame, because I'd given him rent. I told him straight the answer was no. I don't mess with the law."

"Of course you don't," his mother exclaimed.

The detective leaned forward, eyes sharp. "And what was the job he wanted you to do?"

"He wanted me to turn over a shop with him."

"You mean commit a robbery?"

"Yes."

"Which shop?"

"I don't know because I refused to listen. We yelled a lot but in the end I told him he could stuff his flat. And his robbery. Then I walked out."

"You did the right thing, Sam," his mother said.

"This is a very serious offence that McCauley is accused of," Crawford said. "And as he did have an accomplice with him, I would like to go over the exact times of your own movements. I'm sure you understand it is important to clarify the situation. Your mother says you came home about . . ."

The doorbell rang.

"Answer it, Sam," his mother said.

Sam jumped to do as he was told, anything to be able to lick his parched lips without those eyes studying his every move. As he lifted his hand to open the front door, he saw that it was shaking, its muscles trembling like jelly. Even with an effort he could not control it. He stuck a smile on his face.

It was Lloyd Morgan.

"Hi, Lloyd."

"Hello, Sam. Is your mother in? Esther in the teashop told me she had gone up to the flat and I need to have a few words with her. With you as well."

Oh shit, not Lloyd as well. Like wolves closing in all around him.

"Okay, come on up. But I warn you, we've got the fuzz with us at the moment."

"The police?"

"Yes. A Detective Sergeant Crawford."

"What does he want?"

"He's asking about an ex-mate of mine who's got himself into deep shit."

Lloyd stopped, half-way up the stairs. "Zack McCauley?"

"Yes."

"Did you do it, Sam?"

"Do what?"

"Don't play dumb with me."

"I'm not."

"Then let's have the truth."

Sam stared at Lloyd and the concern on his face took him by surprise. It loosened something inside him and suddenly he found himself wanting to cry. Oh shit, that would be a disaster, snivelling like a five-year-old. He had always liked Lloyd, liked the way he was not as grindingly serious as most adults, and for a split second he felt the urge to unburden himself. Grab a bit of male bonding. Like he would have with his father. Except that his father would have been too ashamed of him.

Sam kicked at the stair ahead of him. "I am telling the police the truth."

"That, I will be interested to hear."

They continued up to the flat in silence but when they walked into the sitting-room, Detective Sergeant Crawford was there alone. He stood up at the sight of Lloyd.

"Good afternoon, Mr Morgan."

"Hello, Tony, nice to see you making yourself useful. What have these two scallywags been up to? Not putting enough cream in the scones or watering down the milk?"

Crawford laughed, "No, they're helping with some enquiries I'm making."

"Where's Ma gone?" Sam asked.

"She went to put the kettle on. She's making some tea after all." The sergeant turned back to Lloyd. "My boss tells me you've got most of the traders to agree to finance the installation of the CCTV. That will make a big difference to . . .''

Sam left them to it.

In the kitchen Sam found his mother nowhere near the kettle. She was bent over the sink, head in a bowl, vomiting her guts out.

"Ma, what's the matter? Are you ill?''

She straightened up and he grabbed a square of kitchen-roll for her to clean her mouth. She looked wretched. "What the hell do you think is the matter? I'm scared shitless.''

It was then it hit him, what he'd done to her. Until now he had been so frightened for his own plight that he had not consciously allowed himself to dwell on what she might be going through. If he was honest with himself, he had to admit he had actively avoided thinking of it too much because all it did was deepen the fog of guilt that was suffocating him. He'd thought he could bear it, but seeing his mother vomiting into the sink was the end. It felt as if shreds were being torn off his insides. It was too much for him.

Too much for her.

He went over to his mother, put his arms around her slight shoulders and hugged her close. She leant against him without saying a word and he knew he couldn't let this go on.

"Ma, you were right. Worse luck. I should have done what you said in the first place and gone to the police. I didn't realise it would be like this. Maybe they won't be too hard on me if I co-operate as much as possible. I'll go out there and tell Sergeant Crawford the truth.''

She jerked out of the circle of his arms and stood glaring at him, her hair ruffled into a tufty mane like an angry lioness. "Sam Forrest, you do and I'll wring your bloody neck.'' She stamped her foot furiously. "Don't you dare do anything of the sort.''

Sam stared at her, seriously taken aback. "But I thought that was what you wanted me to do. When I came home, you told me to . . .''

"That was then. This is now. I am not letting you go to prison, and that's final. Not now. Not ever. Do you hear me, Sam?''

"Yes, Ma, I hear you.''

He hugged her once more and this time she hugged him back ferociously.

"Tea everyone?" Anna asked with a shiny smile. She had washed her face, combed her hair and filled the teapot.

Sam watched her and thought what bloody good actors adults learn to be. Actors or hypocrites? He pushed the thought aside and concentrated on Detective Sergeant Crawford. The policeman had climbed off his high horse since Lloyd's arrival and looked less intimidating now sitting drinking his tea and nibbling on a Hobnob. It gave Sam a flicker of hope.

Get me out of this alive, he prayed, and I swear I'll never get into trouble again.

"Now, Sam, let's go over the times once more," Sergeant Crawford said.

Lloyd stood up. "I'll come back later."

"That's not necessary, sir. I only have a couple more questions and then I can leave you all in peace. Or would you prefer that Mr Morgan left?" He looked at Sam.

"No, I don't mind. There's nothing to hide."

"Right then. Exactly what time did you return home after the row with McCauley?"

"I'm not sure, but it was around eleven-thirty. I remember thinking Ma would be very busy in the teashop at that hour, so I had better not disturb her."

The policeman's eyes turned on Anna. "How did you become aware that your son was home at eleven-thirty, if you were in the teashop downstairs?"

"One of my waitresses told me she had seen him at the window when she came to work."

"Which waitress was that?"

"Nella Torrence."

The detective jotted down the name on his pad. It would be checked.

"And what time did she come to work?"

"Two o'clock."

"So before two o'clock you had no idea that your son was home. Is that correct?"

Anna nodded. "Yes."

He looked at Sam and his eyebrows met in a frown. "Is there anyone who can vouch for you between eleven-thirty and two o'clock?"

"Yes, my brother. He came back from swimming and found me at home. We watched a film together on video. I didn't look at the time but I think he arrived about twelve-ish."

They had settled on that time between them, his mother and himself, though the truth was nearer one o'clock. The robbery had taken place shortly after twelve and he knew it wasn't until quarter to one that he'd got home because the Market Square clock had struck as he hurried past.

Crawford was making more notes. "We will need to talk to your brother. Swimming at the leisure centre, was he?"

"Yes."

"Right, we can check the times with them. Someone will remember him leaving, I dare say."

A spasm of fear chilled Sam's bowels. They had banked on nobody being able to pin down exactly when Danny had left. Least of all, Danny. Oh hell, he badly felt like a joint to calm his nerves. He risked a glance at his mother but whatever was going on inside, she was giving nothing away. Lloyd, on the other hand, was watching with blatant interest.

Sam gave the policeman a helpful smile and made his voice as decisive as it would go. "It could have been a bit after twelve that Danny arrived. I'm sorry I can't do better than that."

"Maybe twelve-thirty?"

"Maybe. But I don't think so."

"So in fact, you have no one to vouch for your being at home before twelve o'clock."

"No. But I was here," Sam insisted doggedly.

"Tony," Lloyd interrupted the proceedings very casually, "what day are you talking about? I may be able to help with this. I rang here one morning last week. Last Thursday it was."

Sam snatched a surreptitious deep breath as the policeman's attention veered round to Lloyd.

"Really, Mr Morgan? It is in fact Thursday that we are concerned with."

"Well, there's no problem then, is there, Sam?"

Sam stared, uncertain what was coming.

"Don't you remember? I rang to speak to your mother and you answered the phone. I had an eleven-thirty meeting that morning with the borough planners." He turned to Crawford and said courteously but with an undercurrent of impatience, "You can of course check that."

Sam reached for the lifeline. "Oh yes. I remember now. You wanted Ma but she was busy in the teashop, so you asked me to pass on a message. About the Chamber meeting, I think."

"But you forgot."

"Yes. Sorry." Sam succeeded in looking sheepish but his mind was whirling. What on earth was Lloyd up to?

Lloyd continued, his manner carrying conviction, "I rang just before the planning meeting started, so it would have been about eleven-twenty. There is no question that Sam was in the flat at that time because he answered the telephone. So that should settle it for you, Tony."

"Are you certain of the time of the phone-call, Mr Morgan?"

"I am not a moron, Tony. I rang before the meeting because I wanted to discuss some details with Mrs Forrest, before I discussed them with the planning officer. There is no doubt about the time. You can check it with my secretary."

"And there's no doubt that it was Sam you spoke to, not his brother?"

"None at all," Lloyd said curtly.

"Well, that certainly puts a different light on the matter, Mr Morgan. If Sam was here in the flat, he could not have been the other end of town with McCauley."

"I'm glad that's settled," Lloyd said smoothly. "Sam, you really are your own worst enemy. You forget to pass on my message and then forget my phone call. You had better buck up, my boy, if you expect to get anywhere." But he said it with a smile, as if he chose not to make an issue of the matter.

Sam nodded. He was speechless.

It was Anna who took action. She stood up. "If you have finished the questions now, Sergeant Crawford, I really am very busy downstairs."

The detective rose to his feet but turned once more to Sam.

"Just one last question. Have you any idea where McCauley may be hiding?"

"No, I don't."

"Also, we're looking for a girl. The one who was with you both in the flat this summer. Tara Tucker."

Sam's heart hammered sickeningly. "Why? What's she done?"

"We want to question her about McCauley's present whereabouts. Do you know where she has gone?"

"No."

"All right, I'll leave you to return to your work now. Thank you for your time, Mrs Forrest. And for your valuable help, Mr Morgan."

You slimy creep, Sam thought, just because he's buddy-buddy with your boss. But he hid the thought behind a polite handshake and could feel the pulse in his head begin to slow to a more bearable canter.

He had got away with it. Thanks to Lloyd, he was not going to rot behind bars.

The front door shut and his mother returned to the sitting-room.

"Right, you two," Lloyd said, "I want to know what's gone on. If I'm going to be a party to obstructing the course of justice, I think I deserve to know why, don't you?"

"Yes," Anna said quietly, "you do." She poured him a scotch and said to Sam, "Tell Lloyd what happened."

It scared Sam to let anyone else in on his secret but he knew he had no choice, so he sat down on the floor in front of Lloyd and told him the truth.

Anna wanted to cry with relief. Instead she made another pot of tea and sent Sam back downstairs to help Nella in the teashop. She needed to talk to Lloyd in private.

"Lloyd, are you totally out of your mind?" She was slumped on the sofa, feeling as if a dog had just chewed her up and spat her out. Opposite her, Lloyd was sitting upright in an armchair looking every inch the pillar of society she had been so certain he was. But it would seem that the pillar had feet of clay, and if that was mixing metaphors, then too bad. That was exactly how she felt, all mixed up. "Lying to the police is a serious offence, Lloyd."

"That sounds to me like the pot calling the kettle black." He said it with a laugh, but his eyes weren't smiling.

"Thank you, Lloyd. Thank you for protecting him."

"No need for you to thank me, Anna. Sam has already done that himself, profusely. He's no fool. He knows what I did."

"So do I. And I'm more grateful than I can say."

"Don't be. He's worth saving."

"I know."

"Tell me whose idea it was not to call in the police at the beginning."

"Sam's at first. Then mine. I know it's crazy, but I don't want him to go to gaol for years. I couldn't bear it. I know he did wrong but it would ruin him for ever. I couldn't let that happen, Lloyd, I just couldn't. Not when he hardly did anything in the robbery. I'm certain he would never do it again."

"Can you really be so sure?"

"Yes. Yes, I can. You heard him, he feels ashamed of what he's done, as well as being scared stiff of the police grabbing him. He's got more sense than to put himself through this again. Anyway," she said fiercely, "he's my son."

"That's what I'm relying on, Anna," Lloyd said gently.

There was an awkward silence while both listened to their own thoughts, then Anna pulled herself together and shook her head at him. "You're just as soft in the head, Lloyd Morgan. Don't you make me out to be the only idiot round here."

"As if I would."

"You're no better at choosing between two impossibles than I am. Not when it involves someone you love."

"That's true," he said, with a good attempt at a laugh.

"You can have the rock and I'll take the hard place. How's that for an even distribution of calamity?"

"You're too generous."

They both smiled and their eyes held.

"You mad Welshman, what can I do to show you how grateful I am?"

Lloyd said nothing for a long moment, just looked at her until she felt uncomfortable, then he smiled, "Cook me a slap-up meal and make Sam do the washing-up."

"You've got yourself a deal," Anna laughed and the sound

surprised her. It felt like years since she had laughed. "Lloyd, you have no idea what a relief it is to me to share this with someone. It's been like a ticking bomb inside me, threatening to explode all weekend. I kept thinking that if it blew me into millions of little pieces, I wouldn't be able to guard Sam anymore but at least it might take the town's mind off the robbery."

"A diversionary tactic."

"That's right."

"Too messy. Anyway the Chamber would need you to organise a squad to clean up the pieces."

She laughed again. "It's the inside of my head that needs cleaning up. It's in such a jumble."

He leant forward. "I'm not surprised. It must have been grisly. But Anna, there is one possibility you have to face."

"If it's something horrible, don't tell me."

"I'm sorry, I have to. What if Zack or Tara reappear? Sam is a sitting duck for blackmail."

Anna stared at Lloyd. "Don't."

"It's possible. You've got to be prepared for it."

She lifted her chin and her jaw jutted like a ledge to hang her determination on. "Okay, let them try it. I'll shop them to the police as soon as look at them and if they say Sam was involved, I'll claim it's just sour grapes. I'll say they want to strike back at him for not helping them in their criminal activities. Easy. No sweat."

Lloyd smiled at her. "That's your story and you're sticking to it?"

"You bet I am."

"My money is on you then."

"Wise man." Anna laughed once more because it was better than crying. "Lloyd, you must love him very much."

"Love who?"

"Sam."

His reaction was not what she expected. His blue eyes turned almost navy as if he was struggling in deep water, the heavy brows were drawn together and his jaw was clenched ready to bite off the words on his tongue. There was a silence. Why did he find it so hard to admit that he felt Sam was the son he'd never had? It was so obvious to her. Why not to him?

Finally Lloyd nodded. "I am fond of Sam. He's a nice boy."

"Why else would you perjure yourself for him?"

"Why else, indeed?"

Something had gone. Suddenly their friendship was on ice again. Was this whole stupid world upside-down? When he abruptly stood up to go, she held on to his arm and placed a kiss on his cheek.

"Thank you, Lloyd, for what you did. You are such a good friend to us. I will always be indebted to you. When would you like that slap-up dinner?"

He lingered briefly as though he was going to say something, but then shook his head and replied, "I'm not sure. I'm busy with this Bristol company at the moment and the blasted Chamber affairs. I'll let you know."

He left and after she closed the door behind him, she felt miserable. Something had gone wrong and she didn't know what. God, he was a touchy bastard. What on earth had she said to upset him now?

It was an hour later that Danny arrived home. He tried to slink off to his room but she felt in need of his chirpy smile, so waylaid him in the corridor.

"Did you have a good training session? You were longer than usual, so I thought you had gone to . . ." She stopped. His tee-shirt was shredded from the neck right down to his navel and was covered in dirt. "Danny, what on earth have you been doing?"

He glared at the floor and kicked the toe of his trainers at the carpet. "Nothing."

"You don't rip your shirt doing nothing. What happened?"

He still did not look up. "Nothing much." His tone was angry and resentful.

"Have you and Will had a fight? Is that it?"

He hesitated, then nodded in sullen silence.

"It must have been a bad one to tear your clothes like this." She noticed then that his lower lip was swollen. "Don't worry, you'll soon patch it up and be best of friends again."

She was a fine one to talk. Look at the way Lloyd had just

left. Oh God, she was beginning to think she was some kind of alien changeling, who would never learn to understand human beings.

"Let me get you something to eat and . . ."

"I don't want anything to eat."

That was unheard-of.

She put a hand on his shoulder in a gesture of comfort but he shrugged it off and shuffled a few paces away from her. His eyes were still aiming a belligerent stare at the carpet, but the hand that clutched his sports-bag was clenching and unclenching as he waited for her to finish with him.

"Danny," Anna said gently. "Don't take your quarrel out on me. I've got enough trouble with Sam, and I'm not to blame if . . ."

"Sam," he shouted furiously, "it's always fucking Sam." He stamped his way down the corridor and slammed his bedroom door.

Anna was tempted to hammer it down and talk some sense into his chlorine-sodden head, but instead she leaned against a wall for support and decided to be a celibate nun in her next life.

22

Sam was nervous. The glass double-doors opened automatically when he approached them, making him jump, and a little girl standing on the other side of them giggled. He ignored her and started to walk across the large expanse of reception hall to the desk opposite, but half-way there he changed his mind and veered off through a doorway on his left. A long, impersonal corridor stretched ahead of him, with stairs behind yet more glass doors on his right.

Hospitals made him uneasy. He had only been in one twice and both times had ended in tears. Once was when he was five years old and had been bitten by a bad-tempered poodle and had to have stitches in his leg. The other was worse. His mother had been up on a ladder painting Danny's bedroom ceiling and had fallen off, banging her head on the wardrobe on her way down. He had thought she was dead. She lay there as still as the corpses he'd seen on television. He was eleven at the time and had had the sense to dial 999. He remembered crying with Danny while they waited for the ambulance. It had turned out to be no worse than concussion, and after twenty-four hours in a hospital bed, she had returned home with nothing more than a bump behind her ear and a headache. But he didn't like hospitals. Or poodles.

The problem now was to find intensive-care without drawing attention to himself. It took him some time. After a few false starts, a hospital porter sent him up two flights of stairs where he managed to lose himself in the rabbit-warren of corridors, but then he saw a nurse walking ahead of him who, from the back, could have been Tara. The same small dark head and bird-like legs. His throat tightened and he hurried to overtake her. Of course it wasn't her. The face was all wrong. But he asked for directions anyway just to hear her voice. It didn't have Tara's northern accent but told him where the intensive-care unit was and, without further trouble, he got himself there. Instantly he was accosted by a burly figure of a woman in a tight navy uniform. Sister Hyde, her badge declared.

"Can I help you?"

"I'm looking for Mrs Anstey."

"You're too late, I'm afraid."

No, no, not dead. Don't let her be dead. Please don't let her be dead.

"We transferred Mrs Anstey to Castle Ward yesterday. No need to look so shocked. I didn't mean to frighten you. Her condition has improved, so she no longer needs to be here in intensive."

"Thank you, thank you very much."

"You're welcome." She could not resist a smile for the attractive young lad and told him how to find Castle Ward.

Sam scuttled off and this time had no trouble. He was expecting a large ward with lots of beds, but when he reached it he discovered that she was in a side-room on her own. He stood outside her door, swallowed hard, counted to ten, then knocked. A woman's voice called, "Come in."

He pushed open the door.

Oh shit, she was covered in tubes.

It was the woman he remembered from the off-licence but older, greyer, her eyes no longer so sure of themselves.

"Hello, who are you?" she asked.

Sam was tempted to run. This was harder than it had seemed in his head.

"Are you Mrs Rachel Anstey?"

"Yes, I am." She lifted an arm, trailing tubes like octopus tentacles, and indicated the chair by her bed. "Come and talk to me, I'm bored stiff."

Sam stepped further into the room but hovered at the foot of the bed. "I was asked to deliver a package to you." He held out a fat manila envelope.

She took it, studied its blank surface and asked again, "Who are you?"

"I'm Jason Aggate. I was sitting on the lawn outside, waiting for my mate to finish visiting his sister, when someone came up and offered me ten quid to deliver this to you. So here I am." It was the best he could come up with. He turned to leave.

"Wait!" The voice was accustomed to being obeyed and Sam wondered if she was a headmistress as well as a magistrate. "Describe the person who gave you this package."

"It was a young guy about eighteen or nineteen, I guess." He watched her open the envelope. "Tallish with fair hair." Her eyes widened as she drew out a thick bundle of bank-notes. He stared at it, as if surprised and let his mouth drop open.

"Go on."

"That's a hell of a lot of money, Mrs Anstey."

She looked from the money to him and back to the money. "It certainly is." She started to count it. He watched her. She did it quickly and efficiently despite the tubes, probably the way she did everything. She stopped for a second to say, "Carry on describing him", and continued the counting.

"He was thin. Real thin, and had dark eyes."

"What was he wearing?"

"Jeans and a denim jacket. Nike trainers that were knackered." He took a couple of steps backwards.

She was still counting, her grey head bent over the pile of notes, her fingers flicking through them, making the veins on the back of her hands stand out. High on each side of her nose was a red mark, as if she had been wearing glasses recently. Reading maybe. She looked up suddenly and her grey eyes were sharp and intelligent.

"Nine hundred and twenty pounds."

"Right. I'm off now."

"Did this thin, blond young man give you any message for me?"

"Oh yes. He said he was sorry."

"That's all?"

"Yes."

He turned and walked to the door. She did not say anything until he had his hand on it.

"Nine hundred pounds is, as you put it, a hell of a lot of money. It would come in very useful."

"Sure would." He pulled the door open.

"So why give it to me?"

"Don't ask me. I just delivered the package." He risked a glance at her and knew instantly that he was sunk. She was wearing a patient smile.

"Don't bother pretending any more, young man. It's your eyes that give you away. Everything else about you looks different, so that I might not have recognised you. But those caramel eyes of yours are unmistakable. I noticed them in the shop."

Sam did not know whether to run or talk. He looked at the tired lines on her face and the drips attached to her body because of him. He decided to talk.

"I just wanted to say I was sorry. I thought it could buy you a holiday somewhere. To recover, I mean." He shuffled uncomfortably. "I didn't think you would recognise me."

"I deal with young offenders all the time you know, so I don't look at them as a faceless group. In the shop you struck me as not the kind of face I would have expected to see in that situation."

"I'm sorry."

She gave him a searching look. "So you said. What about the other one? The one that stabbed me."

"He's gone. I don't know where. Honestly."

She nodded and stared down at the money for a long time. "Go away, young man. Satan comes in many guises and one of them is brown honest eyes bearing gifts." She sighed. "My daughter has ME and badly needs a holiday. Go away."

Sam shot out of the door, cursing himself for taking such a bloody stupid risk when he could have put the money in the post. But he had wanted to see her, needed to see for himself that she wasn't dead. Outside the hospital, he lit a cigarette and breathed in great lungfuls of relief.

When Sam arrived home his mother was waiting for him. She was doing it discreetly, but he wasn't fooled by her air of casual interest. It was nearly five o'clock and normally she would be in the teashop at this hour.

"Did you have a good afternoon?" she asked. She was in the sitting-room watching *Countdown*. "What did you do?"

"Yes, it was fine. I went for a walk. And no, I didn't see Tara. Or Zack. And no, I didn't do drugs. And no, I'm not going back to school. Does that cover everything?"

She gave him a look that he didn't like and went back to her programme.

"Sorry, Ma." He plonked himself into a chair and draped his long legs over its arm. "It's just that I feel you're breathing down my neck all the time."

"I am not."

"That's what it feels like."

"Sam, I just want what's best for you."

"I know, Ma. I know that."

She looked tired. Nella Torrence had packed in her job at the teashop now that school had started up, so his mother was putting in more hours. She had been on at him again to return to his A levels this term, and on top of that he was feeling guilty that he had deceived her about the stolen money, but strictly speaking, he had in fact told the truth. They had dumped it, still in the carrier-bag, into a dustbin in the street. But even he wasn't that green. It was obvious that Zack would be back there like a shot as soon as Sam was out of sight. So he'd beaten him to it, that's all. But the knowledge that Zack was somewhere out there, angry and resentful, scared the hell out of him. What Tara had intended, he didn't want to think.

He was missing her like mad.

"What's the matter with Danny?" his mother asked as she turned off the television. "I can't get any sense out of him. He's as prickly as a porcupine."

"Don't ask me. He hardly speaks to me."

"I've noticed that. Why is it?"

"Ask him, not me."

Sam had been hurt and then annoyed by his brother's behaviour towards him over the last few days. He had never known Danny like this. He was in a permanent sulk, making it more than clear that the return of the prodigal son was not to his liking. Last night Sam had been watching a rerun of *Terminator*

II when Danny had come in and switched it off with the weird comment, "With friends like yours, you don't need to watch that film." Sam had been tempted to flatten him, but whatever it was that was eating his little brother, he knew he was in some way responsible.

The telephone rang. His mother went to answer it and he listened to her voice in the hall.

"Hello, Emma, how's the hotel trade? What can I do for you?"

There was a long silence, a few murmurs and then a low, "No, Emma. No, I had no idea. I assumed he was coming back." A short pause. "I'll try to get in touch with him. Yes, I know I recommended him to you. Don't worry, I'll make sure you're not out of pocket." Another pause. "Yes, I'll be in touch. Thanks for letting me know." She hung up.

After a short delay, she came slowly back into the sitting-room.

"What's up, Ma?"

"That was Emma Barton from Barton's Hotel."

"Oh yeah, the one that looks like Jabba the Hutt's sister."

"Don't be rude."

"That's where your artist friend is staying, isn't it?"

"Yes. Nick took a room there only because he had to leave our upstairs flat. Blast the man, what is he up to?"

"What do you mean?"

She ruffled her hair with annoyance. "It seems that when he left to go to his exhibition in London last Monday, he took all his things with him."

"Oh."

"Exactly. And he hasn't paid his bill."

"Done a bunk, has he?"

"I can't believe it. But it looks like it. I'll ring the gallery. The trouble is that I haven't got a permanent address for him, because he said he's been staying with various friends while he sorts out a flat for himself." She frowned, and he could see she feared the worst.

"Sounds shifty, you must admit," Sam said. "Did he pay what he owed when he left here?"

"Not exactly."

"Oh Ma, you've always said get the money up front. Never trust a grockle."

"I know, I know. It's just that . . ." Her words ground to a halt and she stared miserably out the window. "I did trust him. He said he would pay me after the exhibition. I wanted to believe him. I thought he was . . ." She left the words hanging.

"Your friend?"

She nodded and suddenly exclaimed, "The bastard!" She thumped her forehead. "How dumb can I get! Do I wear a notice saying come and wipe your feet here, is that it?"

"Ma . . ."

"He certainly must have seen the signs flashing loud and clear. Lonely widow, come and fleece her. Because . . ."

"Are you lonely?" Sam interrupted.

His mother's anger skidded to a halt and she looked at him defensively. "Of course I get lonely sometimes. That's why I fell for a smooth talker like Nick Steed." She stared off into space as if watching a replay of some scene in her head, and her mouth softened. "But I had some fun this summer."

She said it as though she were talking about deep-sea diving or space exploration, something she never expected to find in her own life, and it occurred to Sam for the first time that adults needed to go off the rails at times as well.

"You could have fun with Lloyd Morgan instead."

She stared at him in surprise. "What is that supposed to mean?"

"Come on, Ma, you can't be that blind. You must be able to see it."

"See what?"

"That he fancies you like mad."

To his amusement, she blushed bright scarlet and turned away to tidy some school-books Danny had left lying around on the sofa. "Don't be stupid."

"It's true."

"Rubbish. Lloyd and I are very good friends, that's all. I know he likes me, but not like that. Anyway, it's obvious even to a blind person that he doesn't want a permanent involvement with anybody, he just likes having an occasional fling."

"You're barmy if you think that."

"No, Sam, you've got it all wrong. You're the one he cares about. Look what he's done for you. Taught you to drive, given you a job at the boatyard, scraped you out of that nightclub and now even lied to the police for you. Since when has he ever done anything like that for me?"

"Try getting in trouble with the police and maybe you'd find out."

She shook her head. "No, he's not interested in anything more than we have already."

"Are you?"

She turned back to the books so that he could not see her face, but a telltale finger of red was creeping down her neck. "Of course not. I'm not interested in anything except getting you and that spiky brother of yours sorted out and keeping this blasted teashop afloat. Forget men!"

Sam felt sorry for her and the feeling gave him a nasty shock. He suddenly became aware of how much things had changed. A few weeks ago they would not have been having this conversation.

"Maybe Lloyd has got it right," his mother continued, getting more heated again. "Relationships cause too much trouble and heart-ache. Look at you and Tara, look at me when your father died and now with Nick. It's all too . . ." She stopped and gave a high-pitched cry. "The money."

"What money?" Sam didn't like seeing his mother like this.

"The money in the desk drawer."

"The three hundred pounds? The money you accused me of taking?"

"Nick was here the night before I found it missing. He asked me if he could take my car and went to get the keys from that drawer. But I said I needed it. Thank God I had that much sense or I might have lost the car as well." She jumped up and paced furiously round the room. "Nick Steed, you dirty rotten thief, you low-down . . ."

"Slow down, Ma. You've got no proof. He'll just deny it. And anyway, it might not have been him. You're jumping to conclusions again."

"Correct conclusions."

"Not necessarily. You said yourself it might have been Zack.

There's no way of knowing for certain. But you've changed the locks now, so calm down and keep cool."

She did not look as if she had any intention of keeping cool. "No, Sam. There are other things that have gone missing since I've known him. I was just too stupid to make the connection." She headed into the hall. "I'm calling that art gallery right now."

But before she reached the telephone, the doorbell rang. Sam heard her go down to open the front door. A moment later she was back in the sitting-room, her face as white as ash. At her side stood Detective Sergeant Crawford.

He walked over to Sam and said very formally, "Sam Forrest, I am arresting you on suspicion of taking part in a robbery in Porter's Off-licence at twelve-fifteen on Thursday the twenty-eighth of August. You do not have to say anything but it may harm your defence if you do not mention, when questioned, something which you may later rely on in court. Anything you do say may be given in evidence. Do you understand?"

"Yes," Sam whispered. "I understand."

The police station terrified Anna. She had only been in one once before, when Danny's bicycle was stolen from Market Square, but on that occasion the uniformed constable had smiled sympathetically at her. This time the officers were scrupulously polite but as grim as gaolers.

They sat in a small room with grey walls and grey floor that smelt of fear and linoleum, and a tape-recorder clicked continuously on the table. They brought her a cup of plastic coffee to scald her palate, while they went through the same questions over and over again with Sam. About Zack's habits and movements, about his past, his friends, his income and then about Tara. Sam supplied the answers readily but claimed he had first met her on the beach and that she came from somewhere vague up north. Neither of them mentioned that she had stayed at their flat or that Anna possessed the address and telephone number of her mother in Sheffield. The police took their time but eventually got round to the questions about Sam himself, his relationship with Zack and Tara, and his movements on the Thursday in question. Anna felt sick with nerves but he handled it extremely convincingly, sticking to their agreed story-lines and conveying just the right touch of remorse for an ill-spent summer. He was better this time than when they had caught him by surprise at the flat.

Lloyd's all-important phone-call was trotted out as an alibi once more and Anna was just beginning to feel on safer ground, when they brought up the subject of drugs.

Had Sam seen Zack use them?

Did Tara?

Did Sam?

And it seemed to Anna that Sam was telling the truth. Yes, Zack used all kinds, even needles, but no, Sam had never seen him dealing. And yes, Tara had popped a few pills and smoked pot. When he came to his own habits, he was careful to avoid looking at herself but openly admitted smoking cannabis a number of times. Anna was just thankful it wasn't worse. But could she be sure? She had turned him into such an expert liar. He was warned about the consequences of using illegal substances by the police officer but that was as far as it went and then they were back on the times again. The time Sam came home, the time Danny finished swimming, the time of Lloyd's phone-call, the time Anna went up to the flat. Over and over. And just when she thought it was finished, they started at the beginning again.

"Lloyd, don't go."

Lloyd was just getting into his car. He was about to leave the boatyard to drive up to Bristol, taking advantage of the quieter evening traffic, and was still in the office only because he had stopped to make a last couple of phone-calls. Half an hour late and awash with caffeine, he had one foot in the Rover when a small red car scooted into the yard, trailing a puff of black smoke, and skidded to a halt. It was Anna.

"Wait, Lloyd. Please."

He waited. And watched as she jumped out, her legs looking summer-tanned and sleek as they preceded her out of the car. He liked her legs. But he forgot them the moment he looked at her face.

"Anna, what is it? What's happened?"

"Sam has been arrested."

"What!"

"The police arrested him. Just now." Her voice was shaking and her blue eyes looked as if they had found the door to hell.

"But why? Surely my phone-call is supposed to have put him in the clear?"

"No, it hasn't. Not now."

"What has changed?"

"That detective has got it into his head that Sam was McCauley's accomplice. They were known to be in each other's pockets and the leisure centre says Danny didn't leave there until around quarter to one. Crawford claims there was enough time for Sam to have had the talk with you at eleven-thirty and still get across town to the off-licence by twelve-fifteen and back again by one."

"Oh hell, no. Poor Sam. Though Crawford must be sure. He has probably timed it all. But I can't place the phone-call any later, Anna. I wish I could. But I was in a meeting after eleven-thirty and there are people who will, unfortunately, vouch for that."

She nodded miserably. "You've stuck your neck out already."

"Is there any other way I can help?"

"Yes, that's why I came. I need the name of a good solicitor. They let Sam out on bail but . . ."

"Well, that's something to cheer about. Where is he?"

"At home."

Lloyd could imagine the state of shock the kid must be in. But it was a case of the old cliché, if you can't do the time, don't do the crime. Sam should have kept his fingers clean. "He must be going through hell right now but, Anna, it's a hell of his own making." He said it gently. "Don't let him drag you down into it. It is his own life and he's the one who chose to cross swords with the justice system."

She bared her teeth at him and he almost expected a snarl. "I don't want justice. I want my son."

"I know. And I'll do everything I can to keep him for you. First, a decent solicitor. David Appleton is the man. He's first-rate. I'll contact him immediately and then pull a few strings to see what else I can find out about what's going on."

Abruptly she put out a hand and gripped his arm, as if to save herself from drowning. "Thank you, Lloyd. You're such a good friend to me. As well as to Sam."

"I'm glad you've noticed," he said, and folded a comforting arm around her.

She burrowed against his shoulder and he expected to feel her crying but instead she gave a long sigh that he wasn't quite sure how to interpret. When a police-siren wailed past somewhere near the harbour, she stepped back from him and aimed a furious glare in its direction.

"They're putting Sam in a line-up," she said.

"An identification parade?"

"Yes."

"Who is doing the identifying?"

"Mr Anstey, as his wife is still in hospital. And the shop assistant. But his glasses were broken, so he's unreliable."

"When is it to be?"

"In two weeks."

So that was it. Their case rested on the main eyewitness. It all depended on how much Sam's change in appearance would fool Mr Anstey and whether the police had discovered that the boy spent twenty-four hours as a blond.

"I'd better warn you," Anna said very seriously, "that I'm taking a machine-gun with me into the line-up and just before Mr Anstey gets to Sam, I'll mow him down. Just like Al Capone used to do. No witness, no case."

"I'll drive the getaway car," Lloyd smiled.

She tried an answering smile, she really did, but it didn't come, so she frowned instead. "I must get home. Sam will need company."

"Anna, he's not a baby, for Christ's sake. Anyway, he's got Danny to hold his hand if necessary, hasn't he?"

"Danny! I don't know what's the matter with that child. He's impossible at the moment. I've tried talking to him but he just clams up and retreats to his room. He's even skipping training sessions now and . . ."

Lloyd took hold of the hand she was waving around in

exasperation and said, "Enough, Anna, enough. You need a break from all this. Come on, I'll buy you a meal to put some meat on your bones."

"Weren't you going somewhere in the car?"

"Nowhere important." He opened the passenger door to tempt her. "Hop in."

She hesitated, then tumbled in as though a string had snapped. "Thanks."

He gave her silence during the drive, to struggle with the mayhem inside her head, but he had no intention of being so generous during the meal. She needed to talk about something other than her children, whether she knew it or not.

23

Anna sat in another grey room, larger than on the previous occasion, but to her eyes even grimmer. It was divided in two by a glass section that made her think of a guillotine blade descending to slice off the heads of the guilty. She shuddered and received a pat from the hand on her left. It belonged to David Appleton, Sam's solicitor, who was sitting beside her at the back of the room, observing fair-play. She was glad he was with her. There was something infinitely reassuring about his pinstripe suit and ample double-chin and eyes that had seen it all before.

To one side stood the Duty Inspector who was conducting the identification parade and who maintained a professional impassivity that only managed to wind her nerves even tighter. When he had read out the instructions earlier – "Look at each member of the parade at least twice" and "Take as much time and care as you like" – his voice had roared in her ears like a chain-saw.

Oddly, Philip Anstey seemed almost as jumpy as she was. Anna had been surprised. She had expected someone bigger and bolder as the husband of a magistrate, but this man was slight, with mild nervous eyes that were not used to the spotlight. Even so, he was jumpier than he should have been. His shirt looked crumpled and not quite clean but maybe that was because his wife was in hospital and he did not know what magic worked the washing-machine. It was the dark patches of sweat under his arms that were the real give-away.

He was standing near the glass and Anna found herself staring obsessively at the back of his head and the neat bristles of his hair-line, wondering if he'd had it cut that morning, so razor sharp was it. She had to force herself to shift her gaze to the row of faces on the other side of the glass partition. There were twelve of them, all young, all male and holding an identifying number, and all looking as guilty as hell. In fact, except for Sam, they had all been picked at random off the streets. Stooges, they called them. David Appleton had told her they were paid for performing this civic service and she wondered how much.

Her mind was veering everywhere except where it should be. On Sam. He looked so vulnerable, it hurt. He had dressed casually in jeans and tee-shirt because he did not want to stand out from the others, but there was a freshness about him that the rest of the stooges did not seem to possess. Her heart rejoiced to see it was still there despite the traumas of the last few weeks, but her head reminded her about mothers and rose-tinted spectacles. Lloyd would no doubt tell her to take them off.

The trouble was, she didn't know how.

Sam was fourth from the right in the line-up, number nine, next to a boy with fair hair and brown eyes that were flitting everywhere. In Anstey's place, Anna would have picked him on the eyes alone. She could not see the witness's face, but followed the gradual turn of the back of his head as his gaze slowly inched down the line. She held her breath when it seemed to reach Sam and yearned for that machine-gun, but he did not seem to linger any longer than on the others. When he reached number twelve, he started on number one again.

During this last fortnight of waiting, while she had been biting her nails down to the knuckle, Sam had seemed irritatingly unconcerned. She couldn't fathom it. He kept saying, "Don't worry, he'll never recognise me now. Look at me. My face is as chubby as a chipmunk's and my hair is totally different."

"How can you be so sure, Sam?"

"The guy was scared in the shop, scared shitless. He won't have noticed anything very clearly. And the shock will have wiped whatever he did see. He won't remember, I promise you. Just relax."

She found his confidence inexplicable.

Suddenly Philip Anstey was speaking and shaking his head. "No, the boy in the shop is not there. He is definitely not one of those, I'm certain." They went through the same routine again with the shop-assistant from the off-licence, but he kept complaining that the assailants had broken his glasses, so he wasn't sure what they looked like. He made no identification.

Sam had been right.

He was safe.

Relief raced over every square-inch of her skin making it sting and tingle like frostbite and she became dimly aware that David Appleton was offering her a handkerchief. She accepted it and realised she must be crying. She mopped at her face, thanked him for accompanying her and stood up, eager to get out of that place. Various officers spoke to her and forms were signed, but it was all a blur. Only one thing reverberated in her head like an echo.

Sam was free to go.

Lloyd left it until three o'clock and then downed tools on the Evinrude engine he was working on, stripped himself of overalls and grease, and took to the Rover. The identification parade would be over by now and he wanted to be there in person to see her face, to be the one to hold her hand, because for Anna he knew it would be a case of either opening the bubbly or opening her wrists.

The second he walked through the teashop door, it was obvious. There was Sam, in waiter's white shirt and black trousers, pen and note-pad in hand and no ball-and-chain in sight. Anna, on the other hand, was sitting at one of her own tables with Harriet Torrence, a Cheshire-cat grin on her face and unable to take her eyes off her son. Her hair looked as if her hands had been ruffling overtime.

"Hello, Anna. Good news?"

"The best," she beamed.

"I'm very glad." He was careful not to say too much in front of Harriet.

"What are you two on about?" Harriet queried.

"Just Chamber business," Lloyd said, and distracted her with "How's Nature's Basket doing?"

"Better and better, touch wood." Harriet tapped her own head.

He pulled up a chair and joined them. The place was very quiet with only a few tables occupied, typical of the post-season lull. For a month or so it would be the tail-end of the coach outings, then it would start to build again with the beginning of Christmas shopping. Without being asked, Sam brought Lloyd a cup and saucer so he could avail himself of Harriet's teapot, and added a hefty slice of mocha gateau on the side.

"What's this? Giving away your mother's profits, are you?" Harriet laughed. "You'll have to watch him, Anna. You can't trust him."

Lloyd almost throttled her but Sam just went about his business and Anna continued to smile happily. Nothing was going to burst her bubble. Lloyd wondered when she would let herself think about the danger to Sam if the police caught McCauley.

"I've got some news you'll both be interested in," he said as Harriet poured him some tea.

"What's that?"

"The Council are about to announce their decision about the coaches. They are to use both Market Square and the beach car park."

Both women groaned.

"But the new plan won't come into operation until next May," he continued, "and will run only until the beginning of September. Then it will revert back to the present parking system for the winter and spring."

Anna beamed at him. "That's not bad at all."

Harriet thumped Lloyd on the back. "A bloody good job you did there, Chairman. I heard from a councillor who shall remain nameless but who bears a striking resemblance to Billy Bunter, that you have done such a brilliant stalling job with proposals and counter-proposals that it delayed the decision until it was too late to put it into operation this summer. I mean to say, who wants to be dumped at the beach on a chilly autumn afternoon. The coaches all want to come into the town centre now and who can blame . . . ?"

The door opened and Nella Torrence walked in. She was in school uniform and looked upset.

"Why aren't you at school, dear daughter?"

Nella dropped her school-bag on the floor. "I went to the shop but Dad said you were here."

"What's the problem, Nella?" Anna asked.

The girl looked round the room uneasily and spotted Sam walking out of the kitchen carrying a laden tray. "Hi, Sam."

He came across to the table, immediately curious. "What are you doing here? Not sunk to having tea with the oldies, surely?"

But she didn't smile. "No."

"Why aren't you at school?" her mother repeated.

Nella shrugged miserably. "I've been kicked out."

"What!"

"Kicked out of school."

"What for? What have you done?" Harriet wailed.

The girl looked at her mother warily. 'I got caught smoking pot in the loo."

"Oh shit, Nella," Sam groaned. "That's tough."

Anna stood up. "That's tough? Is that all you have to say for yourself, Sam?" The laughter and the smiles had gone. "You are the one who has been involved with drugs this summer. I heard you admit it to the police, so don't bother to deny it, and now you've got poor Nella caught up in it so that she's expelled from school. And what do you say? That's tough!"

Sam frowned at his mother, unaware that he was still holding the tray. "You think I am responsible for Nella's actions?"

"Who else?"

"She's a free agent. She makes her own choices."

"Don't tell me you didn't give her a helping hand."

Nella started to speak but her words were drowned by the crash of the tray to the ground. Cups, cakes and plates shattered in an explosion of tea. Without taking his eyes from his mother's, Sam had opened his hands and released the tray, then without a word he walked out of the teashop.

For a moment the silence was total, but suddenly everyone spoke at once. Harriet was talking, Nella was fussing over the mess, customers were chattering and Esther appeared from the kitchen to enquire what had happened. Anna just stared. She stared at her son striding past the window, then at the smashed crockery on the floor.

Lloyd watched her. She was listening to no one, only seeing what was in her own head. Something major had happened in there. He could feel it as sharply as he could feel the hot tea that had soaked into his trousers.

Anna scrubbed at the stains in the hamster's cage with a venom that had nothing to do with cleanliness. She was alone in the flat and free to give vent to her rage with only Hammy's pink ears as witness.

She felt used.

Abused by her own son.

She glared at the hamster, where he sat preening in his temporary residence of a discarded cake-tin.

"How could he do such a thing?" she demanded of the animal. "When he knew what the consequences could be. Hasn't the boy learnt anything?"

The hamster paused in his grooming, long enough to give her a curious beam from his bright eyes, and then resumed work on his rear end.

No amount of denials by Nella had convinced her. The girl was obviously trying to protect Sam and refused to admit he had been her supplier, lying and pretending for him, just as Anna had done to the police. Well, to hell with protection from now on. Time for Sam to grow up. She winced as she thought how easily he had deceived her with his instant remorse, as if crime and drugs had been a momentary aberration that would never be repeated, and because she had wanted so much to believe him, she had been taken in. But all the time he was handing out drugs to Nella Torrence. And who else?

With a fresh cloth Anna rubbed the cage dry, renewed the bedding and filled the water-container and food-dish, then plonked the hamster back in his house. He sniffed suspiciously and set about packing his cheek-pouches with sunflower seeds.

"Make the most of it, Hammy. From now on it's up to Sam to keep you cleaned and fed. You're his responsibility, not mine."

She walked over to the window and looked down at the street below, which had settled into the quieter pace of autumn. A chill drizzle had started falling and was turning the pavements glossy black, so that even though it was still early evening, the day was as dark as her thoughts. Sam couldn't run forever. He would have to come home sooner or later, but it depressed her to find she would rather it was later. She knew she should ring Harriet to find out how Jonathan was taking the news about Nella, but she didn't want to. She liked standing there in the gathering gloom, doing nothing for anybody.

The front door slammed and she waited to hear which of her two sons would walk in. Her money was on Danny.

"Hello, Ma."

Wrong again. It was Sam.

She turned to face him but said nothing.

"Don't you want some light in here?" he asked.

"I can see perfectly clearly, thank you."

He got the point. "Okay, I asked for that one. But I want to explain." He walked over to the light-switch and flicked it on, filling the room with artificial brightness, then sat down in an armchair with his legs outstretched, but to Anna he looked anything but relaxed. "First, I want to say I'm sorry that I have upset you again, but I think you're overreacting." He waited for a response, but received none, so continued, "Secondly, you can't blame me for decisions made by Nella. If she wants to smoke a reefer, that is her choice, not mine. And if she's dumb enough to do it at school, then that can't be dumped on me, because it wasn't my fault she wanted to show off to the kids in her class."

A long silence divided them.

"Well?" he prompted.

"Well what? What is it you want me to say, Sam? That I know you've been a naughty boy again, but I forgive you. Is that it? Well, I'm sorry I can't oblige this time." She turned her back on him and drew the curtains across the window, shutting out the rest of the world.

"No, Ma, that's not what I want. I want you to see that Nella is responsible for her own behaviour, just as I am for mine. And you are for yours."

"Responsibility, Sam, is something you have yet to understand, it seems. You admit it was you who supplied Nella with the drug?"

"Yes. I admit that." He said it defiantly.

"Why?"

"She asked for some."

"And you knew where to get it?"

"Yes."

"Despite the fact that you were already in trouble with the police, you were messing around with drugs."

He nodded uneasily.

"Doesn't that strike you as stupid? As well as deceitful to me."

"It was only a bit of cannabis, Ma, not a stash of heroin. Anyway, Nella never did like that school and wants to finish her A levels at the college instead. It's no big deal, Ma, so get it straight."

"That's the point, Sam. At long last I have got it straight. You caused a young girl to get kicked out of school, you committed an illegal offence, yet you call it no big deal and refuse to accept your share of the responsibility. Just like in the off-licence. You told me you had learnt your lesson there and I believed you, but you lied."

Sam leapt to his feet. "No, I didn't lie. I swear I didn't. The robbery was wrong and I'll never do anything like that ever again. I'm mature enough to know better now."

Anna strode towards him until she was only inches away. "All actions have consequences, Sam, and you have to face up to yours. No more moral cowardice. Maybe then you'll learn what mature means."

He reached out and put a hand on her shoulder. "Ma, I tell you I have already learnt that. I know I have to live with myself and look myself in the face every day." He squeezed her shoulder and his brown eyes searched her face anxiously for a sign of relenting. "I'm not a moral coward, despite what you may think."

"I hope you're right."

"I am, Ma. I know I am. But I'm sorry I have hurt you like this."

"So am I."

"I won't do it again."

"You won't give drugs to Nella ever again? Or to anyone else?"

"No, I promise."

Anna nodded and allowed him to hug her.

"To freedom." Sam raised his glass.

"To freedom," Lloyd echoed.

"To freedom. And to the good health of Mrs Anstey," Anna added. They all sipped their champagne.

It had been Sam's idea. He had rung Lloyd and invited him over for a celebration drink and though Lloyd had to attend a mayoral function that evening, he had promised to sneak away early from it and be at the flat by nine o'clock. The telephone call had come as something of a surprise considering the fracas in the teashop that afternoon, but Sam had made no reference to it.

"Would you like some more?" Sam asked, offering the green bottle that he had produced so proudly and opened with an excess of noise and bubbles.

Champagne was not exactly Lloyd's favourite tipple but he accepted with good grace. Whatever had gone on earlier between Sam and Anna had obviously been settled because they were certainly amicable now. Amicable, that is, except for an undercurrent of wariness. It was as if they had both had enough of each other.

"Good luck, Sam," Lloyd said. "Now you've been given a second chance, it's time to get on with life."

"That's exactly what I intend to do. I want to thank you both for all your help. I am grateful. And I know you must think I've been a complete dork."

Lloyd nodded. "The mind and morals of a lemming. And that's an insult to lemmings."

"Right. I know that."

"So you should, Sam," Anna said. "You've made life hell for us all, including Danny. He has . . ."

The sound of the front door banging open interrupted her.

"Talk of the devil," Sam said with obvious relief. "Hey, Danny boy," he called out, "come in here and get your tongue stuck into these bubbles."

The reply was slow in coming from the hallway. "Nah, I'm

going to bed." Danny's voice, even by his recent moody standards, sounded on the higher scale of uptight.

"Hey, bro, come on, don't be a deadbeat." Sam loped out of the room. "I'm pouring champagne, so you . . ." His words stopped in mid-air. "Fucking hell, Danny, what's happened to you?"

Anna was out of her chair before Lloyd had even registered what he'd heard.

This time it wasn't just the tee-shirt that was shredded. Danny's chest was bisected by long shallow cuts. They had stopped bleeding but looked raw and painful. One cheekbone was wearing an angry bruise.

"Who did this, Danny?" Anna demanded.

But Danny gave Sam a dirty look. "You should know," he said, and walked into the kitchen where he started to dab off some of the dried blood with the dish-cloth.

Anna took it gently from him, brought out the cotton-wool and warm water, and set to work on him. "Lloyd, will you make him a cup of hot chocolate, please, and Sam, go and get him another tee-shirt." Danny squealed like a puppy when the TCP hit the scratches.

"Okay, Danny, what happened and why?" Anna asked quietly.

"It was just some guys. No big deal."

"No, Danny," Lloyd said, "this is a serious attack and must be reported to the police."

"No."

"Yes," his mother said firmly. "This isn't the first time, is it?"

He shook his head reluctantly.

Sam grabbed his brother's shoulder and shook him sharply. "What is this all about? Why do you say I should know? Tell me."

"Or what? Or you'll put a matching bruise on the other cheek?"

"If that's what it takes."

"Sam! Stop it," Anna snapped.

"You are going to have to tell us in the end, Danny," Lloyd interrupted. "You might as well get it over with now."

"I'll break their necks," Sam said fiercely.

Danny broke free from Sam's grip, pulled the clean tee-shirt over his head to hide the damage and capitulated. "Okay, okay, but you'll only go and make it worse for me, I know."

"I'll make it worse for the bastards who . . ."

"Shut up, Sam," Lloyd said.

They waited. Eventually it came out.

"It's someone called Zack, and his mates. Friends of yours, Sam, they say."

"They're not friends of . . ."

"Shut up, Sam. You've done more than enough already." It was Anna this time. "Carry on, Danny."

He sipped his hot chocolate to give himself time. "They've been threatening me for weeks. Three of them. Everywhere I go, they're there. It got so I didn't want to leave the house."

"But why on earth would McCauley threaten you?" Anna asked.

"I can guess," Sam said.

"Why?"

"To make sure I keep quiet, that I'm not tempted to go to the police. He's too stupid to realise they already know it was him."

"Oh Sam," Anna exclaimed. "What have we done? I protect one son, while the other . . ."

"It's your fault, Ma," Danny burst out. "You wouldn't tell me what was going on. You kept everything from me even though it was obvious something was wrong, with the police asking questions and everything. It was like you couldn't trust me or something."

"No, Danny, no. That wasn't the reason. I didn't want to worry or upset you, that's all. I wanted to protect you from it."

"Ma, I'm not a kid any more."

"But why didn't you tell your mother or Sam what was happening to you?" Lloyd asked. "There was no point getting beaten up and not passing on the message."

Danny stuck out his chin stubbornly and glared at Sam. "You two weren't telling me anything, so I wasn't going to tell you anything."

"You're nuts, bro, but I'm sorry. Sorry for what I got you into.

So right now I'm going to get you out of it.'' Sam headed for the door.

"Sam," Anna shouted, "don't you dare go. You'll get into more trouble. Leave it to the police."

He shook his head. "Sorry, but I can't. The police would ask too many questions." He continued into the hall.

Lloyd looked at Anna's panic-stricken face, sighed inwardly and strode after the boy. "No, Sam, forget it. If you go anywhere near McCauley, you risk getting hauled into prison."

"That's a risk I'll have to take. I'm not having him beating up on my brother."

"All very noble. What a pity your ideals weren't quite so high when you walked into that off-licence in the first place."

Sam ducked his head. "Okay, I know. It's my fault. That's why I'm going to sort it out now."

"Where is McCauley hiding?"

"I don't know for sure. But he might be with a kid called Sparky Roberts. He hangs out in the Black Kitten."

"All right, leave it to me. I'll sort McCauley out." Lloyd could not believe what he had just said. Who did he think he was? John Wayne? Somehow, without noticing, he was up to his neck in this family.

"Thank you, Lloyd." It was Anna. She was standing behind him and when he turned and saw her eyes warm with gratitude, he knew he was stuck with it. "I'll come with you," she added.

"No, Anna."

"Don't be daft, Ma."

"Ma, you're a girl."

For a moment, Lloyd thought she was going to tear a strip off them, but instead she smiled softly. "A man's gotta do what a man's gotta do, and all that rubbish, you mean?"

"You bet yer sweet life, little lady."

Anna put a hand on Lloyd's arm. "Take care, cowboy. We've had enough shoot-outs round here." In front of her sons, she leaned up and kissed him on the mouth. Brief maybe, but nevertheless a kiss. A little gratitude, it seems, goes a long way when it comes to families.

*   *   *

Lloyd felt as if he were back in kindergarten. The Black Kitten was strictly for youngsters. Judging by appearances, at least half of them were under-age, but that did not stop them drinking and smoking like veterans. The bouncers on the door must be doing a roaring trade in kick-backs. It was only ten-thirty in the evening, so the serious clubbers were not yet out of bed, which meant it wasn't too much of a struggle to reach both bar and barman.

"Scotch and soda," he ordered, and lit himself a cigarette while he waited.

The club was the usual dark cave with strobe lighting, but this time the walls were riddled with slinky black kittens, all coy and cute. Lloyd took a long drag on his cigarette for something to do and blew a snake of smoke into the blue haze that rose like evening mist off the dance floor. When his drink arrived he hung on to the barman, who was young and pushy, long enough to ask a few questions.

"I'm told a guy called Sparky Roberts hangs around here. Do you know him?"

"Sure, I know him. I know most of the kids that come in here."

"Observant, are you?"

"Yeah." He ran a smug hand over his slicked hair. "Professional, that's me."

"Using your professional expertise, would you therefore point out to me which one is Sparky Roberts?" He slid a five-pound note across the counter.

The barman palmed it smoothly, skimmed a glance round the room and said, "He ain't here."

Lloyd pulled another fiver from his pocket, rustled it ostenta- tiously, then replaced it in his pocket. "Let me know when he arrives."

"Yeah, sure will. You wait there and I'll tip you the wink when I see him."

"Don't take all night. I haven't got that kind of patience." Lloyd parked himself on a stool.

An hour and the rest of his cigarettes later, the barman tapped his shoulder. "He's in the corner, over there by the picture of Cat-Woman."

Lloyd studied the group in question. Two girls of varying shades of Pamela Anderson and a teenage boy who was laughing a lot. "The kid with the big hair and a bad case of freckles?"

"That's him. A crack-head, I hear. Can't keep his hands off blondes."

Lloyd passed over the second fiver and skirted the heaving mass of bodies that gyrated on the dance-floor, until he reached the table he wanted.

"Sparky Roberts?"

The boy was seated between the two girls, an arm around each. "Yeah? That's me."

"Could I have a word with you?"

"I'm busy," he grinned. "I've got my hands full." The girls giggled in unison.

"Your ears don't look too busy, so listen to this. I want you to pass on a message to Zack McCauley."

Instantly the boy's face went blank. "Don't know the bloke."

"That's not what I hear."

"Then you hear wrong."

"I want you to go to see this person you don't know and tell him I've got something for him. Something from his friend, Sam."

"I don't know what shit you're talking about."

"No, but McCauley will. Tell him I'm nothing to do with the police but want a word in private."

"I never heard of no McCauley."

"Just tell him. And don't take long. I'll wait here by the bar for another hour and then I'm gone."

"You've made a mistake. I'm staying here with my sweet angels." He kissed the girl on his right and the other one pouted prettily at Lloyd.

He headed back to the bar. His stool had been taken, so he bought himself another pack of cigarettes and a bottle of Evian, and leaned against a mock-marble pillar to consume them.

The hour was more than up. The Black Kitten had grown increasingly playful with every passing minute, while the noise level and body-count rose hand in hand. Lloyd had noticed the boy slip away a while ago but he was gone for so short a time that he wondered if he had just taken a trip to relieve himself. He gave it another half-hour and was just contemplating the possibility of approaching the boy once more, when suddenly another body was leaning against his pillar with him.

"I hear you've got something for me."

Lloyd looked at him. Tall and thin with malicious pale eyes that had pupils like caverns you could hide in. His bony hands kept fingering his face, as if they were too nervous to keep still.

"That depends on who you are."

"Look, man, I'm not here to play games. I'm the guy you asked for."

"Zack McCauley?"

"Yeah, but who the fuck are you? I've been over this place like one of them sniffer-dogs and I can't smell no fuzz here."

"No, I'm not with the police."

"So who are you?"

"It doesn't matter. I'm a friend of the Forrests and I am here to give you something."

"So what's holding you up?" He held out one of the bony hands.

"Not in here. It's too obvious."

"Don't give me that crap. I'm not going out in no dark alleyways, man. I'm not stupid."

"The gents cloakroom will do."

McCauley peeled his skeleton off the pillar and set off without a word. After a couple of minutes Lloyd followed him. He found him bent over a washbasin, rinsing his nose, and wondered what junk he had just been shoving up it. Christ, Sam must have been really bewitched by that girl to let himself get caught up with this trash. Two other youths were standing at the urinals but immediately recognised that they weren't wanted and hurried out.

As soon as they had left, Lloyd stepped up close to McCauley and said threateningly, "Don't you ever touch the young Forrest kid again. I'm warning you that I'll break your bloody neck if you come anywhere near him."

McCauley backed off. Lloyd was not a person he intended to mess with hand to hand. The man was not tall but looked fucking fit, as if his muscles knew their way around, and McCauley was too smart to tangle with them. His hand started heading for his pocket but before it got there, Lloyd had grabbed him and rammed him fiercely against the wall.

"Do you understand, you scumbag?"

One hand was pressing hard on McCauley's chest and a forearm was jammed across his throat. He tried to speak but the pressure on his windpipe prevented it. He nodded instead.

"Good. I'm glad you're not totally stupid. So get this as well. Stay away from Sam too. Don't you drag your filthy habits and gutter morals anywhere near him. He's clean now and I intend to make sure he stays that way. Got that?"

McCauley's breath was coming in short painful gasps. He blinked his agreement. If he could just get his hand to his pocket, he would show this big bastard where gutter morals got you. On top, that's where. On top. His throat was burning and his head felt as if it would explode if it didn't get more oxygen, but his fingers homed in automatically on the flick-knife. It was like a part of him. The steel was in his hand and ready to slice into flesh, when Lloyd struck.

He seized McCauley's wrist and smashed it against the wall again and again. McCauley tried to scream as he felt a bone crack in his hand, but only a moan escaped past the pain in his throat. The knife dropped to the floor. Lloyd kicked it away.

"You don't seem to have got your head straight yet," he growled. "Let me help you." He yanked him off the wall and smashed him back against it, so that his head cracked numbingly on the hard concrete.

McCauley whimpered and would have fallen to the floor if Lloyd had not been holding him up.

"Now do you get the message?"

At that moment three teenagers burst in through the door, took one look at what was going on and walked out again. Lloyd ignored the interruption.

"Right, now we're getting somewhere. You leave the Forrest family alone and I'll leave you alone. That seems a fair deal to me, especially after what you've put them through. Agreed?"

He nodded weakly.

"Say it, you stinking piece of slime."

McCauley looked as if he would rather kill Lloyd than agree with him, but nevertheless whispered hoarsely, "Agreed."

"That's settled then." Lloyd released his grip on the youth who immediately slid down the wall to the floor, nursing his damaged right hand.

"You fucking bastard," McCauley hissed.

"That was from me. This is from Sam." He tossed an envelope on to the floor.

McCauley reached for it with his good hand and opened it with difficulty. He drew out a thick bundle of ten-pound notes. His pale eyes widened with appreciation, then looked up at Lloyd suspiciously. "What the fuck is this?"

"Four hundred and fifty pounds."

"What for?"

"That's your half of the stolen money from Porter's Off-licence. Sam is being fair. Fairer than you deserve. He wants me to inform you that he has no intention of going to the police and is giving you the money that would have been yours. All you have to do is take it and clear out of this town. Go and pollute somewhere else."

McCauley grinned nastily and rubbed his throat. "What are those kids to you?" he said huskily. "Nothing, I bet. It's the mother, isn't it? A tasty bit of skirt she is. After a quick shag there, are you?" He managed a croaking laugh. "I fancied a go at her myself, those tits of hers are . . ."

The fist thumped into his face and he toppled over on his side, his mouth oozing blood. When he looked up, Lloyd had left.

24

Anna was worried. It was one-thirty in the morning and still Lloyd was not back. She was restless and could not settle, despite a hot bath and steaming mug of camomile. The boys had stuck close to her all evening – whether for her comfort or theirs, she wasn't sure – but at midnight she had packed them off to bed. When she checked them a few minutes ago, Danny was fast asleep but Sam was awake and shifting his furniture around, as if rearranging his life. She had apologised to Danny. He had grunted and groaned a fair bit, but when Sam sat him down and told him the truth about what had happened, he was so shocked that he stopped complaining. But he and she both knew that she had let him down.

Oh hell, this whole business of bringing up kids was impossible. And there was no one else to blame for your mistakes, when you were a single parent. Mistakes like Nick Steed. The thought of her own naïveté made her cringe. She had left messages at the gallery for him, but he had not contacted her. Of course not, why should he? He was on to bigger and better things now, where girls had longer legs and younger skin. She had been a convenience when he was short of cash for the summer, that's all. Whether or not he was the one who had stolen from her, she would never know, but she could kick herself for her wilful stupidity.

She prowled the sitting-room, peering out of the window at intervals to search for headlights in the darkness, but nothing moved out there. Oh, Lloyd, take care of yourself. Please take care. There are vicious thugs out there at night. I couldn't bear it if . . .

Her prowling jerked to a halt.

Oh no you don't. You have already made a fool of yourself over Nick Steed because loneliness got the better of you. Kids growing up and biological urges taking over. Not again. And Lloyd was right about your being a bad judge of character, wasn't he?

Maybe.

Or maybe not. Perhaps the reason she chose the artist was because somewhere deep inside herself, in some dark hidden corner that she didn't want to look at, she knew he was not right for her, so there was no risk of a real relationship. No fear of falling in love. No need to push him away like she did Lloyd. She had fallen in love with Ian and almost died of pain when he was taken away from her. Love was too dangerous. Like a fire that drew you to it with its warmth and dazzling colour and then burnt you to a crisp when you got too close.

With an impatient shake of her head she resumed the prowling.

The Rover drew up outside the teashop and Lloyd switched off the engine. The silence was a sweet relief. His ears were still throbbing from the bruising they had received in the nightclub and he could do with a proper drink to wash out all that clean water swilling around inside him.

He wondered whether Anna was still awake. There were lights on in the flat above but that didn't mean that she hadn't gone to bed while waiting for him to return. He liked the image of her in bed and held on to it while he lit a cigarette, but he had only got as far as speculating about the colour of her sheets and her nightdress, when the street-door to the flat opened and she stood there in that frumpy old dressing-gown of hers that he liked. It made her look so accessible. She must have been watching for his car. That thought gave him an unexpected kick of pleasure somewhere under his ribs and he realised how long it was since he had wanted anyone to tie even a slender string to him.

He got out of the car. "Don't look so worried. I'm still in one piece and so is McCauley. Just about. It's only my reputation as an upright citizen of this town that is shattered because I'm now infamous as a dedicated voyeur at teenage clubs." He said it to make her laugh, but she didn't.

"You found him?"

"Yes."

"No police?"

"None."

She breathed a deep sigh of relief and said, "Come on up." She led the way upstairs but the dressing-gown hid all but her ankles from his view. In the sitting-room, she turned to face him. Her blonde hair was tousled and her brow creased in a frown, as if she had been giving herself a hard time while he was gone, but her eyes were intent on his as she said, "Tell me what happened."

"I found his freckled friend, Sparky Roberts, in the Black Kitten. I left a message that I wanted to see McCauley and, hey presto, up he pops beside me."

"Unpleasant, isn't he?"

"He certainly is." Lloyd recalled McCauley's comments about Anna. "A slimeball of the worst kind."

"I'm surprised he turned up at all, knowing that the police must be looking for him."

"Apparently he checked over the place and myself thoroughly before making his move. A junkie like that has probably learnt to smell coppers at fifty paces." Lloyd sat down on the sofa to distance Anna and her dressing-gown from the range of his hands. He felt tired, too tired to be sure he could control them. Or wanted to, for that matter. "I dangled a juicy bait for him and he came up for it, like the slimy eel that he is. I warned him off the boys fairly forcefully."

Anna gave him a long look, then poured him a scotch from the bottle ready on the table and handed it to him. She sat down next to him on the sofa.

"Do you think McCauley will leave Danny alone now, Lloyd? Or should I go to the police?"

Lloyd swallowed a mouthful of his drink and felt it burn a hole in his tiredness. "That's up to you, Anna, but any involvement with Zack McCauley will drag Sam back into the limelight. I think there's a good chance McCauley will push off elsewhere for a while, but of course he might always come back. Like I said before, Sam is a sitting-duck for blackmail. His only chance is to brazen it out and deny everything."

Anna's eyes darkened and she fiddled with the end of the belt of her dressing-gown. "What bait did you use? To tempt out this eel."

Lloyd hesitated.

"What bait, Lloyd?"

She had a right to know.

"Money."

She did not look surprised. "What money?"

"Money that I said was from Sam to buy him a ticket to another town."

She nodded. "How much money?"

"Does it matter?"

"Yes."

"His share of the robbery."

"But it was thrown away in a dustbin."

"I know."

"How big a share?"

"Half."

"Four hundred and fifty pounds?"

"That's right."

She had wound the belt into a neatly rolled ball in the palm of her hand. "That's a lot of money I owe you."

"Forget it."

"No, I won't forget it. I will repay it all." She said it in a low voice and carefully unravelled the ball. "I won't forget any of it." She raised her eyes to his. "Thank you, Lloyd. Thank you for everything."

Now was the perfect moment to take her in his arms and kiss her, but he was acutely aware that she could hardly say no in the circumstances. And he didn't want gratitude.

"I tell you what," he smiled, "you can repay me in dinners."

"Dinners?"

"Yes. I never did get that slap-up meal you promised me, but how about a few tasty home-cooked meals? With all the trimmings. On a Sunday evening after a hard day's sailing, I reckon that might just about compensate me."

"You should be so lucky!" she exclaimed. "I'm dead on my

feet by then and not even my children get that service. Baked beans on toast is about my limit on a Sunday evening."

"No steak and chips?"

"No chance," she laughed. "But you're welcome to share our beans on toast, if you like."

He swallowed more of his drink and wondered if it was a serious offer, but decided to change the subject. "How has Danny coped with it all? I presume you've told him what really happened."

"Yes, Sam did. He is shocked, of course, a cross between horror and sneaking admiration for big brother's antics, I suspect, but at least he understands the consequences of getting carried away on the wrong track. A timely lesson, I hope. Interestingly, he said he didn't think Sam was that stupid." She shook her head. "Neither did I."

"What did Sam say about the Nella Torrence business?"

"He admitted it. Of course he promised not to do it again but it's too late for poor Nella, isn't it?"

"Come on, Anna, don't chuck in the towel. At least he's seen sense now and is back on the straight and narrow. You're lucky, for Christ's sake."

Abruptly she removed the glass from his hand, finished off the last mouthful of scotch in it and placed it on the floor.

"I know I'm lucky," she said. "And it's not just Sam who has seen sense." She leaned forward, took his face in her hands and kissed him full on the mouth. "To hell with kids."

Lloyd didn't bother wasting time on surprise, but did what he had done in his head ten thousand times, put his arms around her and kissed her long and hard. She tasted sweet and moist, and her skin was as soft as snowflakes on his tongue. He wanted to eat her all up and then ask for more, to take her sailing on his boat and see her blonde hair and her laugh snatched by the wind, and make love to her in a sandy cove where he could gaze at her honey skin in the sunlight and . . .

"Lloyd," she whispered against his mouth, "how can I have been so stupid?"

"Easy," he murmured, and brushed his lips down the smooth slope of her neck. "Look at your sons. It runs in the family."

"You bastard," she laughed. "And don't mention my sons to

me again. Ever." Her hands rippled down his back setting off minor explosions under his skin.

"You mean Sam and Danny?" he teased.

"Never heard of them." She slid out of her dressing-gown and underneath she was wearing the kind of nightshirt that was like an oversized tee-shirt. This one had a big teddy-bear on the front with a balloon growing out of his mouth saying 'I'm cute' right across her left breast.

She saw him looking at it and said with a smile, "A present from Danny last Christmas. If I'd known this was going to happen, I'd have put on my one and only slinky nightdress."

He bent his head and kissed the balloon. "I like cute, just the way it is."

She started to undo the buttons of his shirt. "Lloyd, I would like to go with you on one of your fishing trips to Wales." Her fingers stroked the muscles of his chest.

"Would you now? So you fancy a wet weekend in a tent?"

She grinned at him. "As long as you don't forget your rod."

That did it. He stood up, scooped her up in his arms and carried her to the bedroom.

"Oh hell, I haven't changed the sheets," she wailed.

"It's not the sheets I'll be looking at," he said as he laid her down and lifted the nightshirt over her head. He suppressed the urge to jump her deliciously naked bones and stretched out beside her on the bed, but she twisted her body, soft and hungry, into his arms. Her lips eagerly took possession of his mouth while her fingers set off to discover the texture of his skin, as if searching for forgotten memories. Under his hands, her body felt as smooth and sleek as the lines of a class racing-boat. But infinitely more desirable.

Some time later, he noticed that her sheets were blue.

Anna stretched as luxuriously as a cat in the bed, cuddled the pillow that lay crumpled beside her and gave it a kiss. It still smelt of him. Lloyd had left at six-thirty that morning, before the boys woke, and though he hadn't actually said that was the reason he was leaving her bed so early, they both understood.

It had hurt to let him go.

The kind of hurt she had forgotten she ever knew.

Her body still tingled with pleasure and stirred restlessly as though in search of Lloyd, so she got up and took a cool shower to shut it up. An hour later she was cooking breakfast when Danny bounced in. In the mornings he reminded her of Tigger, he had so much energy.

"Bacon and eggs. Great!" He pinched a rasher from under the grill and wolfed it down. The bruise on his face looked darker, if anything, but he seemed unconcerned about it, as though just the fact of being included in the family secret at last had turned his world around. "What story do you think I should tell them at school to explain my injuries? That I heroically saved an old lady who was being mugged? That I had a wicked fight with my brother? Or . . ." he paused and gave her a toothy smile ". . . that I got beaten up on the way home yesterday?"

"I'd go for the truth, if I were you." She slid two eggs on to a plate.

"Okay," he grinned, "if that's what you want. I'll just tell them my whole family is criminal and misleads the police."

"Danny, would you like these eggs on your head?"

"No thanks." He took the plate from her and added some bacon and toast. "Did Lloyd sort out that McCauley bastard last night?"

"Yes. You won't hear from him again." She prayed that it was true.

"How did he scare him off?"

"Brute force, I think."

"Mental! The turd deserved it. In your face, McCauley."

"I couldn't agree more." She poured him a glass of milk and kissed his cropped blond head to show she was sorry.

"Aw, Ma, leave off."

She laughed and went back to the bacon.

It was like that all morning. She kept laughing, at nothing in particular but at everything in general. The laughs kept bubbling up and popping out quite uninvited, like froth off the happiness inside her.

"Feeling better, are we?" Esther Miller asked as together they made a heap of sandwiches for a nearby office.

Another laugh sneaked out. "Yes."

"I'm delighted to hear it. And I haven't seen that Sam of yours smiling at customers so much for ages."

The smile had started as soon as Anna told him the result of Lloyd's single-handed manhunt of the night before and had remained throughout his morning shift in the teashop.

"It looks like the Forrests are coming out of the woods," Anna laughed, and turned to see Sam walk into the kitchen.

At his side was Tara Tucker.

Anna froze.

The girl had not changed. Except the look on her face. The eyes were huge, and frightened.

"Ma, Tara just arrived. She wants to talk to me, so I brought her here in the kitchen because I thought you might not want your customers to listen."

Tara frowned. "Sam, don't fuck around. Let's go outside."

"No. Here's fine."

Esther looked from Sam to Anna, bundled the sandwiches into a plastic box and said quickly, "I'll go and drop these round next door."

Anna nodded but continued to stare at Tara. "What do you want?"

Esther tactfully disappeared.

"That's between me and Sam." The girl stretched out a thin arm and held on to his hand. "Come on, Sam. Let's go."

"No. Tell me here." But he did not withdraw his hand.

She stepped closer to him and her skittering eyes looked up into his. "Sam, I'm scared."

"Why, what's happened? Not the police nosing around, is it?"

She nodded and chewed on her lower lip.

"After you?"

Again she nodded and looked miserable. "The pigs."

"But why, Tara? Why you? What have they got on you?" He put a hand on top of hers and held it tight.

"I don't know for sure. But it's Zack. Oh Sam, it's Zack." Tears started to run in black rivulets down her cheeks and she buried her head against his arm.

Sam stroked her hair and Anna could see the concern written all over his face. Damn the girl, she knew every trick in the book.

So what was she up to now? But unlike last time Anna saw her pawing Sam in the teashop and had felt the urge to rip her off her son, this time was different. This time she wanted Sam to do the ripping himself.

Instead he continued stroking the little black head, soothing her sobs. "What's Zack into now?"

The girl shook her head, but couldn't speak.

"Tara," Sam said more firmly, "get it out. What is going on?"

She raised her head and rubbed the back of her hand over her cheeks and nose like a child. "He's dead."

"Dead! I don't believe it! What happened?"

"I killed him."

There was an awful silence, broken only by her sniffs. Anna grabbed a sheet of kitchen-roll and pushed it at the girl.

"How?" she demanded.

"He fried and died," Tara wailed. "He didn't chill out, but just kept popping pills until he fried."

"If he overdosed, it was his own fault," Sam said quickly. "Why did you say you killed him?"

The girl blew her nose and dabbed at her cheeks, but only managed to smear the black streaks further. "We've been hiding out at Mandy's place, but last night he went out for a while and when he came back, he asked me to go over to Donovan's to get some stuff for him. He was scared the fuzz might stop him in the streets."

"So you went and bought for him."

"Yeah. A hell of a lot of it. Not crap either."

"Oh Tara, I told you to lay off the heavy junk."

"I know, Sam, but Zack was rolling in it."

"Where did he get money from? Last I knew, he was broke."

She shook her head uncertainly. "I don't know. But he sure had a wad, with hundreds of pounds. He sent me over to Donovan's with it. That's how I killed him. By buying too much for him."

"That's dumb, Tara. If he ODed, that's his own fault. Not yours. He never knew how to stop whenever he got his hands on some money."

Anna listened, appalled. Oh Lloyd, what have I got you into? You intended the money to get rid of him, but not like this. I hated McCauley for what he did to Sam and to Danny, but I wouldn't wish him dead. Then suddenly she was angry. Angry at McCauley for yet again screwing up her family's happiness while it was still so new and shiny. And angry at Tara. The girl's hand was still holding on to Sam's like a tentacle to drag him down into murky depths.

"What exactly happened, Tara?" Anna asked.

Tara ignored her but told Sam, "When I woke this morning, he was lying beside me on the bed. Cold. It was horrible, Sam, I . . ."

"Lying on your bed?" Sam interrupted.

"Yes, but nothing happened between us, I swear. He was off on his trip and collapsed there. I thought he was asleep."

"Did you call an ambulance?"

"No, it was too late. He was real cold and stiff."

Sam shuddered. "So why are you frightened of the police?"

It dawned on Anna how rational Sam was being. Maybe there really was some sense in that head of his, not just hormones.

"When the police find him, they're bound to come after me. And Mandy will tell them I bought the drugs, I know that bitch will. Oh Sam," she leaned her body against his, "I'm so scared."

Sam looked at her a long time and then said, "Just leave, Tara. Go back to Sheffield and you'll be safe."

She tipped her head back and nuzzled his cheek. "Come with me, Sam."

Anna watched and held her breath.

He bent his head and kissed the girl, but not on the mouth. "I have already made up my mind."

"So you'll come?"

"No. I'm staying here."

Anna breathed again.

Tara stepped away from him and released his hand. "Are you going to remain a mummy's boy all your life, you dork? Can't you see what she's doing to you?" She waved a scornful hand towards Anna. "She's got no man of her own, so she's hanging on to you instead."

"Get out of my kitchen," Anna said quietly.

"Come with me, Sam?"

He was breathing heavily, as if fighting for air, but his face remained steady. "No," he said, "I told you, I'm staying here."

"Sam, please come."

"No."

Suddenly Tara was shouting. "You fucking arsehole, I don't need you anyway. It was just your money I wanted. I can get better than you out of the gutter. And just so you know, I *was* sleeping with Zack and he was a hell of a lot better than you in bed." She opened the door and slammed her way out.

Anna had caught a glimpse of Esther and the customers staring with embarrassment. In the kitchen Sam didn't move. She waited until he finally turned his head towards her.

"Sorry about that," he said shakily.

"Are you okay, Sam?"

He managed something like a smile. "I'm okay. But I think I might go for an HIV test."

Anna shuddered inwardly but said without fuss, "Good idea."

He took a couple of deep breaths and burst out with, "Ma, this is as good a time as any to tell you I'm moving out. Now that it looks as if this is all over, I want to get a place of my own."

Anna felt an unexpected shiver of relief. She nodded. "If that's what you want."

"It is. And a proper job." The shock was leaving his eyes.

"Yes, of course."

"I thought I'd ask Lloyd again. The boatyard is expanding, isn't it, so he's bound to need more staff?"

"But Sam, you've already let him down once. He may not be too keen to go through the experience again."

He nodded uncomfortably but tried a smile on her. "I know, but I really do want to get it right this time."

"Good."

There was nothing more to say. They both wanted to end the conversation but did not know how, and a heavy silence slid into the gap between them.

Esther broke it. She pushed open the kitchen door and asked, "All clear?"

"Yes, all clear. Come on in," Anna encouraged. "No more bullets flying around."

"Or teenage girls," Esther chuckled and eyed Sam curiously. "Customers are waiting to order out there, when you're ready."

"Right," he said quickly, and left.

Esther picked up a knife to start work on a baguette but halted when she saw Anna's face. "Come on, love, cheer up. Sam is safe from that girl's clutches, that's obvious from the way she shot out of here like a scalded cat. So no worries there."

"No, she can't hurt him any more."

"Well then, forget about her and concentrate on whatever it was that had you bouncing around this morning like a dog with two tails."

"You're right, Esther. That's exactly what I intend to do. Sam can get on with his own life and I'll get on with mine." She ducked her head and watched Sam through the hatch as he attended to his customers. "No, I won't worry about that boy any more."

Esther wondered where the usual maternal 'my son' had gone, but decided not to comment, especially as Anna had started humming something softly under her breath that sounded suspiciously like a love-song.

"Hello, Harriet. Any news on Nella?"

"Oh, Anna, I'm so glad you've rung. I need help."

It was not until four-thirty that Anna had managed to escape from the teashop up to the privacy of the telephone in the flat. She had two calls to make, so, saving the best till last, she had dialled the number of Nature's Basket first and found Harriet in tears.

"How is Nella taking it?" Anna asked. "Still in shock, I imagine."

"No, no, not at all. That's what is so infuriating. She's as cheerful as a bloody sunbeam and doesn't seem able to regret a thing. She even says she will be able to concentrate better on her exams now that she won't be constantly irritated by the intrusive and patriarchal attitude of school authorities. Her words, not mine."

"Does she really mean it?"

"Oh yes, I'm sure she does. You know what a bolshy creature she is at heart. She says she'll be much happier at the college where she can do her own thing – whatever that means!"

Anna still felt acutely aware that her son was responsible. "So how can I help?"

"It's Jonathan."

"I thought it might be. How has he reacted?"

"He's gone ballistic. If he's not shouting at her, he's shouting at me. And in between that, he's yelling at the school for not doing its job properly."

"Oh Harriet, I'm sorry. Sounds like hell."

"It is." The blast of nose-blowing trumpeted vigorously down the line. "I haven't mentioned Sam's involvement to him."

"Thanks."

"Nella is denying it, of course, and says she got the dreaded weed from a girl at school."

"That's generous of her. I am always impressed by young people's loyalty to each other, but I hate to have to tell you that Sam admitted it to me. That he was her supplier. I'm really sorry, Harriet, more than I . . ."

"Don't be. If it hadn't been Sam, it would have been someone else. If my daughter had made up her mind to start experimenting, nothing was going to stop her, you know what she's like."

Anna poured silent blessings on her friend's head and thought that it wasn't just young people who knew how to be loyal. "So what can I do to help?"

"Speak to Jonathan and make him see reason. You know how he's always been willing to listen to you. He is threatening to pack her off to boarding-school for her final year."

"What!"

"I know. Gruesome, isn't it? Can you imagine our little darling stuck in that kind of strait-jacket?"

"Does Nella want to go to boarding-school?"

Harriet snorted. "Of course not. Anyway, we can't afford it, but he is talking of selling my field to pay for . . ." Her voice disintegrated into tears.

Anna felt like throttling her son.

"Don't worry, Harriet, he won't do that, I'm certain. He knows what it means to you and why it was bought, so when he cools down, he's bound to see sense. Nella is old enough to make her own choices now and he'll have to accept that fact whether he likes it or not.'' Anna listened to herself with a sense of shock.

"So you'll talk to him?''

"Yes, of course I will. I'll do everything I can to help. When do you want me to come over?''

"Anytime.''

"How about tomorrow? I'll give him another twenty-four hours and then I'll come over after he's had a chance to sleep on it.''

"That sounds a good idea, thanks. I'm really sorry to . . .''

"Not as sorry as I am.''

Anna murmured a few more comforting noises, then said goodbye; but as she hung up, she wondered if it was too late to pack her own kids off to boarding-school, warts and all.

She had just dialled the number of the boatyard, when Danny breezed in, dumped school-bag in one corner, swimming-togs in another, shoes in a muddy heap in the hall and looped his tie round her neck with a deprived, "I'm starving.''

"Go make yourself a sandwich, I'm busy.''

"My mother is a hard-hearted woman,'' he groaned and shuffled off into the kitchen.

Anna found herself counting the beeps as the telephone rang the other end and abruptly realised she was holding her breath. She felt acutely self-conscious. Like on a first date. She exhaled the air to dispel her tension, just as the receiver was picked up and Lloyd's voice said, "Morgan's Boatyard''. She liked his voice. It was crisp but approachable, with just a touch of the sing-song Celtic cadence that she now knew increased dramatically when roused. The knowledge made her smile.

"Hello, Lloyd.''

"Anna.'' There was no doubting the pleasure in the word. "You've called in the nick of time. I was just about to wring my foreman's neck.''

"Why, what has he been up to?''

"Mutiny over machining methods. I'm trying to drag him towards the twenty-first century, but it's not easy. He's determined to stick with his stone-age axe.''

"Sounds undesirable to me."

"Don't mention desire. Tell me instead, how was your day?"

"Lonely."

"Mmm, sounds curable to me."

"What do you prescribe?"

"Soft music and wine to be taken at least once a day."

"I don't think your foreman would appreciate the soft music."

He laughed. "It's not for him. That old reprobate is incurable, as well as tone deaf. Bread and water is all he deserves, and keelhauling if he's lucky."

"Captain Bligh isn't your middle name, by any chance?"

His chuckle sent ripples right down to her toes and she kicked off her shoes to give them air. She had spoken her mind to him a thousand times in the past, so why butterflies now? He was still the same Lloyd.

"Lloyd . . ."

"Yes?"

"I've made a decision."

The line went so quiet she thought it was dead and when he eventually spoke, his voice was less intimate. She felt the loss.

"A decision about what?"

"About me. I've decided you were absolutely right about my being too caught up in cakes and cream teas and coaches. And children. I can't see the wood for the trees."

"And?"

"And so I've decided I need a break, to go away from it all. Business is quiet at the moment."

A long sigh whispered down the line like a draught of cold air. "Anna, I hadn't got you pegged as one of those people who, at the first hint of pressure, need 'space' to run off to find their own self. Or rush to counselling or some other such support to prop them up. Have you changed your mind so easily since this morning? Or is it because you think last night was one of the trees that are blocking your view of the wood."

"Lloyd Morgan, I'll come over and block *your* view with a rolling-pin, if you don't retract such insults. Can't you recognise an invitation when you hear one?"

"An invitation?"

"Yes. To go away together."

"Oh Anna, I thought . . ."

"Well you thought wrong."

"I apologise."

"Apology accepted."

"And I retract any insult. Unreservedly."

"I should damn well think so."

"And as we're talking of reservations, how about dinner tonight at the Weary Ploughman? A nicely chilled glass of Chablis would help us decide when and where to take this break of yours."

She could hear his smile. "You've got yourself a date."

It would not have been her own choice of venue for a candlelit dinner but maybe he wanted to dispel the memory of their last meeting there, or perhaps it was just Nick Steed he wanted to erase. But she had to admit they did a half-decent salmon steak there and the view was certainly romantic, so she wasn't going to argue. Anyway, she had a scary feeling that if the meal were served in a mud-hole in the ground with fins still flapping, she wasn't going to notice. Her eyes were elsewhere.

"I'll pick you up at seven-thirty," Lloyd said, and it sounded as if he was still grinning.

"Don't be late," she teased and hung up.

25

When Anna walked into the kitchen, Danny was munching into a foot-long wedge of French bread that was oozing what looked suspiciously like salami, tuna and honey in colourful dollops on to his school trousers.

"Plates have been invented," Anna commented out of habit, but her heart was not in it, so Danny took no notice. He was reading the local paper on the table with an interest usually awarded only to the sports pages.

"It's got McCauley in here, Ma."

Anna peered over his shoulder at the story that was bannered across the front page under the headline, 'Youth found dead in bed'. It went on to outline the sordid circumstances of his death and infer involvement with drugs, but withheld any specifics. Anna shuddered, tore out the offending article, screwed it into a tight, hard ball and banished it to the bin with a very final "Good riddance." When she looked round, Danny was watching her with his mouth open, teeth poised in mid-bite. He looked worried.

"You okay, Ma?"

"Of course I am."

"You look kind of upset."

Anna touched her cheek with the back of her hand and felt the flushed warmth of her skin. "It's hardly surprising if I am. I've just had a difficult conversation with Harriet Torrence that made me feel as guilty as hell even though it's all Sam's fault, and now I come in here to have McCauley leap up in my face again."

Danny looked uncomfortable. Dumping his sandwich down

on the table where it dribbled its innards on to the battered pine, he said, "Chill out, Ma, everything's okay now. No need to get in a stress. You should take it easy."

Anna gave her son a reassuring smile. "Don't worry, I intend to. I'm going to, as you put it, chill out over a meal tonight – one not cooked by me for a change."

"Oh yeah? At Harriet's house, I suppose."

"No, not health food. I mean in a proper restaurant, with rich cream sauces that clog your arteries, and waitresses I haven't had to train myself."

"Who with?"

"Lloyd."

Danny's blue eyes lost interest, as jaunts with Lloyd Morgan were nothing new. "Is Sam going to be around this evening?"

"Yes. As far as I know he has no plans for going out anywhere, so you and he can watch one of those dreadful videos you like so much, while I'm not here to moan about it."

"Great. We'll pig out on Pringles and popcorn and watch a funny. We haven't seen *Ace Ventura* for ages and Jim Carrey is a blast in it, especially when he . . ."

Anna groaned and headed for the door. "I'm going back to work."

"Ma."

She turned. "Yes?"

"Don't give Sam a hard time, will you?"

"What do you mean?"

"He's taken a lot of grief this summer, with Tara and everything. And that business with Nella was her own dumb fault. So give it a rest now."

"I think you're right, Danny. We're all ready to give it a rest and start watching some funnies. But Sam has got to sort himself out properly." She hesitated. "He's moving out, you know. Permanently."

"Yeah, he told me." He pulled a face that was meant to disguise his disappointment. "I'll miss the stupid bozo."

"I know."

"Won't you?"

"That's not the point, is it? He's more than ready to go and even I am capable of seeing that now. But you never know with that brother of yours, he is just as likely to change his mind and end up coming home again."

"Dream on, Ma!"

"No, I'm not dreaming any more."

He stared at her and chewed his lower lip, then said shyly, "I don't think you can really blame him, Ma."

"Blame him for what?"

"For all this mess." He waved an arm around as if to indicate the whole flat and the family it contained.

Anna sat down at the table. "Is that how you see us? A mess?"

"No, no, I didn't mean that, honest." His footwork was fast, suddenly aware of the hole he was digging for himself. "Of course we're not a mess, not really. We're good mates all of us and I know it's not easy, Ma, not on your own, I mean."

Anna passed no comment but waited for more.

Danny swallowed, picked up the remains of his sandwich, inspected it and put it down again, his gaze not ready to meet hers. "It's just that it's been tougher on him."

"Why on him? Why tougher than on you or on me? I know that after your father's death Sam fell into the role of being man about the house while he was still very young, and certainly he has helped me enormously in the teashop, but . . ."

"You see, that's exactly what I mean. I could just doss around and spend all my time swimming and going in for competitions, but he had to help you."

"No, Danny, he didn't have to."

"Yes, he did. Can't you see? He felt so guilty, so shitty, that he had no choice. He had to make up for it."

"Why on earth should Sam feel guilty? Guilty about what, for heaven's sake?"

"About Dad's death."

Anna's stomach twisted on spikes of alarm. Very gently, she asked, "Why should he feel guilty about Ian's death, Danny? It had nothing to do with him. It was an awful shock for you both, I know, to see your father collapse like that – and to have him die in my arms." She shook her head to keep the image at bay. "Of course I realise it has affected you both deeply, but there's no reason for Sam to feel guilty."

Danny picked up his sandwich and took a fierce bite. "Well he does."

"Has he said so?"

"No."

"Then what makes you think he does?"

"I just know."

Anna nodded, trusting her younger son's instincts about his brother. "Okay, Danny," she had to tread softly because he looked ready to clam up, "can you tell me why Sam feels so guilty? Is it because he didn't come over, like you did, to be with Ian when he died on the dance-floor?"

Danny's eyes flicked up at her with astonishment and then headed back to his sandwich. "Of course not."

"Then why?"

No answer.

"Tell me, Danny. Please, tell me."

He prodded a dollop of honey and licked his finger, then took a deep breath as if resigned to finishing the job he had started. "I thought you knew."

"No, I don't."

He shifted his eyes to hers at last and she saw the disappointment in them. "I guess I thought a mother would be able to see inside his head."

"Well, I can't. That's why I need you to tell me."

"He thinks he killed Dad."

"What!" Anna jumped to her feet. "No, that's ludicrous, you must have got it wrong. Sam can't possibly think that. He has no reason to, none at all."

"But it's true. He does, I know he does, because he mumbled something about it at Dad's funeral. He thinks that if he hadn't pushed Dad to dance with you that last time, he would not have died and would still be with us now." His voice was not as steady now, and Anna wondered if her younger son also believed in Sam's guilt.

"Oh Sam, my poor Sam. Is that what he's been carrying around all these years and I never guessed?"

Danny tried to lighten the mood with a shrug. "A dumb dork, isn't he? No wonder he's so screwed up. He's got so much heavy stuff in his head that he can't look at himself straight."

Anna walked over, put her arms around her son and hugged him close. "Dad's death was not Sam's fault, my darling. His heart was in a bad state, and though we didn't know it at the time, he was lucky to have lasted as long as he did. The previous dance could have done it or the next rugby game or cycle ride. At least we were with him when the heart-attack happened, all of us. I've always been grateful for that. I know we haven't talked about this stuff for a long time, but I promise you, Sam wasn't responsible at all."

Danny nodded and stood up, gently extricating himself from her embrace. "Of course he wasn't. I know that, even if he doesn't." He headed for the door, trailing crumbs from the remains of the sandwich in his hand.

"Danny."

"Mmm?"

"Thanks."

He gave her a flash of cornflower-blue and a cheesy grin. "Hey, what are brothers for?"

Anna made a real attempt to be friendly towards Sam when she returned to the teashop, but it didn't work out right despite her efforts. Whatever mess was in his head, she couldn't let it excuse his present behaviour, and it was as if the gap that had opened up between them would need more than good intentions to fill it. But even after they shut up shop and returned to the flat, they could manage no more than a stilted exchange. In glaring contrast was the easy flow of Danny's chatter to them both as he declared his intention of making the most of an evening uncluttered by training or homework.

"The pool is being treated for bugs or something, which means I'm in a swim-free zone. Ma is out on the town tonight, so let's party for two, bro."

"Way to go, tadpole. You and me and Jim Carrey."

The boys chortled and thumped each other's biceps with great gusts of machismo, so Anna knew she had lost them to their boys-own world where she was not welcome. Instead, she treated herself to a brisk hot shower during which she let loose with a lively version of 'Fly Me To The Moon' and thanked her lucky stars that she'd had the sense to produce two sons. They could do their buddy-bonding act. With hardly a pang, she recognised that they mattered more to each other now than she did.

When she stepped out of the shower and towelled herself dry, her scalp tingled and it didn't take much of an effort to nudge the boys out of her head completely and concentrate on the evening to come. Determined not to be late this time, she rummaged through her wardrobe only to find it depressingly thin on the ground where anything sexy was concerned. There hadn't exactly been much demand for it, had there? Holding up a dusky-pink dress that was new but definitely in the smart rather than the erotic category, she groaned and vowed a spending spree on her flexible friend. A spree that included a flimsy silk nightdress, a horrendously expensive one that shimmered in all the right places and made her totally irresistible to Lloyd Morgan.

The thought of him stuck a grin on her face and a tickle of nerves in her throat. Oh hell, she was worse than a teenager. She pulled on the pink dress and brushed her hair hard but it didn't stop snapshot memories of last night from flickering through her head – of the hand on her bare thigh, fingernails clean and square and stroking her flesh with a touch that made her ache inside, of his tongue pink and moist on her stomach, and of the pupils of his eyes, huge and wanting her. She tore the pink dress up over her burning cheeks and replaced it with a delphinium-blue one that, though undeniably older, displayed a decent chunk of cleavage and, she hoped, emphasised slim hips. Anyway, Lloyd had once remarked that he liked her in it and that was good enough for her. It did not surprise her that she had remembered his comment, even though it had been made many months ago. It was just as she was splashing on a liberal dose of scent and hoping it had not gone off in the two years since she bought it, that the doorbell rang.

"Oh Lloyd, you're far too early," she panicked, and grabbed for her box of earrings, sending it tumbling on to the floor instead. "Damn it," she yelled, and called out, "Danny, get the door for me, will you?"

The earrings were scooped back where they belonged and a gold pair that matched the chain round her neck fixed into place.

She stepped back to study the overall effect and was surprised. What struck her most about the woman looking out at her from the mirror was not the dress or the shining blonde hair or the gold at her throat. No, none of that made any impact on her. It was the expression. There was a glow on her face that had nothing to do with make-up, and hope in her eyes that spoke of a future. Anna gazed into the eyes and smiled at them, as at a friend she had not seen for a long time. They smiled back at her.

Abruptly the door burst open and Danny shouted, "Ma, get out here, quickly," and disappeared.

What were those two boys up to now? She left her room and hurried towards the sitting-room where she could hear voices. If they had spilled their cokes over the carpet again just when Lloyd had arrived, she would . . . The sight that hit her stopped her dead on her heels. The room was full of men, big and broad and anything but friendly.

"Are you Mrs Forrest?" He was dark and tough, like he knew his way round the back streets.

Anna nodded. "I am. And who on earth are you?"

"I am Sergeant Collier." He flipped open his badge and at the same time waved a sheet of paper at her. "I have a warrant to search these premises."

"How dare you come into my house like this? This is an invasion of my rights and I intend to report . . ."

Sergeant Collier handed her the sheet of paper. "Here is your copy of the warrant. My officers have legal authority to search your flat."

Anna's brain began to take in the situation and realised with a thud that all these people were police. But they weren't in uniform, nor in suits, so it was obvious they weren't CID making further enquiries about the robbery. That had been her first fear. She tried to remain calm and when she studied them more carefully, she found that there were six of them, including one policewoman she had not noticed earlier. All were casually dressed in jeans and denim jackets, two had stubble on their jaws and one had his hair cut like a skinhead. They had to be a drug squad.

No, not drugs. Please don't let it be drugs.

Three of them hovered round Sam as if they expected him to make a break for it.

"What are you searching for, Sergeant Collier?" The question was unnecessary.

"We have reason to believe that your son, Sam Forrest, is in possession of controlled drugs." He turned away as if tired of talk and ready to get down to business. "Which is your room, Sam?"

"No," Anna objected, "this is a mistake. Sam wouldn't . . ." But she stopped when she looked at her son's face. Of course Sam would.

She felt ill.

The police officers took over the flat, filling it with their quick efficient movements, checking each room briefly, then homing in on Sam's bedroom. Three of them did the searching while one wrote notes down on a pad and the policewoman stayed with Danny in the sitting-room, but one black officer was stationed near the front door to prevent any attempt at escape. They did their work with a professional indifference that made it feel like rape.

Anna hated them. She did not care if they were just doing their job, they had no right to be in her house, treating her and her family as if they were criminals. They wanted only Sam in the bedroom while they searched it, but Anna insisted on being present to make certain they observed legal niceties – like not planting anything on him.

But it was humiliating; humiliating and degrading.

She was bundled with Sam into the corner by the window while they took the room apart. The bed was stripped, mattress overturned, cupboards emptied, shoes searched, socks turned inside-out, books shaken and even CD cases opened. Sam stood rigid beside her, his face like dead ash and his fingers trembling behind his back. He would not look at her. Neither of them spoke.

"Do you have the key to this compartment?"

It was Sergeant Collier. Wearing plastic gloves, he had been through all the drawers of Sam's desk, but had turned up nothing to interest him. There was just the locked cupboard on the left-hand side of his desk, the one that had defeated Anna when she searched this same room at the beginning of the summer – when Sam had still been her child.

Sam shook his head. "No."

"Where is the key?"

"I lost it. Months ago, I lost it."

The officer sighed. "Look, we are going to have to break open that lock if you don't give us the key and that will make an unnecessary mess of the desk. Is that what you want?"

Anna looked at Sam. His lips were white, except for a tiny trickle of blood where his teeth had bitten into one corner.

"Sam," she murmured.

He stared at the desk.

"Is that what you want?" Sergeant Collier repeated. When he still received no response, at a nod from him one of the other officers, the one that looked like a skinhead, approached with a metal implement designed to make mincemeat of unco-operative locks.

At the last minute, Sam whispered, "Don't."

The officer stopped in mid-action and Collier held out a waiting hand. "The key?"

Sam coloured fiercely, walked over to the radiator near the door and, under everyone's watchful scrutiny, extracted a key from behind it that was held in place with sticky tape. No one commented. He looked at it lying in the palm of his hand as if it were the key to a world he was frightened to lose but then, without a word, handed it over. Sergeant Collier wasted no time but immediately unlocked the compartment, let out a contented "Bingo!" and started lifting out objects.

Anna was in shock. Her eyes watched but her brain wouldn't take it in. This was what you saw on television, on one of those fly-on-the-wall documentaries that made you feel good about yourself and thankful to be safe from their intrusive eyes and controlled aggression. This didn't happen in your own home. It just didn't.

First, a flat rectangular box was brought out, black and velvety like a jewellery box, and for one ghastly moment Anna believed Sam had taken to burglary; but when it was opened, it contained just a pair of scales. Miniature brass scales. She stared at them blankly for a second and then realisation hit. Oh no, what more proof was needed? But more came. Neat little blocks of it, like dried-up Oxo cubes, each one wrapped in protective cling-film.

They were handed over to the exhibits officer who placed them in a plastic bag and labelled it.

Sergeant Collier looked up from the desk at Sam. "You know what this substance is?"

Sam hesitated and Anna could see him choosing which way to go. Eventually he nodded. "Yes."

"It looks like skunk cannabis. Is it yours?"

"No."

"Where did it come from?"

"From a friend."

"How did it get into your possession?"

"He asked me to look after it for him."

"Which friend?"

"Zack McCauley."

Oh Sam, they're not stupid, don't lie to them.

It took an effort to keep the words inside her head. An officer in a black leather jacket was writing down everything Sam said and she wanted to tell her son to shut up. A solicitor, that's what he needed right now, she had to ring David Appleton. Her mind was starting to shunt into action once more. Collier was lifting a note-pad out of the desk-locker and as he flicked through it, Anna could see its pages contained lists of names that were all in Sam's handwriting.

"Is this notebook yours?" Sam was asked.

"Yes." He had no option.

Collier nodded, as if satisfied, and handed it over to the exhibits officer for more bagging and labelling. A tin containing Rizlas followed, a lighter and a long manila envelope. When the policeman's hand pulled out from the envelope a neat wad of banknotes, Anna reached screaming-point.

"Sam!"

His brown eyes looked at her wretchedly but he said nothing. Collier went through the "Is this yours?" routine again, but received only a resentful "No."

Anna looked round the wreck of her son's bedroom as if she were seeing the wreck of his life and decided she'd had enough. She walked out, but as she did so, she did not miss the look of relief on Sam's face. Behind her she heard the words, "Sam Forrest, I am arresting you on suspicion of dealing in controlled drugs. You do not have to say anything, but . . .''

She quickened her step. What the hell was going on? This was insane. Just when her life at last seemed smooth and ready to run on straight tracks, this bomb goes off in her lap. Blowing great holes in everything. Surely she had been through this already – the fear that cripples you, the police, the lies and, above all, the sickening knowledge that her son was a criminal. She had been through it once and survived. Only this evening in the shower she had been so happy that Sam was free, and that she was on the starting-blocks of a life of her own and eager to get on with it. Not just with Lloyd, but with everything. So what the hell had gone wrong?

In the sitting-room her other son was talking quietly with the policewoman and both turned round with expectant faces as Anna entered, but she had no desire to voice Sam's guilt. They would find out soon enough. She stood by the window, watching the evening lights flicker invitingly in Market Square, and waited. It was not long before heavy footsteps announced the return of the drug squad and they stood with Sam in their midst, like a posse out for a hanging.

''Mrs Forrest, we have arrested your son, Sam, and are going to take him down to the station for further questioning.'' The policeman's eyes, hard and cold as the metal on his badge, shifted speculatively on to Danny. ''How old are you, son?''

''Fifteen.''

''And which is your room?''

''Down the corridor, second on the left.''

Collier continued to observe the boy, deciding whether it was likely to be worth the effort of a further search, when one of the other officers asked quietly, ''Do you want a body search done?''

Out of the corner of her eye, Anna saw the policewoman step closer. ''No,'' she exclaimed sharply. ''Don't. Danny and I knew nothing about what was in Sam's room and I assure you there's nothing in Danny's, nor hidden in our pockets or anywhere else. He swims, for heaven's sake, he's into health and fitness. Not drugs.''

"I dare say you would have said the same about your other son, Mrs Forrest," Collier commented.

It wasn't true. She felt her cheeks colour and didn't know whether the anger or the humiliation was the harder to control. All she was certain of was that if any one of these officers laid a finger on her family, she would scream rape.

Collier stood assessing her for a moment, then shook his head. "No, no body search. We're finished here." He turned to leave but Anna interrupted him.

"Sergeant, I would like a minute to speak to my son. To Sam. Alone."

Collier shook his head again. "Sorry, no. That's not possible."

"All right, not alone, but let me speak to him. Please."

The policeman glanced across at Sam, who looked quickly away and glared sullenly at the floor as if the last thing he wanted right then was a session with his mother.

"Okay, Denton, in the kitchen with the lad. You've got two minutes, Mrs Forrest."

The policewoman took hold of Sam's arm and escorted him into the kitchen without a word. It took Anna a second to absorb what was happening, then she strode after them and shut the door. The policewoman, with arms folded, placed herself beside it. Anna ignored her.

"Sam."

He stood in the middle of the room and reluctantly lifted his eyes to hers. They were muddy with misery and fear, but a sullen defiance had taken root that she recognised as his flimsy armour.

"Sam, why did you do it?"

His glance flickered briefly to the officer by the door and back to Anna with a frown and a meaningful shake of the head. "I didn't."

"Sam, what about right and wrong?"

His frown deepened. "You don't understand."

"No, it's obviously you who don't understand. I thought I had taught you about moral values, that there is an intrinsic right or wrong to whatever you do. You're just doing what is expedient at the time or what seems a good idea to make a quick buck. I trusted you, Sam."

"Ma, don't go on. I'm in trouble and I don't need this. What I want is to get hold of that solicitor, Appleton."

Anna nodded. "I will ring him immediately. We will both come down to the police station."

He grunted a "Thanks", but she was not to be distracted.

"But I got it wrong before, didn't I? I helped bury your conscience, protected you from the consequences of your actions and so you thought it was okay to carry on as if you were untouchable. Well now you know it doesn't work like that." She stepped closer to him. "Nor *should* it work like that. We both did it wrong, Sam."

"Don't, Ma, please. Just leave me alone." He turned his back on her and she saw his shoulders start to tremble, but he quickly raised his head, sniffed hard and was just about to say something, when the door opened and Collier snapped curtly, "Time's up." Without a word, Sam walked past her, out of the kitchen and into the supervision of the police.

Anna remained standing there, alone, and thought about the future that she wanted.

After several moments the sounds of their preparations to leave roused her and she hurried to the front door.

"That's all, Mrs Forrest. We are taking Sam in custody down to the station now."

The boy was standing between two of the officers, looking slight and very young next to their burly figures, but his chin was still set into stubborn resistance. It was only the subdued droop of his shoulders that told another tale.

"I'll come as soon as I've got hold of Appleton," she assured him. She put out a hand and touched his arm. "We'll do everything we can, you know that."

He nodded, as if he did not trust his voice.

"Don't worry, bro, Appleton will have you sprung in no time. Hang tight and don't let them munch you down." It was Danny. His words earned a stony frown from the nearest officer but a satisfied snort from his brother.

Anna followed the police down the stairs to the street where the car was waiting, and at the last moment she reached up and kissed Sam's cheek. "I love you, Sam, no matter what."

He turned and gave her a fragile smile. "I know," he said, and ducked down into the police-car. Doors slammed and suddenly he was gone.

Back in the flat, Anna immediately dialled the number of David Appleton, and a short conversation was sufficient to impart the necessary information and to arrange an immediate meeting at the police station. When she hung up, Danny was hovering at her elbow, his teeth clicking together anxiously. She gave him a hug.

"Do you think Sam will be sent to gaol?" he asked.

Oh no, not gaol. Surely she'd saved him once. Wasn't that enough, for Christ's sake? Enough. She'd had enough of other people's burdens.

"No, Danny, I don't think so. Maybe to a young offenders' institution. Or perhaps probation, if he's lucky." Please God, let him be lucky.

"It's a first offence, isn't it? So they can't be too heavy on him." He threw himself into a chair and tossed a cushion across the room. "I don't want him banged up in a cell."

"Neither do I. I thought we had beaten them. How can this happen now? It's just not possible, not believable, not . . ."

"Not fair."

"Oh Danny, don't talk about fairness. It will all depend on how much he has been selling, and what kind of drugs. If he's been dealing in a big way at the school, they're bound to come down on him hard."

Danny gave a moan from deep down inside. "The stupid bugger."

"How could he lie to me like that? He made me think it was all over." It made her furious to know that Danny's own name would now be on the school's blacklist, as a result of having a brother arrested for dealing. Nothing ever came without strings. "What I don't understand is how the police found out? What made them barge in here with a warrant?"

"It was Tara."

"Tara? How was she involved?"

"The policewoman told me when you were all in Sam's room. She said Tara went and shopped him to the cops after her row with him. She gave them names and places and it seems they checked out, so he doesn't stand a chance."

Anna felt the final straw of hope slip out of her hand. Her son had made his choices and there was nothing she could do about it now – except be there when he came out.

The doorbell startled the heavy silence in the flat and Danny jerked in his chair. "Who's that?"

"It's okay," Anna soothed, "it won't be the police again. It will be Lloyd. He was coming round tonight, remember?"

"Oh yes, I forgot." He slumped back in his seat.

But Anna hadn't forgotten. She had been waiting for him. It had taken her a long, long time to put herself back together again, piece by piece, when Ian died and she had fallen apart inside. But she had managed it. Just. Then Sam had blown her world to bits again with five minutes of thoughtless stupidity in an off-licence. So she had sold her soul for him, but she was damned if she'd go through that again. Her soul was her own once more and she intended to keep it that way. Nothing was going to stop her now from taking a firm hold on her life with both hands and making something of it, something worth having.

This time she knew where she was going. This time she was not alone, and that knowledge put breath in her lungs. Before the bell could ring again, she hurried to open the door to Lloyd.